SOUTHERN LITERARY CLASSICS SERIES

C. Hugh Holman and Louis D. Rubin, Jr.
General Editors

Previously published

The Partisan Leader

The
Partisan Leader

A TALE OF THE FUTURE

 srs

by
NATHANIEL BEVERLEY TUCKER

With an Introduction by
C. HUGH HOLMAN

THE UNIVERSITY OF NORTH CAROLINA PRESS
Chapel Hill

INTRODUCTION

❦

The Partisan: A Tale of the Future was written as a campaign document supporting the Whigs in the presidential election of 1836, when Martin Van Buren was running for what his opponents claimed to be in fact simply a "third term for Andrew Jackson." Its author, Beverley Tucker, although he respected Jackson's abilities, was a passionate opponent of his policies. For Van Buren, however, he had the contempt that is expressed vigorously in *The Partisan Leader*, which attacks Jackson's actions and Van Buren's character. The intention of the book was not to prophesy disunion and civil strife, as several critics in recent years have claimed, but to warn against the grave dangers to the nation that would result from the election of Van Buren. The warning is directed primarily, however, at Tucker's beloved Virginia, pictured in the novel as suffering the fate of indecision and being caught between a powerful and successful independent Southern Confederacy, burgeoning with the economic fruits of bloodless secession, and a North ruled by the petty potentate Van Buren, in his third term and preparing to seek his fourth in 1849, the supposed time of action of the novel. Virginia in 1836 was divided between its allegiances to the Democratic party of Jackson and to the Whigs who opposed him and supported the strength of the separate states. Thus the representation of Virginia in 1849 as torn between the forces of a Democratic dictator and a successful Whig South merely projects and magnifies the presidential struggle of 1836.[1]

The success of a campaign document must, in one sense, be judged by the outcome of the campaign, and *The Partisan Leader* measured by such standards was a failure. Van Buren won an easy majority over the three Whigs who opposed him, and Virginia, not heeding Tucker's caveat, gave the Democratic party its electoral votes. The novel was, however, to have a longer life than most such works, in that it served as propaganda for both the Union and the Confederacy in the Civil War, which it is sometimes taken as prophesying. Literary works called forth by political issues must have qualities that survive the issues themselves. Washington Irving's *History of New York ... by Diedrich Knickerbocker*, which is in its fourth book a satire on Jefferson himself and his embargo policy, has survived because of its humor and its parody, even though the political significance of the work has long since ceased to matter.[2] *The Partisan Leader* has had a continued life of a much lesser sort because it embodies in almost pure form the complex of sentiments that shaped the southern secessionist movement. In its humorless pages one may find the essence

1. The historical data used in this introduction are drawn from Glyndon G. Van Deusen, *The Jacksonian Era, 1828–1848* (New York, 1959); Arthur M. Schlesinger, Jr., *The Age of Jackson* (Boston, 1945); Frederic Bancroft, *Calhoun and the South Carolina Nullification Movement* (Baltimore, 1928); Chauncey S. Boucher, *The Nullification Controversy in South Carolina* (Chicago, 1916); Henry H. Simms, *The Rise of the Whigs in Virginia, 1824–1840* (Richmond, 1929); and Claude G. Bowers, *The Party Battles of the Jackson Period* (Boston, 1929).

2. See Edwin Greenlaw, "Washington Irving's Comedy of Politics," *Texas Review*, I (1916), 291–306, and Greenlaw's edition of *Knickerbocker's History of New York (Books III–VII)* (New York, 1919).

of militant southern sectionalism and rampant states' rights, long after Van Buren's electoral votes have ceased to matter; for within the fictional framework of the novel are imbedded numerous disquisitions on the cardinal issues that separated South and North in the forty years between the Missouri Compromise and the election of Lincoln. Its continuing value is in the completeness with which it presents an intransigent antebellum aristocrat's attitudes toward states' rights, secession, slavery, the national bank, the tariff, the "American system," the Supreme Court, and that mystical legal concept "sovereignty."

Beverley Tucker was suited by time, temper, training, and experience to be the "fire-eater" *par excellence*. Born in Matoax, Virginia, September 6, 1784, Nathaniel Beverley Tucker (he seems never to have used the "Nathaniel") was the son of St. George Tucker, who became professor of law at the College of William and Mary, and Frances Bland Randolph Tucker, the mother of John Randolph of Roanoke by her earlier marriage.[3] He grew up in Williamsburg and attended the College of William and Mary, where he learned the principles of the famed George Wythe, particularly that of the derivative power of the Federal government. There, too, he learned to reverence the eighteenth-century agrarian-

3. The facts of Tucker's life and the publication of his books are drawn primarily from the massive unpublished dissertation of Percy Winfield Turrentine, "Life and Works of Nathaniel Beverley Tucker," Harvard University, 1952. Also of value have been Norma Lee Goodwin's unpublished master's thesis, "The Published Works of Nathaniel Beverley Tucker," Duke University, 1947; Carl Bridenbaugh's long introduction to the "Americana Deserta" edition of *The Partisan Leader* (New York, 1933); Jay B. Hubbell, *The South in American Literature, 1607–1900* (Durham, N.C., 1954), pp. 424–33; and Maude Howlett Woodfin, "Nathaniel Beverley Tucker: His Writings and Political Theories With a Sketch of His Life," *Richmond College Historical Papers*, II (June, 1917), 9–42.

ism of a stable planter aristocracy. He read law under his
father's direction, but he spent most of his summers at the
Randolph plantation at Roanoke, where he was profoundly
influenced by his half-brother, John Randolph, one of the
most brilliant and at the same time one of the most pathetic
of the Virginia statesmen of the early Nationalist period.
Randolph, a strict-constructionist, an ardent advocate of the
doctrines of the Virginia Resolutions of 1798, and a fervent
states' rights spokesman in their spirit, was, even before his
election to the United States Congress in 1799, a force in
Virginia political thought, and he was an effective but sometimes irrational and irascible sectional leader until his
death in 1833. Beverley Tucker adored him, absorbed his
principles, reverenced his strict integrity, and portrayed him
lovingly as Bernard Trevor in *The Partisan Leader*.

In 1806, Tucker was admitted to the Virginia bar and
began the practice of law at the Charlotte Court House—
seat of the county in which Roanoke was located.[4] With the
aid of land and slaves given him by his half-brother, he
reached a financial state that enabled him to marry in 1809.
He served in the War of 1812, entering the army as a lieutenant in 1813 and being discharged with the rank of
captain in 1815. After the war, discontented with his law
practice at Charlotte Court House—he called it "unprofitable, disgusting, and laborious"[5]—Tucker moved to Missouri in 1816 and settled in what is now Jefferson County.
He was appointed Judge of the Northern Circuit in the Missouri territory in 1817 and was active in political and civic

4. The Roanoke that John Randolph was "of" should not be confused
with the present day Virginia city of that name; it was a community in
Charlotte County.
5. William C. Bruce, *John Randolph of Roanoke, 1773–1833*, 2nd ed.
(New York, 1922), II, 512.

affairs in the territory. In those days of the debates between the slaveholding interests and the abolitionists over whether Missouri should enter the Union as a free or as a slave state, Tucker was a vocal advocate of the principle that the Federal government had no right to dictate such matters to individual states. His opposition to the Missouri Compromise was bitter, for he felt that it was unconstitutional in that it denied the inalienable right of a people to form their own constitution and state government. One of those "rights" which he asserted was that of the people of Missouri to exclude Yankees from the state, a proposal that he made to the Constitutional Convention and which has usually been taken as humorous. However, Tucker was seemingly devoid of a sense of humor, and the suggestion was possibly made in the grimmest earnestness. He proposed that the word "cow" be used as a shibboleth for all persons attempting to cross the Mississippi River from the east bank; if anyone pronounced it "Keow," he said, that person was clearly a Yankee and should be turned back.[6]

The Missouri Compromise marked for him the beginning of a certainty that secession was the only permanent solution to the South's problems. On February 14, 1851, Tucker was to write W. Gilmore Simms, the South Carolina novelist: "I vowed then [in 1820], and I have repeated the vow, *de die in diem*, that I will never give rest to my eyes nor slumber to my eyelids until it [the Union] is shattered into fragments. I strove for it in '33; I strove for it in '50, and I will strive for it while I live . . . there is now no escape from the many-headed despotism of numbers, but by a strong

6. John Francis McDermott, "Nathaniel Beverley Tucker in Missouri," *William and Mary Quarterly*, XX (October, 1940), 507.

and bold stand on the banks of the Potomac. . . . If we will not *have* slaves, we must *be* slaves."[7]

In 1820· Tucker was appointed judge of the Third Judicial Circuit in the new State of Missouri. He continued as a circuit judge until 1830, when he settled as a planter at "Ardmore," his newly completed house on a six-thousand-acre holding in Missouri. His first wife had died in 1826; a second wife, married in 1828, lived only five months after the wedding; and in 1830 he took his third wife, the daughter of a wealthy Missouri landholder, General Thomas A. Smith.

During these years in Missouri he more and more firmly embraced the political doctrines to which he was to hold inflexibly until his death. In matters of politics he responded to principle rather than personality. He opposed John C. Calhoun as early as 1824, when the South Carolinian ran for the vice-presidency on both the Jackson ticket and that of the hated Federalist John Quincy Adams. Tucker said, "The illweaved ambition of that restless aspirant Calhoun has scattered the strength of the South. . . . He is one of the men for whom I never felt respect or confidence."[8] Yet he was to support Calhoun's causes from 1828 until his death. When Jackson vetoed the Turnpike Bill in 1830, marking a defeat for Clay's "American system," Tucker contributed a series of articles to the Fayette (Missouri) *Western Monitor* defending the president's action.[9] Yet he later supported Clay.

The South Carolina Nullification Ordinance in 1832 was for him a crucial event. The tariff it opposed was, like all

7. William P. Trent, *William Gilmore Simms* (Boston, 1892), pp. 183–84.

8. Turrentine, "Life and Works," p. 710.

9. *Western Monitor*, Aug. 25, Sept. 15, Sept. 22, Oct. 13, Nov. 3, Nov. 24, Dec. 1, 1830.

tariffs, an abomination to Tucker, who regarded it as discriminatory against the agricultural South for the benefit of the industrial North and the West. On the other hand, the docrine of nullification itself seemed to him sophistical and paradoxical. As long as a state remained in the Union, he felt, it could not declare the laws of that Union unconstitutional. However, a state had no obligation to remain in a Union that was transgressing against its basic rights. The decision of South Carolina should have been, Tucker believed, not nullification but secession. Tucker's view of the relationship of the states to the Federal Union was shared by many who during the conflict over the tariff saw it as too small an issue for actual secession. W. Gilmore Simms, for example, as editor of the Charleston (S.C.) *City Gazette* took such a stance, and saw nothing contradictory in the name of his particular faction—"The Union and States' Rights Party."[10] Jackson's actions were in a strictly legal sense merely the enforcing of his oath of office, but Tucker felt that his Nullification Proclamation and Force Bill represented very dangerous attempts to elevate the central government over that of the states. Calhoun in his arguments in support of nullification relied heavily on the Virginia and Kentucky Resolutions of 1798 and 1799, occasioned by the Alien and Sedition Laws and defining the limits of the powers of the central government. These resolutions, framed by Madison and Jefferson, were also fountainheads for Tucker's view of the Federal government and, as he read them, defined the sovereignty of the separate states.

10. See Boucher, *Nullification Controversy*, passim; and editorials in the *City Gazette* in late 1831 and 1832. Simms, however, differed from Tucker in not believing the tariff issue a sufficient justification for secession.

Tucker, still supporting Jackson, called upon him in the *United States Telegraph*[11] and at least once in person to renounce the implications of his Nullification Proclamation and to assert secession to be an inalienable right of every sovereign state. By the end of 1833, however, he had despaired of Jackson's preserving the rights of the states, and he made a complete break with the president and the Democratic party and embraced the newly formed Whig party. He was undoubtedly encouraged in this new party alliance by Duff Green, whom he had known when Green was a prominent citizen of Missouri and a member of its Constitutional Convention. Green, who became the editor-publisher of the *United States Telegraph* in Washington, D.C., in 1825, had been a leading Democrat and a member of Jackson's "Kitchen Cabinet," before he followed Calhoun in his split with Old Hickory. In 1832 Green joined the Whigs and became a powerful supporter of Calhoun. Out of this party turmoil surrounding the Nullification Controversy came the fundamental impetus for *The Partisan Leader*.

In 1833 Beverley Tucker was called back to Virginia because of the grave illness of John Randolph, who died while his half-brother was still en route. Now Tucker's sojourn in the Missouri wilderness, a sojourn that had lasted seventeen years, was over. In 1834 he accepted the professorship of law at the College of William and Mary, and he held this position and lived in Williamsburg until his death in 1851. According to all accounts Tucker was a brilliant teacher and found in the classroom the most effective means of spreading his doctrines abroad. At William and Mary he came under the influence of Thomas R. Dew, professor of political

11. February 26, 1833.

law and, after 1836, president of the college. Dew was one
of the most articulate of the defenders of slavery and a
powerful advocate of the doctrine that slavery was a benefit
both to the slave himself and to the civilization into which
he was introduced.[12] Thus it is possible to say that Tucker
learned his conception of the Constitution and states' rights
from John Randolph of Roanoke, his party politics from
Duff Green, and his concept of slavery from Thomas R.
Dew. He seems never to have yielded a principle once it was
embraced, so that by 1834 his mind was set in the patterns
of the Resolutions of 1798, the bitter rejection of the
Missouri Compromise, and the theory of slavery as a "positive good" advanced by Dew in 1832. He was not to yield or
significantly modify one of these principles before his death,
and he was to teach them with persuasively passionate conviction to hundreds of the best young minds of the South
from 1834 to 1851.

In 1835 and 1836 Tucker had his brief career as a novelist. He began *George Balcombe* in November, 1835, and
completed it in February, 1836. It was a novel laid in Virginia and Missouri, whose characters voiced Tucker's sentiments on slavery, states' rights, and the dangers of the rule
of the mob. Although Edgar Allan Poe thought it perhaps
the finest American novel and W. Gilmore Simms praised
it highly,[13] Tucker was much less the romancer they lauded

12. Dew advanced his arguments in his *Review of the Debate in the
Virginia Legislature of 1831 and 1832* (1832), which was reprinted in
The Pro-Slavery Argument (1852). Dew's is usually considered the
classic statement of the "positive good" theory of slavery.

13. *Southern Literary Messenger*, III (1837), 49–58; Simms's opinion
is clearly expressed often in his correspondence, see particularly his letter
to Evert A. Duyckinck, Dec. 6, 1854, *The Letters of William Gilmore
Simms*, ed. Mary C. S. Oliphant, *et al* (Columbia, S.C.), III, 344.

than a teacher of political and social principles through the device of the novel. *The Partisan Leader* was written between February and April, 1836, and it underscored rather than diminished Tucker's hortatory role in his fiction. He turned to the novel only once more; a sentimental domestic serial, *Gertrude*, was published in the *Southern Literary Messenger*.[14] Quite properly it never appeared in book form.

Tucker continued to write polemical material for magazines, to instruct his law students with fervor and fervent prejudice, and to carry on extensive correspondence with such figures as James Henry Hammond, a South Carolina politician who was to become a United States senator, and W. Gilmore Simms, whom he encouraged to make the *Southern Quarterly Review* an increasingly rabid voice of the separate South. In 1850, as a delegate from Virginia, he attended the Nashville Convention called to discuss Clay's proposed compromise. There he voiced again his unrelenting distrust of the North and envisioned for the convention an immensely prosperous Southern Confederacy waxing rich through laissez-faire economic policies. But he believed his call to be in vain, and he went back to what he called his "Divine and spotless, honorable Virginia,"[15] a disillusioned man. On August 26, 1851, he died in Winchester, Virginia.

In his own day Beverley Tucker was renowned for his learning and culture. He was a powerful force in shaping some aspects of the mind of the Old South and a learned expositor of the doctrines of the sovereignty of the states. Vernon L. Parrington has justly said, "In him were richly embodied all the picturesque parochialisms that plantation

14. September, 1844, through December, 1845.
15. Turrentine, "Life and Works," 1462–63.

life encouraged. He was so completely and exclusively Virginian as to deserve the epithet 'Virginianissimus.' "[16] But despite how much his teaching contributed to the growing fever of an increasingly sectionalized South through the words and deeds of his students, Tucker survives for us today primarily as one who wrote his prejudices large in the pages of one impassioned novel that deserves to be remembered as historical fact if not as good fiction. For *The Partisan Leader* was an intensification of the prejudices of its maker and a forceful example of that intemperance of words and deeds which led to the tragedy of the Civil War.

The fact that we today see the chief value of *The Partisan Leader* to be in its qualities as political tract would neither surprise nor displease Tucker. It was in just such terms that he conceived, executed, and published it. Years after its composition, he said: "The book was written under a belief that the conservation of all that makes the Union valuable ... depends on the maintenance of the principles of what constituted the old republican party of '98,[17] which I now denominate the States' Rights Party."[18] Duff Green was certainly instrumental in the writing of the book and may have suggested the idea of the work to Tucker.[19] In February, 1836, Tucker was in correspondence with William C. Preston, United States senator from South Carolina, about his new novel and about Preston's serving as Tucker's emissary to a publisher, in order to preserve his anonymity.

16. *Main Currents in American Thought* (New York, 1927), II, 35.
17. I.e., the framers of the Virginia Resolutions of 1798.
18. Turrentine, "Life and Works," 1096.
19. Fletcher Green, "Duff Green, Militant Journalist of the Old School," *American Historical Review*, LII (1946–47), 248.

Preston entered into the scheme enthusiastically.[20] Quite plainly Tucker saw the need for secrecy from the very beginning of his work on *The Partisan Leader*. Preston submitted the manuscript to A. S. Johnson, the proprietor of the Columbia (S.C.) *Telescope*, but he was unable to publish the book before fall. Haste, as well as secrecy, was essential, if the work was to be effective in the presidential campaign; and Tucker entered into an agreement with Duff Green to publish immediately. Yet the book was slow in coming, and on June 5, Preston wrote, "I think it of great importance to bring out the *Partisan* at once. It will have its effect, tho I think the [Democratic] *party* is about to hoist by its own petard."[21] But it was late summer before it went to press. Green printed the work in Washington, using two "confidential compositors" to prevent its being recognized as coming from him.[22] He planned secret publication but distribution on a broad, almost national, scale, using bookselling connections in South Carolina, Georgia, Louisiana, Virginia, Missouri, Pennsylvania, and Massachusetts.[23]

When the book appeared, its title page read: "*The Partisan Leader; A Tale of the Future*. By Edward William Sidney. . . . Printed for the [unnamed] publishers, by James Caxton. 1856." It was in two volumes, and Green's total costs for printing and binding were $983.50.[24] An 1836 New York edition is listed in Roorbach's *Bibliotheca Americana*, but there is no evidence to support the entry, which may very well represent a bookseller's marketing of Green's

20. "Correspondence of Judge Tucker," *William and Mary Quarterly*, XII (October, 1903), 93.
21. Ibid., 94.
22. Turrentine, "Life and Works," 1089.
23. Goodwin, "Published Works," p. 121.
24. Ibid.

edition.[25] The statement is often made that the government suppressed it, although just how is uncertain.[26] For whatever reason, the book did not sell well, and in January, 1837, Green complained that he had lost money on it.[27]

When the Civil War, which it had warned against, finally came in 1861, *The Partisan Leader* at last found a substantial audience, and on Tucker's intended terms. It was published in New York in a two-volume edition, with an "Explanatory Introduction," which claims that the novel shows that "the fratricidal contest into which our country has been led is not a thing of chance, but of deliberate design, and that it has been gradually preparing for almost thirty years." This two-volume edition was reprinted on June 7, and seven thousand copies of this edition had been sold before June 29, when a one-volume edition appeared. The book clearly had propaganda value for those who would prove that the "Southern Conspiracy" had a long history. It also had value as a statement of the grievances of the South, a prophecy of triumph, and a statement of principles. In 1862 an edition with an introduction by the Reverend Thomas Ware was published in Richmond by West and Johnston, who advertised it as "A Novel, and an Apocalypse of the Origin

25. Both Turrentine and Bridenbaugh discount the existence of such an edition on the quite sound grounds that no mention of it occurs in either the Duff Green or the Tucker correspondence. However, neither seems aware of the actual condition and methods of publishing in the 1830's.

26. The title page of the 1861 New York edition reads, "Secretly Printed in Washington (in the year 1836) by Duff Green, for Circulation in the Southern States. but afterwards suppressed." The Library of Congress cards on *The Partisan Leader* carry a notice that the 1836 edition was suppressed. Similar assertions are made in Woodfin, "Writings and Political Theories," p. 14, and Hubbell, *South in American Literature*, p. 429.

27. Goodwin, "Published Works," p. 121.

and Struggles of the Southern Confederacy."[28] It is, in a sense, a tribute to the accuracy with which Tucker expressed the issues of the antebellum political struggle that both sides should see his arguments as contributing to the righteousness of their cause.

Although Tucker said in 1850, "I would rather be known, ten years hence, as the author of that book, than any thing ever published on this continent,"[29] he could hardly have been thinking of its intrinsic literary qualities. *The Partisan Leader* is clumsily written, despite some effective polemical rhetoric and some striking descriptive passages. Its plot is handled with a carelessness unusual even in the heyday of the influence of Sir Walter Scott, when plots tended to be, as Scott asserted in the Introduction to *The Fortunes of Nigel*, merely devices "to bring in fine things."[30] The basic situation of families in which brothers are aligned on opposite sides in civil conflict was almost a commonplace of the period. It can be found repeatedly in Scott—notably in *Waverley*—and in the highly influential *Die Räuber*, by Schiller, which seems to be behind Tucker's central situation, as it was to be behind that of Simms's Revolutionary romance, *The Kinsmen* (1841), entitled *The Scout* in later editions.[31] Furthermore, Tucker is so much less interested in the progress of his hero than he is in the exposition of his doctrines that apparently the need to hasten the work to the printer resulted in his simply abandoning his hero while he

28. Hubbell, *South in American Literature*, p. 430.
29. Ibid.
30. Sir Walter Scott, *The Fortunes of Nigel* (Riverside Edition of the *Complete Works of Scott*; Boston, 1923), p. xxvi.
31. C. Hugh Holman, "European Influences on Southern American Literature: A Preliminary Survey," *Proceedings of the Second Congress of the International Comparative Literature Association* (Chapel Hill, N.C., 1959), II, 454.

is in distress. The suggestion made in the Explanatory Introduction to the New York edition that the first two volumes were the beginning of a serial publication that was abandoned seems ingenious—and, surprisingly, friendly to Tucker as a novelist—but there is no reason whatever to accept it.

Certainly Tucker is greatly influenced by Sir Walter Scott and particularly by his Scottish novels. This influence is plain in the perfunctory love story within the conflict of divided loyalties in a civil struggle; it is more convincingly and attractively present in the carefully drawn pictures of the mountain yeomen, similar to Scott's simple Scotsmen, in the delight Tucker takes in the description of wild scenery, and in the detail and vigor with which he can handle military skirmishes and guerilla warfare. The tale is only partially complete and it is frequently forgotten while the characters expatiate on political and social issues, but from time to time its scene and its action catch our attention. Richard M. Weaver lamented, "A vehement advocate of state rights and the agrarian order, Tucker accepted the gage which he felt had been thrown down by the North and poured forth a stream of political treatises [after *The Partisan Leader*], but in so doing he silenced one more literary voice for the South."[32] He is being more generous than accurate, for, although there are passages in Tucker's novels that make the reader aware of a talent for fiction, there is nothing to indicate that he ever intended it as an end in itself or struggled with the artistic issues of his work.

But if Tucker's novels are aesthetic failures, what of his portrayal of personages from his time? There are enough

32. *The Southern Tradition at Bay* (New Rochelle, N.Y., 1968), p. 93.

parallels between the characters in *The Partisan Leader* and actual persons to give the question some validity. Christian Witt was based on an actual person named Saunders Witt, and Schwartz was based on a John Switzler whom Tucker had known in Missouri.[33] Perhaps some of the vitality of these characters results from their having real-life models. Bernard Trevor seems directly drawn from Tucker's half-brother John Randolph, both in his principles and in his place and way of life. Hugh Trevor resembled Henry St. George Tucker, Beverley's brother and an opponent of secession, enough for Henry to recognize and be angered by the picture.[34] It is tempting, then, to see Beverley as representing himself in the young hero Douglas Trevor, but that at best is only a half-truth. It has been customary to see Mr. B—— as a literal portrait of John C. Calhoun,[35] but this too is highly questionable. Despite the fact than an emissary from the successful Southern Confederacy could not be a Virginian, Mr. B—— is made a North Carolinian, not a South Carolinian. Furthermore, he clearly enunciates the doctrines that Beverley Tucker spent his life preaching. Also at the time that *The Partisan Leader* was written Tucker disliked and distrusted Calhoun, although he approved his policies in general. The temptation is strong to say that Mr. B—— is really Mr. Beverley himself and that he is what Tucker would like to be as a powerful statesman, as Douglas is what he would like to be as a man of action. So that, even on the level of characterization, everything in *The Partisan Leader* is an expression of the intelligent,

33. Hubbell, *South in American Literature*, pp. 430–31.
34. Ibid.
35. For example, Parrington, *Main Currents*, II, 37, and Bridenbaugh, "Introduction," 1933 edition, p. xxix.

prejudiced, and embittered man that Beverley Tucker was in 1836 and remained for the rest of his life. Carl Bridenbaugh lamented that "one of the most vivid actors in the drama of States Rights remains unnoticed. Jurist, poet, publicist, gentleman of the old school, novelist and archangel of the Old Dominion, Beverley Tucker well deserves to be res-urrected."[36] To read *The Partisan Leader* is indeed to res-urrect him and to learn the angers and ambitions, the prin-ciples and prejudices that he shared with his class in his time and that moved him and them toward the tragedy of fratricidal war.

36. Bridenbaugh, "Introduction," 1933 edition, p. ix.

A NOTE ON THE TEXT

There are four distinct editions of *The Partisan Leader* that
are verifiable, although references have been made to editions that seem not to be extant, if they ever existed, and for
which there is no evidence. The novel was secretly published
in two volumes in Washington in 1836. Rudd and Carleton
published the book in two volumes in New York in 1861.
After it had gone through two impressions, it was re-issued
as two volumes in one in June, 1861. West and Johnson
published *The Partisan Leader* in Richmond in 1862. An
edition, reproducing the 1836 one, edited by Carl Bridenbaugh, was published in the "Americana Deserta" series in
New York in 1933.

The present text is a reproduction of the third impression
of the 1861 edition, that is, the two-volumes-in-one impression. It purports to be a "Fac-Simile Of the Original Edition, printed at Washington in 1836." A comparison of this
edition with the first edition seems to verify this claim with
one exception: through Chapter XXII (the first chapter of
the second volume), material bearing particularly on the
issue of the "Southern Conspiracy" has been italicized for
emphasis although it was in Roman type in the 1836 edition. The "Explanatory Introduction" has been retained,
despite its inaccuracies, for the light it casts on how the
book looked to Northern patriots during the Civil War.

THE PARTISAN LEADER

A Key to the Disunion Conspiracy.

THE PARTISAN LEADER.

BY BEVERLY TUCKER,
OF VIRGINIA.

Secretly Printed in Washington (in the year 1836) by DUFF GREEN, for Circulation in the Southern States.

BUT AFTERWARDS SUPPRESSED.

NEW YORK:
REPRINTED BY RUDD & CARLETON.
M DCCC LXI.

R. CRAIGHEAD,
Printer, Stereotyper, and Electrotyper,
Carton Building,
81, 83, and 85 Centre Street.

EXPLANATORY INTRODUCTION.

THE reader will learn from the following pages that the fratricidal contest into which our country has been led is not a thing of chance, but of deliberate design, and that it has been gradually preparing for almost thirty years. The dark plotters of South Carolina and Virginia, who in 1832 and 1833 were defeated in their nullification and disunion schemes by the fidelity and decision of Jackson, though abashed and discomfited, did not relinquish their purpose, notwithstanding they changed their plans. At first they resolved on organizing a direct resistance to the Federal authority throughout the South as soon as the "Southern heart" could be "fired" for that purpose; but, fearing a second reverse from the popularity of the Democratic party, they veered from a policy of open assault against that party and the Union, to one of sapping and mining both. Hence Mr. Calhoun and his secession allies, in 1837, joined the Democratic party, that from 1833 to 1836 they had hated and denounced. By little and little the Secessionists, after having attained admission to its counsels, modified the policy of the party, continually changing it more and more in conformity with their own ideas. Thus it was in pursuit of aims, purely Southern and sectional, that the Mexican province of Texas was overrun and conquered by American adventurers in 1835 and 1836; that Texas was annexed in 1845; and that the war with Mexico was inaugurated. It was to subserve Southern, and eventually Disunion, purposes that the Missouri Compromise was repealed, and all the evil enginery of Lecomptonism put into operation. It was to further the accursed cause of national disruption that just such a Cabinet as that of Buchanan was gathered up, whereby the army might be dispersed, the navy scattered, and the national treasury plundered and bank-

Explanatory Introduction.

rupted—so that Secession might march unmolested over the prostrate form of our noble Government. The one purpose of disunion has been for the greater part of the time the animating principle of State rights' policy, since Calhoun and his adherents stealthily wormed themselves into the citadel of the Democracy. Even so apparently insignificant a matter as the repair and return of the English ship Resolute to the British Government, was undoubtedly due to the anxiety of the Southern Confederates to conciliate the good will of England, and secure for them her future alliance. The Secessionnists courted and used the Democratic party from 1837 to 1860, and in the latter year, at Charleston, having no further use for that organization, ruthlessly rent it asunder. Without dispute our country is suffering from the effects of a conspiracy unparalleled in its nature and extent in the history of mankind. In comparison with it the conspiracy of Catiline and Cethegus in ancient Rome fades into meanness and insignificance. The American conspiracy is now and may ever continue its own only parallel.

In addition to the testimony furnished by the past history and present circumstances of the country, in proof of the above positions, there is happily a piece of irresistible evidence supplied us in the pages of a most remarkable work written and secretly printed in the years 1835 and 1836, in which nearly every important point of the great conspiracy which is developing itself in our own immediate day, stands distinctly shadowed forth. Composed in the form of a novel, its twin object was to excite the South to rebellion, and to teach how to make that rebellion successful. It was "a tale of the future," and most wonderfully is that "future" fulfilling its predictions. Indeed, the Jeff. Davises, Yanceys, Pryors, Rhetts, Letchers, etc., seem to have done little else than servilely to follow out the programme sketched for them in this remarkable book. Its author, Professor BEVERLY TUCKER, of William and Mary College, Virginia, and but recently deceased, was one of the most trusted friends and devoted partisans of Mr. Calhoun, and had he lived till to-day, would have witnessed no feeble promise of the complete fulfilment of his own prophecies. The circumstances under which "The Partisan Leader" was ushered into existence sufficiently indicate its object and character. The manuscript was placed in the hands of Mr. Calhoun's connexion and con-

Explanatory Introduction.

fidant, Duff Green, then proprietor of the "Telegraph," published in Washington City. It was accordingly printed in Green's office on "Capitol Hill," but with a fictitious imprint, and a false date of twenty years in advance, because, as is known from the best living testimony, Green confessed the book to be "Treason." When the "Partisan Leader" was commenced in 1836, it was the intention of its author to make it a serial, to be issued at frequent intervals or until the whole South should have become impregnated with disunion. But only two parts were printed and distributed, because after the election of Mr. Van Buren in November 1836, the Secession leaders had resolved upon a change of programme from open opposition to the Democracy, to a close but treacherous connexion with it. This was effected under color of a great admiration for the sub-treasury feature in the Jackson-Van Buren policy; at all events Mr. Calhoun and his friends thenceforward held foremost seats in the Democratic synagogue.

It is remarkable that the revolution thus skilfully projected in the Partisan Leader is nowhere in the whole book sought to be justified on the grounds of alleged aggressions by the North in respect to slavery. Like the abettors of secession on the floors of Congress, Professor Tucker seems to have been unable to make out the semblance of a good case. After the merest allusion to the grounds for dissolution, he says in one of the pages of this book—

"If any farther account of *the causes* of the rebellion be required, . have none to give. It was through the eyes and hearts of the South that conviction entered. Outrage to the laws; outrage to the freedom of elections; outrage to one respected and beloved (Mr. Calhoun), left nothing for *reason* to do."

It was in the administration of General Jackson that the Partisan Leader found or made motives for the disruption of the Confederacy. Negro slavery had not then, nor has it now, any necessary connexion with that design.

We close this introduction by appending a quotation from an editorial article in the *National Intelligencer* of January 25th, 1851, in which the editor, Mr. Gales, had alluded to the remarkable character of this political novel, as furnishing a key to some of the profoundest intricacies in American politics.

Explanatory Introduction.

" No one," said Mr. Gales, "who has been familiar with the topics and tone of the discussions in the South for the last two years but will at once recognise in this fiction—a fiction not at all more strange than the reality—the projected shadow of what has already come to pass. From that day to this these defeated 'partisans' have spared no pains to make their story come true, by diffusing doubts and discontents into the quiet homes as well as the political circles of the South, with a view to bring about a revolution, which, had their ambition succeeded, would, in its consequences, have desolated those homes, broken up those abodes of peace and happiness, and devastated the country with the flames of a fierce, unsparing, and unrelenting civil war."

Alas, that the revolution which Mr. Gales supposed to have been averted by the passage of the Compromise of 1850, should have been brought back upon the pathway of our country by the fatal repeal of the Missouri Compromise, the abominations and bloodshed in Kansas, the proceeding in the Charleston Convention of last year, and the crowning derelictions and treason of the Buchanan administration.

FAC-SIMILE

Of the Original Edition, printed at Washington

in 1836.

THE

PARTISAN LEADER;

A TALE OF THE FUTURE.

BY

EDWARD   WILLIAM   SIDNEY.

"SIC SEMPER TYRANNIS."
The Motto of Virginia.
"PARS FUI." . . . . . Virgil.

IN TWO VOLUMES.

VOL. I.

PRINTED

FOR THE PUBLISHERS, BY JAMES CAXTON.

1856.

DEDICATION.

———

THE part I bore in the transactions which form the subject of the following narrative, is my voucher for its authenticity. My admiration of the gallant people, whose struggle for freedom I witnessed and partook; the cherished friendships contracted among them, at a time of life when the heart is warm, and under circumstances which called all its best feelings into action; and, above all, the connexion then formed, which has identified me with Virginia, and which, during the last five years, has been the source of all my happiness; are my inducements to dedicate this work to you. The approbation which, in acknowledging, more than rewarded my humble services, is my warrant for hoping, that this tribute of grateful veneration will be favorably received.

Dedication.

Among those whom Virginia, at this time, honors with high places in her councils, I see with pride, the names of many with whom I once stood, shoulder to shoulder, in the eye of danger. Of my regard for these, this is not the place to speak, for *they* are not thus to learn my sentiments concerning them. The record of their praise, and the reward of their glorious deeds, is on the page of history.

But there are others who will die without their fame, and whose names will sink with them into the tomb, of whose unpretending devotion to their native country I am proud to testify. They belong to that class, peculiar to a society whose institutions are based on domestic slavery; the honest, brave, hardy, and high-spirited peasantry of Virginia. Among them, I saw examples of simple virtue and instinctive patriotism; and from their lips I heard lessons of that untaught wisdom, which finds its place in minds uncorrupted by artificial systems of education, and undebased by abject and menial occupations. The names of Jacob Schwartz and Christian Witt deserve to live in history. But the narrative, in which I have endeavored to preserve them, will, in after times, be classed among romances. Such is the fate of all men, whose deeds shame the vaunted achievements of those the world calls great.

Dedication.

Be it so. It is not the less my duty to testify of what I have witnessed. Remembering the virtues which I saw displayed by such, I take pride in dedicating to the *whole* people of Virginia, in all ranks and classes, this imperfect record of what I witnessed in her *late glorious struggle*.

E. W. S.

P. S. My date reminds me that this is the anniversary of that glorious day, on which Virginia first declared herself an independent State. May its auspicious return ever find you FREE, HAPPY, and GLORIOUS!

PARTISAN LEADER.

CHAPTER I.

And whomsoe'er, along the path you meet,
Bears in his cap the badge of crimson hue,
Which tells you whom to shun, and whom to greet.
                                        BYRON.

TOWARD the latter end of the month of October, 1849, about the hour of noon, a horseman was seen ascending a narrow valley at the eastern foot of the Blue Ridge. His road nearly followed the course of a small stream, which, issuing from a deep gorge of the mountain, winds its way between lofty hills, and terminates its brief and brawling course in one of the larger tributaries of the Dan. A glance of the eye took in the whole of the little settlement that lined its banks, and measured the resources of its inhabitants. The different tenements were so near to each other as to allow but a small patch of arable land to each. Of manufactures there was no appearance, save only a rude shed at the entrance of the valley, on the door of which the oft repeated brand of the horse-shoe gave token of a smithy. There too the rivulet, increased by the innumerable springs which afforded to every habitation the unappreciated, but inappreciable luxury of water, cold, clear, and sparkling, had gathered strength enough to turn a tiny mill. Of trade there could be none. The bleak and rugged barrier, which closed the scene on the west, and the narrow road, fading to a foot-path, gave assurance to the traveller that he had here reached the *ne plus ultra* of social life in that direction.

Indeed, the appearance of discomfort and poverty in every dwelling well accorded with the scanty territory belonging to each. The walls and chimneys of unhewn logs, the roofs of loose boards laid on long rib-poles, that projected from the gables, and held down by similar poles placed above them, together with the smoked and sooty appearance of the whole, betokened an abundance of timber, but a dearth of everything else. Contiguous to each was a sort of rude garden, denominated, in the ruder language of the country, a "truck-patch." Beyond this lay a small field, a part of which had produced a crop of oats, while on the remainder the Indian corn still hung on the stalk, waiting to be gathered. Add to this a small meadow, and the reader will have an outline equally descriptive of each of the little farms which, for the distance of three miles, bordered the stream.

But, though the valley thus bore the marks of a

crowded population, a deep stillness pervaded it.
The visible signs of life were few. Of sounds there
were none. A solitary youngster, male or female,
alone was seen loitering about every door. These,
as the traveller passed along, would skulk from
observation, and then steal out, and, mounting a
fence, indulge their curiosity, at safe distances, by
looking after him.

At length he heard a sound of voices, and then a
shrill whistle, and all was still. Immediately, some
half a dozen men, leaping a fence, ranged themselves across the road and faced him. He observed
that each, as he touched the ground, laid hold of a
rifle that leaned against the enclosure, and this cir
cumstance drew his attention to twenty or more :
these formidable weapons, ranged along in the same
position. The first impulse of the traveller was to
draw a pistol; but seeing that the men, as they
posted themselves, rested their guns upon the ground
and leaned upon them, he quietly withdrew his
hand from his holster. It was plain that no violence
was intended, and that this movement was nothing
but a measure of precaution, such as the unsettled
condition of the country required. He therefore
advanced steadily but slowly, and, on reaching the
party, reined in his horse, and silently invited the
intended parley.

The men, though somewhat variously attired, were
all chiefly clad in half-dressed buck-skin. They
seemed to have been engaged in gathering corn in

the adjoining field. Their companions, who still continued the same occupation, seemed numerous enough (including women and boys, of both of which there was a full proportion,) to have secured the little crop in a few hours. Indeed, it would seem that the whole working population of the neighborhood, both male and female, was assembled there.

As the traveller drew up his horse, one of the men, speaking in a low and quiet tone, said, "We want a word with you, stranger, before you go any farther."

"As many as you please," replied the other, "for I am tired and hungry, and so is my horse; and I am glad to find some one, at last, of whom I may hope to purchase something for both of us to eat."

"*That* you can have quite handy," said the countryman, "for we have been gathering corn, and were just going to our dinner. If you will only just 'light, sir, one of the boys can feed your horse, and you can take such as we have got to give you."

The invitation was accepted; the horse was taken in charge by a long-legged lad of fifteen, without hat or shoes; and the whole party crossed the fence together.

At the moment, a man was seen advancing toward them, who, observing their approach, fell back a few steps, and threw himself on the ground at the foot of a large old apple-tree. Around this were clustered a motley group of men, women, and boys, who opened and made way for the stranger. He advanced, and, bowing gracefully, took off his forage cap, from beneath which a quantity of soft curling flaxen hair fell over his brow and cheeks. Every eye was now fixed on him, with an expression rather of interest than mere curiosity. Every countenance was serious and composed, and all wore an air of business, except that a slight titter was heard among the girls, who, hovering behind the backs of their mothers, peeped through the crowd, to get a look at the handsome stranger.

He was indeed a handsome youth, about twenty years of age, whose fair complexion and regular features made him seem yet younger. He was tall, slightly, but elegantly formed, with a countenance in which softness and spirit were happily blended. His dress was plain and cheap, though not unfashionable. A short grey coat, waistcoat, and pantaloons, that neatly fitted and set off his handsome person, showed by the quality of the cloth that his means were limited; or that he had too much sense to waste, in foppery, that which might be better expended in the service of his suffering country. But, even in this plain dress, he was apparelled like a king in comparison with the rustics that surrounded him; and his whole air would have passed him for a gentleman, in any dress and any company, where the constituents of that character are rightly understood.

In the present assembly there seemed to be none, indeed, who could be supposed to have had much experience in that line. But dignity is felt, and courtesy appreciated by all, and the expression of frankness and truth is everywhere understood.

As the youth approached, the man at the foot of the tree arose, and returned the salutation, which seemed unheeded by the rest. He advanced a step or two, and invited the stranger to be seated. This action, and the looks turned toward him by the others, showed that he was in authority of some sort among them. With him, therefore, our traveller concluded that the proposed conference was to be held. There was nothing in his appearance which would have led a careless observer to assign him any pre-eminence. But a second glance might have discovered something intellectual in his countenance, with less of boorishness in his air and manner than the rest of the company displayed. In all, indeed, there was the negative courtesy of that quiet and serious demeanor which solemn occasions impart to the rudest and most frivolous. It was plain to see that they had a common purpose, and that neither ferocity nor rapacity entered into their feeling toward the newcomer. Whether he was to be treated as a friend or an enemy, obviously depended on some high consideration, not yet disclosed.

He was at length asked whence he came, and answered from the neighborhood of Richmond. From which side of the r.ver?—From the north side. Did he know anything of Van Courtlandt?—His camp was at Bacon's branch, just above the town. What force had he?

"I cannot say, certainly," he replied, "but common fame made his numbers about four thousand."

"Is that all, on both sides of the river?" said his interrogator.

"O, no! Col. Loyal's regiment is at Petersburg, and Col. Cole's at Manchester; each about five hundred strong; and there is a piquet on the Bridge island."

"Did you cross there?"

"I did not."

"Where then?" he was asked.

"I can hardly tell you," he replied, "it was at a private ford, several miles above Cartersville."

"Was not that mightily out of the way? What made you come so far around?"

"It was safer travelling on that side of the river."

"Then the people on that side of the river are your friends?"

"No. They are not. But, as they are all of a color there, they would let me pass, and ask no questions, as long as I travelled due west. On this side, if you are one man's friend, you are the next man's enemy; and I had no mind to answer questions."

"You seem to answer them now mighty freely."

"That is true. I am like a letter that tells all it knows as soon as it gets to the right hand; but it does not want to be opened before that."

"And how do you know that you have got to the right hand now?"

"Because I know where I am."

" And where are you ? "

" Just at the foot of the Devil's Back-bone," re-plied the youth.

" Were you ever here before ? "

" Never in my life."

" How do you know then where you are ? " asked the mountaineer.

" Because the right way to avoid questions is to ask none. So I took care to know all about the road, and the country, and the place, before I left home."

" And who told you all about it ? "

" Suppose I should tell you," answered the young man, " that Van Courtlandt had a map of the country made, and gave it to me."

" I should say, you were a traitor to him, or a spy upon us," was the stern reply.

At the same moment, a startled hum was heard from the crowd, and the press moved and swayed for an instant, as if a sort of spasm had pervaded the whole mass.

" You are a good hand at questioning," said the youth, with a smile, " but, without asking a single question, I have found out all I wanted to know."

" And what was that ? " asked the other.

" Whether you were friends to the Yorkers and Yankees, or to poor old Virginia."

" And which *are* we for ? " added the laconic mountaineer.

" For OLD VIRGINIA FOR EVER," replied the youth,

in a tone in which exultation rung through a deeper emotion, that half stifled his voice.

It reached the hearts of his auditors, and was echoed in a shout that pealed along the mountain sides their proud war-cry of " OLD VIRGINIA FOR EVER." The leader looked around in silence, but with a countenance that spoke all that the voices of his comrades had uttered.

" Quiet, boys," said he, " never shout till the war is ended—unless it be when you see the enemy." Then turning again to the traveller, he said, " And how did you know we were for old Virginia?"

" I knew it by the place where I find you. I heard it in *your voice;* I saw it in *their eyes;* and I felt it in *my heart;*" said the young man, extending his hand.

His inquisitor returned the cordial pressure with an iron grasp, strong, but not convulsive, and went on : " You are a sharp youth," said he, " and if you are of the right metal that will hold an edge, you will make somebody feel it. But I don't know rightly yet who that is to be, only just I will say, that if you are not ready to live and die by old Virginia, your heart and face are not of the same color, that's all."

He then resumed his steady look and quiet tone, and added, " You must not make me forget what I am about. How *did* you learn the way here?"

" I can answer that *now;*" said the youth. " I learned it from Captain Douglas."

" Captain Douglas !" exclaimed the other. "If you were never here before, you have never seen him since he knew it himself."

"True enough;" was the reply. "But I have heard from him."

" I should like to see his letter."

" I have no letter."

" How then ?"

" Go with me to my horse, and I will show you."

The youth, accompanied by his interrogator, now returned toward the fence. Many of the crowd were about to follow; but the chief (for such he seemed) waved them back with a silent motion of his hand, while a glance of meaning at two of the company invited them to proceed. As soon as the stranger reached his horse, he drew out, from between the padding and seat of his saddle, a paper closely folded. On opening this, it was found to be a map of his route from Richmond to a point in the mountains, a few miles west of the spot where they stood. On this were traced the roads and streams, with the names of a few places, written in a hand which was known to the leader of the mountaineers to be that of Captain Douglas. A red line marked the devious route the traveller had been directed to pursue.

He said that, after crossing the river, between Lynchburg and Cartersville, to avoid the parties of the enemy stationed at both places, he had lain by, until dark, at the house of a true Virginian. Then, turning south, and riding hard all night, he had crossed the Appomattox above Farmville, (which he avoided for a like reason,) and, before day, had left behind him all the hostile posts and scouting parties. He soon reached the Staunton river, and, having passed it, resumed his westward course in comparative safety.

"You know this hand," said he to the chief, "and now, I suppose, you are satisfied."

"I am satisfied," replied the other, "and glad to see you. I have not a doubt about you, young man, and you are heartily welcome among us—to all we can give you—and that an't much—and all we can do for you; and that will depend upon whether stout hearts, and willing minds, and good rifles can help you. But you said you were hungry; so, I dare say, you'll be glad enough of a part of our sorry dinner."

CHAPTER II.

Heus! etiam Mensas consumimus.—VIRGIL.

RETURNING to the party which they had left, they found the women in the act of placing their meal before them, under the apple-tree. There was a patch of grass there, but no shade; nor was any needed in that lofty region; the frost had already done its work by stripping the trees of their leaves, and letting in the welcome rays of the sun through the naked branches. The meal consisted of fresh pork and venison, roasted or broiled on the coals, which looked tempting enough, though served up in wooden trays. There were no knives but such as each hunter carries in his belt. Our traveller's dirk supplied the place of one to him. Their plates were truly classical, consisting of cakes of Indian corn, baked in the ashes, so that, like the soldiers of Æneas, each man ate up his platter before his hunger was appeased.

Our traveller, though sharp-set, could not help perceiving a woful insipidity in his food, for which his entertainer apologized. "We ha'nt got no salt to give you, stranger," said he. "The little that's made on the waters of Holston is all used there; and what comes by way of the sound is too dear for the like of us, that fight one half the year, and work the other half, and then with our rifles in our hands. *As long as we let the Yankees hold James river, we must make up our minds to eat our hogs when they are fat, and to do without salt to our bread.* But it is not worth grumbling about; and bread without salt is more than men deserve that will give up their country without fighting for it."

When the meal was finished, our traveller, expressing a due sense of the courtesy of his entertainers, asked what was to pay, and proposed to continue his journey.

" As to what you are to pay, my friend," said the spokesman of the party, in the same cold, quiet tone, " that is just nothing. If you come here by Captain Douglas's invitation, you are one of us; and if you do not, we are bound to find you as long as we keep you. But, as to your going just yet, it is quite against our rules."

" How is that?" asked the traveller, with some expression of impatience.

"That is what I cannot tell you," replied the other.

" But what right," exclaimed the youth—then checking himself, he added: " But I see you mean nothing but what is right and prudent; and you must take your own way to find out all you wish to know about me. But I thought you said you did not doubt me."

"No more I do," replied the other; "but that is not the thing. May be, our rules are not satisfied, though I am."

"And what are your rules?"

"It is against rule to tell them," said the mountaineer, dryly. "But make yourself easy, stranger. We mean you no harm, and I will see and have every thing laid straight before sun-rise. You are heartily welcome. Such as we've got we give you; and that is better than you will find where you are going. For our parts, except it be for salt, we are about as well off here as common; because there is little else we use that comes from foreign parts. I dare say, it will go hard with you for a while, sir; but, if your heart's right, you will not mind it, and you will soon get used to it."

"It would be a great shame," said the youth, "if I cannot bear for a while what you have borne for life."

"Yes," said the other, "that is the way people talk. But (axing your pardon, sir,) there an't no sense in it. Because the longer a man bears a thing, the less he minds it; and after a while, it an't no hardship at all. *And that's the way with the poor negroes that the Yankees pretend to be so sorry for, and tried to get them to rise against their masters.* There's few of them, stranger, but what's happier than I am; but I should be mighty unhappy, if you were to catch me now, in my old days, and make a slave of me. *So when the Yankees want to set the negroes free, and to make me a slave, they want to put*

us both to what we are not fit for. And so it will be
with you for a while, among these mountains, sleep-
ing on the ground, and eating your meat without salt,
or bread either, may be. But after a while you will
not mind it. But as to whether it is to be long or
short, young man, you must not think about that.
You have no business here, if you have not made up
your mind to stand the like of that for life ; and may
be that not so mighty long neither."

At this moment a signal from the road gave notice
of the approach of a traveller ; and the leader of the
mountaineers, accompanied by his guest, went forward in obedience to it. But, before he reached the
fence, he saw several of the party leap it, and run
eagerly forward to meet the new-comer. A little man
now appeared, walking slowly and wearily, whose
dress differed but little from that of the natives ; and
who bore, like them, a rifle, with its proper accompaniments of knife, tomahawk, and powder-horn. His
arrival awakened a tumult of joy among the younger
persons present, while he whom I have designated as
the chief stood still, looking toward him with a countenance in which an expression of thoughtful interest
was mingled with a sort of quiet satisfaction, and great
kindness and good will. Yet he moved but a step to
meet him, and extending his hand, said, in his usual
cold tone, " How is it, Schwartz ?" to which the
other, in a voice somewhat more cheery, replied
"Well; how is it with you, Witt?" " Well," was
the grave answer.

The two now drew apart to converse privately to-gether. Crossing the road, they seated themselves on the fence in front of the stranger, so that during their conference they could keep an eye on him.

"Who is this you have got here?" asked Schwartz.

"A young fellow that says he wants to go to the camp," replied the other.

"Has he got the word and signs?"

"No. He does not know any thing about it. I have a notion he is a friend of the captain's."

"What makes you think so?"

"He has got a paper in the captain's hand-write to show him the way. But there's no name to it; and if there was, I could not tell that he was the man. Sure and certain the captain wrote the paper, but then somebody may have stolen it. A man that knows as much about the country as he does, after looking at that paper and travelling by it away here, is the last man we ought to let go any farther, or know any more, unless he is of the right sort."

"I should like to see that paper;" said Schwartz.

"Here it is," replied his companion. "I don't much mistrust the young fellow; but I did not like to let him have it again till I knew more."

Schwartz now looked at the paper and inquired the stranger's name.

"I did not ask his name," said Witt, "because he could just tell me what name he pleased. As there was no name on the paper, it did not make any odds. Besides, I wanted to be civil to him, and your high gentlemen down about Richmond are affronted sometimes if you ask their names. The young fellow is all right, or all wrong, any how; and his name don't make any odds. If the captain knows him, when he sees him, it's all one what his name is."

"But I know," said Schwartz, "who ought to have that paper; and if he don't answer to that name it's no use troubling the captain with him."

"I should be sorry for any harm to him," said Witt, "for he is a smart lad; and if he is not a true Virginian, then he is the greatest hypocrite that ever was born."

They now recrossed the road, and Schwartz, addressing the stranger, said, "I must make so bold, young man, as to ask your name."

The young fellow colored, and, turning to Witt, said, "I thought you were satisfied, and done asking questions."

"So I was," said Witt, "but there is a reason for asking your name now, that I did not know of. I owe you nothing but good will, young man," added he with earnest solicitude; "and if your name is what I hope it is, be sure by all means and tell the truth; for there is but one name in the world that will save your neck."

"Then I shall tell you no name at all," rejoined the youth, somewhat appalled at this startling intimation. "Why did not you ask me at once, when I was in the humor to keep nothing from you. I was willing to answer any civil question, or indeed any question *you* would have put to me, but I will not submit to be examined, over and over, by every chance-comer."

"There's where you are wrong, young man," replied Witt. "This is no chance-comer. He is my head man, and I am just nobody when he is here."

Surprised at this ascription of authority to the diminutive and mean-looking new-comer, our traveller looked at him again, and was confirmed in a resolution to resist it. He had patiently borne to be questioned by Witt, who had something of an air of dignity. He was a tall, clean-limbed, and powerful man, of about forty, remarkable for the sobriety of his demeanor, and the thoughtful gravity of his countenance. The other was a little, old fellow, not less than sixty years of age, in whose manner and carriage there was nothing to supply the want of dignity in his diminutive form and features. A sharp little black eye was the only point about him to attract attention; and in that the youth thought he saw an impertinent and knowing twinkle, which rendered his inquiries yet more offensive.

"I thought," said he to Witt, "that Captain Douglas was your captain."

"So he is," was his reply. "That is, he commands all here. But that is only so long as we choose. I did not tell you this was my *captain*. He is nc

captain, nor *lieutenant,* nor *ensign* neither.	But all of
us here follow him; and, when he is away, the rest
follow me."

"You all follow *him!*" said the traveller, looking
contemptuously on the puny figure before him.

"To be sure they do;" said Schwartz, with a quiz-
zical smile, and answering the stranger's thoughts.
"To be sure they do.	Don't you see I am the like
liest man here?"

"I cannot say I do," said the youth, offended at
the impertinent manner of the question.

"Well, I am the strongest man in the whole com
pany."

"I should hardly think that;" replied the traveller,
scornfully.

"Any how, then, I *am* the biggest," rejoined
Schwartz, laughing.	"That you must own.	What!
do you dispute that too?	Well then, look here,
stranger!	I ha'nt got no commission, and these men
are as free as I am.	What *do* you think makes them
obey my orders?"

"I really cannot say," replied the young man.

"Well," said Schwartz, "it is a curious business,
and well worth your considering; because, you see,
I have a notion if you could find that out, you would
find out a pretty good reason why you ought to tell
me your name.	But that is your business.	Some
name you must have, and the right one too.	And
you see, stranger, it makes no odds whether it is no
name or the wrong one.	It is all the same thing;

because, if you are the man that ought to have that paper, you would tell your name in a minute."

"Do *you* know who ought to have it?" asked the youth.

"May be I do," said Schwartz.

"Question for question," said the other. "*Do* you know?"

"I do."

"Well, then, my name is Arthur Trevor. Is that right?"

"That's as it may be," said Schwartz. "But now I want to know how you came by this paper."

"What need you care about that, if I am the person that ought to have it."

"Just because I want to know if you *are* the one that ought to have it."

"I tell you," replied the youth, "that my name is Arthur Trevor."

"But *I* do not *know* that it is," replied Schwartz, carelessly.

"Do you doubt my word, then?" exclaimed the youth; his eye flashing, and the blood rushing to his face, as if it would burst through his clear skin.

"Look here, stranger," said Schwartz, in a tone of quiet expostulation; "I don't mean no offence, and you'll think so too, if you'll just look at it rightly; because, you see, I don't know who you are. I don't doubt Arthur Trevor's word; and, if you are Arthur Trevor, I don't doubt your word. Now, if you have any way to show that you are Arthur Trevor, you have but to do it, and it will set all as straight as if I had axed you ten thousand pardons."

"But I have no means of showing it," said the young man, in some perplexity. "I took care to bring nothing with me to show who I am. The name of Trevor might have brought me into trouble in some parts of the country."

"That is true enough," replied Schwartz; "and so I asked you how you came by the paper, because I knew how Arthur Trevor should have come by it; and, if you got it that way, why then you are the very man."

By this time the youth saw the folly of his anger, and answered, calmly, that he got it from a man he never saw before.

"What sort of a man was he?" asked Schwartz.

"Nothing uncommon, except that he was lame."

"Did he give you anything else at the same time?"

"Yes; he gave me this;" said the youth, producing a dirty piece of paper, on which were scrawled these words:

"Sur. If you hav occashun to go of a jurney, carry this with you, bekase it mout be of sum sarvice to you."

"Well," said Schwartz, "that will do. You are Arthur Trevor, sure enough. And I reckon, Witt, you would have said so too, if you had seen this."

Witt looked at the paper, and merely nodded assent.

" Well," said the young man, " now I suppose I may go on to my friend."

" Not just yet," said Schwartz.

" Why so?" asked the youth, again relapsing into petulance.

" Just because you could not get there," was the answer.

" Why not," said he, " after finding my way thus far ?"

" For the same reason that you could not have got any farther if I had not come. You would meet with rougher customers than these between here and the camp. Come, come, my son. You must learn to take things easy. The captain has not got a better friend than me in the world ; nor you neither, if you did but know all. And, you see, you are going to a new trade ; and I thought I would just give you a lesson. Now you may see, that, when you mean nothing but what is fair and honorable, (and *you* always know how that is,) the naked truth is your best friend ; and then, the sooner it comes the better. I am pretty much of an old fox ; and I reckon I have told more lies than you ever dreamed of, but, for all that, I have seen the day when the truth was better than the cunningest lie that ever was told. And then again, it an't no use to mind what a man says when he don't know you ; because, you see, it an't you he is talking to, but just a stranger."

" But I have travelled desperate hard to-day, Witt," continued Schwartz ; " and I must push on to the camp to-night.   So just give me a mouthful, and I'll be off, and pilot Mr. Trevor through among the guards."

"My horse is at your service, as you are tired," said Arthur, whose feelings toward his new acquaintance were now quite mollified.

"I have had riding enough for one day," said Schwartz; "and was glad enough to get to where I could leave my horse.   It an't much good a horse will do you, or me either, where we are going.   By the time we climb to the top of the Devil's Backbone, you'll be more tired than me; and the horse will be worst off of any."

He now told one of the boys to make ready Arthur's horse, and, snatching a hasty morsel, seized his rifle.   "It will not do," said he, "to starve when a man is on fatigue, and it will not do to eat too much. And see here, Witt," added he, taking him apart, and speaking in a low tone, "if a long-legged, red-headed fellow comes along here, and tells you he is from Currituck, and seems to think he knows all the signs, never let him find out but what he does.   Only just make an excuse to keep him a while, and send a runner on to me, that I may have time to get out of the way, because he must not see me.   Then you can start him off again with a couple of fellows to show him the way."

CHAPTER III.

———————— The forest's shady scene,
Where things that own not man's dominion dwell,
And mortal foot hath ne'er or rarely been.

BYRON.

THE travellers now moved off together, Arthur walking, and leading his horse. They soon reached a point where a sharp ridge, jutting like a buttress from the side of the mountain, came down abruptly to the very bank of the rivulet. Up this ridge, not unaptly called "the Devil's Back-bone," the path led. Leaning, as it were, against the mountain—its position, the narrow, ridgy edge along which the traveller clambered, and the rough nodules which interrupted the ascent, like the notches in a hen's ladder, gave it no small resemblance to this house-wifely contrivance. The steep descent on either hand into deep dells, craggy and hirsute with stinted trees bristling from the sides, together with the similarity of these same nodules to the joints of the spine, had suggested a name strictly descriptive of the place. The ruggedness, steepness, and vast height of the ascent, would naturally provoke some spiteful epithet; and were the spot to be named again, a hundred to one it would receive the same name, and no other.

At the summit of this narrow stair, the travellers stopped to take breath, and look back on the scene below. Arthur, who was at the romantic age when young men are taught to affect an enthusiasm for the beauties of nature, and to prate about hues and scents, and light and shade, and prospects in all the variety of the grand, the beautiful, and the picturesque, had been feasting his imagination with the thought of the glorious view to be seen from the pinnacle before him. Like an epicure about to feast on turtle, who will not taste a biscuit beforehand lest he should spoil his dinner, so our young traveller steadily kept his face toward the hill as he ascended it. Even when he stopped to take breath, he was careful not to look behind. Schwartz, on the contrary, who was in advance, always faced about on such occasions, filling the pauses with conversation, and looking as if unconscious of the glorious scene over which his eye glanced unheeding. Arthur was vexed to see such indifference, and wondered whether this was the effect of use, or of the total absence of a faculty of which poets so much delight to speak.

At length the summit was attained; and now the youth looked around in anticipated exultation. At first he felt bound to admire, and, forgetting the unromantic character of his matter-of-fact companion, exclaimed: " Oh! how grand! how beautiful!"

"For my part," said Schwartz, indifferently, "I cannot say that I see any thing at all rightly, except it be the little branch down there, with its patches of meadow and corn-fields, and its smoky cabins. In the spring of the year, when you cannot see the cabins for the shaders, and the corn, and oats, and meadow is all of a color, it looks mightily like a little green snake. What it is like just now, I cannot say, as I never saw one of them snakes half-scaled, and with a parcel of warts on his back: but I have a notion he would look pretty much so. As to any thing else—there *is* something there, to be sure, but what it is, I am sartain I could never tell, if I did not know. And as to the distance I hear some folks talk about—why the farther you look, the less you see, that's all; until you get away yonder, t'other side of nowhere; and then you see just nothing at all."

"But the vastness of the view!" said Arthur. "The idea of immensity!"

"As to that," replied Schwartz, "you have only just to look up, and you can look a heap farther, and still see nothing. All the difference is, you know it is nothing; and down there, you know there is something, and you cannot see what it is."

"I am afraid your eyes are bad," said Arthur.

"I cannot see as well as I could once," replied Schwartz; "but if there was anything to be seen down there, I should be right apt to see it. I have clomb this hill, Mr. Trevor, when I could see the head of a nail in a target fifty yards off, and drive it with my rifle ; and I don't think I saw any thing more then than I do now ; and that is only just because there an't nothing there to see.—egad ! but there is, though ! There's that chap a coming along ; and I must see the Captain, and tell him all about it before he comes."

" I see nobody," said Arthur.

" That is because you don't look in the right place," replied Schwartz. " Look along the road."

" I don't see the road, except just at the foot of the mountain."

" Well ! Look through the sights of my rifle. There ! Don't you see a man on horseback ?"

" I see something moving," said Arthur ; " but I cannot tell what it is."

" Well," said Schwartz, " when he comes, you'll see it's a man riding on a white horse, and then, may be, you'll think if there was anything else there, I could see that too."

He now sounded a small whistle, which hung by a leathern thong from his shoulder-belt. The signal was answered from the point of a projecting crag which jutted out from the face of the cliff, not more than fifty yards off. At the same moment, a man was seen to rise up from behind a rock, which had hitherto concealed him; though, from his look-out place, he must have had a distinct view of our travellers from the moment they left the valley. He now approached and accosted Schwartz in a manner which showed that he had already recognized him. Schwartz returned the salutation, and, pointing out the man on the white horse, said : " If that fellow should happen to get by without *their* seeing him, I want you just to fall in with him, like as if you was a hunting, and so go with him to the piquet. Never let on but he knows all the signs, and keep with him : and when you get him to the piquet, make him believe that is the camp, and that the Captain will be there after a while ; and so keep him there till the Captain comes."

Having said this, he again turned his eye toward the object moving below, and gazed intently for a few minutes. Arthur, in the mean time, was left to admire the prospect, and soon began to suspect that Schwartz's ideas of the picturesque were not so far wrong. Indeed, there is nothing to admire from the spot, but the road that leads to it. From the foot of the mountain to the coast, there is an expanse of nearly three hundred miles, with no secondary ridges. As seen from that elevation, the whole is level to the eye, and presents one sheet of unbroken forest. Arthur found time to correct his preconceptions by the testimony of his own senses, while Schwartz continued to observe the movements of the distant traveller. At last he said : " That will do. They have stopped him ; and he will not get away to-night."

They now moved on quietly through a forest of lofty chestnuts, and along a path which wound its way among the scorched trunks of innumerable trees, prostrated by the fires that annually sweep through such uninhabited tracts. The soil seemed fertile, and abounding in luxuriant though coarse pasturage; and the high table-land of the mountain was more level than the peopled district below. Yet all was solitary and silent; nor was a vestige of habitation seen for miles. On inquiring the cause of this, Arthur was told that the country, at that elevation, was too cold to be inviting, as nothing would grow there but grass and oats, and that it was all shingled over with conflicting patents.

"They that claim the land," said Schwartz, "will not go to law about it with one another; because they would have to survey it, and that would cost a mint of money; so they all club to keep it as a summer range for their stock. It belongs to *some* of them, and that is enough."

He had not long done speaking, when he suddenly stopped, and, raising his rifle, fired, and began quietly to load again.

"What did you shoot at?" asked Arthur, looking in the direction of the shot.

"A monstrous fine buck," replied Schwartz.

"Where is he? I did not see him."

"You did not look in the right place. He is down and kicking; and I always like to load my gun before I go up to them, because, you see, a deer, when he is wounded, is as dangerous as a *painter*."

"A *painter!*" said Arthur. "What harm is there in a painter, more than another man?"

"O!" said Schwartz, laughing, "it an't no man at all. I don't just rightly know how you high larnt gentlemen call his name, but he is as ugly a varmint as you'd wish to see; most like a big cat. Sometimes the drotted Yankees gets hold of them and puts them in a cage; and then they call them tigers. Egad! I catched a young one once and sold him to one of these fellows; and the next time I seed him, he was carrying the creetur about with him for a show. And he did not remember me; and so I axed him what it was; and he said 'twas an Effrican tiger right from Duck river! Lord! how the folks did laugh; 'cause you see, sir, Duck river is just a little way down here in Tennessee, not over five hundred miles off; and Effrica, they tell me, is away t'other side of the her-ring-pond, where the negurs come from."

By this time the rifle was loaded, and they advanced toward the fallen deer. They were quite near before Arthur discovered him; and, at the moment, the ani-mal (a noble buck of ten branches) recovered himself so far as to regain his feet. He still staggered, but the sudden sight of his enemy seemed, at once, to stiffen his limbs with horror, and give them strength to support him. In an instant his formidable antlers were pointed; and, with eyes glaring and blood-shot, and his hair all turned the wrong way, he was in act to spring forward. At the instant, the report of the rifle was again heard, and, pitching on the points of his horns, he turned fairly heels over head, and lay with his legs in air, and quivering in death. Schwartz now drew his knife across the animal's throat, and proceeded to disembowel him, when Arthur asked what he would do with the carcass.

"I'll just hang him up in a sapling," said he, "'till I meet one of our men. There ought to be one close by, and I can send him for him. Where there's a hundred mouths to feed, such a buck as this is a cash article."

At this moment, the snapping of a dry stick caught his ear; and, looking up, he saw a man approaching.

"I don't know that fellow," said he, looking hard at him. "But it's all one. I can make him know me."

The usual salutation now passed, and the stranger said: "If I may be so bold, stranger, I'd be glad to know what parts you are from?"

"From Passamaquoddy," said Schwartz.

"Can you tell me the price of skins down there away?"

"Twenty-five cents and a quarter a pound," replied Schwartz.

A few more simple questions and out-of-the-way answers were exchanged, when Schwartz, addressing the other, in an under tone, said: "You are one of the new recruits, I reckon?" The other nodded; and Schwartz went on to ask their number. Being told they were fifty, he said, gravely: "Now, there you are wrong. You are right enough to pass me, after I gave you the word; but that's no reason you should tell me anything. I just asked you, you see, to give you a 'caution ; cause a fellow might come along here that would give you the word as straight as any body, and be a spy all the time. So the right way would be, just to pass him and keep dark, that's the rule ; and, by the time he'd find out how many men we've got, may be he'd find out something else he would not like quite so well. But come, let us take the deer up the road, and you can walk your post and watch it, till I can send somebody for it from the piquet."

The sturdy mountaineer at once shouldered the animal ; and, striding along to the road, threw him down, and quietly betook himself to eating the chestnuts that covered the ground. The traveller moved on, and presently came to the piquet.

Here was a small party quartered in a rude and ruinous cabin, near which was an enclosure around a beautiful fountain, that welled up from a natural basin of stone. In this were confined twenty or thirty calves. A few horses were piqueted at hand, and the sides of the adjoining hills were covered with a numerous herd of fat cattle, browsing on the faded, but still succulent vegetation. The time was come when they should have been driven down for the winter, to the farms of their owners below, but they were left here that the men might have the use of their milk. Should the hunting at any time prove unsuccessful, there was always a beef at hand.

Here Schwartz was known, and joyfully welcomed. He stopped only to tell of the deer, and moved on. "You have a curious system here," said Arthur; "I see the people here know you, but how did you manage with that new recruit? I watched you, and I did not see you give him any sign, and he did not ask for a countersign."

"That is all because you don't know what foolish answers I gave to his questions. You see, we ha'nt got no countersign rightly; 'cause you see, when I stop a man, I want to know who he is, but I don't want to tell him anything about myself. But if I ax a man for the countersign, just so I might as well tell him I am on guard at once. So we've just got, may be, twenty simple questions; and when we ask them, our own folks know what answer to give, and the answer is sure to be one that nobody would give unless he was in the secret."

"And pray how did you find out that I was Arthur Trevor?"

"O! nothing easier, sir. That man that gave you the map was not no more lame than you. But I told him to be sure and not give it to nobody but you, and then to limp so as you'd be sure to notice it. You see, it was I that was to try fall in with you, and pilot you; but, after that, I got up another scheme. As to the other paper, that was to serve you with our folks, because there was a mark there you did not notice, that any of them would know; and then they would be middling sure you were the man you said you were. They would have been civil to you, and let you pass, but then they would have sent a man or two to the camp with you. And now, Mr. Trevor, *here is* something that I *can* see, and I have a notion it's worth looking at."

While he was yet speaking, Arthur's ears had been saluted by a brawling sound, which he now recognized as the rush of water. Turning his head towards it, he perceived that it proceeded from a deep and shaggy dell, which the path was now approaching, and along the verge of which it presently wound. Here the plain broke sheer down into a gulph of vast depth, at the bottom of which a considerable stream was seen. It dashed rapidly along, pouring its sparkling waters over successive barriers of yellow rock, that sent up a golden gleam from beneath the crystal sheet that covered them. The mountain-pine, the fir, the kalmia, and numberless other evergreens, which nearly filled the gorge, afforded only occasional glimpses of the water; while they set off the picturesque appearance of so much as they permitted to be seen. As they advanced, they came to a part where the trees had been cut from the brow of the cliff; and, several of those below having been removed, a clearer view was afforded.

Here, at the depth of two hundred feet, figures were seen moving to and fro, while, right opposite, under a beetling cliff, that screened them from above, were groups clustered around fires, kindled against the rock, behind a rude breast-work of logs. The whole breadth of the stream was here exposed

to view, apparently twenty or thirty yards wide.
Though shallow, by reason of its rapidity it seemed
to pour a vast volume of water.

Standing on the brow of the cliff, Schwartz now
uttered a shout, and immediately half a dozen men,
seizing their rifles, moved up the glen, and were
soon hidden under the bank on which the travellers
stood. They now went on, and presently reached a
point at which the path, turning short to the left,
dived into the abyss, leading down a rugged ledge
that sloped along the face of the cliff, in the direction opposite to that of their approach. It reached
the very bottom, nearly under the point from which
the shout of Schwartz had given notice of his presence. Here he stopped; and, requesting Arthur
to wait a moment, he descended. He had not gone
far before his name was repeated by a dozen voices,
and immediately he was heard to say: "Yes, it is
Schwartz; and I have a friend with me."

"Bring him down," was the answer; upon which
Schwartz, returning, requested Arthur to follow
him, and mind his footing. Arthur obeyed, and
descended, not without some appearance of danger,
sometimes leaping and sometimes crawling, until he
reached the group stationed at the foot of this rude
stairway. Here let us leave him for a while, and
go back to inquire who and whence he was.

CHAPTER IV.

—— Handmaid of Prudence, Fortune comes
Prompt to her bidding, ready to fulfil
Her mistress' pleasure; whether she demand
The treasures of the South, the applause of men,
Or the calm sunshine of domestic bliss,
Lo! they are hers!　　　　　　　　ANONYMOUS.

ARTHUR TREVOR was the youngest son of a gentleman who resided in the neighborhood of Richmond.
He was a man in affluent circumstances, and had long
and honorably filled various important and dignified
stations in the service of his native State.　Endowed
with handsome talents, an amiable disposition, and all
the accomplishments that can adorn a gentleman, he
added to these the most exemplary virtues.　His
influence in society had, of course, been great, and
though now, at the age of seventy, withdrawn from
public life, his opinions were inquired of, and his counsel sought, by all who had access to him.　Through
life he had been remarkable for firmness, and yet
more for prudence.　The steadiness of his principles
could never be questioned, but, it was thought, he
had sometimes deemed it wise to compromise, when
men of less cautious temper would have found safety
in prudent boldness.

To this temperament had been attributed his conduct in regard to the politics of the last twenty years.
*Bred up in the school of State rights, and thoroughly
imbued with its doctrines, he had, even before that time,
been accustomed to look, with a jealous eye, on the progressive usurpations of the Federal Government. In the
hope of arresting these, he had exerted more than his
usual activity in aiding to put down the younger Adams,
and to elevate his successor. Though no candidate for
the spoils of victory, no man rejoiced more sincerely in
the result of that contest ; and, until the emanation of the
proclamation of December, 1832, he had given his hearty
approbation, and steady, though quiet support, to the
administration of Andrew Jackson.*

From that moment he seemed to look with fearful
bodings on the affairs of his country. His disap-
probation of that instrument was expressed with as
much freedom and force as was consistent with his
habitual reserve and moderation. He was, indeed,
alarmed into a degree of excitement unusual with
him, and might have gone farther than he did, had
he not found that others were disposed to go, as he
thought, too far. He had entirely disapproved the
nullifying ordinance of South Carolina ; and, though
he recognized the right of secession, he deprecated
all thought of resorting to that remedy. He was
aware that many of his best friends, thinking that
its necessity would be eventually felt by all, feared
that that conviction might come too late. They
remarked the steady tendency of Federal measures to

weaken the malcontent States in the South, and to increase the resources of their northern oppressors and those of the General Government. Hence they feared, that whenever Virginia, or any other of the slave-holding States, should find itself driven to secession, the other party, in the confidence of superior strength, might be tempted forcibly to resist the exercise of the right. They thus arrived at the conclusion that separation (which they deemed inevitable) to be peaceable, must be prompt.

These ideas had been laid before Mr. Trevor, and, in proportion to the urgency with which they were pressed, was his alarm and his disposition to adhere to the Union. He, at last, had brought himself to believe union, on any terms, better than disunion, under any circumstances. As the lesser evil, therefore, he determined to forget the proclamation, and, striving to reconcile himself to all the acts of the administration, he regarded every attempt to unite the South, in support of a southern president, as a prelude to the formation of a southern confederacy. By consequence, he became a partisan of Martin Van Buren; and united with Ritchie, and others of the same kidney, in endeavoring to subdue the spirit, and tame down the State pride of Virginia. These endeavors, aided by the lavish use of federal patronage in the State, were so far successful, that when, at the end of Van Buren's second term, he demanded a third election, she alone, in the South, supported his pretensions.

By the steady employment of the same pernicious influences, the elections throughout the State had been so regulated, as to produce returns of a majority of members devoted to the views of the usurper. This had continued until the spring of 1848, at which time the results of the elections were essentially the same which had taken place since the memorable 1836 ; when Virginia, at one stroke of the pen, *expunged* her name from the chronicles of honor, *expunged* the history of all her glories, *expunged herself.* From that time the land of Washington, and Henry, and Mason, of Jefferson, Madison, and Randolph, sunk to the rank of a province, administered and managed by the Riveses and Ritchies, the Barbours and Stevensons, the Watkinses and Wilsons, whose chance to be remembered in history depends, like that of Erostratus, on the glories of that temple of liberty which they first desecrated and then destroyed.

> " Where once the Cæsars dwelt,
>   There dwelt, tuneless, the birds of night."

From some cause, not understood at the time, an unexpected reaction had taken place between the spring elections and the recurrence of that *form* of presidential election in the fall, the observance of which was still deemed necessary to display, and, by displaying, to perpetuate the usurper's power. This reaction appeared to show itself chiefly in those counties heretofore most distinguished for their loyalty.

It would have seemed as if the spirit of John Randolph had risen from the sleep of death, and walked abroad through the scenes where his youthful shoulders had received the mantle of *his* eloquence from the hand of Henry. For the first time, in twelve years, the vote of Virginia was recorded against the re-election of Martin Van Buren to the presidential throne.

But not the less subservient were the proceedings of the Legislature elected for his use, the spring before. Yet enough had been done to justify the hope that the ancient spirit of old Virginia would yet show itself in the descendants of the men who had defied Cromwell, in the plenitude of his power, and had cast off the yoke of George the Third, without waiting for the co-operation of the other colonies. At the same time, the power and the will of a fixed majority in the North, to give a master to the South, had been made manifest. It was clearly seen, too, that he had determined to use the power thus obtained, and to administer the government solely with a view to the interest of that sectional faction, by which he had been supported. " *Væ victis !*" " Woe to the vanquished!" was the word. It had gone forth ; and northern cupidity and northern fanaticism were seen to march, hand in hand, to the plunder and desolation of the South.

Under these circumstances, the Southern States had been, at length, forced to see that the day for decisive action had arrived. They therefore deter-

mined no longer to abide the obligations of a constitution, the form of which alone remained, and
having, by a movement nearly simultaneous, seceded
from the Union, they had immediately formed a
Southern Confederacy. *The suddenness of these
measures was less remarkable than the prudence with
which they had been conducted. The two together
left little doubt that there had been a preconcert
among the leading men of the several States, arrang-
ing provisionally what should be done, whenever circumstances should throw power into the hands of those
whom, at the bidding of the usurper, the people had
once driven from their councils. It is now known
that there was such concert. Nor was it confined to
the seceding States alone. In Virginia, also, there
were men who entered into the same views.* But
while the President believed that no decisive step
would be taken by the more Southern States without her co-operation, he had devoted all his power,
direct and indirect, to control and influence her elections. Of tumultuary insurrection he had no fear.
The organized operation of the State Government
was what he dreaded. By this alone could the measure of secession be effected ; and this was effectually prevented by operating on the elections of
members of the Legislature of Virginia. From the
November vote on the Presidential election, less
evil had been apprehended, and less pains had been
taken to control it. In consequence of this, something more of the real sentiments of the people had

been allowed to appear on that occasion; and, from this manifestation, the more Southern States were encouraged to hope for the ultimate accession of Virginia to their Confederacy. *They had therefore determined to wait for her no longer, but to proceed to the execution of their plan, leaving her to follow.*

The disposition of the usurper, at first, was to treat them as revolted provinces; and to take measures for putting down, by force, their resistance to his authority. But circumstances, to be mentioned hereafter, made it impolitic to resort to this measure. But these did not operate to prevent him from using the most efficacious means to prevent Virginia from following their example. Though restrained from attacking them, nothing prevented him from affecting to fear an attack *from* them. This gave a pretext for raising troops; and the position of Virginia, as the frontier State, afforded an excuse for stationing them within her borders. Under these pretences, small corps were established in many of the disaffected counties. Should the presence of these be ineffectual to secure the return of delegates devoted to the crown, an ultimate security was taken against the action of the Legislature. Richmond, the seat of government, became the head-quarters of the army of observation, as it was called, and, surrounded by this, the mock deliberations of the General Assembly were to be held.

The money thus thrown into the country seduced the corrupt, while terror subdued the timid. On

Mr. Trevor, who was neither, these things had a contrary effect. He now, when it was too late, saw
and lamented the error of his former overcaution.
He now began to suspect that they had been right
who had urged him, eighteen years before, to lend
his aid in the work of arousing the people to a sense
of their danger, and preparing them to meet it as
one man.

CHAPTER V.

A sponge that soaks up the king's countenance.
HAMLET.

AMONG those who had been most prompt to take this view of the subject, and most vehement in recommending it, was a younger brother of Mr. Trevor. In all, but the great essentials of moral worth, this gentleman was the very reverse of his brother. The difference was, perhaps, mainly attributable to the character of his intellect. Quick in conception, and clear in his views, he was strong in his convictions, and habitually satisfied with his conclusions. This, added to a hasty temper, gave him the appearance and character of a man rash, inconsiderate, and precipitate, always in advance of the progress of public opinion, and too impatient to wait for it. His ill success in life seemed to justify this construction. Though eminently gifted by nature, and possessing all the advantages of education, he had never occupied any of those stations in which distinction is to be gained. In his private affairs, he had been alike unprosperous. Though his habits were not expensive, his patrimony had been but little increased by his own exertions. He had married a lady of handsome property, but had added little to it. With only

two daughters, he had not the means of endowing
them with more than a decent competency; while
his elder brother, with a family of a dozen children,
had educated the whole, and provided handsomely
for such as had set out in life, and retained the where-
withal to give the rest nearly as much as the children
of the younger could expect. In short, the career
of Mr. Hugh Trevor had been one of uninterrupted
prosperity. In all his undertakings he had been
successful. Wealth had flowed into his coffers, and
honors had been showered on his head. "When the
eye saw him, then it blessed him." Men pointed
him out to their children, and said to them: "Copy
his example, and follow his steps."

The life of Bernard, the younger brother, had been
passed in comparative obscurity. Beloved by a few,
but misunderstood by many, his existence was unknown to the multitude, and unheeded by most who
were aware of it. They, indeed, who knew him
well, saw in him qualities which, under discreet re-
gulation, might have won for him distinction and
affluence. None knew him better, and none saw this
more clearly, than his elder brother. No man gave
him more credit for talent and honor, or less for prudence and common sense. A habit of doubting the
correctness of his opinions, and condemning his
measures, had thus taken possession of the mind of
Mr. Hugh Trevor: and, as the quick and intuitive
Bernard was commonly the first to come to a conclusion, the knowledge of that created, in the other, a

predisposition to arrive at a different result. In proportion as the one was clear, so did the other doubt. When the former was ardent, the latter was always cold; and in all matters in which they had a common interest, the cautious foresight of Hugh never failed to see a lion in the path which Bernard wished to pursue. They were the opposite poles of the same needle. The clear convictions of the latter on the subject of secession had shaken the faith of the former in his own, and had finally driven him to the conclusion already intimated, "that *union, on any terms,* was better than disunion, *under any circumstances.*"

The same habit of thinking had retarded the change, which the events of the last three years had been working in the mind of Mr. Hugh Trevor. His native candor and modesty made it easy for him to believe that he had been wrong, and, being convinced of error, to admit it. But a corollary from this admission would be, that the inconsiderate and imprudent Bernard had, all the time, been right. Of the correctness of such an admission Mr. Trevor felt an habitual diffidence, that made him among the last to avow a change of opinion which, perhaps, commenced in no mind sooner than in his. But the change was now complete, and it brought to the conscientious old gentleman a conviction that on him, above all men, it was incumbent to spare no means in his power to remove the mischiefs of which he felt his own supineness to have been in part the cause.

He was now a private man; but he had sons. To
have given a direction to their political course, might
not have been difficult. But, in the act of repenting
an acknowledged error, how could he presume so far
on his new convictions, as to endeavor to bind them
on the minds of others? Was it even right to use
any portion of his paternal influence for the purpose
of giving to the future course of his children's lives
such a tendency as might lead them into error, to
the disappointment of their hopes, and perhaps to
crime? The answer to these questions led to a determination to leave them to their own thoughts,
guided by such lights as circumstances might throw
upon these important subjects.

It happened unfortunately, that, about the time
of Mr. Van Buren's accession to the presidency, his
eldest son had just reached the time of life when it
is necessary to choose a profession. Without any
particular purpose of devoting him to the army, he
had been educated at West Point. The favor of
President Jackson had offered this advantage, which,
by the father of so large a family, was not to be
declined. But the young man acquired a taste for
military life, and there was no man in Virginia whom
the new President was more desirous to bind to his
service than Mr. Hugh Trevor; his wishes had been
ascertained, and the ready advancement of his son
was the consequence. The promotion of Owen Trevor
had accordingly been hastened by all means consistent with the rules of the service. Even these were

sometimes violated in his favor. In one instance, he had been elevated over the head of a senior officer of acknowledged merit. The impatience of this gentleman, which had tempted him to offer his resignation, had been soothed by a staff appointment, accompanied by an understanding that he should not, unnecessarily, be placed under the immediate command of young Trevor. The latter, at the date of which we speak, had risen to the command of a regiment, which was now encamped in the neighborhood of Washington, in daily expectation of being ordered on active duty.

Colonel Owen Trevor had received his first impressions, on political subjects, at a time when circumstances made his father anxious to establish in his mind a conviction that union was the one thing needful. To the maintenance of this he had taught him to devote himself, and, *overlooking his allegiance to his native State, to consider himself as the sworn soldier of the Federal Government. It was certainly not the wish of Mr. Trevor to teach his son to regard Virginia merely as a municipal division of a great consolidated empire.* But while he taught him to act on precepts which seemed drawn from such premises, it was natural that the young man should adopt them.

He did adopt them. He had learned to deride the idea of State sovereignty; and his long residence in the North had given him a disgust at all that is peculiar in the manners, habits, institutions, and character of Virginia. Among his boon companions he had been accustomed to express these sentiments; and, being repeated at court, they had made him a favorite there. He had been treated by the President with distinguished attention. He seemed honored, too, with the personal friendship of that favorite son, whom he had elevated to the chief command of the army. Him he had consecrated to the purple; proposing to cast on him the mantle of his authority, so as to unite, in the person of his chosen successor, the whole military and civil power of the empire.

It was impossible that a young man, like Col. Trevor, should fail to feel himself flattered by such notice. He had been thought, when a boy, to be warm-hearted and generous, and his devotion to his patrons, which was unbounded, was placed to the account of gratitude by his friends. The President, on his part, was anxiously watching for an opportunity to reward this personal zeal, which is so strong a recommendation to the favor of the great. It was intimated to Col. Trevor that nothing was wanting to ensure him speedy promotion to the rank of brigadier, but some act of service which might be magnified, by a pensioned press, into a pretext for advancing him beyond his equals in rank. Apprised of this, he burned for active employment, and earnestly begged to be marched to the theatre of war.

This theatre was Virginia. But he had long since ceased to attribute any political personality to the State, and it was a matter of no consequence to him that the enemies, against whom he was to act, had been born or resided there. Personally they were strangers to him; and he only knew them as men denying the supremacy of the Federal Government, and hostile to the President and his intended successor (Van Buren).

One person, indeed, he might possibly meet in arms, whom he would gladly avoid. His younger brother, Douglas Trevor, had been, like himself, educated at West Point, had entered the army, and served some years. *Having spent a winter at home, it was suspected that he had become infected with the treasonable heresies of southern politicians. He had resigned his commission and travelled into South Carolina. The effect of this journey on his opinions was not a matter of doubt. Letters had been received from him, by his brother and several young officers of his own regiment, avowing a total change of sentiment. These letters left no doubt, that should Virginia declare for secession, or even in case of collision between the Southern League and the old United States, he would be found fighting against the latter.* The avowal of such sentiments and purposes had so excited the displeasure of the Colonel, that he had cut short the correspondence by begging that he might never again be reminded that he was the brother of a traitor. His letter to this effect, being laid before the commander-in-chief, had given the most decisive proof of the zeal of one brother and the defection of the other.

How this had been brought about, Colonel Trevor knew not. He was not aware of any alteration in his father's sentiments; and, indeed, Douglas himself had not been so, at the time when he was awakened to a sense of his country's wrongs and his own duty. The change in his mind had been wrought by other means; for his father was, at that time, doubting, and, with him, to doubt was to be profoundly silent.

CHAPTER VI.

——————————— The boy is grown
So like your brother that he seems his own.

CRABBE.

DIFFERENCE of political opinion had produced no
estrangement between Mr. Hugh Trevor and his brother, though it had interrupted their intercourse by
rendering it less agreeable. Men cannot take much
pleasure in each other's society, when the subject on
which both think and feel most deeply, is one on
which they widely differ. They accordingly saw little
of each other, though an occasional letter passed
between them in token of unabated affection.

I believe I have mentioned that the children of Mr.
Bernard Trevor were both daughters. The eldest,
then seventeen years of age, had been invited to
spend, with her uncle, in the vicinity of Richmond,
the winter of Douglas's furlough. He was at that
time about five-and-twenty. His long residence in
the North had not weaned him from his native State.
He had not been flattered into a contempt of every
thing Virginian. Neither his age nor rank gave him
consequence enough to be the object of that sort of
attention. Perhaps, too, it had been seen that he was

a less fit subject for it than his elder brother. Though much the younger, he had a range, originality, and independence of thought, of which the other was incapable. Resting in the esteem of his friends and the approbation of his own conscience, the applause of the multitude, the flattery of sycophants, and the seducing attentions of superiors, had small charms for him. His heart had never ceased to glow at the name of Virginia, and he returned to her as the wanderer should return to the bosom of his home—to his friends—to his native land. In appearance, manners, and intelligence, he was much improved; in feeling, the same warm-hearted, generous, unsophisticated youth, as formerly.

In the meantime, his cousin Delia had already reached his father's house, and was domesticated in the family. There she found the younger brothers and sisters of Douglas impatiently expecting his arrival; and so much occupied with the thought of him, that, had she been of a jealous disposition, she might have deemed her welcome somewhat careless. But she already knew her cousins, her uncle, and her aunt. This was not the first time that their house was her temporary home; and she had learned to consider herself as one of the family. As such, she was expected to enter into all their feelings. Douglas was their common favorite. During his long absence, his heart had never cooled toward them. In this he differed widely from Owen, in whom the pleasures of an idle life and the schemes of ambition had left little thought of the simple joys of his childhood's home. The contrast between him and Douglas, in this respect, rendered the latter yet more popular with the single-hearted beings who were impatiently waiting his return.

" Do you remember brother Douglas ?" said Virginia Trevor (a girl one year younger than Delia). " Mamma says you were a great pet with him, when a child, and used to call him your Douglas."

" I could not have been more than three years old at the time you speak of," said Delia ; " but I have heard of it so often, that I seem to myself to remember him. But, of course, I do not remember him."

" And, of course, he does not remember you," said Mrs. Trevor. " At least he would not know you. But I doubt if he ever has forgotten you, as you were then. He was to be your husband, you know; and your father gave him a set of rules to walk by. He was to do so and so, and to be so and so ; and Harry Sanford was to be his model. He said nothing about it ; but ' Sanford and Merton' was hardly ever out of his hands, and we could see that he was always trying to square his conduct by your father's maxims. I believe in my heart it made a difference in the boy ; and that is the reason why he is less like his own father, and more like yours, than any of the rest of my boys."

" I shall certainly love him, then," said Delia, her eyes filling as she spoke, "if he is like my dear old father."

"Indeed, and you may," said Mrs. Trevor; "but, for all that, I would rather have him like his own father. But you must not be affronted, Delia; you know I claim the right to brag about my old man, and to set him up over everybody—even the President himself."

"*I never saw the President*," said Delia, "*but I should be sorry to compare my father with him.*"

"I can assure you," replied the aunt, "there are very few men that would *bear* the comparison. Oh! he is the most elegant, agreeable old gentleman, that ever I saw."

"Except my uncle," said Delia, smiling.

"Pshaw! Yes, to be sure. I always except him."

"*I* will not except *my father*," said Delia, gravely. "I should not like to hear him and Martin Van Buren praised in the same breath."

"Well, my dear," said the good-humored old lady, "we must not quarrel about it. *But you must take care not to talk so before Douglas, because he is the President's soldier.*"

"*I thought*," said Delia, "*he was in the service of the United States.*"

"Well! and is not that all the same thing? *I* do not pretend to know anything about it, but my husband says so, and that is enough for me."

Mr. Trevor, who had sat by the while, listening with grave complacency, now said: "I am afraid you don't report me truly, my dear." Then, extending his hand to Delia, he drew her gently to him, and placing her on his knee, kissed her. "You are a good girl," said he, "and shall love and honor your father as much as you please. He is a noble, gene‑ rous man, and a wise man too. I would to God," added he, sighing heavily, "that I had had half his wisdom."

"Why, bless my soul, Mr. Trevor!" exclaimed his wife, "what does this mean?"

"Nothing," replied he, "but a just compliment to the self‑renouncing generosity and far‑sighted sagacity of my brother."

Saying this, he rose and left the room, while his wife gazed after him in amazement. She had never heard him say so much before, and now perceived that he had thoughts that she was not apprised of. Believing him faultless and incapable of error, even when he differed from himself, she at once concluded that she had lost her cue, and determined to say no more about politics until she recovered it. But he never adverted to the subject again, in her presence, during the whole winter; and her niece, consequently, heard no farther allusion to it from her.

This was no unwelcome relief to Delia. She was no politician; but she was not incapable of under‑ standing what passed in her presence on the subject, except when the interlocutors chose to mystify their meaning. Her father, a man of no reserves, never spoke but with a purpose of expressing his thoughts clearly and fully; and no man better knew how to express them than he. Though deficient, as I have said, in that cold prudence which takes advantage of circumstances, he was eminently gifted with that more vigorous faculty *which makes them.* In the piping times of peace, he was a man of no mark. But when society was breaking up from its foundations, he was the man with whom the timid and doubting would seek safety and counsel. Infirmity had now overtaken him, and he could do little more than think and speak. Consulted by all the bold spirits who sought to lift up, from the dust, the soiled and tattered banner of his native State, and spread it to the wind, he never failed to converse freely with such, and often in the presence of his daughters.

By this means, if he had not imbued them with his opinions, or charged their minds with the arguments by which he was accustomed to support them, he had made them full partakers of his feelings. It seemed, indeed, as if he had a purpose in this. What that purpose was, time would show. One end, at least, it answered. It increased their opinion of his powers, their confidence in his wisdom, and their love for his person. Mrs. Hugh Trevor herself did not hold her husband's wisdom in more reverence than was cherished by Delia for that of her father.

And never did man better deserve the confiding affection of a daughter. He had been her principal instructor from infancy. He had formed her mind; he had trained her to self-command, and taught her to find her happiness in virtue. Educated at home,

her manners were formed in a domestic circle—cha
racterized by refinement, and delicate, but frank propriety. Her love of reading had been cultivated by
throwing books in her way; and, the taste once
formed, her attention had been directed to such as
might best qualify her for the duties of woman's only
appropriate station. Herein she had an example in
her mother; a lady of the old school, courteous and
gentle, but high-spirited, generous, and full of her
husband's enthusiasm in the cause of his country.
Mr. Bernard Trevor was, indeed, a man to be loved
passionately, if loved at all; and to shed the vivid
hue of his mind on those of his associates. It was
the delight of his wife to witness, and to cherish, the
dutiful affection and ardent admiration of her daughters for their father. The consequence was, that his
power over their thoughts, feelings, and inclinations
was unbounded.

It will be readily believed, that, in the mind of
Delia Trevor, thus pre-occupied, there was no room
for any very favorable predispositions toward a young
man, trained from his boyhood in the service of her
country's oppressors. She had heard his mother
speak of him as the sworn soldier of the arch-enemy
of her beloved Virginia; and a sentiment of abhor-
rence arose in her mind at the words. But she reflected that he was her cousin; the son of her good
uncle; the brother of her dearest friend; and, trying
to remember his fondness for her when a child, she
chided down the feeling of disgust, as unnatural and

wicked. But, after all this discipline of her own mind, she found it impossible to think of him with complacency, or to anticipate his arrival with pleasure. *Her imagination always painted him in the hateful dress, which she had been taught to regard as the badge of slavery—the livery of a tyrant. She would try to love him, as a kinsman, but she never could like him or respect him.*

At length he made his appearance, and, to her great relief, in the plain attire of a citizen. He was a handsome youth, whose native grace had been improved by his military education, and in his manners uniting the frankness of a boy with the polish and elegance of an accomplished gentleman. Whether he had been admonished by his father to respect the feelings of his fair cousin, or had caught his reserve, on the subject of politics, by contagion, she had no means of knowing. Certain it is, that, on that subject, he was uniformly silent, and Delia soon learned to converse with him on other topics, without dreading an allusion to that. She thus saw him as he was, and, by degrees, lost the prejudice which, for a time, blinded her to any merit he might possess.

And he did possess great merit. A high sense of honor, strict principles, great openness, and generosity, were united in him with talents of no common order. Quick, apprehensive, and clear in his perceptions, there was a boldness, vividness, and distinctness in his thoughts and language, that continually reminded her of him she most loved and honored. Of her father

he frequently spoke with great veneration and affection. He remembered, as his mother had conjectured,
many of his uncle's precepts. He frequently quoted
them as of high authority with him; and it was plain
to see, that, cherished during fourteen years, they had
exercised a decided influence in the formation of his
character. Indeed, it might be doubted whether his
imagination had ever dismissed the idea, which had
first disposed him to lend a willing ear to the suggestions of his uncle. That which was sport to the elder
members of the family, had seemed to him, at the
time, a serious business. The thought that the little
girl, who loved to hang on his neck and kiss him,
might one day be his wife, had certainly taken possession of his boyish mind. How long he had con-
sciously retained it could not be known; but the
traces of it were still there, and were certainly not
obliterated by the change which time had wrought in
his cousin.

Of her personal appearance I have said nothing.
Were I writing a novel, I should be bound, by all
precedent, to give an exact account of Delia's whole
exterior. Her person, her countenance, her hair, her
eyes, her complexion, should all be described, and
the whole summed up in a *tout ensemble* of surpassing
beauty. But, in this true history, I am unfortunately
bound down by facts, and I lament, that to the best
of my recollection, I shall not have occasion to speak
of a single female, in the progress of my narrative,
whose beauty can be made a theme of just praise. I

do sincerely lament this; for such is the constitution of human nature, that female beauty influences the heart and mind of man, even by report. We read, in Oriental tales, of great princes deeply enamored of descriptions. The grey eyes of Queen Elizabeth have always made her unpopular with the youthful reader; and the beauty of Mary of Scotland, three hundred years after the worms have eaten her, still continues to gild her history and gloss over her crimes. I can say nothing so much in favor of the beauty of Delia Trevor, as that she was good and intelligent, reminding the reader of the sage adage of Mrs. Dorothy Primrose, to wit: "Handsome is, that handsome does." I can only add, that, when I saw her afterwards hanging on the arm of Douglas, and looking up in his face with all the deep and heartfelt devotion of a woman's love, I saw enough of the constituents of beauty to make her an object of love, and enough of the soul of truth and tenderness to make her seem transcendently beautiful in the eyes of a lover.

I say this, to account for the fact that her cousin Douglas soon found himself taking great pleasure in her society, and anxious to please her, not more from duty than inclination. He was, perhaps, chiefly attracted by her conversation, which was always cheerful, sprightly, and intelligent. He may have yielded to a spell of hardly less magic than that of beauty; the spell of a voice melodious, distinct, articulate, and richly flexible, varying its tones unconsciously with every change and grade of thought or feeling.

It may have been the effect of what Byron would call "blind contact," and the sage Mrs. Broadhurst "propinquity;" or it may have been that his hour was come. If one in ten of my married friends can tell exactly how *he* came to fall in love with his wife, I shall hold myself bound to inquire farther into this matter.

But I do not mean to intimate that Lieutenant Trevor, turning his·back on the belles of Boston and New York, and Philadelphia, and Baltimore, and Washington, came home, and tumbled forthwith into love with a plain country girl, just because she was his cousin, and he had loved her when a child. I do not mean to say he was in love with her at all. He had a sincere affection for her; he liked her conversation; he admired her talents much, and her virtues more. He liked very much to be with her, and he was very much with her.

What came of this, the reader shall be told when we have disposed of some matters of higher concernment.

CHAPTER VII.

Nero fiddled while Rome was burning.

DOUGLAS TREVOR reached his father's house just after the Virginia Legislature had assembled. The presidential election was just over, and the partisans of Van Buren, exulting in their success, made their leader the more hateful to his opponents by the insolence of their triumph. Though he had lost the vote of Virginia, it will be remembered that he still commanded a majority in the Legislature, elected before the revolution in public sentiment was complete. The more recent expression of public sentiment showed that the time was come when power must be held by means far different from those by which it had been acquired. Opinion, which at first had been in their favor, was now against them. Corruption had for a time supplied the place; but the fund of corruption was all insufficient to buy off the important interests which were now roused to defend themselves. To add to its efficiency by all practicable means, and to bring to its aid the arm of force, was all that remained.

To organize measures for this purpose, and to enrich themselves from the profuse disbursement of public money, which formed a part of the plan of

operations, were the great objects which engaged
the minds of the majority in the Virginia Legislature. But these, important as they were, could not
entirely wean them from those indulgences which,
for many years, had made Richmond, during the
winter season, the scene of so much revel and
debauchery. To these, as well as to personal intri-
gues and the great interests of the faction, much
time was given. *But the necessity of attending
especially to the latter was made daily more apparent
by the startling intelligence which every mail brought
from the South and Southwest. The nearly simultaneous secession of the States in that quarter, and
the measures to be taken for the formation of a
southern confederacy, were things which had been
talked off until they were no longer dreaded. But
causes had gradually wrought their necessary effects,
and the ultimate cooperation of Virginia, if left to
act freely, was now sure.*

I have already spoken of those men, in each of the
southern States, of cool heads, long views, and stout
hearts, who, watching the progress of events, had
clearly seen the point to which they tended. It is
not here that their names and deeds are to be regis-
tered. They are already recorded in history, and
blazoned on the tomb of that hateful tyranny which
they overthrew. They had been discarded from the
service of the people, so long as the popularity of the
President had blinded the multitude to his usurpations. "The oppressions of the northern faction,

and the fierce assaults of rapacity and fanaticism, *Rapacity*
hounded on by ambition to the destruction of the
South, had restored them [the 'State-rights men']
to public favor. They had seen that secession must
come, and that, come when it might, their influence
would be proportioned to their past disgraces. Pre-
suming on this, they had consulted much together.
Not only had they sketched provisionally the plan
of a southern confederacy, but they had taken
measures to regulate their relations with foreign
powers." One of their number, travelling abroad,
had been instructed to prepare the way for the
negotiation of a commercial treaty with Great
Britain. One of the first acts of the new confederacy was to invest him publicly with the diplomatic
character, and it was at once understood that commercial arrangements would be made, the value of
which would secure to the infant League all the
advantages of an alliance with that powerful nation.
The designation of a gentleman, as minister, who
had so long, without any ostensible motive, resided
near the Court of St. James, left no doubt that all
things had been already arranged. The treaty soon
after promulgated, therefore, surprised nobody, except indeed that some of its details were too obviously beneficial to both parties to have been expected. Not only in war, but in peace, do nations seem
to think it less important to do good to themselves
than to do harm to each other. The system of free *free*
trade now established, which has restored to the *trade*

South the full benefit of its natural advantages, and made it once more the most flourishing and prosperous country on earth ; which has multiplied the manufactories of Great Britain, and increased her revenue by an increase of consumption and resources, even while some branches of revenue were cut off; and which, at the same time, has broken the power of her envious rival in the North, and put an end for ever to that artificial prosperity engendered by the oppression and plunder of the southern States ; is such an anomaly in modern diplomacy, that the rulers at Richmond, or even at Washington, might well have been surprised at it. But the bare nomination of the plenipotentiary was enough to leave no doubt that a treaty was ready for promulgation, and that its terms must be such as to secure the co-operation of Great Britain.

But, while the leaders of the ruling faction thought of these things, and anxiously consulted for the preservation of their power, there was still found among the members of the Legislature the ordinary proportion of men who think of nothing but the enjoyment of the present moment. Such men are often like sailors in a storm, who, becoming desperate, break into the spirit room, and drink the more eagerly because they drink for the last time. When the devil's "time is short, he has great wrath;" and this point in his character he always displays, whether he exhibits himself in the form of cruelty, rapacity, or debauchery.

The amusements, therefore, of the legislators assembled at Richmond suffered little interruption, and the dinner and the galas, the ball and the theatre, and the gaming-table, with revel, dissipation, and extravagance, consumed the time of the servants of the country, and swallowed up the wasted plunder of the treasury.

Respected by all, beloved by individuals of both parties, and courted by that to which he was supposed to belong, Mr. Hugh Trevor was an object of the most flattering attention. His house was the favorite resort of such as enjoyed the envied privilege of the *entrée*. His gallant and accomplished son was the glass before which aspirants for court favor dressed themselves. The budding youth of his daughter had, for years, been watched with impatient anticipation of the time when her hand might be seized as the passport to present wealth and future honor.

Her cousin Delia was not recommended to notice by *all* these considerations ; but the most prevailing of the whole was one that made her claims to attention fully equal to those of Virginia. Her father, though in comparatively humble circumstances, could give with his daughter a handsomer dowry than the elder and wealthier brother could afford with his. He was notorious for generosity, and his infirmities made it probable that he was not long for this world. Delia was therefore universally regarded as an heiress. Add to this, that in the

affection of her uncle she seemed hardly to be postponed to his own daughter, and it was obvious to
anticipate that the same influence which had procured office and emolument for himself and his
sons, would be readily exerted in favor of her future
husband.

It followed, that, whatever were the amusements
of the day, whether ball or theatre, or party of
pleasure by land or by water, the presence of Delia
and Virginia was eagerly sought. The latter, simple
and artless, saw in all who approached her the
friends of her father. If she thought at all of
political differences, it was only to recognize in most
of them the adherents of the man to whose fortunes
he had so long attached himself, and *in* whose
fortunes he had flourished. To all, her welcome
was alike cordial and her smile always bright.

With Delia, the case was far different. Much
more conversant than her cousin with the politics of
the day, she was aware that her father was obnoxious to many that she met. On some of those who
sought her favor, she knew that he looked with
detestation and scorn. To such she was as cold and
repulsive as a real lady can ever permit herself to be
to one who approaches her as a gentleman in genteel
society. The height of the modern mode would,
indeed, have countenanced in such cases that sort of
negative insolence, the practice of which is regarded
as the most decisive indication of high breeding.
But she had been trained in a different school. She

had been taught that, *in society*, self-respect is the
first duty of woman; and that the only inviolable
safeguard for that, is a care never to offend the self-
respect of others.

Thus, while a part of those who approached her,
were made to feel that their attentions were not
acceptable, she never afforded them occasion to
complain of any want of courtesy on her part.
Without being rebuffed, they felt themselves constrained to stand aloof. There was nothing of which
they could complain; no pretext for resentment—
no opening for sarcasm—no material for scandal.

But in proportion to the impotence of malice, so
is the malignity of its hoarded venom. All were
aware of the political opinions and connexions of
Mr. Bernard Trevor; and it was easy to make
remarks in the presence of his daughter, not only
offensive, but painful to her feelings. To this purpose, no allusion to him was necessary. It was
enough to speak injuriously of those whom she
knew to be his friends, and whose public characters
made them legitimate subjects of applause or cen-
sure. By this, and other means of the like character,
she was always open to annoyance; and to such
means the dastard insolence of those whom her
coldness had repelled, habitually resorted for revenge.
On such occasions she frequently found that her
cousin Douglas came to her aid. Unrestrained by
the considerations that imposed silence on her, he
was always ready to speak on behalf of the party

attacked. If he could not directly vindicate, he would palliate or excuse. If even this were inconsistent with his own opinions, he would take occasion to speak approvingly of the talents or private worth of those who were assailed. Whether she regarded this as a proof of good breeding, or of kindness to herself, or of an incipient change in his opinions, such conduct always commanded her gratitude and approbation.

CHAPTER VIII.

He was, in logic, a great critic,
Profoundly skilled in analytic.
He could distinguish and divide
A hair, 'twixt south and southwest side.
                                        HUDIBRAS.

AMONG those who had thus manifested a disposition to win the favor of Delia Trevor, was a young man who had, not long since, entered public life under the auspices of a father, who, fifteen years before, had openly bartered his principles for office. Besides some talent, the son possessed the yet higher merit, in the eyes of his superiors, of devotion to his party and its leader. He never permitted himself to be restrained, by any regard to time or place, from making his zeal conspicuous. Taught, from his infancy, that the true way to recommend his pretensions was to rate them highly himself, he seemed determined never to exchange his place in the Legislature for any in the gift of the Court, unless some distinguished station should be offered to his acceptance. For any such, in any department, he was understood to be a candidate.

At first, he supposed that a private intimation to this effect, through his father, would be all-sufficient.

But he was overlooked, and post after post, that he would gladly have accepted, was conferred on others. Fearful that he might be deemed deficient in zeal, he redoubled his diligence, and with increased eagerness sought every opportunity to display his talents and his ardor in the service of his master. Still he seemed no nearer to his object. Whether it was thought that he was most serviceable in his actual station, or that the wily President deemed it a needless waste of patronage to buy what was his by hereditary title and gratuitous devotion, it is hard to say. The gentleman sometimes seemed on the point of becoming malcontent; but his father, who had trained him in the school of Sir Pertinax McSycophant, convinced him that more was to be got by "booing," and resolute subserviency and flattery of the great, than in any other way. Under such impressions, he would kindle anew the fervor of his zeal and send up his incense in clouds. Again disappointed, and sickening into the moroseness of hope deferred, he would become moody and reserved, as if watching for an opportunity of profitable defection.

Such an opportunity, at such a moment, had seemed to present itself in his acquaintance with Delia Trevor. A connection with her seemed exactly suited to his interested and ambidextrous policy. A handsome and amiable girl were items in the account of secondary consideration. But her fortune was not to be overlooked. Then, should his

services, at length, seem likely to meet their long
deserved reward, she could be presented to the
court as the niece of Mr. Hugh Trevor, the tried and
cherished friend of the President. Should the cold
ingratitude of his superiors at length drive him into
the opposition for advancement, he was sure of being
well received as the son-in-law of a patriot so
devoted as Mr. Bernard Trevor. *Utrinque paratus*,
could he secure the hand of Delia, he felt sure that
he must win, let the cards fall as they might.

Having taken this view of the subject, and
examined it in all its bearings, he made up to Delia
with a directness which startled, and a confidence
that offended her. But the gentleman had little to
recommend him to the favor of the fair. His person
was awkward, and disfigured by a mortal stoop.
His features, at once diminutive and irregular, were
either shrouded with an expression of solemn importance, or set off by a smile of yet more offensive self-
complacency. His manners bore the same general
character of conceit, alternately pert and grave; and
his conversation wavered between resolute, though
abortive, attempts at wit, and a sort of chopt logic,
elaborately employed in proving, by incontestable
arguments, what nobody ever pretended to deny.
He had been taught by his learned and astute
father, to lay his foundations so deep that his
arguments and the patience of his hearers were apt
to be exhausted by the time he got back to the
surface of things. Yet he reasoned with great

precision, and rarely failed to establish, as unques·
tionable, the *premises* from which other men com·
monly *begin* to reason.

This talent, and this use of it, are more applauded
by the world than one would think. Men like to be
confirmed in their opinions ; and, the fewer and
more simple these may be, the more grateful are
they for anything that looks like a demonstration of
their truth. To a man whose knowledge of arithme-
tic only extends to the profound maxim " that two
and two make four," how gratifying to find a distinguished man condescending to prove it by elaborate argument!

But ladies have little taste for these things, and
still less for the harsh dogmatism and fierce denunciations of hostile, but absent politicians, with which
Mr. P. Baker, the younger, occasionally varied his
discourse. To Delia, therefore, the gentleman, in
and of himself, and apart from all extrinsic considerations, was absolutely disagreeable. His first
advances drove her within the safe defences of
female pride and reserve. But when the manifest
audacity of his pretensions led her to think of him
as the supple slave of power, as one who had prosti-
tuted himself to the service of his master, with an
eagerness which condemned his zeal to be its own
reward, her disgust increased to loathing, and her
pride was kindled into resentment. Without showing more of these feelings than became her, she
showed enough to make her the object of his inso-

lent and malignant hatred. But she was fortified by her position in a family which he dared not offend, and his paltry malice found vent in such allusions to the politics of the day as he knew must wound her.

Things were about coming to this pass, when Douglas Trevor arrived. The first time he met Mr. Baker in company with his cousin, he saw a disposition on his part to pay attentions which were obviously annoying to her. Both duty and inclination impelled him to come to her relief; and, in doing this, he awakened the jealousy and incurred the displeasure of the gentleman. But these were feelings he had no mind to display toward one who wore a sword, and especially toward the son of a man so influential at Washington as Mr. Hugh Trevor. He accordingly drew off, in morose discomfiture, and Delia, relieved from his offensive attentions, felt that she owed her deliverance to her cousin. He was, of course, bound to occupy the place at her side from which he had driven Baker; and she was bound to requite the service by making the duty he had imposed on himself as little irksome as possible. She exerted herself to be agreeable, and succeeded so well, that Douglas went to bed that night in the firm belief that he had never passed a more pleasant evening, or seen a girl of more charming manners than Delia.

This circumstance led to a sort of tacit convention, which established him in the character of her special attendant, in all parties where Mr. Baker made his appearance. By an easy progress, this engagement was extended to all societies and all places. He knows little of human nature who needs to be told the natural consequences of these things.

But, leaving the reader to form his own judgment, and to anticipate such result as he may, my present business is with the repulsed and irritated Baker. Though it consoled his pride and self-love to impute his discomfitures, not to any absolute dislike of himself, but to a preference for another, there was nothing in that preference to soothe his resentment. As Douglas had, in the first instance, come somewhat cavalierly between him and the object of his wishes, he, perhaps, had reasonable grounds of displeasure against him. But, as it might be quite inconvenient to give vent to his feelings in that direction, they were carefully repressed. In such assaults on those of the lady, as her cousin might not observe, or might think it unwise to notice, did his malice indulge itself.

So matters stood when the astounding intelligence reached Richmond, that a diplomatic agent from the State of South Carolina had been long secretly entertained at the Court of St. James, and that he was supposed to have negotiated an informal arrangement for a commercial treaty between that government and the confederacy then forming in the South. Something was rumored as to the terms of the contemplated treaty, which filled the whole

northern faction in Virginia with consternation.
It was feared that that State could not be withheld from joining the Southern League, except by
force, and that, in a contest of force, she would
be backed, not only by the southern States, but
by the power of Great Britain.

CHAPTER IX.

" If I had known he had been so cunning of fence, I'd have seen
nim damned ere I had fought with him."

OLD PLAY.

IT was now the month of February; and a plea
sant day had tempted our young people to a jaunt
of amusement to the head of the falls. Mr. Baker,
stealing away from his duties as a legislator, was
one of the party. Repulsed by Delia, he was beginning an attempt on the heart of Virginia, of whose
loyalty, as the daughter of Mr. Hugh Trevor, he
could entertain no doubt.

Here his reception would have been little better
than with the other, had not Virginia been held in
check by a respect for the supposed opinions of her
father. Born at the very moment when the good
old gentleman was in the act of making up his mind
*to sacrifice the sovereignty of his native State to the
necessity of preserving the Union,* he seemed to
seize on the opportunity of compensating the impiety
to which he felt himself driven, by giving to his
infant daughter the name he had so long cherished
and honored. It was a moment of one of those re
lentings of the heart, in which nature asserts her

supremacy, and compels its homage to those whom
we have been accustomed to reverence and obey.
If even the prodigal or the traitor be subject to be
so affected, how much stronger must be such an im
pulse in the mind of a pure and upright man, impel
led by a sense of duty to his country to dishonor her
venerated name. This poor tribute was as the kiss
of peace with which the executioner implores the
pardon of some illustrious victim of State policy, who
is about to bleed under his hand. Had he yielded
to his feelings, he would have taken up the self-
accusing lamentation of the returned prodigal. But
his sense of duty was deep and abiding, and was
always most sure to command his exact obedience
when the duty was most painful. He could not
doubt the correctness of a conviction, which even
his cherished devotion to his native State could not
make him shake off entirely. In such a case, t
doubt was, with him, to be convinced.

But the name thus bestowed upon his daughter
was not without an effect on her mind. She knew
little of politics, but, from her very infancy, *self-love
had made her jealous of the honor of the State whose
name she bore*. The name itself was a spell of power
on the heart of Delia. It had disposed her to love
her cousin before she knew her. It had drawn them
together on their first acquaintance, and had often
been the theme of conversation between them.
Somewhat older, and much the superior in intellec
tual power, Delia had unwittingly exercised an

influence over the mind of Virginia which inclined her to listen favorably to all that could be urged against the usurper's claim to a dominion, unchecked by the authority of the State.

For more than a year past, Mr. Trevor had him-self begun to doubt the wisdom of his former opinions. Doubting, he was silent, but he had not been unwilling to subject his daughter to the action of her cousin's more vigorous mind. For many years, he would as soon have exposed his children to the contagion of the plague, as permit them to visit their uncle. During the last summer he had suffered Arthur and Virginia to spent a month with him; and he was not sorry to observe that the former came home with deeper thoughts than he chose to express. Of their love and admiration of their uncle neither made any secret. He was not only unlike their father, but so unlike any other man, that he had been a curious study to them during their whole visit. The originality of his thoughts, and the vividness with which he expressed them, afforded them constant amusement. He had that faculty of making truth look like truth, in the exhibition of which the young mind so much delights. Then he was so frank, so ardent, and withal so kind, that it was impossible to know and not to love him.

After all this, the reader will not be like to par-take of the surprise of Mr. Philip Baker, when he found, on shifting his battery, that he was not much more in favor with Virginia Trevor than with her cousin. The consequence was, that whenever he attempted, in company, to attach himself to the immediate party of these young ladies, he was apt to find himself a supernumerary. But, as Virginia had shown no marked dislike to him, his vanity easily adopted the idea that she considered him as the property of Delia. He took some pains to undeceive her, and would have been mortified at her unconcern on the occasion, had he not thought some allowance should be made for her indifference to a man who did but take her as a *pis aller*. He did not, therefore, at once withdraw himself from their *coterie*, but continued to hang about, and take his part in conversation, whenever nothing particularly exclusive in the manner of the interlocutors forbade it. He could not come between whispers; but he could answer any observation that met his ear. Being, as I have said, something between a prose and a declaimer, he thought himself eloquent, and would seize occasions to hold forth to the general edification, in a style intended to dazzle the bystanders.

On the day of which we speak, he had been in close attendance on Virginia, until, rather by address than by direct repulse, she had contrived to shake him off. Is so happened, that the rest of the company were all paired off, leaving him in the enviable condition of a half pair of shears, when relief appeared in the person of a gentleman just from Richmond.

This gentleman, originally one of the devisers of the *pic nic*, had stayed behind for the mail, and now arrived with the news alluded to in the last chapter. Baker, being disengaged at the moment, was the first to receive the intelligence, and he lost no time in awakening the attention of the company by vol leys of oaths and imprecations. While he continued to exercise himself in calling down the vengeance of " the Eternal," according to the most approved formula of the old court, on those whom he denounced as traitors, the rest listened in amazement, disgust, or alarm, to this boisterous effusion of his rage. At length, as he stopped to take breath, Douglas availed himself of the pause to ask what was the matter. The whole story now came out, and Mr. Baker, having put his audience in possession of his text, went on with his discourse. Unmindful of the presence of the ladies, he vented his wrath in language with which I do not choose to stain my paper. *Every man who had held a conspicuous place among the advocates of State rights for the last twenty years, was condemned, ex cathedra. The dead were especially recommended to the tender mercies of the devil, in whose clutches he supposed them to be; while the living were indiscriminately devoted to the same doom.*

Against the person by whom the treaty was said to have been negotiated, his wrath burned most fiercely. In the midst of one of his most savage denunciations of that gentleman, he happened to

recollect having heard Delia speak of him as the
intimate friend of her father. The thought turned
his eye upon her. She was already pale and trem
bling with emotion, when she caught his insulting
glance. In an instant the blood gushed to her face,
and tears to her eyes. He saw it, and went on to
comprehend in his denunciation all the aiders, abettors, and *friends* of the *traitor*, whom in one breath
he devoted to the gallows.

This was more than Delia could bear, and more
than Douglas was disposed to suffer. He had caught
the glance which Baker had cast at his cousin; he
saw the effect on her feelings; he witnessed her increasing emotion, and felt it his duty to come to her
relief. He approached Baker, and passing him, as
if with no particular design, touched him gently,
and said in a low voice: "Such language is im-
proper in this company."

"How so," exclaimed Baker, aloud. "I hope there
is no man here disposed to take the part of a traitor."

Douglas turned, and, biting his lip, said in a tone
not loud, but from its distinctness and marked
emphasis, audible to all present: "I spoke so as to
be heard by none but you, and invited you by a
sign to go apart, where I might explain my meaning
in private. But, as you will have the explanation
here, I say, that *you know there is no man* here disposed to take the part of a traitor. If you had
thought there was, sir, I suspect your denunciations
would have been less violent."

"I don't understand you, sir," said Baker, reddening.

"My meaning is as plain as becomes this presence," said Douglas, coldly, and again walking away. Baker looked around, and read in every eye that he was expected to follow. He did so, and, joining Douglas, they both walked on together.

"I shall be glad to receive a farther explanation, sir," said he in an agitated tone.

"Speak lower, then," replied Douglas, calmly, slipping his arm within that of Baker; "and use no gesture. My meaning is this: That he who is regardless of the presence and feelings of a lady, is not apt to overlook those of a man. To make my meaning yet plainer, sir, your language would have been more guarded, had my uncle been represented here, not by a *daughter*, but by a *son*."

The quiet tone of Douglas's voice, the equivocal meaning of the first words he had uttered, and the pacific action intended to deceive those who looked on, had calmed for a moment the alarm of Baker. He had recovered himself before he was made to perceive what was really meant; and ere he had time to reflect on his situation, the dangerous temptation of a repartee assailed him. Glancing back at the company, he said: "If I may judge by appearances, sir, you have the right as well as the inclination to assume that character."

Douglas had turned his head, instinctively, as Baker looked back, and saw that they had rounded a point of rock, and were out of sight. In an instant, he disengaged his arm with a push that nearly threw the legislator down the bank, and stepping back, glared upon him with an eye that instantly brought the other to his senses. While he stood blenching and cowering under this fierce glance, Douglas recovered his self-command, and said, with stern calmness: "You had nearly made me forget myself, sir. But we understand each other now. Take a turn along the shore to compose yourself. I will wait here for you, and we will return to the company together."

He seated himself on a rock, and the other obeyed mechanically. How he succeeded in recovering his composure is another affair. He walked on, and on, and fain would he have followed the course of the river to the mountain cave from which it issues, there to hide himself from the consequences of his own folly and impertinence. What would he not have given to recall that last speech? Until then, he was the party aggrieved. Douglas's offence against him had not been so gross as to admit of no explanation; and, to all appearance, an amicable one had been given. The truth might not have come out until he had had time to escape to his constituents; and before the next session the affair might have been forgotten. But now, Douglas had been insulted, and how he felt and how he would resent the insult, was awfully certain.

Baker continued his walk so far, that the girls

became uneasy at the absence of the two young men. They begged some of the gentlemen to go in quest of them, but the request was evaded. At last, they arose from their seats on the rocks, and declared they would themselves go. They accordingly set out followed by the rest, and in a few yards came to where Douglas was quietly seated on a flat stone, and playing checks with pebbles on the smooth sand.

"Where is Mr. Baker?" exclaimed Virginia, eagerly.

"Yonder he goes," replied Douglas, calmly. "He has a mind for a longer walk than I like; and I am just waiting for him here. But I must not detain you, girls. His taste for the picturesque will probably be satisfied by the time we get to our horses, and he will soon overtake us."

He said this with an air so careless as to deceive every person present but Delia. But the heart will speak from the eye, and a glance at her, as she searched his countenance, unconsciously said: "I have redressed you." Coloring deeply, she strove to hide her emotion,—taking his arm and busying herself at the same time with the adjustment of her veil. In spite of some undefined apprehensions, she was grateful, relieved, and pleased; and a slight pressure on the arm she held, spoke her feelings perhaps as distinctly as they were understood by herself.

Douglas returned the pressure with more energy

The words of Baker yet tingled in his ears; and while they burned with the insult, the pain was more than soothed by the thoughts they had awakened. Were then the day-dreams of his boyhood to become realities? He was not, as yet, conscious of any but a cousin's love for Delia. He could impute no other feeling to her. But *should* this mutual affection ripen into a more tender sentiment! With whom could a man pass his days more happily, than with a woman so intelligent, so amiable, so prudent, so much a lady? He did not love her. But he felt that to love her, and be beloved by her, would be a happy lot. The slight weight she rested on his arm was sweet to him. He wished the pressure was heavier. But she walked on, self-poised, and with a light and steady step over the rugged ground. Was not that step more confident, because she felt that he was there to aid her in case of need? Even so, she seemed sufficient for herself in the resources of her own mind. Yet had she needed and accepted, and gratefully, though silently, acknowledged his protection. He was happy in having had occasion to protect her. Was not she the happier for it too? The heart will ask questions. Time gives the answer.

CHAPTER X.

——————— Oh! speak it not!
Let silence be the tribute of your homage!
The mute respect, that gives not woman's name
To the rude breath, which, trumpeting her praises,
Taints by applauding.

ANONYMOUS.

A FEW days after, Douglas handed his cousin the following paper:

"Mr. Baker begs leave to throw himself on the mercy of Miss Delia Trevor. He confesses his offence against her on Saturday last. He admits, with shame, that he did intend to wound her feelings, and that he has nothing to offer in extenuation of his offence. He does not even presume to ask a pardon, which he acknowledges to be unmerited, and respectfully tenders the only atonement in his power, by assuring Miss Trevor that he will never again, intentionally, offend her by his presence.
          Signed,   PHILIP BAKER."

Delia read this curious document in silence, and, on looking up, found that Douglas had left the room. She ran after him, but he was gone, and for a day or two avoided any opportunity for farther explanation.

At length she found one, and asked by what means the paper had been procured.

"By *proper* means, my dear coz," said he, "if the paper is a proper one."

"Proper!" exclaimed she, "for me to receive, certainly. But for him to give! Indeed, I pity any poor wretch who can be so abject. I am glad, at least, I am to see him no more. I should find it hard to behave to him as becomes myself!"

"It would be hard," said Douglas, "but as you always will behave as becomes yourself, hard though it be, it was right you should be spared the trial."

"This *is* your doing then?" said she.

"No questions, coz," replied Douglas. "I must behave as becomes me too."

This put an effectual stop to farther inquiry, and the slight concealment did but deepen Delia's sense of the service Douglas had rendered her. While she admired the delicacy which, at once, veiled and adorned his chivalrous character; he, on his part, felt greater pleasure at having redressed her wrong, because the affair had taken such a turn as to conceal the part that he had acted. The ties thus formed in secret, are doubly sacred and doubly sweet. The heart involuntarily classes them with those chaste mysteries which the vulgar eye must not profane They become the theme of thoughts which some times rise up, and kindle the cheek, and light the eye, and then sink down again and hide themselves deep in the silent breast.

But this privacy was destined to be invaded by one person, at least; and that, the very one from whom Douglas would most anxiously have concealed the whole affair. Yet there was no person to whose tenderness, delicacy, and affection for both parties, it could have been more fitly confided. In short, Mr. Trevor, one day, placed in the hands of his son a letter, in the President's own hand-writing, of which the following is a copy:

WASHINGTON, March 3d, 1849.

MY DEAR SIR : I hasten to lay before you a piece of information which touches you nearly. Though I receive it at the hands of one who has the highest claims to my confidence, I yet trust it will prove to have originated in mistake.

It is said that your son, Lieutenant Trevor, on receiving the news of the late treasonable proceedings of some of the southern States, openly vindicated them ; and that he spoke freely in defence of the principal agent in their most wicked attempt to league themselves with the enemies of their country. It is said, moreover, that, in doing this, he insulted and fastened a quarrel on one, whom I have great reason to esteem for his uniform devotion to the Union. The regular course for such a charge against an officer, holding a commission in the army of the United States, is one which I would not willingly pursue, in the case of the son of one of my earliest and most cherished friends. As Lieutenant Trevor is now at home, on furlough, I address this letter to you to be laid before him. I have no doubt he will readily give the necessary explanations, and, in so doing, afford me a new occasion for displaying that regard for you and yours, with which I am,

Dear sir, your friend,

MARTIN VAN BUREN.

"Can you tell me what this means?" said the mild old gentleman to his son.

"As I remember," replied Douglas, "the circumstances under which I heard of the events alluded to, I think, I can give a guess at the meaning. It means that my cousin was insulted, in my presence, and that I protected her, as was my duty."

"And how does it happen that I never heard of it? Who was the person, and what has become of the affair?"

"It has all blown over," said Douglas, "and I had hardly expected it would ever be spoken of again. Delia alone knew of it from me, as it was right she should. I have never mentioned, nor has my friend. I am sure she has not; and what the other party can promise himself from the exposure, I am sure I cannot tell."

"The thing is now made public, at all events; and both as your father and as the friend of the President, it is right that I should know all about it."

"Certainly, sir," replied Douglas, "you shall know

all; and when you do, I need not explain why I
have never told you before."

He left the room, and soon returned with a bundle
of papers. From this he handed one to his father,
which proved to be a challenge, in the most approved
form, from him, the said Douglas Trevor, to Philip
Baker, Esq. Then came a proposition to discuss
from the other party; then a flat demand of apology, or the alternative of, what is called, gentlemanly satisfaction; then an offer to apologize;
then the paper we have already seen; and then the
following:

"Philip Baker declares, on his honor, that he meant
no offence to Lieutenant Trevor by any words
addressed to him on Saturday last; and that he
deeply regrets having spoken any which may
have sounded offensively in the ears of Lieutenant
Trevor."

"This will do," said Mr. Trevor. "It only shows
that you have acted as became a soldier and a gentleman. These papers show clearly that the quarrel
began in an insult to your cousin, which you were
bound to resent. This will be perfectly satisfactory
to the President."

"Doubtless it *would* be," said Douglas, promptly;
"but so much of the affair as implicates my cousin's
name must go no farther."

"But it is that," replied Mr. Trevor, "which
shows the cause of the quarrel. The other papers
only show that you fancied an intention to insult

where none existed. This would tally too well with
what the President has heard."

"Be it so," answered Douglas calmly. "If the
President is never satisfied till I furnish a paper
which is to blend my cousin's name with a public
discussion, he must remain dissatisfied. I cannot
help it. Better to have suffered the insult to pass
unnoticed, than to make a lady's name the theme of
guard-house wit."

"Bless you, my noble boy," said the admiring
father. "You are right, and there is no help for it.
But what shall I say to the President?"

"What you please. The *conclusions* you draw
from what you know, he is welcome to. The *facts*
are with you."

"Certainly," said Mr. Trevor, after a musing
pause; "certainly he will trust in my general assurance that his information is, *to my certain knowledge*,
erroneous. This *will* do. It *must* be sufficient."

"It *must* do," said Douglas, "whether it will or
no. In the mean time, my dear sir, let me beg that
the affair may go no farther, even in the family.
Delia alone knows of it, and she only knows as much
as may be gathered from that paper, a duplicate of
which is her's by right. I therefore beg that you
will say nothing about it, even to her."

And he did say nothing to her; but Douglas
observed that that night, when she held up her lip
for his paternal kiss, the kind old gentleman gave it
with more than his usual tenderness. He held her

off, parted the hair from her forehead, gazed earnestly and affectionately upon her; and then, kissing her again, bade God bless her, in a voice choked with emotion. From that moment, she was to him as a daughter.

CHAPTER XI.

That proud humility—that dignified obedience.—BURKE.

THE visit of Delia to her uncle now drew to a close, and she prepared for her return home. It was settled that she should be accompanied by Douglas, Arthur, and Virginia, who were to spend a few weeks with her father.

On the road, Douglas felt more and more the duty and the privilege of being the protector of his cousin, and, by the time they reached the end of their journey, he had discovered that the latter was as precious as the former was sacred. Some such thought had stolen into his mind while he was yet at home, but that was not the place to mention the subject to her; and he had determined to impose upon himself the most scrupulous restraint, until he should have restored her honorably to her father's arms.

Two days' travel brought them to the residence of Mr. Bernard Trevor, on the banks of the Roanoke. They found him laid up with a fit of the gout, which, while it confined him to the house, produced its usual salutary effect on his general health. At the sight of his daughter and her companions, his pain was, for the moment, forgotten; and, flinging away his flannels and crutches, he sprang to his feet and caught her in his arms. At the same time, Arthur and Virginia pressed forward for their wel come, which they, in their turn, received.

Unfortunately, Mr. Trevor was not the only one who forgot himself at the sight of Delia. Poor old Carlo, starting from his slumbers on the hearth-rug, had recognized his young mistress, and was mani-festing his joy at her return with boisterous fond-ness, when one of his feet saluted the inflamed toe of his master. In an agony, which none but they who have felt it can conceive, the old gentleman sank into his chair. Here he remained for some minutes, unconscious of every thing but his suffer-ings, while the soft hand of his daughter replaced and soothed the tortured limb.

At length, recovering enough to look around, his eye fell on Douglas, who stood aloof, waiting to be introduced. Some little tag of military foppery, which always clings to the undress of an officer, satisfied Mr. Trevor who he was. Stretching out his hand, he said: "Ah! Douglas, my dear boy! How glad I am to see you! But I ought not to have recognized you, you dog! standing back there with your hat under your arm, as if waiting your turn of presentation at a levee. Perhaps you don't remember me. I certainly should not have known you, but for the circumstances under which I see you. But what of that? Was it not yesterday you were sitting on my knee, and hanging about my neck? Yes, it was yesterday; though we have both dreamed a great deal since. But dreams must give way to realities; so let us vote it yesterday, and meet to-day as we parted last night."

This singular *accoste* had the desired effect, and Douglas felt, at once, as if he had been with his uncle all his life.

" You forget, my dear sir," said he, " that I was intercepted by one whose privilege, I am sure, you would not have me dispute, though he has abused it so cruelly."

" You mean the dog?" said Mr. Trevor. " Poor old Carlo! Come to your master, my poor fellow! No; your privilege shall never be invaded. We are both past service now, and must learn to sympathize with each other. If you cannot understand the nature of a gouty toe, I hope I shall always have heart enough to understand yours. Give me a rough coat, or a black skin, for a true friend; one that will not grudge any superior advantages that I may possess. Tom," added he, in a tone of marked gentleness, " the fire is low. No, not yourself, old man," he continued, as the negro whom he addressed moved toward the door; " not you, my good old friend. Just ring the bell, and let one of those lazy dogs in the kitchen bring in some wood. But why don't you speak to your master Douglas? I am sure you remember what cronies you were, when you were teaching him to ride."

"I'm mighty proud to see you, sir," said the old man, taking the offered hand of Douglas, with an air of affectionate humility. "But it was not my place, sir," added he, answering his master's words, "to speak first. I made sure master Douglas would remember me after a while."*

"I do remember you, Tom," said Douglas, cordially, "and many a time, on parade, have I been thankful to you for teaching me to hold my reins and manage my horse."

"You will find it hard," said Mr. Trevor, gravely, "to convince Tom that you remember him, if you call him by that name. Tom is Delia's daddy, and Lucia's, and Arthur's, and Virginia's daddy, and so will be to the day of his death. If ever he ceases to be your daddy, too, Douglas, I shall move to reconsider the vote that we just now passed unanimously."

"It is a vice the northern air has blown upon

---

* I crave the forbearance of all critics, who have taken their ideas of a Virginia house-servant from Cæsar Thompson, or any such caricatures, for giving Tom's own words, and his own pronunciation of them. It is not my fault if there is but little peculiarity in his phraseology. His language was never elegant, and frequently ungrammatical. But he spoke better than the peasantry of most countries, though he said some things that a white man would not say; perhaps, because he had some feelings to which the white man is a stranger. A white man, for example, would have said he was *glad* to see Douglas, whether he were so or not. Old Tom said he was *proud* to see him, because he *was* proud to recognize his former pet in the handsome and graceful youth before him.

me," said Douglas, blushing. "I felt the truth of what you said just now, and am not more sure of being affectionately remembered by any that I used to know, than by my good old daddy."

Mr. Trevor now requested Tom to see that the horses of the travellers were properly attended to; and the negro left the room.

"What a graceful and gentlemanly old man!" said Douglas, looking after him.

"His manners," said Mr. Trevor, "are exactly suited to his situation. Their characteristic is proud humility. The opposite is servile sulkiness, of which, I suspect, Douglas, you have seen no little."

"I have seen nothing else," said Douglas, "among the servants in the North. If the tempers of our negroes were as ferocious, and their feelings as hostile, we should have to cut their throats in self-defence in six months."

"I am glad," said Mr. Trevor, "that you have not learned to sacrifice your own experience to the fanciful theories of the *Amis de Noirs*, at least on this point. The time, I hope, will come when you will see, if you do not already, the fallacy of all their cant and sophistry on the subject of domestic slavery. You will then bless God that your lot has been cast where the freedom of all, who, in the economy of Providence, are capable of freedom, is rendered practicable by the particular form in which the subordination of those who must be slaves is cast."

"I am not sure," said Douglas, "that I exactly comprehend you."

"Perhaps not," replied the uncle. "And that reminds me that I am trespassing on forbidden ground. Just there, the differences of opinion between your father and myself commence; and from that point they diverge so much, that I do not feel at liberty to speak to his son on certain topics."

"But why not, my dear sir? You surely cannot expect me to think with my father on all subjects; and you would not have me do so, when you thought him wrong. I do not profess to be deeply studied in these matters; but, between your lights and his, I might hope to find my way to the truth."

"There are some subjects, Douglas," replied Mr. Trevor, with solemnity, "on which it is better to be in error than to differ, totally and conscientiously, from a father. Delia is but a girl; but should she have come back to me changed in her sentiments (opinions she cannot have) in regard to certain matters, I should feel that I had been grievously wronged by any one who had wrought the change. I know your father has not done this; and I must do as I would be done by, and as I am sure I have been done by."

"I cannot conceive," said Douglas, "what sort of subjects those can be, concerning which error in opinion is better than truth, under any circumstances."

"Those," replied Mr. Trevor, "in which truth would bring duty in conflict with duty."

"Nay, then," said Douglas, "there is no danger of my conversion in such cases. I should take that as an infallible proof that doctrines leading to such consequences must be false."

"Your proposed test of truth is so specious," observed Mr. Trevor, "that I will go so far as to say one word to convince you of its fallacy. If ever I take you in hand, my lad, my first lesson will be to teach you to examine plausibilities closely, and to distrust summary and simple arguments on topics about which men differ."

"Does any one, then, maintain," asked Douglas, "that two opinions which impose conflicting duties can both be right?"

"I shall not answer that," answered Mr. Trevor. "*You shall answer it yourself. You are a soldier of the United States. Suppose an insurrection. What, in that case, would be your duty?*"

"*To fight against the rebels*," replied Douglas, promptly.

"*And, thinking as you do, so it would be. Now, suppose your father to be one of those same rebels.*"

"I see," said Douglas, after a pause, in which he colored to the tips of his ears; "I see that you are right."

"In what?" asked Mr. Trevor.

"In maintaining," he replied, "that two opinions which prescribe conflicting duties, may both be right."

"But I have not said so," replied Mr. Trevor, smiling.

"But you have proved it."

"I am not quite sure of that. Here is another summary and simple looking argument, on a difficult question. My own rule is, '*distrust and re-examine.*'"

He stopped short, while Douglas looked at him with a perplexed and wondering eye. He at length went on : "I shall not break faith with your father by teaching you to think. You have the propositions ; and you see there is fallacy somewhere. Analyse the subject, and find your own result. But come, my boy—this is poor entertainment for a hungry traveller. Your aunt has some dinner for you by this time, and here is Tom come to tell us so. Come, give me your arm, and help me to the dining room."

"My dear father," said Delia, "that is my office."

"Both ! both ! my children !" exclaimed the old man, throwing away his other crutch. "Why, now I am better off than a man with sound limbs."

In the dining room, Mrs. Trevor awaited them. A hasty greeting was all she had allowed herself on the first arrival of the party ; after which, she betook herself to the duties of housewifery and hospitality. They found her standing at the back of her chair ; and Douglas, as he entered, thought he had rarely seen a more striking figure. She was matronly in her dress and air ; tall, majestic, and graceful in her person ; and with a countenance beaming with frankness, animation, and intelligence. She had been a beautiful woman, and, being much younger than her husband, was still handsome. She extended her hand to Douglas as he entered, and placing him near her, so mingled the courtesy due to a stranger with the cordiality of an old acquaintance, as to make him feel all the comfort and ease of home, without ever losing a sense of that bland influence, which, while it secures decorum, imposes no constraint.

" Would you have known me ?" asked the lady.

" I cannot say I could have *identified* you," he replied ; " but I should have recognized you as one I ought to know."

" And your uncle ?"

" Not by sight, certainly," said Douglas. " I remember him too distinctly for that. He is too much altered. But I know him by his manners and conversation. These I never could forget; and these are the same, and peculiarly his own. I remember how he used to exercise my mind, and make me talk ; and yet never let me talk without thinking."

" And has he been at the old game already ?"

" O yes ! He has set me to revising and doubting what have seemed to me to be self-evident truths, and proposes to leave me to work out the problem by myself. What conclusion I am to settle in, I cannot guess ; but, from present appearances, I shall not be surprised if I go away convinced that I have seven fingers on one hand, and but two on the other; nine in all."

" He has not touched on politics ?"

" *O no ! That subject he has tabooed ; and I am truly sorry for it ; for while I never desire to waver in my allegiance to the United States, I am anxious to understand what may become me as a Virginian.* If I may judge from what my father says, there is no man from whom I could learn more on that subject than my uncle."

"His lesson would not be a short one," replied the lady. "His commandments on behalf of the State are only second in authority with him to the decalogue; and they do not lie in as small a compass. But he fears he might teach you some things your father would wish you to unlearn."

"I am not so sure of that," answered Douglas. "I meant to say that there is no man whose judgment my father holds in higher respect."

"That is something new," said Mrs. Trevor, coloring, and with a countenance in which there was some expression of wounded pride. "I should be glad to be convinced of that."

"Why should you doubt it?" asked the young man, with surprise.

"Because it has not always been so; and, as I claim a woman's privilege to admire my husband above all men, I have felt hurt at it. Your uncle thinks so highly of his brother's wisdom and prudence, that he has always borne to be thought the reverse of him in these things, and quietly submitted to be condemned as a heretic on account of opinions, of the correctness of which he found it impossible to doubt."

"There may *have been* something of this," said Douglas, earnestly ; "but I assure you it is not so now. I do believe one motive with my father for wishing me to make this visit, is his desire that I should hear both sides; and have the benefit of the sagacity and manly sense which he imputes to my uncle."

"He will have to tell him so plainly," replied Mrs. Trevor, "before he will open his mouth to you. But I shall be less scrupulous; and I am in daily expectation of a friend whose frankness will leave you no cause to regret your uncle's reserve."

"Who is that?" asked Douglas.

"I shall leave you to find out. You will see many here who feel and think with your uncle, and who come to him to compare thoughts and concert measures. Among them is the man on whom the destinies of his country depend."

"The only man of whom I should predicate that," replied Douglas, with some quickness, "is one who, I am very sure, never comes here."

"There is a good and an evil principle," said Mrs. Trevor. "Events alike depend on both. *You* speak of the one of these—*I* of the other."

Douglas felt his cheek burn at this remark. His aunt, observing it, added : "You see, you will run the risk of adopting dangerous heresies if you encou rage us to be too unreserved. But your candor and good sense may be trusted to lead you right, without our guidance."

Douglas felt the truth of the first part of this speech. Whether anything more than a complimentary turn of expression was meant in the closing words, he did not know. But if the lady intended to express a hope that he might become a convert to the disorganizing notions which he feared were prevalent in her circle, he took the liberty to doubt whether her anticipations would ever be realized. He now changed the conversation, and determined to take a second thought before he invited discussions which might mislead him. He found he had to do with active and vigorous minds, against which he might, perhaps, vainly strive to defend himself, even with truth on his side. He resolved, therefore, to yield to the inclination which led him to pass his time with his young friends, and chiefly with Delia.

CHAPTER XII.

My heart, sweet boy, shall be thy sepulchre;
I'll bear thee hence, and let them fight that will,
For I have murdered where I would not kill.
                              SHAKSPEARE.

I SHOULD detain the reader with matters not worthy
of a place in this grave history, if I descended to the
particulars of the intercourse between Douglas Trevor
and his charming cousin. It is enough to say, that
he found himself, daily, more and more happy in her
society; and was more and more convinced that it
was a necessary ingredient in his happiness. It was
not long before he concluded that he would not live
without her; and, having told her so, was referred by
her to her father.

Nothing doubting that his communication would be
favorably received, Douglas was eager to break the
matter to his uncle, and ask his approbation of his
suit. To his utter amazement, the old gentleman,
assuming an air at once serious and tender, said: "My
dear boy, had I the world to choose from, there is no
man to whom I would sooner trust my daughter's
happiness. But circumstances forbid your union. I
speak advisedly and sadly. I have seen what was

passing. I anticipated this communication, and delı berately decided on my answer."

" For God's sake, sir!" exclaimed Douglas, trembling with impatience, " what do you mean ; and what is your answer ? "

" I mean," said Mr. Trevor, " and my answer is, that circumstances forbid it."

" Surely," said Douglas, " your objection is not to the nearness of blood."

" I am not addicted to any such exploded superstition," said Mr. Trevor. " But my daughter must never marry one that wears that dress."

" I like my profession, sir," said Douglas, " but will change it without hesitation."

" God forbid ! " replied the old gentleman. " I would not have you do so ; and were you so inclined, it would not be in your choice."

" I can resign when I will, and my resignation will certainly be accepted."

" Still you would be a soldier, and you must be a soldier. Peace is not in our choice, and the time is at hand when every man, who can wield a sword, must do so."

" I do not understand you, sir," said Douglas in amazement.

" I am aware you do not. It is time you should. You have now a right to understand me ; and I have a right to be understood by you. We are on the eve of what you will call rebellion. I shall call it a war of right and liberty. I am old and infirm ; but

I am not always imprisoned by the gout ; and nothing but physical inability shall keep me from sus-
taining, with my sword, a cause that I have always
advocated with tongue and pen.   It will be bad
enough to meet the sons of my brother in arms
against my country.   That I cannot help.   But it is
in my choice whether I shall thus meet my daughter's husband.   That must never be."

He ceased to speak, and the young man, dizzy
with mixed thoughts and feelings, sat gazing at him
in mute astonishment.   At length, starting up, he
was about to leave the room, when the old gentleman held out his hand.   Douglas gave his, and his
uncle, pressing it cordially, went on : "My son,"
said he, " you are the only male of my race in whom
I recognize any thing which tells me that the same
blood flows in our veins.   We cannot help the selfishness that disposes us to love those who resemble
us even in our faults.   It might be better for you not
to resemble me, and perhaps I ought to wish that
you did not.   But I cannot.   I find it easier to forget
that you are not my son, and to love you as if you
were.   The hope that you may yet be so, is hardly
less dear to me than to you.   That you will be so, if
' you outlive the envy ' of those awful events which
shall open your eyes, I can hardly doubt.   But these
things must do their work.   The convictions which
shall make you throw off the badges of allegiance
to him whose sworn foe I am, must come of themselves.   While you wear them, I am bound to

respect your honor by saying nothing to shake your faith in him, and to his cause. In the mean time, I can but hope for the best. I do hope; and I invite you to hope. But for the present, hope must be our all. Things must remain as they are until it pleases God so to order events as to make your sense of duty to your country consistent with that which, as my daughter's husband, you will owe to her and to her father."

I leave the reader to imagine the consternation of Douglas at this decisive condemnation of his proposed plan of happiness, and at the astounding intelligence that accompanied it. He saw plainly that his uncle spoke not conjecturally, but from certain knowledge; and he was sure, that under such circumstances, no attachment could tempt Delia to marry him. He did not therefore attempt to continue the discussion of the subject, but left the house and wandered into the fields.

The tumult of his mind rendered him incapable of reflexion. I shall not attempt to analyze the chaos of his thoughts. But light, not darkness, floated on the surface. The hand of Delia was indeed withheld for a season, but he was not forbidden to hope that it might one day or other be his. Should it ever be true that rebellion was awake, and that civil war was at hand, he was not told that fidelity to his standard would be imputed to him as a crime. The strife must end one way or the other, and that being past, he would no longer be condemned to the hard alternative of relinquishing the object of his most ardent wish, or exhibiting the shocking spectacle of a husband warring against the father of his wife.

But what was to be done in the mean time? Should the old gentleman take the field, he must find some other theatre of action, and his father's influence with the President would readily procure him that indulgence. *As to the idea of renouncing what he had been taught to call his allegiance to the Federal Government, and aiding to maintain the dishonored sovereignty of his native State, it did not enter his mind.* Yet there was something in its workings that suddenly awakened an undefined interest in the late correspondence between his father and the President. He no sooner thought of this, than his restless wanderings received a definite direction to the neighboring post-office.

Here he found a letter from his father, containing litle more than the copy of one from the President. Its contents were as follows:

"WASHINGTON, *March* 20, 1849.

"MY DEAR SIR: Your letter has been received, and, *to me*, is entirely satisfactory. But I regret to inform you that, to those friends whom I feel myself bound to consult, it is not so. Such of them, indeed, as are acquainted with your high character, do not intimate a doubt that a full explanation of the affair would entirely justify your assurance that I have been misinformed.

" But they remind me that my information comes from a source entitled to all respect and confidence, and that, by making thus light of it, I may estrange a friend, whom they regard as hardly less valuable and meritorious than him whose feelings I wish to save. They represent, moreover, that the affair is bruited in the army, and that some officers are malcontent at the thought that a charge so serious should be passed over without inquiry, on the bare assurance of a father's confidence in the innocence of his son.

" Under these circumstances, should Lieutenant Trevor not demand a court of inquiry, I am fearful I may be constrained, against my wish, to order a court-martial. Need I tell you, my dear sir, how earnestly I deprecate the necessity of a measure, which must so nearly touch one to whose friendship I feel so much indebted, and whose loyalty to the Union and its officers has always been so conspicuous and steady.

"I remain, my dear sir,
"Your assured friend,
"M. V. B."

To this copy Mr. Trevor added these words:

" The discretion, good sense, and proper feeling you have already manifested in this affair, have been so conspicuous, that I choose rather to trust its future conduct entirely to yourself than to embarrass you by any advice of mine. Yet, there is one person,

my dear boy, with whom I would have you to advise.
Your uncle has been a soldier in his youth, and is
profoundly versed in all matters of military etiquette.
He is, moreover, a clear-sighted and sagacious man,
who will, at once, see this matter in all its bearings
and relations to other subjects. His views are not
only, in general, more comprehensive than mine, but
I suspect he is, at this moment, aware of considerations which might properly influence you, and which
are hidden from me. I know his guarded and delicate reserve, in all his communications with my
children, where he apprehends a difference of opinion
between himself and me. Tell him that he has my
thanks for it; but that I shall be yet more obliged,
if, in this instance, he will cast it aside entirely, and
give you the benefit of all his thoughts, as if you
were *his own* son. I fear my last days may be spent
in bitter regrets that I myself have not heretofore
made more avail of them."

CHAPTER XIII.

It is enough to grieve the heart,
To think that God's fair world hath been
The footstool of a thing so mean.

BYRON.

THE evening was far advanced, when Douglas again reached his uncle's house. He went immediately to his room, and sent to request a private interview with Mr. Trevor. He was accordingly invited into the little study of the old gentleman, where he commonly sat surrounded by books and papers. On entering the room, he observed an elderly gentleman, whom he had never seen before, pass out at a door communicating with the drawing-room.

Douglas now silently handed his father's letter to his uncle. Mr. Trevor read it attentively, and again and again looked over it, resting his eye on particular passages, as if to possess himself of the full meaning of every expression. The subject was in itself interesting, and quite new to him. But he felt a yet deeper interest in the obscure intimations of a change in his brother's mind in regard to those matters about which they had so long and so painfully differed. Even if he was mistaken in this, it was

consoling to find himself rising in the estimation of
Mr. Hugh Trevor; no longer regarded by him as
rash, reckless, and inconsiderate, but consulted as a
" clear-sighted and sagacious man " in an affair of
very great importance. He alone, who has been
conscious of being thus undervalued by a friend at
once beloved and respected, can estimate the satisfaction which Mr. Trevor felt at that moment. If
there was any mixture of alloy with this pleasure, it
flowed from self-reproach. He had sometimes found
it impossible to repress some little risings of resent
ment, at finding his judgment habitually disabled by
his elder brother. He had indeed been once a little
white-headed boy, when the other was a highly intelligent and promising youth. But, at sixty, he was
not quite content to be still looked on as a child.
Yet, when he remarked the candor of his brother's
language, and the self-abasing sadness of his tone,
he was vexed to think that one unkind thought
toward him had ever entered his mind.

At length, he interrupted this train of thought, to
ask of Douglas an explanation of the President's
letter. In answer, he received a detailed account
of the scene at the falls, and was permitted to read
the correspondence which had grown out of it.

" I have heard something of this before," said
Mr. Trevor. " Delia told me all that passed in her
presence, and showed me Baker's palinode, which is
rather the most extraordinary document that I ever
saw. Why, the dog acknowledges that he actually

intended to insult a lady. He might, at least, have had the grace to lie about it. *False* shame is better than no shame at all."

" He would have been glad to put the matter on that footing," said Douglas, " could he have got leave to do so. He sent me such a paper as you suppose, but I refused to receive it. His apology to me I knew to be false. It was, therefore, the more satisfactory because the more humiliating. But I sent him word that I would not take any thing to my cousin but the truth. Here," continued Douglas, " is his first *project* of an apology, and of my rejection of it."

Mr. Trevor read them, and then said : " This is well. I knew you had acted handsomely, but *how* handsomely, I had not conceived of. But let me hear, I pray you, how all this has been tortured into an offence against majesty."

Douglas colored slightly at the word, and handed his uncle a copy of the President's first letter to his father. He had but to add an account of his subsequent conversation with his father, and Mr. Trevor was in possession of the whole affair.

" You see," said Douglas, " that I am referred to you for advice, and that you are invited to say to me, unreservedly, what you will."

" *I do see*," *replied Mr. Trevor*, " *that I have carte blanche*, as far as depends on your father. But there are some things I would *now* say to *his son*, which it would not be proper to say to a *soldier of*

the United States. I cannot, therefore, discard all reserve, but *all* that *he* has ever imposed on me, I now shake off. Indeed, I should have done this now, without his permission. You are my son, as well as his. You have shown that you know how to protect my daughter, and have fairly earned a right to protect her through life. Nay, no raptures : no thanks ! The exercise of this right must be postponed until affairs have taken a different shape from that they bear at present. But *revenons à nos moutons !*" The question is, what you are to do to save this despicable, heartless wretch from the necessity of offending a wretch even baser than himself, whom he despises."

" Whom do you mean ?" asked Douglas.

" I mean," replied the other, " the President and the elder Baker, that tame slave of power, that shameless, mercenary pander, who, having both talent and reputation, sold the one and sacrificed the other for office and infamy."

" And is it for such a man," exclaimed Douglas, " that I am required to make disclosures before a court of inquiry, or a court-martial, which delicacy and self-respect forbid ? Never ! Be the alternative what it may, I shall never consent to it."

" You are right, my son," said Mr. Trevor, " nor can I relieve you from the difficulty by authorizing the profanation of my daughter's name, to which such an investigation would lead. My duty on that head is peremptory, not discretionary. If your

father were any thing but the perfect gentleman he
is, I might suspect that his reference to me was
intended to elicit some such suggestion. But I
know him better. I infer from his letter more than
you discover there; and I am not sure that the
advice which I am most disposed to give, is that
which he would be best pleased to see you follow."

"What would that advice be ?" asked Douglas,
anxiously.

"Nay," replied the old gentleman, "when I have
made up my mind, you shall know."

"But why not give me your thoughts," said the
youth, "and let us discuss them ?"

"Because, circumstanced as you are, we cannot
properly discuss them. I can but give you my judgment, when I have formed it, and leave you to find
out the reasons for it."

"My own first thought," said Douglas, "is to
resign. Let us discuss that."

"It was mine too," said the uncle, "and there is
therefore no occasion to discuss it. Though I had
not sufficiently matured my opinion to announce it
to you, I think I may promise, that if you come to
that conclusion, I shall not dissent from it."

"The only difficulty that I see in the way," said
Douglas, "is that an offer to resign is, under such
circumstances, generally understood as a shrinking
from inquiry."

"It is so; and the opinion is so far right, that,
when the charge is infamous, resignation doubles

the infamy. It is a tacit consent to be infamous, only on condition that one may be safe."

"You state the point with startling force," said the youth. "And how would you distinguish this case from the one you suppose?"

"By distinguishing the accusation from one of falsehood, peculation, or cowardice. Should you plead guilty to such charges as these, or seek to evade them by resignation, you stand dishonored. But read over the President's bill of indictment. Now suppose it true that you had entertained and avowed the sentiments there imputed to you, would there be any dishonor in that?"

"Certainly not; unless my being an officer of the United States would make a difference."

"Should that prevent you from thinking, or take away a freeman's right to express his thoughts?"

"It would seem not. But does it not make some difference?"

"Certainly. Shall I tell you what it is? Such sentiments would make it your duty (not to the United States, but to Virginia and to yourself,) to resign. Now, it is because I have no mind to seduce a soldier from his standard that I have been careful not to infuse such sentiments into you. *If once you lay aside the panoply of the uniform*, and throw away the amulet of the commission, I would not ensure you against opinions which you may have to maintain at the hazard of your life. But time presses. Your own suggestion disposes me to speak more promptly and decidedly than I should otherwise have done. *I therefore say, tender your resignation.* But, if you have no objection, I should like to consult a friend, on whose most hasty opinions I rely more than on the coolest judgment of others."

"If you mean my aunt," said Douglas, "I know few persons on whose instinctive sense of propriety I should place more reliance."

"She would well deserve your confidence; but I mean the gentleman who left the room as you entered. He has been her friend for thirty years, and mine for more than half that time."

"But to me," said Douglas, "he is an utter stranger, and I feel some delicacy in consulting a stranger on such an occasion."

"You forget," said Mr. Trevor, "that all there is of delicacy in the case touches me as nearly as you. It is not you, a stranger, but I, an intimate friend, who propose to ask his advice. Charge that matter to my account, then, and merely decide for yourself, whether it may not be desirable to have the counsel of one as remarkable for scrupulous delicacy, as for sagacity and resource?"

"There can be but one answer to that question," replied Douglas, "and I shall therefore gladly take the benefit of his advice."

The hand-bell sounded, and the ever-ready Tom appeared. "My respects to Mr. B——," said Mr. Trevor. "Ask him, if he pleases, to walk into this room."

Tom disappeared, and soon returned marshalling in Mr. B———. He was a man apparently of sixty years of age, or more, slightly formed, but tall, erect, clean-limbed, and sinewy. His vigor seemed little impaired by time, though his high and strong features made him look at least as old as he was. A light blue eye, clear and sparkling, quick in its glance, but settled and searching in its gaze, was the striking feature of his face. The sun had burned out all traces of his original complexion, and a silver hue had usurped the color of his hair. His whole appearance was impos-ing, and while it commanded the respect due to the wisdom of age, seemed to claim no pity for its infir-mities. To this sentiment, which enters so largely into the composition of that character which the world calls *venerable*, he certainly made no pretensions. No one would have called *him* venerable, though no man was held in higher veneration by those who knew him.

CHAPTER XIV.

I had not loved thee, dear, so much,
Loved I not honor more.   LOVELACE.

THE frankness and cordiality of his manner, when introduced to Douglas, gave assurance that he took a great interest in the young man; who felt, on his part, that he was in the presence of a man of no common mould, and that in that man he had found an efficient friend.

"And now, Tom," said Mr. Trevor, "pass the word for coffee and privacy in this room."

Tom bowed and withdrew, and Mr. Trevor, without preface or apology, proceeded to lay the case before his friend. This he did with great precision of statement, while the other listened with an air which showed that no word was lost on him. Having got through, Mr. Trevor added: "We now wish you to advise what should be done in this case."

"Resign, by all means," said Mr. B——. "Resign immediately!"

"Your reasons?" asked Mr. Trevor.

"There are plenty of them, of which you are aware," said B——, "and with which our young

friend shall be made acquainted after resignation—
not before. But there are others which may be spoken
of now. The alternative is a court of inquiry, a court-
martial, or resignation. To the two first the same
objection applies. Your nephew cannot expect any
satisfactory result from either, but by the use of
means which, I am sure, his delicacy would not permit him to use—I mean the public use of a lady's
name. Some people have a taste for that, and in
other parts of the world it is all the rage. I thank
God that the fashion has not reached us. A woman,
exposed to notoriety, learns to bear and then to love
it. When she gets to that, she should go North;
write books; patronize abolition societies; or keep a
boarding-school. She is no longer fit to be the wife
of a Virginia gentleman. But there is no need to
say this. You, Trevor, were your nephew so inclined,
would never permit the name of your daughter to be
thus profaned."

"I could oppose nothing to it," said Mr. Trevor,
"but my displeasure. And though I might not wish
it, could I have a right to be displeased with Douglas for vindicating himself from a charge which has
grown out of his gallant defence of her? Think of
the favorable standing of his family; observe the
rapid promotion of his brother; and consider whether
a punctilio of this sort should bind him to renounce
prospects so flattering?"

"Were the prospect more flattering than you state
it," said B——, "it would not change my opinion.

But what prospect is there?   Colonel Trevor is perhaps a favorite at court. So, doubtless, is your brother.
But he is not a man whose fidelity is either to be
bought or rewarded ; and he and his will be, at any
moment, postponed and sacrificed to the mercenary,
who might desert, and even mutiny for want of pay.
Here is proof of it.

" Look at the shallow pretext for this proposed
court-martial. The President is pleased to say that
he believes your brother ; but that *there are those*
who do not. Who are they? Who can they be?
Who is there, worthy to be accounted among his
advisers, that can disbelieve anything that Hugh
Trevor shall assert ? Don't you see the cheat ?
Don't you see that your brother, whose attachment
to the Union, based as it is on principle, may be
safely trusted, is to have his feelings wounded to
gratify the mortified pride of the elder Baker, and
the skulking malice of his son ? You, Mr. Trevor,
know better than I do, who are about the President.
Is there one among them to whom your father's
word would need the support of other testimony ?
Good old man ! So little has he of pride or jealousy,
that this thought never occurs to him. He is modestly
asking himself what right he has to expect credence
from those who do not know him. And who are
these malcontent officers ? Think you there is one
of them who would venture to express his dissatisfaction to you ? No. There is no one malcontent. No one dissatisfied but that son of the horse-

leech, whose mouth is ever agape, and never can be filled.

" Do look at this letter," continued B——, address-ing Mr. Trevor. " How perfectly in character. Not one traversable allegation (as the lawyers say) except that of his friendship for your brother. ' Those friends whom I feel bound to consult ! ' Who are they ? Press him, and I dare say some fellow below contempt, some scullion of the kitchen political or the kitchen gastronomical, may be found to father what it is alleged that these friends have said. ' His information is from a source entitled to all confi-dence ! ' Does he even say that as of himself? No. He charges that too on his friends, though it might not be easy to find a sponsor for that compliment to old Baker. Since the death of his brother pimp Ritchie, I think that sort of thing has gone out of fashion. ' Hardly less valuable and meritorious than your brother.' The same authority. ' On dit,' ' they say.' I think this last On, would be as hard to find as that universal author of mischief, Nobody.

" But, when we come to the dissatisfaction of the army, it is worse still. Here is on dit upon on dit. Somebody says that somebody else is dissatisfied ; and such are the gossamer threads, woven into a veil to hide this insult to your brother, and this indignity to your nephew. Take away these, and what remains but a wish to soothe Baker? And what must be the force of those favorable dispositions to your young friend, which are to be counteracted by such a motive?

By a reluctance to offend an abject wretch too spirit-
less to resent, and without influence to make his
resentment at all formidable."

"Enough!" said Douglas. "I will send on my
resignation by the next mail."

"No, my dear sir," said B——, "don't yield too
readily to my suggestions."

"It was his own suggestion, and already approved
by me," said Mr. Trevor. "Had you dissented, we
would have reconsidered the matter. As it is, we are
but confirmed in our decision."

"That being the case," said B——, "I have only to
say distinctly that the thing admits of no doubt with
me. I am not only sure that, in resigning, your
nephew will do what best becomes him as a gentleman, but that he will make a fortunate escape from
the service of one whose maxim it is to reward none
but the mercenary."

"Then go to work, my boy," said Mr. Trevor.
"The mail goes at day-light. Enclose your letter of
resignation, unsealed, in one to your father. I will
have them mailed to-night, and you will get an
answer in a week. Here are the materials. Write,
and we will chat and take our coffee. By the way,
Douglas, you have not dined."

"Thank you, my dear uncle, I am too busy to be
hungry," said the youth.

"Be it so," said the old gentleman. "It is not
so long since I was young, but that I understand your
trim. Starving is better than blood-letting, and a full
heart needs the one or the other."

When Douglas's letters were finished, he would gladly have put them into Delia's hands before he sent them off. But he found, what most men have been surprised to find, that after what had passed in the morning between him and Delia, it was much harder to obtain an interview with her than before. When a young gentleman makes a visit of some days to a friend in the country, whose daughter suspects that he has something to say to her that she is impatient to hear, it is amusing to see how many chances will bring them together. Each of them is always happening to have some call to go where the other happens to be; and, when together, each is apt to be detained in the room by some interesting occupation until the rest of the company have left it. They are continually meeting in passages, and on staircases; and, in pleasant weather, they are almost sure to stroll into the garden about the same time. But let the decisive word be once spoken, and all is changed. Then, bless us, how we blush! and how we glide through half-open doors, and slip away around corners!

Still it will happen, as love makes people restless, that both will rise early, and so meet in the parlor before others are awake. And then there is "the dewy eve and rising moon," and the quiet walk "by wimpling burn and leafy shaw;" but as to a private word in the bustling hours of the day, that is out of the question.

All this is the result of sheer accident. See how

innocent and artless she looks! And how light and elastic is her step as she moves along; her swan-like neck outstretched, her face slightly upturned, her eye swimming in light, and looking as if the veil of futu ~ity were raised before her, and all the gay visions of hope stood disclosed in bright reality. Is she not beautiful? O the charm of mutual love! Who can wonder that each man's mistress, wearing this Cytherean zone, is in his eyes the Queen of Beauty herself?

But I forget myself. What place for thoughts like these in a chronicle of wars and revolutions? True, it is in such causes that the spring of great events is found. But these belong to the history of man in all ages, in all countries, under all circumstances. It was so "*before Helen;*" and will be so while the world stands. But it may not be unprofitable to look into the chain of cause and consequence, and to trace the leliverance of Virginia from thraldom, and the defeat of the usurper's well-laid plans, to the impertinent speech of one of his minions to a country girl, during a *pic nic* party at the falls of James river.

But to return. Douglas took a copy of his letter of resignation, and, meeting Delia the next morning, put it into her hands. She read it with a grave and thoughtful countenance, and then, looking sadly in his face, said: "This is what I feared."

"What you feared!" replied he, in amazement. "Can you then wish me to retain my place in the army?"

"Until you resign it to conviction and a sense of duty, certainly!"

"And can you doubt that I have done so?"

"How can it be so?" she replied. "But yesterday we spoke on this subject. What has since happened. O! can it be that my noble father has imposed dishonorable conditions; and that you have been weak enough to comply with them? O! Douglas! Is my love fated to destroy the very qualities that engaged it?"

"Dear Delia," said Douglas, "I understand you now. Your beautiful indignation reminds me that you do not know what has passed."

"What can have passed?" asked she, with earnest and reproachful sadness. "All the eloquence and address of Mr. B—— himself could not have convinced your unbiassed mind in two hours' conversation. I know his power. I know the wonders he has wrought; and I trembled when I heard the watchword, 'coffee and privacy.' I feared your love for me might be used to sway your judgment, and hoped to have found an opportunity to invoke it for the worthier purpose of guarding your honor. I did not dream that, when I rose so early this morning, I was already too late."

"Sweet youth, I pray you chide a year together,"

said Douglas, playfully. "Your indignation is so eloquent, that, cruel as it is, I would not interrupt you to undeceive you. Your father and Mr. B——

have made no attack on my opinions or allegiance , and what was done last night you have had no agency in, since our party at the Falls. It all originated there."

He now gave her the full history of the affair, and succeeded in convincing her that his standard of honor was even higher than she had imagined. If she requited him for her unjust suspicions with a kiss, he never told of it. Perhaps she did. For although, according to the refinements of the Yankees, kissing was in very bad taste, yet the northern regime had not reached the banks of the Roanoke. The ladies there still continued to walk in the steps of their chaste mothers—safe in that high sense of honor which protects at once from pollution and suspicion.

It is true, that when a people become corrupt, they must learn to be fastidious, and invent safeguards to prevent vice, and blinds to conceal it when it is to be indulged. Duennas are necessary in Spain. They are at once the guarantee of a lady's honor, and the safe instruments of her pleasures. Black eunuchs perform the same functions in Turkey. In the northern factories, boys and girls are not permitted to work together. In their churches, the gentlemen and ladies do not sit in the same pew. What a pitch of refinement! Sterne's story of the Abbé in the theatre at Paris affords the only parallel.

Thank God! the frame of our society has kept us free from the cause and its consequences. Whatever corruption there may be among us is restrained to a particular class, instead of diffusing itself by continuous contact through all grades and ranks. If it were true, as the wise, and eloquent, and pious, and benevolent, and discreet Dr. Channing had said, some fifteen years before, that below a certain line all was corrupt, it was equally true that above it all was pure. Nature had marked the line, and established there a boundary which the gangrene of the social body could never pass.

CHAPTER XV.

Mammon, the least erected spirit, that fell
From heaven, for e'en in heav'n his looks and thoughts
Were always downward bent, admiring more
The riches of heav'n's pavement, trodden gold,
Than aught divine or holy else enjoyed
In vision beatific.　　　　　　　MILTON.

ON the evening of the third day from that of
which I have just been speaking, the President of
the United States was sitting alone in a small room
in his palace, which, in conformity to the nomencla-
ture of foreign courts, it had become the fashion to
call his closet. The furniture of this little apartment
was characterized at once by neatness, taste, and
convenience. Without being splendid, it was rich
and costly; and, in its structure and arrangement,
adapted to the use of a man, who, devoted to business, yet loved his ease. The weariness of seden-
tary application was relieved by the most tasteful
and commodious variety of chairs, couches, and sofas,
while the utmost ingenuity was displayed in the
construction of desks, tables, and other conveniences
for reading and writing. In the appearance of the
distinguished personage, to whose privacy I have

introduced the reader, there was a mixture of thought and carelessness very much in character with the implements of business and the appliances for ease and comfort which surrounded him. He occasionally looked at his watch, and at the door, with the countenance of one who expects a visitor ; and then throwing himself against the arm of his sofa, resumed his disengaged air. That something was on his mind was apparent. But, interesting as the subject might be, it did not seem to touch *him* nearly. His whole manner was that of a man who is somewhat at a loss to know what may be best for others, but finds full consolation in knowing precisely what is best for himself.

As the events of the last ten years make it probable that none of my younger readers have ever seen the august dignitary of whom I speak, and as few of us are like to have occasion to see him in future, a particular description of his person may not be unacceptable. Though far advanced in life, he was tastily and even daintily dressed, his whole costume being exactly adapted to a diminutive and dapper person, a fair complexion, a light and brilliant blue eye, and a head which might have formed a study for the phrenologist, whether we consider its ample developments or its egg-like baldness. The place of hair was supplied by powder, which his illustrious example had again made fashionable. The revolution in public sentiment which, commencing sixty years ago, had abolished all the privi-

leges of rank and age ; which trained up the young
to mock at the infirmities of their fathers, and
encouraged the unwashed artificer to elbow the
duke from his place of precedence ; this revolution
had now completed its cycle. While the sovereignty
of numbers was acknowledged, the convenience of
the multitude had set the fashions. But the reign
of an individual had been restored, and the taste of
that individual gave law to the general taste. Had
he worn a wig, wigs would have been the rage.
But as phrenology had taught him to be justly
proud of his high and polished forehead, and the
intellectual developments of the whole cranium, he
eschewed hair in all its forms, and barely screened
his naked crown from the air with a light covering
of powder. He seemed, too, not wholly unconscious
of something worthy of admiration in a foot, the
beauty of which was displayed to the best advantage by the tight fit and high finish of his delicate
slipper. As he lay back on the sofa, his eye rested
complacently on this member, which was stretched
out before him, its position shifting, as if unconsciously, into every variety of grace. Returning from
thence, his glance rested on his hand, fair, delicate,
small, and richly jewelled. It hung carelessly on
the arm of the sofa, and the fingers of this, too, as if
rather from instinct than volition, performed sun-
dry evolutions on which the eye of majesty dwelt
with gentle complacency.

This complacent reverie was frequently broken by

the sound of the door-bell. At such moments, the President would raise his head with a look of awakened expectation, which subsided instantly; until, by frequent repetition, it called up some expression of displeased impatience: At last, the sound was echoed by a single stroke, which rang from what looked like a clock within the room. He immediately sat erect, assuming an air of dignified and complacent composure, suited to the reception of a respected visiter.

The door opened, and the gentleman in waiting bowed into the room a person who well deserves a particular description, and then withdrew.

The individual thus introduced was a gentleman whose age could not be much short of seventy. In person he had probably been once nearly six feet high, but time had at once crushed and bowed him to a much shorter stature. Indeed, the stoop of his shoulders, the protrusion of the neck, and the projecting position of the chin, made together that peculiar complex curvature which brings the top of the cape of the coat exactly against the top of the head. The expression of his countenance was, at once, fawning and consequential. His face had been originally something between round and square. It was now shortened by the loss of his teeth. The muscular fulness of youth had not been replaced by any accession of fat, nor had the skin of his face shrunk, as it often does, on the retiring flesh. The consequence was, that his cheeks hung down in loose pouches, and all his features, originally small and mean, seemed involved in the folds of his shrivelled and puckered skin. His voice was harsh and grating, and the more so from an attempt at suavity in the tones, which produced nothing more than a drawling prolongation of each word. Thus, though he spoke slowly, the stream of sound flowed continually from his lips, reminding the hearer of the never-ending chant of the locust.

As the President rose and gracefully advanced to welcome him, he shuffled forward as if wishing to prevent the honor thus done him, while the increased curve of his back and the eager humility of his upturned countenance, betokened the prostration of his spirit in the presence of the dispenser of honor and emolument. Having bowed himself on the hand which had been graciously extended to him, he remained standing on the floor as if unmindful of repeated invitations to be seated. The President had not yet so entirely forgotten the manners which once distinguished him as a most accomplished gentleman, and was not at first aware of the necessity of seating himself before his deferential guest. At length, he resumed his place on the sofa, and then the other, with a new prostration, which seemed to apologize for sitting in the presence of majesty, followed his example. He did not, indeed, presume to share the sofa, though invited to do so, but took his place on a seat equally luxurious on the opposite side of the fire-place. But the luxury of the *chaise longue* was lost on him. He felt that to lean against the back or arm would be quite unbecoming, and sat as nearly erect as he could, in that precise posture which indicates a readiness to spring to the feet and do the bidding of a superior.

"I had begun to despair of seeing you this evening, my dear sir," said the President, in a tone at once kind and reproachful. "I had given orders that I should be denied to all but you."

"You do me great and undeserved honor," replied the other, "but I—— "

"I wished to speak to you in private," continued Mr. Van Buren, not noticing the interruption, "of a matter which deeply interests us both. Here is a letter which I received this morning, which makes it at least doubtful whether the last step which I took in regard to that young man, Trevor, is quite such as should have been taken."

He then took from a bundle of papers, one which he read as follows:

"SIR: I have just learned that charges of a serious nature have been made against Lieutenant Trevor, which, it seems, grow out of certain occurrences to which I am privy. I can have little doubt that the affair, to which I allude, has not been truly reported to you. Had it been, you would have seen that Lieutenant T. acted no otherwise than as became a soldier and a gentleman, in whose presence a lady, under his protection, had been insulted. The enclosed documents, to the authenticity of which I beg leave to testify, will place the transaction in its true light. Were Lieutenant T. at Washington, I should not lay these papers before you, without authority from him. As it is, I trust I do no more than my duty by him, and by your Excellency, in furnishing such evidences of the real facts of the case, as may aid you in deciding on the course to be pursued in regard to it.

"It may be proper to add, that, having acted as Lieutenant T.'s friend on the occasion, these documents were left in my possession in that character. It is this same character, in which I feel it especially my duty to step forward as the guardian of his honor and interests.

"Hoping that your Excellency will excuse the freedom which calls your notice to so humble a name,

  "I have the honor to be,
   "Your Excellency's most obedient,
    "Humble servant,
     "EDGAR WHITING,
     "*Lieut.* 12*th Inf. U. S. A.*"

Having read this letter aloud, the President, without comment, placed in the hands of his guest a bundle of papers. It is only necessary to tell the reader that they were copies of the same documents which Douglas had laid before his father and uncle, each one duly authenticated by the attestation o Lieutenant Whiting.

Mr. Van Buren now threw himself back upon the sofa, and fixed his eye on the face of his companion with an expression which betokened some concern, not unmixed with a slight enjoyment of the perplexity with which the purblind old man pored over the papers. Indeed, his uneasiness could hardly have escaped the observation of a casual spectator. He shifted his seat; he read; then wiped his spectacles, and read again; then wiped his brow; and having gone through all the documents, again took them up in order, and read them all over again. When, at length, he had extracted all their substance, he turned on the President a perplexed and anxious look, and remained silent.

At length, the latter spoke. "I fear we have made an unlucky blunder in this business, my dear sir," said he.

"I fear so too, sir," said the other. "But I beg leave to assure your Excellency that the information I took the liberty to communicate was a simple and exact statement of what I learned from my son, which, I trust, your Excellency will see is in nowise contravened by these documents. I certainly was not apprised of the provocation which, it is here said, was offered to a lady under Lieutenant Trevor's protection."

"Make yourself perfectly easy on that head, my dear sir," said the President. "I give myself small concern on Lieutenant Trevor's account. My obligations to his father are more than discharged by the rapid advancement of his elder brother; and he can have no right to complain that proceedings have been instituted to inquire into a matter which, even thus explained, places his loyalty in no very favorable light. My concern is, lest the prosecution of this investigation should lead to results undesirable to you."

"I understand your Excellency," replied the honorable Mr. Baker. "The object of this communication is to convey a covert intimation that, if proceedings against Lieutenant Trevor are not stayed, he will revenge himself by endeavoring to dishonor my son. I never brought him up to be the 'butcher of a silk button,' and don't wonder that his notions of gallantry, &c. &c., do not exactly square with those of these *preux chevaliers*."

"That view of the subject is doubtless quite philosophical," said the President; "and if you regard it in that light, it will remove all difficulty out of the way."

"I cannot exactly say," replied the other, "that I should be quite willing to expose my son to the pain of seeing these documents made public; concocted, as they manifestly have been, by men who have learned to quarrel by the book, and contrived on purpose to shut the door against inquiry. I dare say he would hardly have made the communication I received, could he have anticipated the step which I deemed it my duty to your Excellency to take in consequence of it."

"The misfortune is," replied the President, "that I have already caused an intimation to be given to Lieutenant Trevor that it may be necessary to order a court-martial, unless he thinks proper to demand a court of inquiry. Either way, the whole affair must come out."

"Is there no other alternative?" asked the anxious father. "Could not these papers be suppressed? There is no other authentic evidence of these facts."

"Unfortunately," said the President, to whom habitual intercourse with the base had made the feeling of contempt so familiar that he repressed it without difficulty, "unfortunately these papers are but copies. The originals are doubtless in the hands of Lieutenant Whiting, whose honor cannot be questioned, and probably they will be farther verified by the handwriting of your son."

"What then can be done?" asked the honorable Mr. Baker, in a state of unutterable perplexity. Receiving no answer, he sat musing, with the restless and fidgeting air of a man who seeks in vain for some starting point for his thoughts. He was at length roused from his reverie by two strokes of the bell, which issued from the clock-case at the President's back. The signal was answered by the touch of a hand-bell, which stood on a table near him. The door opened. The gentleman in waiting entered, advanced to the table, laid a packet of letters before the President, and withdrew in silence.

He took them up, shuffled them through his hands

as a whist player runs over his cards, and having fixed his eye on one, took it out of the parcel, and threw the rest on the table. His companion having in the mean time relapsed into unconscious reverie, he opened this, and ran his eye over the contents.

"Here is good news for us, my dear sir," said he. "Lieutenant Trevor here tenders his resignation, which, perhaps, may put an end to the difficulty."

"Perhaps!" exclaimed the other, eagerly. "There can be no doubt about it, I hope."

"None at all; if his accounts are all adjusted, of which I have little doubt. But it is not customary to let go our hold on an officer by accepting his resignation, until that matter has been inquired into."

"It will be a great relief to me," faltered out Mr. Baker, looking at the President with an anxious and imploring countenance—

"To have this explained at once" said Mr. Van Buren, interrupting him. "You shall be gratified, my dear sir."

The hand-bell was again sounded. The gentleman in waiting re-appeared; a few words were spoken to him in a low tone, and he again withdrew.

CHAPTER XVI.

——————— His thoughts were low,
To vice industrious, but to noble deeds
Timorous and slothful.

MILTON.

"THERE is something in this business," said the President, after a silence of a few minutes, "which I do not well understand. I was not prepared to find Lieutenant Trevor so ready to resign, and still less to receive his letter of resignation through the hands of his father, without one word of expostulation to his son, or to me. He does not even intimate any the least regret at the event. What can this mean?"

"It does not at all surprise me," said Mr. Baker. "Hugh Trevor was always a visionary and uncertain man; and his influence over his sons is such, that I should consider the manifest defection of Lieutenant Trevor as a sure proof of the estrangement of the father."

"I thought," said the President, "that he had been always remarkable for his steadiness and fidelity."

"In one sense he is so," replied Baker. "But his steadiness is of the wrong sort. He is one of those men who professes to be governed, and I dare say is governed, by principles. But his principles are so numerous, and so hedge him around and beset him on every side, that they have kept him standing still the greater part of his life. When he moves, it would take an expert mathematician to calculate the result of all the compound forces which act upon him, and to decide certainly what course he might take."

"How happens it, then," asked the President, "that I have always found him so loyal and faithful in his devotion to me?"

"*Because he identified your Excellency in his own mind with the Union, to which he is determined to sacrifice every thing else. But now that disunion has come, and the question is whether Virginia shall adhere to the North or join the South, he has a new problem to work, and how he may work it, no man can anticipate. Hence I say he is uncertain.*"

"But does he think nothing of the advancement of his family?"

"It seems not, in this instance. That is what I meant when I said that his principles were too many. Your Excellency knows," continued the honorable gentleman, with a contortion of the mouth meant for a smile, and which, but for the loss of his teeth, might have produced a grin, "that the *cardinal number* of standard principles is the only one which can be counted on."

"Have you then any information," asked the President, "which leads you to suspect him of disaffection?"

"None," replied Baker; "I do but speak from my knowledge of the man. I do not think him capable of that gratitude for the many favors he and his family have received which should bind him indissolubly to your Excellency's service."

"It is well, at least," said the President, "that one of his sons, on whom most of those favors have been lavished, is made of different materials. The principles of Colonel Trevor are exactly of the right sort; or, as you would say, my dear sir, they are of just the right number. Could I obtain any information of the father's movements, which might give me just cause to doubt him, I would take occasion to show the difference I make between the faithful and the unstable. I would refuse to receive this young man's resignation, and order a court-martial immediately. I mistake if the father would not be glad to extricate him from the difficulty, by renouncing some of these fantastic notions which he dignifies by the name of principles."

"I beseech your Excellency," said Baker, forgetting his envious spleen against the virtuous and upright friend of his early youth, in his alarm at the mention of the court-martial; "I beseech your Excellency not to understand me as preferring any charge against Mr. Hugh Trevor. He is an excellent man, who well deserves all the favors he has received, and will, doubtless, merit many more. I pray that what I have said may not at all influence you to any harsh measures against him or his."

The tact of the President at once detected the revulsion of Baker's feelings, and the cause. Indeed, he well knew both the men. He was aware that all that had been said of Mr. Trevor was essentially true. He had, therefore, the more highly prized his friendship, as one of the brightest jewels in his crown. He had taught his advocates and minions to point to him as one, whose support it was known would not be given to any man but from a sense of duty. He was himself not so dead to virtue as not to respect it in another; and his favorable dispositions toward Mr. Trevor, and the benefits bestowed on his family, had more of respect and gratitude than commonly mingled in his feelings or actions. Of Baker, he had rightly formed a different estimate. He found him in the shambles, and had bought and used him. To Baker, too, Mr. Trevor appeared only as one, in whose life there was a "daily beauty that made his ugly;" and he had seen, with malignant envy, the honors and emoluments for which he had toiled through all the drudgery of a partisan, freely bestowed on the unasking and unpretending merit of a rival. Gladly would he have improved the distrust, which he saw had entered into the mind of the President, had he not been warned that the first effect of it might be to press an inquiry which must eventuate in the irreparable dishonor of his own son.

While he sat meditating on these things, and subduing his malice to his fears and his interest, the door-bell sounded; the single stroke from the clock-case

echoed the sound; the door opened; and a new character appeared on the stage.

No person whose name appears in this history better deserves a particular description than he who now
entered. Fortunately I am saved the necessity of
going into it, by having it in my power to refer the
reader to a most graphic delineation of his exact pro
totype in person, mind, manners, and principles.

In Oliver Dain, or Oliver le Diable, as he was
called, the favorite instrument of the crimes of that
remorseless tyrant Louis XI., he had found his great
exemplar. The picture of that worthy, as drawn
by Sir Walter Scott, in Quentin Durward, is the
most exact likeness of one man ever taken for
another. It is not even worth while to change the
costume ; for although he did not appear with a bar-
ber's apron girded around his waist, and the basin
in his hands, it was impossible to look upon him
without seeing that his undoubted talents, and the
high stations he had filled, still left him fit to be
employed in the most abject and menial services.

This happy compound of meanness, malignity,
treachery, and talent, was welcomed by the President with a nod and smile at once careless and
gracious. At the sight of him, Mr. Baker made
haste to rise, and bustled forward to meet and salute
him with an air, in which, if there was less of servility, there was more of the eagerness of adulation
than he had displayed toward the President himself.
The earnest inquiries of Mr. Baker after his health,

&c., &c., were answered with the fawning air of one who feels himself much obliged by the notice of a superior, and he then turned to the President as if waiting his commands. These were communicated by putting into his hands the letters of Mr. Hugh Trevor and his son, which he was requested to read.

While he read, the President, turning to Mr. Baker, said : " While I thought of ordering a court-martial on the case of Lieutenant Trevor, I deemed it advisable to have all his military transactions looked into, intending, if any thing were amiss, to make it the subject of a distinct charge." Then, turning to the other, he added : " You have, I presume, acquainted yourself with the state of the young man's accounts."

" I have, sir," was the reply. " They have been all settled punctually."

" Then there is nothing to prevent the acceptance of his resignation ?"

" Nothing of that sort, certainly, sir. But has your Excellency observed the date of this letter of his ? You may see that he does not date from his father's house. I happen to know this place, Truro, to be the residence of that pestilent traitor, his uncle. Now, if the charge be well founded, I submit to your Excellency whether the offender should be permitted to escape prosecution by resigning. If it be not exactly capable of being substantiated, yet his readiness to resign on so slight an intimation renders his disaffection at least probable, and his date renders it nearly certain. Might it not then be

advisable to retain the hold we have upon him?
The court-martial being once ordered, additional
charges might be preferred ; and I much mistake
the temper of the country where he is, if he does
not furnish matter for additional charges before the
month of April passes by."

"Why the month of April?" asked the President.

"Because then the elections come on ; and there
is little doubt that exertions will be made to obtain
a majority in the Legislature of men disposed to
secede, and join the southern confederacy. In that
county, in particular, I am well advised that such
exertions will be made. A hen-hearted fellow has
been put forward as the candidate of the malcontents, who can be easily driven from the canvass by
his personal fears. Let the affair once take that
shape, and immediately the fantastic notions of what
southern men call chivalry, which infest the brain
of this old drawcansir, will push him forward as a
candidate. I had made some arrangements which,
with your Excellency's approbation, I had proposed
to carry into effect for accomplishing this result, in
the hope of bringing him into collision with the law
of treason, and so getting rid at once of a dangerous
enemy. Now, if this young man's resignation be
rejected, and a court-martial be ordered, the part he
will act in the affair can hardly fail to be such as to
make his a ball-cartridge case."

"Your plan is exceedingly well aimed," said the

President, "but on farther reflection, my good friend Mr. Baker is led by feelings of delicacy to wish to withdraw his charges. I am loth to deny any thing to one who merits so much at my hands, but still there are difficulties in the way which will not permit us to pursue that course. The acceptance of this resignation will effectually remove them, and indirectly gratify the wish of Mr. Baker. Now, what do you advise?"

In the act of asking this question, the President shifted his position so suddenly as to call the minion's attention to the motion. He looked up and saw his master's face averted from Mr. Baker, and thought he read there an intimation that he should press his former objection. This he therefore did, expressing his reluctance to give advice unfavorable to the wishes of one so much respected as Mr. Baker, and highly complimenting the delicacy of his scruples.

"But suppose," asked the President, "we press the passage of the law authorizing a court to sit here for the trial, by a jury of this District, of offences committed in Virginia. In that case, should our young cock crow too loud, we might find means to cut his comb without a court-martial."

"That Congress will pass such a law cannot be doubted," said the other, "were it not vain to do so, when it seems to be understood that none of the judges would be willing to execute it. I am tired of hearing of constitutional scruples."

"I am bound to respect them," replied the President, meekly. "But I really do not see the grounds for them in such a case as this. I beg pardon, Judge Baker. I know it is against rule to ask a judge's opinion out of court. But I beg you to enlighten me so far as to explain to me what are the scruples which the bench are supposed to feel on this subject. I make the inquiry, because I am anxious to accept this young fellow's resignation, if, in doing so, I shall not lose the means of punishing the offences which there is too much reason to think he meditates. To try him in Virginia would be vain. Indeed, I doubt whether your court could sit there in safety."

"I fear it could not," replied the Judge, "and have therefore no difficulty in saying, that the necessity of the case should overrule all constitutional scruples. I have no delicacy in answering your Excellency's question out of court. It is merely an inquiry, which I hope is superfluous, whether I would do my duty. I trust it is not doubted that I would; and should I be honored with your Excellency's commands in that behalf, I should hold myself bound to execute them. To speak more precisely : should the court be established, and I appointed to preside in it, I should cheerfully do so."

"That then removes all difficulty," said the President. "The young man's resignation, therefore, will be accepted, and measures must be taken to distribute troops through the disaffected counties in such numbers as may either control the display of the malcontent spirit at the polls, or invite it to show itself in such a shape as shall bring it within the scope of your authority, and the compass of a halter."

Some desultory conversation now arose on various topics, more and more remote from public affairs. On these Mr. Baker would have been glad to descant, and perhaps to hear the thoughts of the President and his minister. But all his attempts to detain them from talking exclusively of lighter matters were effectually baffled by the address of the former. All this was so managed as to wear out the evening, without giving the gentleman the least reason to suspect that he was in the way, or that the great men who had seemed to admit him to their confidence, placed themselves under the least constraint in his presence. At length he took his leave.

CHAPTER XVII.

That just habitual scorn, which could contemn
Men and their thoughts, 'twas wise to feel.

BYRON.

As the door closed behind him, the countenance of the President relaxed into a smile, indicative of great satisfaction and self-applause, along with an uncontrollable disposition to merriment. The smile soon became a quiet laugh, which increased in violence without ever becoming loud, until he lay back against the arm of the sofa, and covered his face with his handkerchief. At length, his mirth exhausted itself, and he sat erect, looking at the Minister with the countenance of one about to make some amusing communication. But he waited to be spoken to, and remained silent. His minion took the hint, and addressing himself to what he supposed to be passing in his master's mind, said : " I beseech your Excellency to tell me by what sleight, by what *tour de main*, this hard knot about jurisdiction has been made to slip as easily as a hangman's noose ? I feared we should have had to cut it with the sword, and behold it unites itself."

"How can you ask such a question?" said the President, with mock gravity. "Did you not hear the elaborate and lucid argument by which the Judge proved incontestably that it could not be unconstitutional to do his duty? The wonder is how they ever contrived to make a difficulty. Surely none who shall ever hear that demonstration can doubt again."

"But may I be permitted to ask by what means such a flood of light has been poured upon his mind? But yesterday he was dark as the moon in its perihelion. Has the golden ray of additional favors again caused its face to shine?"

"No," said the President.

"No new emoluments to him or his?"

"None at all," was the laughing answer.

"No new honors?"

"None; but the honor of doing additional duty, for the first time in his life, without additional compensation."

"In the name of witchcraft, then, what has wrought upon him?"

"That I shall not tell you," said the President, still laughing. "That is my secret. That part of my art you shall never know. It is one of the jokes that a man enjoys the better for having it all to himself. I keep it for my own diversion. It is a sort of royal game. You, I am sure, may be satisfied with your share in the sport, having been admitted to hear that argument. It was a lesson in dialectics worth a course at a German university. But come! There is a time to laugh, and a time to be serious. What do you propose on the subject of these Virginia elections?"

"I propose," said the Minister, "to distribute some five hundred men in certain counties, with the dispositions of which I have made myself acquainted, to preserve order at the elections, as we should say to the uninitiated ; but in plain English, to control them. They will succeed in this, or provoke violence. Either way, we carry our point. We prevail in the elections, or we involve the members elect in a charge of treason. I think we may trust Judge Baker for the rest. The more dangerous of our enemies will thus fall under the edge of the law, and the less efficient, if not left in a minority, will be powerless for want of leaders."

"But the scene of action," said the President, "is close to the line. The offenders may escape into North Carolina, and from thence keep up a communication with their friends. They may even venture to Richmond at a critical moment, and effect their great purpose, or they may adjourn to some place of greater security."

"It will certainly be necessary," said the Minister, "to guard against that, by increasing the number of troops at the seat of government. Besides, if we can but get one day to ourselves, their chance of legislative action may be broken up by adjournment *sine die.*"

"Then, with so many points in the game in our

favor," replied the President, " we have but to play it boldly and we must win. It shall go hard, too, if, in the end, we do not make this superfluous State Legislature, this absurd relic of *imperium in imperio,* abolish itself. At all events, the course of conduct which they will necessarily pursue, must sink the body in public estimation, and dispose the people to acquiesce in the union of all power in the hands of the Central Government. We can then restore them all the benefits of real and efficient local legislation, by erecting these degraded sovereignties into what they ought always to have been —municipal corporations, exercising such powers as we choose to grant."

Some farther conversation ensued, in which details were settled. A minute was made of the points at which troops should be stationed; the number of men to be placed at each ; and the corps from which they were to be drawn. It was left to the Minister to fix on proper persons to command each party, and to devise instructions as to the part to be acted. In some places it was proposed simply to awe the elections by the mere presence of the military. In some, to control them by actual or threatened violence. In others, insult was to be used, tumult excited, resistance provoked, and dangerous men drawn in, to commit acts which might be denounced as criminal. Having thus possessed himself of his master's will, this modern Sejanus withdrew to give necessary orders for effecting it

"The only truly wise man that I know in the world," said the President, looking after him. "The only one who knows man as he is; who takes no account of human virtue, but as one form of human weakness. In his enemies, it gives him a power over them which he always knows how to use. In his instruments, he desires none of it. Why cannot I profit more by his instruction and example? Fool that I am! I will try to practise a lesson."

He rang the bell, and directed that the Minister should be requested to return.

He had not yet left the palace, and soon re-appeared. As he entered, the President said: "This young Trevor! He has talent, has he not?"

"Talent of every kind," said the Minister.

"That he has a superabundance of what fools call honor and gallantry, I happen to know. I suppose his other *virtues* are in proportion?"

"I suspect so, from the example of the father, and all I can learn of the son."

"Can you then doubt of his ultimate course? or even that of his father? Do you doubt that if the standard of rebellion is once raised, the young man will be found fighting under it, with the old man's approbation?"

"Not at all. I know no man who would raise it sooner than himself, after he has had time to be thoroughly indoctrinated by his uncle."

"Then the sooner the better. He is but a cocke-rel yet. What if he can be brought to commit himself before his spurs have acquired their full length?"

"Nothing could be more judicious, and nothing easier."

"How would you go about it?"

"Let him have a letter neither accepting nor rejecting. Intimating the necessity of farther investigation of his accounts, &c., &c., before we let him off, and requiring him, for the convenience of farther correspondence, to remain at the place from whence his letter is dated. Keep him fretted in this until the election is near at hand, and, a day or two before, let him receive a letter accepting his resignation. My life upon it, he will spring to his destruction like a bow, when the string is cut, that snaps by its own violence."

"You are right," said the President. "That will do. Much will depend on the style of that letter. You have your hands too full to be troubled with such things, or I should ask you to do what no man can do so well. But you have your pupils, who have learned of you to say what is to be said, so as just to produce the desired effect, and no other."

The instrument of the royal pleasure again withdrew. Again the President looked after him, and said, musingly: "Were I not myself, I would be that man. I should even owe him a higher compliment could one be devised, for, but for him, I had never been what I am. What then? Is he the creator, and am I his creature? No. I am wrong

Could he have made himself what I am, he would have done so. He has but fulfilled my destiny, and I his. He has made me what I alone was capable of becoming, and I, in turn, have made him all that he ever can be. I owe him nothing, therefore; and should he ever be guilty of any thing like virtue, there is nothing to hinder me from lopping off any such superfluous excrescence, even if his head should go with it. But he is in no danger on that score. If he held his life by no other tenure, his immortality would be sure."

While the master thus soliloquized, the minion was wending his way home, to the performance of the various duties assigned him. Our present business is with the letter to Douglas alone. The pen of a ready and skilful writer was employed, the document was prepared, submitted to the inspection of the President, approved by him, signed " by order" by the Secretary of War, committed to the mail, and forwarded to Douglas. Let us accompany it.

CHAPTER XVIII.

—————— Behold the tools,
The broken tools that tyrants cast away
By myriads.——————   BYRON.

BEHOLD us then, once more, at the door of Mr. Bernard Trevor's little study. The uncle and nephew are together. A servant enters with letters from the post-office, and we enter with him. The letters are opened, and Douglas having read that of the Secretary of War, hands it to his uncle. Let us read with him.

" SIR : *I have it in command from his Excellency the President to say, that your letter of resignation has been received with surprise and regret.*

" *He has seen with surprise that, at a moment of such critical importance, one who had been, as it were, the foster-child of the Union, should seize, with apparent eagerness, a pretext to desert the banner of his too partial sovereign.*

" His regret is not at the loss of service, which, rendered by one capable even of meditating such a step, would, at best, be merely nominal ; but at the thought that that one is the son of a friend so long cherished and so much respected as your father.

" I am farther charged to remind you, that resignation, when resorted to for the purpose of evading
military prosecution, is always deemed little short
of a confession of guilt. In most cases, this pro-
duces no embarrassment. The loss of the commission is generally an adequate punishment ; and it is,
in such cases, well to leave the conscience and the
fears of the accused to inflict that punishment, rati-
fying the sentence by prompt acceptance of the
proffered resignation.

" But this does not hold in all cases. The President bids me say that he is not yet prepared how to
act in one of so serious a character as this. His
regard for your father is the source of this perplexity. He requires time to reflect how far he can
reconcile to his public duty that tenderness to the
feelings of a friend which makes him desirous, if
possible, to stay inquiry by accepting your resignation. Under other circumstances, he would not
hesitate to reject it, and instantly order a court-
martial, as the proper means of bringing to prompt
and merited punishment an offence which, I am
charged to say, he considers as virtually admitted
by your attempt to evade a trial ; when, if innocent,
you would certainly wish an investigation, in order
to establish your innocence.

" In conclusion, I am instructed to say, that for
the purpose of further communication, if necessary,
and to facilitate such measures as it may be deemed
proper to take in relation to you, I am required to

keep myself advised of your locality. To save
trouble, therefore, I deem it advisable to command
you to remain at the place from whence your letter
of resignation was dated, and to which this is
directed, until farther orders.

        " Yours, &c., &c.
(" By order of the President.")

This letter Mr. Trevor read with calm and quiet
attention, carefully weighing every phrase and word,
while Douglas, perceiving the handwriting of his
friend Whiting on the back of another, hastily tore
it open, and read as follows :

" I never performed a more painful duty in my
life, my dear Trevor, than in putting the seal and
superscription to the accompanying letter from the
Secretary.

" My situation in the Department should have
given me earlier notice of what was passing, but I
got no hint of it until yesterday. I immediately
did what I believed to be my duty as a friend ;
though I am now fearful that what I did may not
meet your entire approbation. I am sensible you
would not have done it for yourself ; but there are
some things which delicacy forbids us to do in our
own case, which we are not displeased to have done
by others. Indeed, had I known that the matter
had gone so far, I should have left it in your own
hands. But I had no reason to believe that any
intimation of it had, as yet, been given to you, and

I wished to prevent any step whatever from being taken.

"With this view I ventured to lay the whole correspondence before the President. I know that he received and read it. You will therefore judge my surprise at being required, to-day, to forward the unprecedented document which accompanies this.

"I am guilty of no breach of duty when I assure you that that paper is sent, as it imports on its face, 'by the order of the President.' The Secretary is not responsible even for one word of it. The very handwriting is unknown to me, and it was sent to the department precisely in the shape in which you receive it.

"Knowing what I did, I should have doubted whether it had not been surreptitiously placed among other papers transmitted to us at the same time. But there is no room for mistake. It came accompanied by the most authentic evidence that it had been read and approved by the President himself.

"I find *myself* placed in a delicate situation. Here is an avowal of full faith in a charge disproved by my positive assurance : a charge that no one can believe, who does not believe me capable of basely fabricating the documents, copies of which the President has, authenticated under my hand.

"Your own course leaves no doubt what you would advise me to do, under such circumstances.

But my lot in life is different from yours. Impatient as I am of this indignity, I fear I shall be constrained to bear it. 'My poverty but not my will consents.' I do not, therefore, ask you to advise me, for I would not do so, unless prepared to give to your advice more weight than I can allow it. It could add nothing to the convictions of my own mind, and the indignant writhings of my own wounded honor; and even these, God help me, I am forced to resist!

"This affair has, as yet, made no noise. It is not at all known of in the army; but I think I can assure you of the sympathy of all whose regard you value, and their unabated confidence in your honor and fidelity. I shall make it my business, be the consequence to myself what it may, to do you ample justice. Indeed, my indignation makes me so reckless of consequences, that, apart from the necessity of bearing insult from one from whom no redress can be demanded, I am not sure that I do not envy your lot.

"That your resignation will eventually be accepted, cannot be doubted. What is the motive to this letter, it is hard to say; but certainly it does not proceed from such a disposition as would willingly afford you an opportunity of triumphant vindication.

"*God bless you, my dear Trevor. We have indications that stirring times are at hand, which will tempt me to exchange the pen for the sword. Where duty may call me, I cannot anticipate; but it will*

be strange if the charms of a life of active service
don't bring us together again.   Meet when we may,
you will find still and unalterably, your friend,
" E. W."

Having read this second letter, Douglas passed it
also to his uncle, and, rising, hastily left the house.
It is needless to scan the thoughts that accompanied
him in his ramble.   They were bitter and fierce
enough.   But he had learned, in early life, to master
his feelings, and never to venture into the presence
of others until the mastery had been established.
Many a weary mile did he walk that day before his
purpose was accomplished, but having at last effected
it, he returned.

Mr. Trevor had found leisure, in the mean time,
to scrutinize the letters in whole and in detail, and
had, at length, arrived at a conclusion not far from
the truth.   He was prepared, therefore, to welcome
the return of Douglas with a cheerful smile; and
instead of adding to his excitement by any expression of resentment or disgust, endeavored to calm
and soothe him.   For such conduct the young man
was altogether unprepared.   Aware of his uncle's
wishes in regard to him, he had looked for something different, and had endeavored to fortify his
mind against such impressions as he feared he might
attempt to make on it.   The great principles by
which he had been taught to govern himself were
not false because he had been wronged.   *His duty*

*to the Union was not affected by the injustice of the
President.* So his father would have reasoned the
matter, and like his father, he determined, if possible, to think and act. But he had no idea that in
this attempt he would receive countenance and even
aid from his uncle. It may, therefore, be readily
believed that the old gentleman rose yet higher in
his esteem and confidence, from the delicacy and
forbearance which he so unexpectedly practised.

CHAPTER XIX.

Stone walls do not a prison make,
Nor iron bars a cage.   LOVELACE.

It was settled, on consultation, that he should abide the final event; and that, until then, nothing of what had passed should be made known to his father, to Delia, or to any of the family but Mrs. Trevor. In her he had learnèd to seek an adviser, and in her he always found one—sincere, sagacious, and discreet. Mr. Trevor, as I have said, was not a man from whose opinions his wife would probably dissent, but he had not contented himself to command her blind, unreasoning acquiescence. He had trained her mind; he had furnished her with materials for thought; and he had taught her to think. She was in all his confidence, and he consulted with her habitually on plans which involved the welfare of his country. From her, therefore, the history of Douglas's entanglement with the authorities at Washington was not concealed. From the rest of the family it was a profound secret; and, as Mr. Trevor's health was now much restored, it did not interrupt the enjoyments of the genial season which invited them to seek amusement out of doors.   By means of this, the impatience of Douglas was diverted, and he found it quite easy to accomplish his philosophical determination to wait the result of the affair in patience.

When, at length, a week had been allowed him to fret his heart out, the deferred acceptance of his resignation was received.   This, too, was couched in phrases of decorous and studied insult.   But he had learned to think that the dastard blow struck by one who screens himself behind the authority of office, inflicts no dishonor.   The interval, which had been intended to give his passions time to work themselves into a tempest, had subdued them.   Reason had taken the ascendant, and though his reflections had not been much more favorable to the authority of his former master, than the promptings of his resentment, they were much less suited to his present purpose.   He was effectually weaned; divested of all former prepossessions, and ready to yield to the dictates of calm, unbiassed reason.   He sought his uncle, and with a quiet and cheerful smile, handed him the letter.

As soon as Mr. Trevor read it, he exclaimed, ' Thank God ! you are now a freeman."

" I am truly thankful for it," replied Douglas, " though I feel as if I shall never lose the mark of the collar which reminds me that I have been a slave.   But, until within a short time past, I have never felt that I was."

" When the bondage reaches to the mind," said Mr. Trevor, " it is not felt."

" And was mine enslaved," asked Douglas, " when my thoughts were as free as air ? "

" Their prison was airy," replied the old gentle man, " and roomy, and splendidly fitted up. But look at the President's letters, and see the penalties you might have incurred, had your freedom of thought rambled into such opinions as many of your best friends entertain."

" Still," replied Douglas, " the penalty would have attached, not to the opinion, but to the expression of it."

" And do you think your mind would work without constraint, in deciding between opinions which it might be unsafe to express, and those which would be regarded as meritorious !"

" I can, at least, assure you that such a thought as that never occurred to me."

" But it occurred to your friends. It tied my tongue, and, I suspect, your father's too, of late. Now that I am free to speak, let me ask, wherein would have been the criminality of *expressing* the opinions imputed to you ? "

" It would have been inconsistent with my duty of allegiance."

" *Allegiance ! To whom ? You will not say to King Martin the First ? To what ?*

" *To the constitution of the United States. I was bound by oath to support that.*"

"*And what if your views of the constitution had shown you that the acts of the Government were violations of the constitution*, and that the men denounced by Baker as traitors were its most steady supporters. What duty would your oath have prescribed in that case? Would you support the constitution by taking part with those who trampled it under foot, against those who upheld it as long as there was hope?"

"I should have distrusted my own judgment. Surely, you would not have me set up that against the opinions of the legislative, executive, and judiciary, all concurrently expressed according to the forms of the constitution."

"What then must *I* do?" asked Mr. Trevor. "Be the opinions of all these men what they may, the constitution, after all, is what it is. As such, I am bound to support it. Now, when I have schooled myself into all possible respect for their judgment, and all possible diffidence of my own, if I still think that they are clearly in error, *is it by conforming to their opinion or my own that I shall satisfy my own conscience, to which my oath binds me, that I do actually support the constitution?*"

"I suppose," said Douglas, "you must, in that case, conform to your own convictions."

"Then I may, at last, trust to my own judgment when I have no longer any doubt."

"You must of necessity."

"And you," said Mr. Trevor, "who were not free

to do so—who, in the matter of an oath, were to be guided, not by your own conscience, but by the consciences of other men—was your mind free?"

Douglas colored high, and, after a long pause, said : "I see that I have been swinging in a gilded cage, and mistook its motions for those of my own will. I see it, and again respond cordially to your ejaculation : Thank God ! I am free."

"I rejoice at it, especially," said Mr. Trevor, "because now all reserve is at an end between us. Heretofore, in all my intercourse with you, my tongue has been tied on the subject of which I think most, and on which I feel most deeply. *I find it hard to speak to a son of Virginia without speaking of her wrongs, and the means of redressing them. It is harder still, when he to whom I speak is my own son too.*"

"*I have long ago learned from my father,*" said Douglas, "*that the whole South has been much oppressed. I know, too, that he attributes the oppression to the exercise of powers not granted by the constitution. But, with every disposition to resist this oppression, he taught me to bear it sooner than incur the evils of disunion.*"

"What are they ?"

"Weakness, dissention, and the danger to liberty from the standing armies of distinct and rival powers."

"Hence you have never permitted yourself to look narrowly into the question."

"I never have. I have no doubt of our wrongs; but I have never suffered myself to weigh them against disunion. That I have been taught to regard as the *maximum* of evil."

"But disunion has now come. The question now is, whether you shall continue to bear these wrongs, or seek the remedy offered by an invitation to join the Southern Confederacy. The evils of which you speak would certainly not be increased by such a step. We might weaken the North, but not ourselves. As to standing armies, here we have one among us. The motive which that danger presented is now reversed in its operation. While we remain as we are, the standing army is fastened upon us. By the proposed change we shake it off. Then, as to dissension, if there is no cause of war now, there would be none then. Indeed the only cause would be removed, and it would be seen that both parties had every inducement to peace. Even in the present unnatural condition, you see that the separation having once taken place, there remains nothing to quarrel about."

"What, then," said Douglas, "is the meaning of all this military array that I see? *Are no hostile movements apprehended from the Southern Confederacy?*"

"Not at all. They have no such thought. The talk of such things is nothing but a pretext for muzzling Virginia."

"How do you mean?" asked Douglas.

" You will know if you attend the election in this county to-morrow. You will then see that a detachment of troops has been ordered here on the eve of the election. The ostensible use of it, is to aid in the prevention of smuggling, or, in other words, in the enforcement of the odious tariff, and a participation in the advantages our southern neighbors enjoy since they have shaken it off. But you will see this force employed to brow-beat and intimidate the people, and to drive from the polls such as cannot be brought to vote in conformity to the will of our rulers. *Go back to Richmond next winter, and you will see the force stationed there increased to what will be called an army of observation.* In the midst of this, the Legislature will hold its mock deliberations ; and you will find advanced posts so arranged as to bridle the disaffected counties, and prevent the people from marching to the relief of their representatives. By one or the other, or both of these operations, Virginia will be prevented from expressing her will in the only legitimate way, and her sons, who take up arms in her behalf, will be stigmatised as traitors, not only to the United States, but to her.

CHAPTER XX.

Ah, villain! thou wilt betray me, and get a thousand crowns of the King for carrying my head to him.

SHAKSPEARE.

As Mr. Trevor had intimated, the next day was the day for the election of members to the State Legislature. The old gentleman, in spite of his infirmities, determined to be present. He ordered his barouche, and provided with arms both the servant who drove him, and one who attended on horseback. He armed himself also with pistols and a dirk, and recommended a like precaution to Douglas. "You must go on horseback," said he. "It *may* enable you to act with more efficiency on an emergency. At all events, were you to drive me, I should have no excuse for taking one whose services I would not willingly dispense with. Give me the world to choose from, and old Tom's son Jack is the man I would wish to have beside me in the hour of danger. As to you, my son, I think your late master would not be sorry to get you into a scrape. You should, therefore, be on your guard. My infirmities will render your personal aid necessary to help me to the polls. Keep near me, therefore; but keep cool, and leave me to fight my own battles. Prudence and forbearance are necessary for you. As to me, I have nothing to hazard. The measure of my offences is full already. I have sinned the unpardonable sin, and although there is no name for it in the statute book, *I have no doubt if they had me before their new Court of High Commission at Washington*, your special friend, Judge Baker, would find one."

"Why do you call him my special friend?" asked Douglas.

"Because I have means of being advised of what is doing among our rulers, and know that he was at the bottom of the whole proceeding against you. Therefore, I warn you to be prudent to-day. Depend upon it, if you can be taken in a fault, he will find means 'to feed fat his grudge' against you."

On reaching the election ground, the stars and stripes were seen floating above the door of the court-house, which was still closed. A military parade was "being enacted" for the amusement of the boys and cake-women, and the uniform showed that the men were regulars in the service of the United States. They were twenty or thirty in number, all completely armed and equipped. As soon as Mr. Trevor appeared, they were dismissed from parade, the door was thrown open, and they rushed into the house. Presently after, it was proclaimed that the polls were opened.

As Mr. Trevor approached the door, Douglas

observed that a multitude of persons, who before
had been looking on, in silent observance of what was
passing, advanced to salute him, and, falling behind
him, followed to the court-house. On reaching the
door, they found it effectually blocked up by half a
dozen soldiers, who stood in and about, as if by
accident and inadvertence. But the unaccommodat-
ing stiffness with which each maintained his position, left no doubt that they were there by design.
They were silent, but their brutish countenances
spoke their purpose and feelings. Mr. Trevor might
have endeavored in vain to force his passage, had
not the weight of the crowd behind pressed him
through the door. In this process he was exposed
to some suffering, but made no complaint. The
effect appeared only in the flush of his cheek, and
the twitching of his features. The blood of Douglas
began to boil, and, for the first time in his life, the
uniform he had so long worn was hateful in his
sight.

On entering the house, they were nearly deafened
with the din. It proceeded from quite a small
number, but they made amends for their deficiency
in this respect, by clamorously shouting their *hurras*
for the President, and his favored candidate. Besides the soldiery, there were present the sheriff,
who conducted the election, and some twenty or
thirty of the lowest rabble. On the bench were two
candidates. The countenance of one of those was
flushed with insolent triumph. The other looked

pale and agitated. He was placed between his
competitor and a subaltern officer of the United
States army. He seemed to have been saying some
thing, and at the moment when Mr. Trevor and his
party entered, was about to withdraw.

Meeting him at the foot of the stair leading down
from the bench, that gentleman asked him the
meaning of what he saw; to which he answered
that he had been compelled to withdraw. The
meeting of these two gentlemen had attracted
attention, and curiosity to hear what might pass
between them, for a moment stilled the many-
tongued clamor. Mr. Trevor took advantage of the
temporary silence, and said aloud: "You have been
compelled to withdraw. Speak out distinctly, then,
and say that you are no longer a candidate."

" Fellow-citizens," responded the other, in the
loudest tones his tremor enabled him to command,
" I am no longer a candidate."

" AND I AM A CANDIDATE," cried Mr. Trevor in
a voice which rang through the house. " I am a
candidate on behalf of VIRGINIA, her RIGHTS, and
her SOVEREIGNTY."

The shout from behind the bar, at this annuncia-
tion, somewhat daunted the blue coats, and Mr.
Trevor was lifted to the bench on the shoulders of
his friends ; when the officer was heard to cry out,
" Close the polls."

" Place me near that officer," said Mr. Trevor, in
a quiet tone. The sheriff, a worthy but timid man,

looked at him imploringly. He was set down by the side of the officer, and, leaning on the shoulder of Douglas, thus addressed him—

"I shall say nothing, sir," said he, "to the sherifl about his duty. He is the judge of that, and he knows that, without my consent, he has no right to close the polls before sunset. Unless compelled by force, he will not do it. He *shall not* be compelled by force; and, if force is used, I shall know whence it comes. Now mark me, sir; I am determined that this election *shall* go on, and that peaceably. If force is used, it must be used first on me. Now, sir, my friends are numerous and brave, and well armed, and I warn you that my fall will be the signal of your doom. Not one of your bayoneted crew would leave this house alive. As to *you*, sir, I keep *my* eye upon *you*. You stir not from my side, till the polls are closed. I hold you as a hostage for the safety of the sheriff. If an attaek is made on him, I shall know you for the instigator. And, more than that, sir, I know he is disposed to do his duty, and will not think of closing the polls prematurely. A menace addressed to him may escape my ear. If he offers to do it, if he does but open his mouth to declare that the polls are closed, I blow your brains out on the spot."

Suiting the action to the word, he, at the same moment, showed a pistol, the finish of which gave assurance that it would not miss fire. The officer started back in evident alarm, and made a movement to withdraw ; but he found himself hedged in by brawny countrymen, who closed around him, while every hand was seen to gripe the handle ol some concealed weapon.

"Be patient, sir," said Mr. Trevor, "you had no business here ; but, being here, you shall remain. No harm shall be done you. I will ensure you against every thing but the consequences of your own violence. Offer none. For if you do but lift your hand, or touch your weapons, or utter one word to your myrmidons, you die."

These words were uttered in a tone in which, though loud enough to be heard by all, there was as much of mildness as of firmness. Indeed his last fearful expression was actually spoken as in kindness. The officer seemed to take it so, and quietly seated himself.

Not so the rival candidate. He rose, with a great parade of indignation, saying : "Let *me* pass, at least. This is no place for me."

"Do you mean to leave us, sir?" said Mr. Trevor, with great courtesy.

"I do," said the other. "To what purpose should I remain ?"

"Do you then decline? Are you no longer a candidate ?"

"I am ; but I will not remain here beset by armed violence."

"Will you leave one to represent you ?"

"No ; I leave you to work your will. I have no

farther part in the matter.   I shall do nothing, and
consent to nothing.   When the law closes the poll,
it will be closed."

Saying this, he withdrew, and Mr. Trevor observed
that, as he went out, he spoke aside to the sergeant
of the company, who followed him from the house.
Soon after, the men, one by one, dropped off, and all
at length disappeared.

The election now went on peaceably, and nearly
every vote was cast for Mr. Trevor.   But it did not
escape his observation that there were persons present whom he knew to be hostile to him, and devoted
to the rulers at Washington, who yet did not vote.
He saw the motive of this conduct, but determined
to make it manifest to others as well as himself, and
to expose the disingenuous and unmanly artifice
which he saw his enemies were using against him.
Catching the eye of a well dressed man he said,
" You have not voted, I think, Mr. A—— ?"

" I have not," was the answer, " and I don't mean
to vote."

"I beg that you will, sir," said Mr. Trevor.   " I
know you to be my enemy, personal as well as political; but I sincerely wish the name of every voter
in the county to appear on the poll book, though
my defeat should be the consequence."

" It may be so, sir," replied the other; "but I
shall not vote at an election, controlled by force, and
where those commissioned by the Government to keep
order, are either driven off or detained in durance."

" I do not understand you, sir," said Mr. Trevor.
" Am I to infer that the presence of the military here
is under the *avowed* orders of their master ?"

" I dare say," replied the other, " that Lieutenant
Johnson will show you his orders, if you will conde-
scend to look at them."

" I will do so, with great pleasure," said Mr. Trevor, " and promise myself great edification from the
perusal."

" I will read them, sir," said the officer, taking a
paper from his pocket, which he read accordingly in
the following words:

" As there is reason to believe that evil disposed
persons design to overawe or disturb the election of
members of the Legislature from the county of ——,
Lieutenant Johnson will attend at the day and place
of election with the troops under his command, for
the purpose of preserving order. Should his authority be opposed, he is, if permitted to do so, to make
known that he acts by the command of the President, to the end that all who may be disposed to
resist him, may be duly warned that in so doing
they resist the authority of the United States, and
take heed lest they incur the penalties of the law."

" Why, this is well," said Mr. Trevor. " And it
is to give color and countenance to a charge of resistance to the authority of the United States, that you,
Mr. A——, refuse to vote."

" No, sir," replied A——; " it is because I never
will vote at an election controlled by force."

" Be it so," said Mr. Trevor. " I perceive your drift. Go, then, and tell your master that the means used to vindicate the freedom of election were used to control it. Go, sir, and show that you are as much an enemy to truth and honor as to me."

To this A—— made no reply, and soon after withdrew. Indeed, hardly any person remained but the friends of Mr. Trevor, and it was obvious that the result of the election was not to be changed by any votes which could be given. The necessity of keeping open the poll till sunset was, nevertheless, imperious. But the scene became dull and irksome. Douglas, therefore, proposed that his uncle should return home.

" By no means," said he. " You don't understand this game. Should we disband, the sheriff would be required, at the peril of his life, to make a false return. But he shall have his will. Mr. Sheriff, shall I withdraw also ?"

" No ! no ! For God's sake, stay, sir !" exclaimed the alarmed sheriff; " and either see me home, or take me home with you. I have not the influence which makes you safe in the midst of enemies, and am not ashamed to say that I fear my life."

" I will protect you, then, sir," said Mr. Trevor, " until you have made out your return, and given your certificate. When these are done, I hope you will be safe."

The scene again subsided into its former dulness The enemy had disappeared, with the exception of the captive officer, who looked on ruefully, while an occasional vote was given at long intervals. At length, Mr. Trevor observed that some of the voters were about to withdraw. He therefore rose, and begged them to remain.

"This business is not over," said he. "It is not for nothing that the polls are to be kept open until sunset, when all who have not voted have withdrawn. An attack on the sheriff or myself is certainly intended. Perhaps on both. I beseech you, therefore, not to disperse, but to see us both safe to my house. When once among my own people, I will take care of him and myself. I am sorry, sir," continued he, addressing the officer, "that the movements of your friends make it necessary to detain you longer than I had intended. You must be a hostage for us all, until this day's work is over. But assure yourself of being treated with all courtesy and kindness. Should I even find it necessary to compel your company to my own house, doubt not that you will receive every attention due to an honored guest. I beg you to observe that I do not even disarm you. The warning you have received is my only security that you will attempt no violence."

This speech was heard in sullen silence by him to whom it was addressed. But some conversation with others ensued, in which Mr. Trevor took pains to enlighten the minds of his hearers in regard to public affairs. The day wore away somewhat less wearily; the sun went down, and Bernard Trevor was proclaimed to be duly elected.

Our party now took up the line of march. The sheriff and officer were placed in Mr. Trevor's barouche; the former by his side—the latter in front of him, by the side of the driver. A numerous company on horseback surrounded them.

They were scarcely in motion, before the drum was heard, and the regulars were seen advancing to meet them in military array. Mr. Trevor immediately commanded the driver to stop, and draw his pistol. Then calling to the servant on horseback, he made him station himself, pistol in hand, close to the officer. Having made this arrangement, he addressed him :

" You see your situation, sir. Those fellows would not scruple to shoot your master himself at my bidding; and my orders to you both, boys, are, that if we are attacked, you are both to shoot this gentleman upon the spot. I shall do the same thing, sir; so that between us you cannot escape. Now, sir, stand up and show yourself to your men, and speak distinctly the words of command that I shall dictate."

The officer did as he was directed. The advancing platoon was halted, and wheeled backward to the side of the road; the arms were ordered, and the barouche passed on. After passing, a momentary stop was made, while the sergeant was ordered to march the men back to their quarters. This was done, and as

soon as the two parties were at safe distance asunder,
Lieutenant Johnson was released, and courteously dismissed.   Mr. Trevor and his friends reached home in
safety, and without interruption, and thus ended the
election day.

CHAPTER XXI.

I tell you, my lord fool, that out of this nettle, Danger, we pluck this flower, Safety.

SHAKSPEARE.

THE domestic party that we left at the house of Mr. Trevor were variously affected by the history of the occurrences detailed in the last chapter. Arthur had been slightly indisposed, and his uncle had made that a pretext for keeping him out of harm's way. But when he heard what had passed, his spirit was roused, and he felt as a soldier who hears the history of some well-fought battle where he was not permitted to be present. To Virginia the whole story was a subject of wonderment and alarm. The idea that her dear uncle, and her dearer brother, had been engaged in an affair where "dirk and pistol" was the word, threw her into a flutter of trepidation. She could not refrain from asking the former whether he would have shot the poor man sure enough; and received his affirmative answer with a shudder. The feelings of Lucia did not much differ from hers, except in intensity. She had heard too much to be wholly unprepared for such things, and her mind

was too much accustomed to take its tone from those
of her mother and sister.

On these ladies the impression made by the events
of the day was wholly different. If the countenance
of Mrs. Trevor was more thoughtful than before, it
only spoke of higher thoughts. Her eye was brighter,
her carriage more erect, her step more free, while her
smile had less, perhaps, of quiet satisfaction, but
more of hope. The flutter of youthful feelings, and
the sweeter and more tender thoughts proper to one
newly betrothed, made the chief difference between
Delia and her mother. But while Douglas saw in
the latter all the evidence of those high qualities
which fit a woman to be not merely the consolation
and joy of her husband, but his sage adviser and
useful friend, he saw enough in Delia to show that
she, in due time, would be to him all that her mother
was to his uncle.

A few days afterwards, Mr. B—— arrived, and his
appearance was a signal of joy to the whole family.
Douglas now, for the first time, discovered that he
stood in some interesting, though undefined relation
to them, and especially to his aunt. That there was
no connexion of blood or marriage he knew, yet the
feelings of the parties towards each other were mu-
tually filial and paternal. The imposing dignity of
Mrs. Trevor's manner seemed to be surrendered in
his presence. Her maiden name of Margaret, which
no other lip but that of her husband would have ventured to profane, was that by which alone he ever

accosted her, and that generally accompanied with some endearing epithet. The girls would sit upon his knee, and play familiarly and affectionately with his grey locks; while the servants, in the proud humility of their attention to his wants and wishes, seemed hardly to distinguish between him and their beloved and honored master. It was not to be believed that the family kept any secrets from him, so that Douglas could not doubt that he was privy to his little affair of the heart. And so he was; and his manner toward the young man was, from the first, that of a near kinsman, hardly differing in any thing from that of his uncle. As far as coincidence of sentiment and similarity of character could explain this close intimacy, it stood explained. Between him and Mr. Trevor there were many points of strong similitude. But to Mrs. Trevor the resemblance was more striking. Age and sex seemed to make the only difference between them.

But, in addition to this domestic relation, which embraced every member of the household down to the scullion and shoe-black, there was obviously some understanding between the gentlemen in regard to matters of much higher concernment. Indeed, no pains were taken to conceal this fact, though, during Mr. B——'s former visit, Douglas had not been admitted to any of their consultations but that which concerned himself.

It was not long before the two were closeted, in the little study, in close conclave; and soon after, a message was delivered to Douglas requesting his presence.

"I am the bearer of important intelligence," said B——. holding out his hand to the youth as he entered; "and as it particularly concerns you, as well as your uncle, you must perforce consent to become privy to our council."

"I am not sorry to hear it," replied Douglas. "If any thing was wanting to banish all reserve between us, I would be content to suffer some loss to effect that object."

"I believe you," said B——, "and therefore expect you will the less regret an unpleasant circumstance, which, without your act or consent, and even in spite of you, binds you in the same bundle with us."

"That was already done," said Douglas. "What new tie can there be?"

"One of the strongest. The union of your name with your uncle's in a warrant for high treason from the court of high commission at Washington."

"You speak riddles," said Douglas. "The only instance in which I ever incurred the displeasure of the President, was one which no human ingenuity could torture into treason; and certainly my uncle had no hand in that."

"But, having *then* incurred the displeasure of the Government, what if you should *since* have been concerned in any matter which might be called treason?"

"But there has been no such matter."

"My dear boy," said Mr. Trevor, "the question is not of what we *have* done. Had we actually done any thing culpable, there would be no occasion for this warrant from Washington. Our own courts, and a jury of peers, may be trusted to try the guilty. But when men are to be tried for what they have not done, then resort must be had to this new court of high commission at Washington, and to a jury of office-holders."

"But where," asked Douglas, "is the warrant of which you speak?"

"That I cannot exactly say," said B——. "I am not even sure that it is yet in existence. But that it is, or will be, is certain. I need not explain to you my means of knowledge. Your uncle is acquainted with them, and knows that what I tell you is certain. The transactions of the election day will be made the subject of a capital charge, and it is intended to convey you both to Washington to answer it there. I am come to advise you both of this, that you may determine what course to pursue."

"My course is plain," said Douglas. "To meet the charge, and refute it."

"Are you aware," said B——, "who is the Judge of this court of high commission?"

"I think I have somehow understood that it is Judge Baker."

"The father of your friend, Philip Baker, the younger. Now are you aware that, but a few days before the court was constituted, he and other judges

were consulted, and declared it to be so grossly unconstitutional that no judge would preside in it?"

"I see that so it should be declared, but did not
know that such opinion had been given."

"Yet so it was. Now where, do you think, the
considerations were found by which the honorable
gentleman's honorable scruples were overcome? Of
course, you cannot conjecture. You *would* find it,
all too late, if you, by placing yourself in his power,
afforded him an opportunity of gratifying the malice
of his son, without exposing his cowardice and
meanness. I see you doubt my means of knowledge.
Your uncle told me nothing of young Whiting's
communication to the President. Yet I knew of it.
I know," continued B——, not regarding the amazement of Douglas, "that, but for that letter, you
would not have been permitted to resign; and that
Judge Baker's scruples about presiding in this new
court were overcome by hushing up the inquiry,
which would have dishonored his son, and substitut-
ing a proceeding which should number you among
the victims of his power, without implicating the
name of his son. As to my means of knowledge,
when knaves can get honest men to be the instruments of their villany, they may expect not to be
betrayed. Until then, they must bear the fate of all
who work with sharp tools."

"There can be no doubt," said Mr. Trevor, "of
the fate prepared for us, should we fall into the hands
of our enemies. To be summoned to trial before a

court constituted for the sole purpose of entertaining prosecutions which cannot be sustained elsewhere, is to be notified of a sentence already passed. To obey such a summons, is to give the neck to the halter. The question is, then, what is to be done to evade it. Our friend B—— proposes that your brother and sister be sent home, and that you and I, and my family, withdraw to Carolina. How say you?"

"I have the same difficulty that I had, the other day, about tendering my resignation. But, in this instance, it appears with more force. To fly from justice is always taken as evidence of conscious guilt."

"About that," said Mr. Trevor, "I feel small concern on my own account, as I certainly *mean* to commit what all who deny the sovereignty of Virginia will call high treason."

"Then why not take up arms at once? I have much misunderstood appearances, since I have been here, if the means, not of evading, but resisting this attack, are not already organized."

"The time is not yet ripe for action," said Mr. Trevor. "Had it been so, I should not have waited until my own head was in jeopardy, before striking the blow. Nor should my own personal danger precipitate it."

"But what fitter time can there be to call the people to arms, than at this moment, when their minds are heated by the late violent invasion of the elective franchise? What more exciting spectacle could be presented than the sight of a citizen seized as a traitor, and dragged away in chains, to answer, before an unconstitutional tribunal, for maintaining this franchise?"

"Are *you* then prepared to resist, at the point of the bayonet, this unconstitutional warrant, as a thing void and of no authority?"

"I *am*," replied Douglas, with energy. "And I will say more," said he, speaking with solemn earnestness. "I have seen enough to make my duty plain; and I am prepared to go as far as you, yourself, in asserting and maintaining the sovereignty of Virginia at every hazard."

"That being the case," said B——, "as you will not disagree about the end, you must not differ about the means, nor lose time discussing them. *We* are not thinking of this subject for the first time. We see the whole ground, and act under the influence of considerations which we have no time to detail. Are you then, my young friend, prepared to give us so much of your confidence as this? We say to you, 'Go with us where we go, and trust our assurance that when we have leisure to explain all, you will find our plan the best.' Are you content? Are you now ready to carry into execution our matured plan, so far as it has been disclosed to you, trusting all the details to us? Remember—if you say yes to this, we stop no more to deliberate or explain until we are in a place of safety. Until then, you place yourself under orders; and you have learned how to obey. How say you? Are you content?"

Douglas paused, reflected a minute or two, and then, extending a hand to Mr. B——, and one to his uncle, said earnestly : " I am ; command, and I will obey. But which of you am I to obey ?"

" Mr. B——," said Mr. Trevor, " under whose command I now place myself."

" Then to business," said B——. " Warn your brother, at once, of the necessity of returning home with your sister, and see that he makes the needful preparations for his departure at an early hour to-morrow. The boy's heart will have some hankerings that will make it necessary for you to look after him, and urge him to exertion. You, Trevor, must expedite the arrangements for the removal of your family. Pass the word to Margaret and Delia. You may trust much to their efficiency. I am afraid we cannot expect much more from my poor little Lucia, just now, than from Arthur. Now, Trevor, give me the keys of your arm-room ; let Douglas join me there, as soon as he has set Arthur to work, and, in the meantime, send Jack to me there. I will play quartermaster, while you make arrangements for the muster of the black watch."

" The *black watch !*" said Douglas, with an inquiring look.

" Aye," said B——. " The *sidier dhu*—the trusty body-guard of a Virginia gentleman. His own faithful slaves."

" The slaves !" said Douglas. " What use shall we have for them ?"

"I have no time to answer now," said B——. "Ask me that when you come to me in the arm-room.   At present you must attend to Arthur.   We have no time to lose."

Douglas now remembered his enlistment, and betook himself, with the prompt alacrity of an old soldier, to the fulfilment of his orders.

END OF VOL. I.

THE

PARTISAN LEADER;

A TALE OF THE FUTURE.

BY

EDWARD WILLIAM SIDNEY.

"SIC SEMPER TYRANNIS."
The Motto of Virginia.
"PARS FUI." . . . . . Virgil.

IN TWO VOLUMES.

VOL. II.

PRINTED

FOR THE PUBLISHERS, BY JAMES CAXTON.

1856.

THE

PARTISAN LEADER.

CHAPTER XXII.

"I have nursed him at this withered breast," said the old woman, folding her hands on her bosom as if pressing an infant to it; "and man can never ken what woman feels for the bairn that she has first held to her bosom."   SCOTT.

POOR ARTHUR! B—— had predicted too truly that his heart would have some hankerings at the thought of leaving the house where he had, of late, spent so many pleasant hours. It is so long that I have said nothing about him, that the reader may think him forgotten, or may, himself, have forgotten that there was such a person. He had, in truth, no part in the transactions of which we have been speaking. He was at that time of life when the mind, chameleon-like, takes its hue from surrounding objects. He was too young to be advised with, or trusted with important secrets. I have already mentioned that, on the day of the election, he had been detained at home by indisposition. But he had heard of the oc-

currences of that day ; and he was, moreover, unconsciously exposed to influences from every member of
the family, all tending to the same point. Least apparent, but not least efficacious, was that of his cousin
Lucia. They were of that age when hearts, soft and
warm, grow together by mere contact. With thought
of love, but without thinking of it, they had become
deeply enamored of each other. The thing came
about so simply and so naturally, that the result alone
needs to be told.

They were now to part, and the thought of parting
first made them both feel that something was the
matter. They talked of the separation, and Lucia
shed some tears. Arthur kissed them off, and then
she smiled ; and then she wept again ; and then they
agreed never to forget each other ; and so on, till the
secret was out, and their innocent hearts were fondly
plighted.

Such things do not pass unmarked by older eyes.
The maternal instinct of Mrs. Trevor, and the sagacity
of her husband, had detected that of which the parties themselves were unconscious. And now, in the
few hours that they were to remain together, occupied
as the old people were with important engagements,
neither the glowing cheek, the swimming eye, and
the abstracted look of Lucia, nor the rapt enthusiasm of Arthur's countenance, escaped observation.
But as no disclosure was made of what had passed,
their fancied privacy was not invaded by question or
insinuation. They were too young to marry, and secret

love is so sweet! Why not let the innocent creatures enjoy the idea that their attachment was not
suspected? Their friends smiled indeed, but ten-
derly, not significantly. To them, they did but
seem kinder than ever; and that, at a moment when
they were most sensible to kindness, and most ready
to reciprocate it. In this heart-searching sympathy,
Arthur found himself indissolubly united to the
destiny, the opinions, and the feelings, whatever
these might be, of those who so loved his dear
Lucia.

But I am not writing a love-tale. I am but interested that the reader should understand by what
process two principal actors in the *scenes of which
I am about to speak, were diverted from a zealous
devotion to the authority of the United States, in
which they had been educated, to a devotion yet
more enthusiastic in the cause of Virginia.* Enough
of them has been seen to show that I must be
anxious to vindicate them from any charge of incon-
sistency. I trust the reader enters into this feeling,
and deems them worthy of it. If he requires any
farther account of the causes which wrought so great
a change, I have none to give. It was through their
eyes and hearts that conviction entered. Outrage
to the laws; outrage to the freedom of election;
outrage to one respected and beloved; left nothing
for reason to do. Doubtless much had been said to
them by their uncle and Mr. B——, in explanation
of the great principles of the American Union,

which had been trampled on by the Federal Government. But I am not aware that any ideas were presented to their minds on this subject, with which the reading public had not been familiar for twenty years before, and I shall not repeat them here. Let us rather accompany Douglas to Mr. Trevor's magazine of arms. It was in a garret room, where he found Mr. B—— busy in the examination of arms, and portioning out ammunition, with the aid of Jack.

"You come in good time," said B——. "Here is work that you understand. Come help me examine these arms, and see that they are all clean, dry, and well flinted."

"What do you propose to do with them?" asked Douglas, lending a hand to the work.

"We propose," said B——, "to arm the negroes in defence of their master, in case of need."

"But what need can there be, if we set out for Carolina in the morning?"

"They may be wanted before morning," said B——, coolly. "Lieutenant Johnson left the county on the night of the election, and travelled express to Washington. His intelligence was anticipated, and, no doubt, the warrants were all ready before he got there. I daresay they had a ready-made affidavit for him to swear to. This plot was got up so suddenly, that I was hardly advised of it in time. But I hope it is not too late. I have no mind to fire the train too soon. I would rather you should get off peaceably, but, if we do come to blows, I shall take care that the blue-coats have the worst of it."

"You move in this business," said Douglas, "like a man not unused to danger. I presume you have taken the precaution to warn in the hardy and reso- lute neighbors, whom I saw stand by my uncle the other day."

"By no means," answered B. "Were we so minded, we could command a force that would de- molish any that will be sent against us. But it is not desirable to show the strength of our hand. I should be glad, if possible, that the temper of the people were unsuspected. At the same time, there is an exhibition to be made, which will have a good effect on friend and foe—I mean an exhibition of the staunch loyalty and heart-felt devotion of the slave to his master. We must show that that which our enemies, and some even of ourselves, consider as our weakness, is, in truth, our strength."

"Is such your own clear opinion?" asked Doug- las. "I have lived so long in the North, that I have imbibed too many of the ideas that prevail there. But, on this point, it appears to me that they must be right."

"You have not lived there long enough," said B——, "to forget your earliest and strongest attach- ments. You had a black nurse, I presume. Do you love her?"

"My mammy!" exclaimed Douglas; "to be sure I do. I should be the most ungrateful creature on earth, if I did not love one who loves me like a mother."

"And your foster-brother?" asked B——; "and his brothers and sisters? Do not they, too, love him their mother loves so fondly?"

"I have no doubt they do, especially as I have always been kind to them."

"From these, then, I presume, you would fear nothing. Then your brothers and sisters. They, too, have their mammies and foster-brethren. Among you, you must have a strong hold on the hearts of many of your father's slaves. Would they, think you, taken as a body, rise against your family?"

"I have not the least apprehension that they would," replied Douglas.

"Yet they, thus considered, are one integral part of the great black family, which, in all its branches, is united by similar ligaments to the great white family. You have the benefit of the parental feeling of the old who nursed your infancy, and watched your growth. You have the equal friendship of those with whom you ran races, and played at bandy, and wrestled in your boyhood. If sometimes a dry blow passed between you, they love you none the less for that; because, unless you were differently trained from what is common among our boys, you were taught not to claim any privilege, in a fight, over those whom you treated as equals in play. Then you have the grateful and admiring affection of the little urchin whose head you patted when you came home, making him proud by asking his name, and his mammy's name, and his daddy's name. These are the filaments which the heart puts out to lay hold on what it clings to. Great interests, like large branches, are too stiff to twine. These are the fibres from which the ties that bind man to man are spun. The finer the staple, the stronger the cord. You will probably see its strength exemplified before morning. There are twenty true hearts which will shed their last drop, before one hair of your uncle's head shall fall."

" You present the matter in a new light," said Douglas. " I wish our northern brethren could be made to take the same view of it."

" Our northern *brethren*, as you call them," said B—, " never can take this view of it. They have not the qualities which would enable them to comprehend the negro character. Their calculating selfishness can never understand his disinterested devotion. Their artificial benevolence is no interpreter of the affections of the unsophisticated heart. They think our friend Jack here to be even such as themselves, and cannot therefore conceive that he is not ready to cut his master's throat, if there is anything to be got by it. They know no more of the feelings of our slaves, than their fathers could comprehend of the loyalty of the gallant cavaliers from whom we spring; and for the same reason. The generous and self-renouncing must ever be a riddle to the selfish. The only instance in which they have ever seemed to understand us, has been in the estimate they have made of our attachment to a Union, the benefits of which have all been theirs, the burthens ours. Reverse the case, and they would have dissolved the partnership thirty years ago. But they have presumed upon the difference between us, and heaped oppression on oppression, until we can bear no more. But, when we throw off the yoke, they will still not understand us. They will impute to us none but selfish motives, and take no note of the scorn and loathing which their base abuse of our better feelings has awakened. Would they but forbear so much as not to force us to hate and despise them, they might still use us as their hewers of wood and drawers of water. But he who gives all where he loves, will give nothing where he detests. But this, too, is a riddle for them."

"I must own," said Douglas, "that these ideas are new to me, too."

"Not the ideas, but the application of them. Three months ago, you were the devoted soldier of Martin Van Buren. Had you then believed him capable of a conspiracy so base as that which has been plotted against your honor and life, could you still have served him?"

"I should still have wished to serve my country," replied Douglas; "but I should, probably, have doubted whether I could have served her in serving him."

" And do you think you would view the matter differently, had another been the intended victim, and not yourself? "

" I trust not. My personal concern in the affair, I think, has done no more than to emancipate me from my thraldom. But the display of his character is what makes me detest him; and the scenes of the election day have opened my eyes to the wrongs, and the rights, and the interests of Virginia. The scales have now fallen from them, and I am impatient for the day when I may apply in her service the lessons learned in the school of her oppressors."

" You shall have your wish," said B——. " The flint you are now fitting may yet be snapped against the myrmidons of the usurper."

CHAPTER XXIII.

Osric . . . How is it, Laertes?
Laertes . . Why, as a woodcock to my own springe, Osric.
SHAKSPEARE.

WHILE this conversation was going on, the arms had been all examined, loaded, and ranged against the wall, and due portions of powder and ball allotted to each firelock. Their work being nearly completed, Douglas was dispatched with some message to his uncle. As he descended the stairs, he heard, not without a smile, the quick, impatient step of Arthur, pacing to and fro the length of a passage leading from the front door through the building. Arthur was just turning at the end next to the door, when a rap on the knocker arrested him. The door was instantly opened, and he was heard to ask some one to walk in. It was night, and the passage was dark. Arthur conducted the stranger to the door of his uncle's study, which was the common reception room, ushered him in, drew back, and having closed the door behind him, resumed his musing promenade.

Douglas went on, suspecting nothing. He was not aware that the servants had been cautioned against admitting strangers; and poor Arthur was not *au fait* to what was passing. He entered the room. His uncle had risen from his chair in the corner farthest from the door, and was standing behind a large table, at which he usually wrote. He heard him say: "Please to be seated, sir," in a voice between compliment and command, and with a countenance in which courtesy and fierceness were strangely blended. As the stranger, not regarding this stern invitation, continued to advance, the glare of the old man's eyes became fearful, and he laid his hand on a pistol which lay on the table before him. "Stand back, sir," said he, in a low and resolute tone. "Stand back, on your life."

The stranger wore a long surtout, in which Douglas, dazzled by coming into the light, did not at first discover the usual characteristics of an officer's undress. It was thrown open in front, and the badges of his rank were displayed to Mr. Trevor, who stood before him. He was arrested by Mr. Trevor's startling words and gesture, and was beginning to speak when Douglas exclaimed: "What does this mean?"

The stranger turned, extended both his arms, and Douglas rushed into them.

"My dear Trevor!" "My dear Whiting!" were the mutual exclamations of two young men, who had long been to each other as brothers.

"To what on earth," asked Douglas, "do I owe this pleasure?"

"I come," said the other, with a melancholy smile,

and in the kindest tone, while he still held the hand of Douglas, " to make you prisoner."

Douglas started violently, and tried to disengage his hand; but the other held him firmly and went on : " Be calm, my dear fellow. I am your friend as ever, but yet I do not jest. You are my prisoner, on the absurd charge of high treason against the United States. My warrant is against you and your uncle. As it was thought a military force might be wanted to support the arrest, I volunteered myself to receive a deputation from the marshal that I might shield you both from any indignity. You, on your part, I am sure, will do nothing to make my task more painful than it is. Is not that gentleman——bless me! where is he? Was not that Mr. Bernard Trevor who just left the room ? "

"I *am* Mr. Bernard Trevor," said a voice behind. Whiting turned again, and saw Mr. Trevor•standing where he had been before. He now observed that there was a door beside him, at which he had stepped out and returned. " I am Mr. Bernard Trevor, sir, and am sorry that I cannot welcome, as I would, the friend of my nephew. You see that I have no mind to leave the room, and I therefore hope you will content yourself to accept my invitation to be seated. You say that you wish to shield me from indignity. Of course you will not unnecessarily offer what I shall feel as such. The *hand* of authority must not be laid on *me*."

" I shall gladly dispense with an unpleasant form,

sir," said Whiting, "and I trust I shall have the satisfaction of convincing you that my errand, though painful to all of us, is an errand of friendship."

"I have no doubt of it, sir. I have heard of you from my nephew, and from under your own hand, in terms that give full assurance of that. I shall be happy, therefore, to do by you all the duties of hospitality. I merely ask of you to give your word of honor, that, while charged with your present functions, you will be careful not to touch my person."

"I should be most happy," said the young man, "to take by the hand one whom I so highly respect, but I find I must forego that pleasure; and I give the required pledge most cheerfully."

The courteous old gentleman now summoned Tom, and ordered some refreshment for his guest; then throwing into his manner all the frank courtesy of a polished Virginian, he led the way in a desultory conversation on all sorts of indifferent subjects. Half an hour passed in this way, when Tom appeared and summoned the gentlemen to supper.

"I fear," said Whiting, "I am abusing my authority over my poor fellows without. I have a sergeant and half-a-dozen men waiting at the gate, on whose behalf I would fain invoke your hospitality. But it would be much more agreeable to me, if you and my friend Douglas will pass your words that their aid shall not be necessary, and permit me to order them back to the next public-house."

"I am sorry to say," replied Mr. Trevor, "that

I cannot do either; but I pray you to postpone the discussion until after supper."

"How, sir?" exclaimed Whiting. "You surely do not mean to try to escape me?"

"Nothing is farther from my thoughts, sir," said the old man, with a proud smile, "than to try to *escape* you, or permit you to escape me."

"*To escape you*, sir! What do you mean?" asked Whiting.

"I mean not to wound your ear with a word I would not have endured to have applied to myself. I will not say that you are *my* prisoner; but I will say that *we* will leave this house as free as you entered it. Come, my dear sir, while I endeavor to requite your courtesy, permit me also to appropriate your words, and say, as you said to Douglas, that I trust you will not render it necessary to avail ourselves of our superior force."

"I am not sure you possess that superiority," said Whiting; "I have a strong guard without."

"But they *are* without, and you are within. Besides, you will be readily excused from availing yourself of them, when it is known that they are prisoners, in close custody."

"Prisoners!" exclaimed Whiting. "To whom?"

"To my negroes," said Mr. Trevor.

"Regular soldiers prisoners to negroes!" said Whiting, in amazement. "It is not credible; and you manifestly speak by conjecture, as you have had no means of communicating with your friends without."

"I am not in the habit, young gentleman," said
Mr. Trevor, in a tone of grave rebuke, "of speaking positively, when I speak by conjecture. My
orders were, that I should not be called to supper
until they were secured. As to the strangeness of
the affair," continued he, resuming his cheerful and
good-humored smile, "think nothing of that. Remember that night is what the negroes call 'their
time of day.' The eagle is no match for the owl in the
dark. The thing is as I tell you; so make yourself
easy, and let me have the pleasure of doing the
duties of hospitality by my nephew's friend. You
shall not be unnecessarily detained. We must ask
the pleasure of your company for a three hours' ride
across the line in the morning. I will there give
you a clear acquittance against all the responsibility
you may have incurred, for what you have done, or
left undone; and, as soon as you return, to restrain
your men from acts of license, they shall be given
up to you."

There was no remonstrating against this arrangement; and Lieutenant Whiting, putting the best
face he could on the matter, permitted himself to be
conducted to supper.

At the head of the supper table stood, as usual,
Mrs. Trevor. She seemed some six inches higher
than common, her cheek flushed, her nostril spread,
her eye beaming; yet with all her high feelings subdued to the duties of hospitality and courtesy. She
met and returned the salutation of Whiting with the

stately grace of a high-bred-lady, and then her eye glanced to her husband with a look of irrepressible pride. His glance answered it, and, as they stood for a moment facing each other at the opposite ends of the table, Whiting felt a sense of admiring awe, such as the presence of majesty in full court had never inspired. But this feeling, in a moment, passed away, with its cause. The urbanity of the gentleman and the suavity of the lady soon removed all the painfulness of constraint, and the evening passed as it should pass between persons who in heart were friends.

Neither Mr. B—— nor Arthur made their appearance. The girls, indeed, were present. The air and manner of Delia reflected those of her mother. Virginia looked a little alarmed, and Lucia blushing, tender, and abstracted. The interest of the realities that surrounded her could not quite dispel the visions of excited fancy.

With these exceptions, which a stranger would not observe, everything passed as in the company of an invited and cherished guest, and Whiting could not be sorry, at heart, that he had been baffled in his attempt to disturb so sweet a domestic party. The evening wore away not unpleasantly, and he retired to rest in the same room with Douglas, to guard him, or be guarded by him, according as it suited his fancy to consider himself or his friend as the other's prisoner.

A word of explanation is due on the subject of the captive guard, which will be given in the next chapter.

CHAPTER XXIV.

Massa mighty cunning—watch he nigger like a hawk;
But nigger like a owl—he watch massa in e dark.

JIM CROW.

THE first words which passed between Mr. Trevor and Lieutenant Whiting, had been overheard by Tom, who was in the act of leaving the room at the moment. He gave the alarm to his mistress, who hastening to her husband, met him at the door, and just received from him the instructions already mentioned. She immediately sent for Mr. B——, who, with Jack's aid, was in the act of distributing arms and ammunition to the negroes. To him the management of the whole affair was committed. No doubt was entertained that Lieutenant Whiting had not come unattended. The first thing to be done was to ascertain the force by which he was supported, and the place where he had posted his men.

They, meantime, quietly awaited the return of their officer at the great gate, a quarter of a mile from the house. Rather as a point of military etiquette than from an idea that any precaution was necessary, they had stacked their arms in form before the gate, and stationed a sentinel, who, with head erect and military step, walked his post in front of them. They had not long been there, before they heard a negro's voice, who, as he approached from the house, sung merrily a song, of which only the following lines could be distinguished:

> "Peep froo de winder; see break o' day;
> Run down to riber; canoe gone away.
> Put foot in water; water mighty cold;
> Hear O'sur call me; hear Missis scold.
> O dear! my dear! what shall I do?
> My Massa whip me, cause I love you."

The song ceased, and cuffee advanced in silence, but with a heavy swinging step, that rung audibly on the hard ground. As soon as his dusky figure began to be distinguishable, which was not until he was quite near, he was arrested by the sharp challenge of the sentry.

"High!" exclaimed the negro, in a tone of amazement and alarm: "Law-Gorramighty! what dis?"

"Advance!" said the sentinel, mechanically, "and give the countersign."

"What dat, Massa? I never see such a ting in my life."

"Advance!" repeated the sentry, bringing his piece down with a rattling sound against his right side.

The metal glimmered in the light from the windows, The negro caught the gleam, and, falling flat on his face, roared lustily for mercy.

The Sergeant now went to him, raised him up, calmed his fears, and, as soon as he could be made to understand anything, asked if Lieutenant Whiting was at the house.

"I hear 'em say, sir, one mighty grand gentleman went there while ago. Old Tom say, he Mass Douglas' old crony, and Massa and Mass Douglas, and all, mighty glad to see him."

"The devil they are!" said the Sergeant. "Well, I hope they'll be mighty glad to see us, too. I do not care how soon, for this night air is something of the sharpest; and I have drawn better rations than we had at that damned tavern. I say, darkee; the old man keeps good liquor, and plenty of belly-timber, don't he?"

"Ah, Lord! Yes, Massa, I reckon he does. But it an't much I knows about it. Old Massa mighty hard man, sir. Poor negur don't see much o' he good ting."

"But, I suppose, he gives his friends a plenty?"

"Oh, to be sure, sir! Massa mighty proud. Great gentleman come see him, he an't got nothing too good for *him*. But poor white folks and poor negur! —pshaw!"

"A bad look-out for us, Rogers," said the Sergeant to one of his men. "Damn the old hunks, I hope he don't mean to leave us to bivouack here all night. Well, we must wait our hour, as the Lieutenant told us, and then he'll come back to us, or we have to march to the house. Damn it! I shall be pretty sharp-set by that time, and if it comes to that the old gentleman's kitchen and wine-cellar may look out for a storm."

"You talk like you hungry, Massa," said the negro, in a tone of sympathy. "I mighty sorry I an't got nothing to give you."

"But could not you *get* something, cuffee? Is there no key to your master's cellar and smoke-house besides the one he keeps? Don't you think, now, you could get us some of his old apple-brandy? I hear he has it of all ages."

"Ah, Lord, Massa; dat you may be sure of. I hear old Tom say brandy dare older an he; and he most a hundred. 'Spose I bring you some o' dat, Massa, what you gwine give me?"

"Will a quarter do for a bottle of it?"

"Law, Massa! Why he same like gold. *Half* a dolla, Massa!"

"Well, bring us a bottle of the *right old* stuff, mind!—and you shall have half a dollar. And see, darkee; cannot you bring us a little cold bread and meat?"

"I don't know, Massa, what de cook say. I try her."

"Well, go; and, while your hand is in, help your-self well. If the liquor is good, maybe we'll take two or three bottles."

"Well, Massa, I try old Tom. He keep de key. Ah, Lord! Old Massa tink Tom mighty desperate honest; and he tink Tom love him so—better an he own self. He better mind; one o' dese days Tom show him how dat is."

"I don't think you love him much yourself, Sambo."

Who?—I, Massa? My name Jack, sir. Lord, no sir! What I love him for? Hard work and little bread, and no meat? No, Massa, I love soldier; cause I hear 'em say soldier come after a while, set poor nigur free."

"That is true enough. I hope it will not be long before we set you all free from these damned man-stealers. How would you like to go with us?"

"Lord, Massa, you joking. Go wid you? I reckon the old man find it right hard to get somebody to saddle his horse if all our folks was here."

"Well, cuffee, the old man's in hockley by this time; and when we march him off in the morning, you will have nobody to stop you. But bring us the brandy, and then we'll talk about it."

"Ees, Massa! tank ye, Massa! But, Massa, I got two boys big as me, and my brother, and my wife, and all; I don't want to leave them. And, Massa, my boys got some apples. You want some, sir?"

"To be sure I do. Bring them along; but mind and bring the brandy, at all events."

The negro disappeared, and the soldiers occupied themselves in discussing the means of making a profitable speculation on their disposition to leave their master. They were still on this topic when they heard Jack returning, with several more. One brought a chunk of fire; another a basket of apples; another one of eggs; a fourth came provided with some cold provisions; Jack himself brandished a couple of bottles of brandy; and one of his boys brought a pail of water and a tin cup. The liquor was tasted, approved, paid for, and eagerly swallowed. A torch of light wood being kindled, a chaffering commenced, interrupted by occasional allusions to the interesting subjects of slavery, hard masters, and emancipation. The brandy, however, chiefly engaged the attention of the soldiers. The sentry, whose duty was but formal, was permitted to join, as the guns were but a few feet off, just without the gate, which stood open. The light of the torch glittered strongly on the arms, and seemed to make all things distinct, while in fact its unsteady flickering did little more than dazzle their eyes. The negro held it aloft, and, as if to brighten the flame, occasionally waved it to and fro. Suddenly it dropped from his hand into the pail of water, and in an instant the blackness of impenetrable darkness shrouded every eye.

At the same moment, a heavy trampling, as from a rush of many feet, was heard without the gate, and a shivering clash from the stack of arms, as if it had fallen down. The soldiers groped their way towards it, feeling where they supposed it to be. They felt in vain. They winked hard, as if to free their eyes from the blinding impression left by the flaring light, then opened them, and looked about. Judge their astonishment, when, as they began to recover their sight, they found themselves surrounded by a dusky ring, from which issued a voice, not unlike that of their friend Jack, which informed them, in good English, that they were prisoners. The prick of a bayonet on one or two who endeavored to pass through the circle, convinced them that such was the fact; and, after a short parley, they permitted themselves to be marched off, and safely stowed away in a strong outhouse.

I would not have the reader give the negroes the credit of this stratagem. It had been devised by B——, who knew that he could depend upon the address and quick wit of Jack for drawing the soldiers into the snare. All that part of the business had been left to his own discretion. As soon as he had secured the amicable reception of himself and a few others, the rest, dividing into two parties, left the house, and, crossing the fence at some distance from the gate, and on each side of it, advanced stealthily toward it. Here they met, and having arranged themselves for a sudden rush on the stack of arms, an agreed signal was given by a negro who possessed a faculty of mimicking the voices of all animals. As soon as the light was extinguished, the necessary number rushed forward to the object on which their eyes had been fixed; seized the arms, and, falling back, ranged themselves in a half circle outside of the gate. Those who had been with the soldiers, and who all wore concealed arms, closed in behind them, and completely hemmed them in.

B——, in the mean time, who had his reasons for not wishing to be seen, kept aloof; and, as soon as he knew that the soldiers were secured, returned to the house. There, too, he took care not to show himself; and Arthur was advised that he should not, by making his appearance, at all involve himself in what had been done.

CHAPTER XXV.

And even there, his eye being big with tears,
Turning his face, he put his hand behind him,
And, with affection wondrous sensible,
He wrung Bassanio's hand, and so they parted.
                                    SHAKSPEARE.

AT daylight, all was in motion. Arthur and Virginia, being affectionately dismissed by their friends, were first upon the road, before Lieutenant Whiting was awake. Much of the night had been spent in preparations, and long before sunrise Douglas handed his aunt and cousins into their carriage. His uncle mounted the barouche, with Jack for driver, by whose side old Tom was placed; while the lady's maid took her seat by her single-minded master, with a freedom from which an amalgamationist would have drawn the most pleasing inferences. No other white person was seen; but a body-guard of twenty negroes, well armed, and mounted on plough horses, some saddled, some cushioned, and some barebacked, surrounded the carriages and baggage-wagon. In the midst rode Douglas and his friend on horseback.

"You see," said Mr. Trevor to Whiting, as he took his place in the barouche, "that the part these faithful creatures took in last night's work, drives them into exile as well as me. I must not leave them behind to be the victims of baffled malice. What is to become of my plantation, is a question of less importance. I suppose I may say with Cincinnatus, when honor was forced on him as it is on me, my fields must go untilled this year! You see here, sir, my whole male force. Not one proved recreant."

"This affair is altogether unaccountable to me," said Whiting to Douglas, as they moved off together; "and this the strangest feature of the whole. Do men, then, act without motives; and against all assignable motives?"

"I asked the same question myself last night," said Douglas, "and was referred to coming events for the answer. I was partly taught, at the same time, to account for what I was told to expect."

"And how can it be accounted for?"

"I cannot say I have my lesson perfect; but something was said about the difference of character produced by peculiar training, and habitudes of mind formed by circumstances. For my part, it appears to me that there must be something, by nature, in the moral constitution of the negro, intrinsically different from the white man."

"It would, indeed, seem so," said Whiting, "if we are to credit what we see. But, in that case, we must reject the authority which tells us that all are of one race."

"So are all dogs," said Douglas; "and dogs can no more act without motive than man. It depends on temper and character what shall be motives of action. The wolf would be sadly puzzled to judge of the motives of the Newfoundland dog. May not circumstances, which have made the difference between them, have produced the much less difference between the white man and the negro? I have no measure for the effect of such causes. If am put to choose between rejecting the evidence of my own senses, or the evidence of God's word, or the philosophy which teaches that man is to be considered as a unit, because all of one race, philosophy must go by the board. It may be that what is best for me is best for my friend Jack there, and *vice versa;* but as long as neither of us thinks so, why not leave each to his choice? Besides, there is more room in the world for both of us, than if both always wanted the same things."

A ride of a few hours carried the party across the line into North Carolina. Here they stopped at the first public-house; and Mr. Trevor drew up a hasty statement of the events of the night, which *should* have the effect of acquitting Lieutenant Whiting of all blame, on account of his own escape from the fangs of his enemies. In this he set forth that, having been warned of the intended prosecution, he had made his preparations accordingly, and that the officer had but fallen into a snare from which no vigilance could have saved him. This he signed, and gave, moreover, a clear acquittance to Lieutenant Whiting for all he had done; and having thus placed him, as far as depended on himself, *rectus in curia*, he announced to him that he was now at liberty to go whither he would.

"And now, sir," said he, "as the spell which would have made your touch degrading is broken by the State line, let me have the pleasure of taking you by the hand, not only as my nephew's friend, but as one who, in the extremes of victory and defeat, as captor and as prisoner, has borne himself as became a gentleman."

Saying this, he extended his hand, which Whiting grasped with fervor, and they parted as friends cordial and sincere.

Douglas accompanied his friend a short distance on his return, the latter walking, and leading his horse. They conversed of the past and the future.

"I have been a volunteer in this business," said Whiting. "I shall not disguise that my friendship for you led me to offer my services, and I fear that no excuse will be received for my failure. There is a spirit somewhere at work, to which I will give no name, that will be implacable at the thought that any advantage may have been lost by my respect for your feelings."

"I am afraid it may prove so," replied Douglas. "The consequence may be fatal to your advancement in the army, and perhaps you may be driven from it, as I have been. Should it be so, my dear Whiting

——but I will not profit so little by the example of delicacy set me while I wore the epaulette, as to say any thing to you now. I would content myself with telling you where I shall be found, if I myself knew. But shall I keep you advised of my movements?"

"By all means," said Whiting. "I shall always wish to know your fate, whether good or ill."

"I know that," replied Douglas. "But that is not my meaning. Shall I let you know where to find me, in case circumstances should lead you to share my fate?"

"Don't ask me that, Trevor. The question implies ideas which I must not entertain. But should such a time as you suppose ever arrive, I shall know where to find you, should my opinions make it right to seek you."

"Then, God bless you, Whiting! That we shall meet again is sure. That we shall stand shoulder to shoulder in the strife of battle, as, in our day dreams, we have so often thought of doing, I cannot doubt."

And thus parted these gallant and generous youths; the one into exile from the country that he loved, the other to return to the service of an unthankful master.

A farther ride of a few miles brought our party to the village, in which Mr. Trevor wished to take up his temporary residence. Here he found Mr. B——, who had been engaged in investigating the comforts and capabilities of the different public-houses, and having fixed on that he liked best, met Mr. Trevor in the street, and conducted the party to it. The two friends soon drew apart to discuss with the landlord the necessary arrangements for the comfort of the family during their proposed stay.

While they were thus engaged, Douglas seated himself, after the manner of the country, in the bar-room, in which, besides some travellers, there was a motley assemblage of the inhabitants of the village, who had come in to stare at and talk about the new comers. By the time Douglas had taken care of the ladies and baggage, they were deep into the merits of the whole party ; and, when he entered the room, they were too busy talking to pay any attention to him. The principal interlocutors were three. First, a well-dressed, middle-aged man, whose dapper air and delicate hands bespoke one accustomed to bowing across a counter over lace patterns and painted muslins ; and whose style of eloquence was exactly adapted to the praise of such articles. Then there was a coarse, strong man, with a bacon-fed look, plainly, cheaply, and untastefully dressed, in clothes which, by their substantial goodness, indicated at once the wearer's prudence, and the length of his purse. His voice was loud, strong, and self-important, entirely devoid of melody, and incapable of inflection or modulation. His whole appearance showed him to be a substantial planter, ignorant of every thing but corn and tobacco. A huge whip in the hand of the third, together with his dusty and travel-soiled appearance, denoted the driver of a wagon which stood before the door.

Their conversation I reserve for the next chapter.

CHAPTER XXVI.

If she be not kind to me,
What care I how kind she be ?   SUCKLING.

"I CANNOT say I like it altogether, Squire," said
the planter. "It may suit my neighbor Jones, here,
well enough to have one of them high-headed Roanoke planters to come here with his family, and spend
his money. I dare say he will make a pretty good
spec out of them; but, for my part, I would rather
they would stay at home, and live under their own
laws. I ha'nt got no notion, after they saddled that
damned rascal Van Buren upon us so long, that now,
the minute we have shook him off and made a good
government, and good treaties, and all, they should
be wanting to have a sop in our pan. If that's what
they are after, in rebelling against their government,
I don't want to give them no countenance. What
we have done, we have done for ourselves, and we
have a right to all the good of it. They have fixed
their market to their liking, and let it stand so. If
we can get thirty dollars for our tobacco, and they
cannot get ten, I reckon we ha'nt got nobody to thank
for it but ourselves. I dare say, now they see how

the thing works, they would be glad enough to share with us, but I see plain enough that all they would get by joining us, we would lose, and may be more too."

"You are right there, Mr. Hobson," said the merchant; "and that is not all. There's an advantage in buying as well as selling. Now as to this Mr. Trevor, or whatever his name is, coming over here, and buying things cheaper than he could get them at home—why that he is welcome to. Though you may be sure, neighbor, I don't let him have them as cheap as I sell to you. But as to letting in the Norfolk merchants to all the advantage of our treaty with England, that is another matter. For though, when we deepen the bar at Ocracock, I have no doubt our town down there will be another sort of a place to what Norfolk ever was, yet if Virginia was to join us now, right away, the most of the trade would go to Norfolk again, and they would get their goods there as cheap as we get them here, and may be a little cheaper. So you see it is against my interest as well as yours; and I don't like the thoughts of putting in a crop, and letting another man gather it, any more than you do."

"It would be harder upon me than any of you," said the wagoner; "for if that was the case, that damned railroad would break up my business, stock and fluke. As it is, there never was such a time for wagoning before. Instead of just hauling the little tobacco that is made here to the end of the railroad, *now* I have the hauling of the Virginia tobacco, and all, down to *Commerce*."*

It is hard to say whether surprise or disgust most prevailed in the mind of Douglas at hearing these remarks. The idea of the advantages lost to Virginia, by her connexion with the North, had never entered his mind; but still less had he conceived it possible that a sordid desire to monopolize these advantages, could stifle, in the minds of the North Carolinians, every feeling of sympathy with the oppressed and persecuted assertors of the rights of Virginia. The reply of Mr. Hobson to the remark of the wagoner gave him a yet deeper insight into that dark and foul corner of the human heart, where self predominates over all the better affections.

" I don't think that's right fair in you wagoners," said he. "You haul the Virginian tobacco down to Commerce, and when it gets there it is all the same as mine. Now, if it was not for that, I am not so mighty sure but I'd get forty dollars instead of thirty; and I don't like to lose ten dollars to give you a chance to get one."

" It is all one to me," said the wagoner. " You

---

* The reader will look, in vain, on the map, for the name of this place. It was somewhere on the waters of the Sound, and, doubtless, would have become a place of some consequence, had not the union of Virginia to the Southern Confederacy laid the foundation for a degree of prosperity in Norfolk, which bids fair to make it the first city on the continent. The town of Commerce, of course, went down with the necessity which gave rise to it.

may just pay me the same for not hauling that they pay me for hauling, or only half as much, and I will not haul another hogshead."

" But if you won't, another will," said Hobson.

" Like enough," replied the wagoner; " for all trades must live; and if them poor devils get a chance to sell a hogshead or two, instead of leaving it all to rot, you ought not to grudge them that."

" Certainly not," said the merchant, " for I guess that whatever they get, they take care to lay it all out in goods on this side of the line. So the money stays with us after all, and friend Stubbs's hauling does good to more besides him."

" I see," said Hobson, " how it does good to you, but none to me."

" But that an't all, Mr. Hobson," said the landlord, who had entered while this conversation was going on. " Them hot-headed fellows over the line there, like this old Squire Trevor, will be getting themselves into hot water every now and then ; and when they run away and come to us, if they did not bring no money, we'd have to feed them free gratis for nothing. Now Stubbs hauls Squire Trevor's tobacco to Commerce, and he gets a good price ; and then he gets into trouble, and comes over here to stay with me, and so he is able to pay me a good price ; and here it is," added he, showing a roll of notes.

" Still," said Hobson, " I don't see how that does

me any good. If they were to come here begging,
damn the mouthful I'd give them."

" Then you would leave the whole burden on the
poor tavern-keepers," said the landlord.

" No—I would not. I would not let them come;
or, if they did, just give them up to their own government. If they had not a chance to be running
over here, as soon as they got into trouble, they
would keep quiet, and never get a chance to separate, and so ruin our business, whether they joined
us or no."

" Old Rip is wide awake at last," said a voice
from behind ; " but it is to his interest only."

Douglas turned to the voice of the speaker, the
tone of which expressed a scorn and derision most
acceptable to his feelings. He was a tall and fine-
looking man, powerfully made, and inclined to be
fat, but not at all unwieldy. The half laughing
expression of his large, blue eye, and the protrusion
of his under lip, spoke his careless contempt of those
whose conversation had called forth his sarcasm.
The attention of the whole company was drawn to
him at the same moment; all looking as if they
wished to say something, without knowing what.
At length the wagoner spoke, on the well understood principle that, when men talk of what they
understand imperfectly, he who knows least should
be always first to show his ignorance.

" I cannot say I understand rightly what you
mean, stranger," said he; " but I guess, by the cut

of your jib, that you are one of them high dons from South Carolina, that always have money to throw away, and think a body ought never to care any more for himself than another. But this business don't consarn you, no how, because these people don't interfere with your cotton crop."

"Yes, but they do, though," said Hobson; "for if they drive me from tobacco, I shall make cotton. But, if I can keep them out of the tobacco market, I shall be willing to give up the making of cotton to South Carolina."

"Why, that is true," said the stranger, with a sudden change of his countenance, from which he discharged, in a moment, every appearance of intelligence, but that which seemed to reflect the superior wisdom of Mr. Hobson. "That is true," said he, looking as if making a stupid attempt to think; "I had not thought of that before."

As he said this, he sunk slowly and thoughtfully into a chair, his knees falling far asunder, his arms dropping across his thighs, his body bent forward, and his face turned up toward Mr. Hobson, with the look of one who desires and expects to receive important information. The whole action spoke so eloquently to Mr. Hobson's self-esteem, that he went on, with an air of the most gracious complacency.

"You see, stranger, just shutting only a part of the Virginian tobacco out of the market, makes a difference of ten dollars, at the very least, in the price of mine. Now, we used to make a heap of

cotton in this country, but we are all going to give
it up quite entirely, and then, you see, it stands to
reason it will make a difference of five cents a pound,
or may be ten, in your cotton."

This interesting proposition was received by the
stranger with a sluggish start of dull surprise, from
which he sunk again into the same appearance of
stolid musing. "To think what a fool I have been,"
said he, after a long pause. Then, scratching his
head, and twisting in his chair, he added: "You are
right. You are right; and the only way to manage
the matter is to get your Legislature to pass a law,
as you say, to make those fellows stay at home."

"To be sure it would," said the gratified Hobson;
"but then there are so many conceited fellows in the
Legislature, with a fool's notion in their heads about
taking sides with them that cannot help themselves,
that there is no getting anything done."

"Well," said the stranger, "this gentleman guessed
right when he said I was from South Carolina. So
I don't know any thing about your laws here. But
I suppose you have no law to hurt a man for taking
up one that runs away from the law in Virginia, and
carrying him back. I expect old Van would pay
well for them."

Hobson looked hard at the stranger, and only
answered with that compound motion of the head,
which, partaking at once of a shake and a nod,
expresses both assent and caution.

The landlord and merchant both exclaimed against

this suggestion, the one illustrating his argument by
the freedom with which his guest had ordered wine
from the bar ; the other, by his former experience of
his liberality as a purchaser of goods, while he kept
a store in Mr. Trevor's neighborhood, which he had
withdrawn since the revolution. Among the bystanders there was no expression of opinion, but that sort
of silence which betokens an idea that what has been
said is well worth considering.

CHAPTER XXVII.

Sic vos non vobis.—VIRGIL.

In the meantime, Mr. B—— had entered the room, and, hearing the stranger's voice, placed himself at the back of his chair, looking on with a playful smile. He now spoke—

"Have you played out the play?" said he.

The stranger sprang to his feet in a moment, and, facing B——, caught him by the hand, which he shook with an energy which seemed to threaten dislocation. The two then turned off, and left the room together.

"This is most fortunate, my dear sir," said the stranger; "but, pray tell me, how happens it that I find you here?"

"Do you not perceive," said B——, "that I have a friend in trouble, and that I am here with him? Did you not hear the name of Trevor just now?"

"Trevor! No—I did not distinguish the name. What Trevor? Bernard? Is he here? In trouble? About what? I came this far to see you both, and not choosing to go into Virginia, was listening to the conversation of those fellows, in hopes to find some one among them whom I could trust to send with a request that you would both meet me here."

" Here we both are," said B———, " and here Trevor is like to remain for a while. He has been
elected to the Legislature, and they have gotten up
a prosecution against him before that iniquitous
court of high commission at Washington, to hang
him, if they can, or at least to drive him off."

" Can you think him safe here," asked the stranger,
" among such mercenary wretches as those we have
just left ?"

" O yes! You must not judge of this people by
those muck-worms. The best of the three is a Yankee tin-pedler, turned merchant. The other two are
the worst specimens of their respective species. I
dare say there are many more like them, but there
are fifty gentlemen of property in this county who
would stand by us; and are ready, in their individual capacity, to aid us with purse and sword, whenever we raise our banner."

" But where is Trevor ?" said the stranger. " I
am impatient to see him."

" We will go to him," said B———; " but first let
me introduce you to a young friend of ours, whom
you must receive as a friend. He is the sort of man
we should cherish, and, besides that, he has been in
trouble on your account. You must understand
that he was an officer in the army of the United
States, and incurred the mortal displeasure of his
master for not joining one of his minions in abuse of
you, when the news of your successful negotiation
with the British Government was received."

Douglas was now called into the room, and introduced to the stranger; and the three gentlemen repaired together to the parlor of Mr. Trevor. A cordial greeting between the two friends, and a sprightly conversation on various topics, ensued; but at length the ladies left the room, and affairs of moment came under discussion.

"I am come," said the stranger, " to learn your plans, and to consult of the best means of affording such aid as we can. When, where, and how, do you mean to move?"

" We have carried the elections," said B——, " so as to be sure of a majority in the Legislature, if they can be freed from the presence of the Federal army. But, unless that can be done, our friends here, and many others, will not be permitted to attend, and the weaker brethren will be overawed."

" Of course, then, you will attempt that. What measures do you propose to take?"

" None that shall attract observation," said B——. " It is impossible, at this time, to draw together any force which might not at once be overwhelmed by the army at Richmond. We are, therefore, obliged to lie quiet, and suffer our people to see for themselves the advantages they are losing. They are beginning to understand this. They perceive that your commercial arrangements are making their neighbors in this State rich, while they can sell nothing that they make, and are obliged to give double price for all they buy. The abatement of duty in the English ports on your tobacco, and the corresponding abatement of your impost on British manufactures, is driving trade, money, and even population, to the South; and nothing but separation from the northern States can prevent our whole tobacco country from being deserted. This, of course, will open the eyes of the people in time, and we hope, that when the Legislature meets, it may be practicable to draw together, on the sudden, such a force as may drive the enemy from Richmond, and give time at least to adjourn to a place where they may deliberate in safety.

"Is there any such place in the State?" asked the stranger.

"I am not aware that there is at this moment, but such a one must be provided for the emergency, should it arise."

"And what means do you propose to use for that purpose?"

"There is a section of the State," replied B——, "where circumstances enable me to exert a powerful influence, and where, from its localities, a partisan corps might maintain itself, in spite of the enemy, and might give so decided a disposition to the surrounding population, as to establish perfect security within a pretty extensive district."

"But is there no danger," said the southron, "that such a corps would induce an increase of the force at Richmond and elsewhere, and so make the first step in your enterprise more difficult?"

"It would have that effect," said B——, "were not the scene of action remote from Richmond, and unless the operations of the corps were so conducted as to create no alarm for that place. Of course, there should be no appearance of concert with this lower country; and, so far from increasing apprehension of our ulterior designs, our failure to rally to the banner of a successful leader might disarm suspicion."

"Then it seems that all you want is a Marion, a Sumpter, or a Pickens?"

"We have such a one," said B——; "and it is well that you are here with us to aid in consecrating him to his task. Here he stands."

As he said this, he laid his hand, solemnly, gently, and respectfully, on the head of the astonished Douglas.

"What, I!" exclaimed he. "For God's sake, my dear.sir, what qualification have I for such a service."

"Courage, talent, address, and military education," said B——, with a quiet smile.

"And where should I find men willing to be commanded by me, in an enterprise which, of course, supposes the absence of all legal authority?"

"Suppose them provided," said B——. "Is there any other difficulty to be removed?"

"I should still be bound to inquire," said Douglas, "what good end is proposed,before I could agree to enter on a course of conduct which nothing but the most important considerations could justify."

" All that you have a right to ask, and are bound to understand clearly. You would have understood it long before this, but that as long as one shred remained of the tie that bound you to the army of the United States, a delicate respect to you imposed silence on your uncle and myself. You now require that we show you some prevailing reason why Virginia should detach herself from the Northern Confederacy, and either form a separate State, which we do not propose, or unite herself to the South, which we do. Is not that your difficulty ! "

"It is," replied Douglas. " I have long been sensible that there were views of the subject which my situation had hidden from me, and have frequently lamented (while I was grateful for) the resolute reserve which my friends have maintained."

" You must be sensible," said B——, " that the southern States, including Virginia, are properly and almost exclusively agricultural. The quality of their soil and climate, and the peculiar character of their laboring population, concur to make agriculture the most profitable employment among them. Apart from the influence of artificial causes, it is not certain that any labor can be judiciously taken from the soil to be applied to any other object whatever. When Lord Chatham said that America ought not to manufacture a hob-nail for herself, he spoke as a true and judicious friend of the colonies. The labor

necessary to make a hob-nail, if applied to the cul-
tivation of the earth, might produce that for which
the British manufacturer would gladly give two hob-
nails. By coming between the manufacturer and
the farmer, and interrupting this interchange by
perverse legislation, the Government broke the tie
which bound the colonies to the mother country.

" When that tie was severed and peace established,
it was the interest of both parties that this interchange
should be restored, and put upon such a footing as
to enable each, reciprocally, to obtain for the products of his own labor as much as possible of the
products of the labor of the other.

" Why was not this done? Because laws are not
made for the benefit of the people, but for that of
their rulers. The monopolizing spirit of the landed
aristocracy in England led to the exclusion of our
bread-stuffs, and the necessities of the British treasury tempted to the levying of enormous revenue from
our other agricultural products. The interchange
between the farmer and manufacturer was thus interrupted. In part it was absolutely prevented; the
profit being swallowed up by the impost, the inducement was taken away.

" What did the American Government under these
circumstances? Did they say to Great Britain, ' relax
your corn-laws; reduce your duties on tobacco;
make no discrimination between our cotton and that
from the East Indies; and we will refrain from lay-
ing a high duty on your manufactures. You will

thus enrich your own people, and it is by no means sure that their increased prosperity may not give you, through the excise and other channels of revenue, more than an equivalent for the taxes we propose to you to withdraw.'

" Did we say this ? No. And why ? Because, in the northern States, there was a manufacturing interest to be advanced by the very course of legislation most fatal to the South. With a dense population, occupying a small extent of barren country, with mountain streams tumbling into deep tidewater, and bringing commerce to the aid of manufactures, they wanted nothing but a monopoly of the southern market to enable them to enrich themselves. The alternative was before us. To invite the great European manufacturer to reciprocate the benefits of free trade, whereby the South might enjoy all the advantages of its fertile soil and fine climate, or to transfer these advantages to the North, by meeting Great Britain on the ground of prohibition and exaction. The latter was preferred, because to the interest of that section, which, having the local majority, had the power.

" Under this system, Great Britain has never wanted a pretext for her corn-laws, and her high duties on all our products. Thus we sell all we make, subject to these deductions, which, in many instances, leave much less to us than what goes into the British treasury.

" Here, too, is the pretext to the Government of

the United States for their exactions in return. The misfortune is, that the southern planter had to bear both burthens. One half the price of his products is seized by the British Government, and half the value of what he gets for the other half is seized by the Government of the United States.

"This they called retaliation and indemnification. It was indemnifying an interest which had not been injured, by the farther injury of one which had been injured. It was impoverishing the South for the benefit of the North, to requite the South for having been already impoverished for the benefit of Great Britain. Still it was 'indemnifying *ourselves*.' Much virtue in that word, '*ourselves*.' It is the language used by the giant to the dwarf in the fable ; the language of the brazen pot to the earthen pot; the language of all dangerous or interested friendship.

"I remember seeing an illustration of this sort of indemnity in the case of a woman who was whipt by her husband. She went complaining to her father, who whipped her again, and sent her back. 'Tell your husband,' said he, 'that as often as he whips *my daughter*, I will whip *his wife*.'"

"But what remedy has been proposed for these things ?" asked Douglas.

"A remedy has been proposed and applied," replied B——. "The remedy of legislation for the benefit, not of the rulers, but of the ruled."

"But in what sense will you say that our legislation has been for the benefit of the rulers alone ? Are we not all our own rulers ?"

" Yes," replied B——, " if you again have recourse to the use of that comprehensive word ' WE,' which identifies things most dissimilar, and binds up, in the same bundle, things most discordant. If the South and North are one ; if the Yankee and the Virginian are one ; if light and darkness, heat and cold, life and death, can all be identified ; then WE are our own rulers. Just so, if the State will consent to be identified with the Church, then we pay tithes with one hand, and receive them with the other. While the Commons identify themselves with the Crown, ' WE' do but pay taxes to *ourselves*. And if Virginians can be fooled into identifying themselves with the Yankees—a fixed tax-paying minority, with a fixed tax-receiving majority—it will still be the same thing; and they will continue to hold a distinguished place among the innumerable WES that have been gulled into their own ruin ever since the world began. It is owing to this sort of deception, played off on the unthinking multitude, that in the two freest countries in the world, the most important interests are taxed for the benefit of lesser interests. In England, a country of manufacturers, *they* have been starved that agriculture may thrive. In this, a country of farmers and planters, *they* have been taxed that manufacturers may thrive. Now I will requite Lord Chatham's well-intentioned declaration, by saying that England ought not to make a barrel

of flour for herself. I say, too, that if her rulers, and
the rulers of the people of America, were true to
their trust, both sayings would be fulfilled. She
would be the work-house, and here would be the
granary of the world. What would become of the
Yankees? As *I* don't call them WE, I leave *them* to
find the answer to that question."

CHAPTER XXVIII.

Such is the aspect of this shore ;
'Tis Greece—but living Greece no more.

BYRON.

THE impression made on Douglas by these obser-
vations was so strong and so obvious, that his friend
paused and left him to meditate upon them. Some
minutes elapsed before he made any reply. When
he did speak, he acknowledged the existence and
magnitude of the grievance, and again inquired,
with increased solicitude, what remedy had been
found.

"You heard what passed in the bar-room, just
now," said the stranger.

"I did," replied Douglas; "and I was as much
surprised at the facts hinted at, as disgusted at the
sentiments of the speakers."

"Then your surprise must have been extreme,"
said the other; "for I hardly know which amused
me most: their unblushing display of selfish meanness, or the glow of indignation in your countenance,
which showed how little you know of this world of
philanthropy and benevolence that we live in. But
had you no suspicion of the cause of these enviable

advantages which these sons of Mammon are so anxious to monopolize?"

"Not at all, and hence my surprise; for I had supposed heretofore, that, between the two States, all the advantage lay on the side of Virginia."

"You judge rightly," replied the other. "In the way of commerce, nature has done nothing for the one, and everything for the other. But the conversation you have heard is a proof that the sand which chokes the waters of the Sound is a trivial obstacle, in comparison with the legislative barriers which have shut out prosperity from the noble Chesapeake. Look at your rivers and bay, and you will see that Virginia ought to be the most prosperous country in the world. Look at the ruins which strew the face of your lower country, the remains of churches and the fragments of tombstones, and you will see that she once was so. Ask for the descendants of the men whose names are sculptured on those monuments, and their present condition will tell you that her prosperity has passed away. Then ask all history. Go to the finest countries in the world—to Asia Minor, to Greece, to Italy; ask what has laid them desolate, and you will receive but one answer, 'misgovernment.'"

"But may not the fault be in the people themselves?" asked Douglas.

"The fault of submitting to be misgoverned, certainly. But no more than that. Let the *country* enjoy its natural advantages, and they who are too ignorant or too slothful to use them will soon give place to others of a different character. What has there been to prevent the Yankee from selling his barren hills at high prices and coming South, where he might buy the fertile shores of the Chesapeake for a song? No local attachment, certainly; for his home is everywhere. What is there now to prevent the planter of this neighborhood from exchanging his thirsty fields for the rich and long coveted low grounds of James River, or Roanoke, in Virginia? Are these people wiser, better, more energetic and industrious than they were twelve months ago, that their lands have multiplied in value five fold? Is it your uncle's fault, that, were he now at home the tame slave of power, he could hardly give away his fine estate? The difference is, that this country now enjoys its natural advantages, while Virginia remains under the crushing weight of a system devised for the benefit of her oppressors."

"I see the effect," said Douglas. "But tell me, I beseech you, the cause of this change in your condition here."

"The cause is free trade."

"And how has that been obtained?"

"I will answer that," said B——; "because my friend's modesty might restrain him from giving the true answer. It has been obtained by intelligence, manly frankness, and fair dealing. It has been obtained by offering to other nations terms most favorable to their peculiar and distinctive interests,

in consideration of receiving the like advantage
Instead of nursing artificial interests to rival the iron
and cotton fabrics, and the shipping of England, the
wine of France, the silk and oil of Italy, and enviously
snatching at whatever benefit nature may have vouch-
safed to other parts of the world, this people only ask
to exchange for these things their own peculiar pro-
ductions.   A trade perfectly free, totally discharged
from all duties, would certainly be best for all.   But
revenue must be had, and the impost is the best
source of revenue.   No state can be expected to give
that up.   But it has been found practicable so to
regulate that matter as to reduce the charges which
have heretofore incumbered exchanges to a mere
trifle."

"How has that been effected?" asked Douglas.

"If that question were to be answered in detail,"
said B——, "I should leave the answer to him by
whom the details have been arranged.   I will give you
the outline in a few words.   These States were first
driven to think of separation by a tariff of protection.
Their federal constitution guards against it by express prohibition, and by requiring that the impost,
like the tax laws of Virginia, should be annual.

"They have felt the danger to liberty from exces-
sive revenue.   Their constitution requires that the
estimates of the expense of the current year shall be
made the measure of revenue to be raised for that
year.   The imports of the preceding year are taken
as a basis of calculation, and credit being given for

any surplus in the treasury, a tariff is laid which, on that basis, would produce the sum required."

" Then there never can be any surplus for an emergency," said Douglas.

" Always," replied B——; " in the right place, and the only safe place—the pockets of a prosperous pec ple. There is no place in the treasury to keep money. The till of the treasury has a hole in the bottom, and the money always finds its way into the pockets of sharpers, parasites, man-worshippers, and pseudo-patriots. But let that pass. You see that a small revenue alone will probably be wanting, and being raised annually, the tariff can be annually adjusted.

" Now, what says justice, as to the revenue to be raised by two nations on the trade between the two, seeing that it is equally levied on the citizens of both ?"

" On that hypothesis each should receive an equal share of it," said Douglas.

" Precisely so," answered B——; " and let these terms be held out to all nations, and if one will not accept them another will. On this principle a system of commercial arrangements has been set on foot which, by restoring to these States the benefit of their natural advantages, is at once producing an effect which explains their former prosperity. It places in stronger relief the evils of the opposite system to Virginia, and really leaves her, while she retains her present connexion with the North, with-out any resource. Tobacco she cannot sell at all. *Invita natura,* she will have to raise cotton to supply

the beggared manufactories of the North, from which
she will not receive in return the third part as much
of the manufactured article as the Carolina planter
will get for his. This is her fate. She sees it, and
would throw off the yoke. But her northern masters
see it too. She is all that remains to them of their
southern dependencies, which, though not *their* colonies, they have so long governed *as* colonies. Take
her away, and they are in the condition of the wolf
when there are no sheep left. Wolf eat wolf, and
Yankee cheat Yankee. This they will guard against
by all means lawful and unlawful, for Virginia alone
mitigates the ruin that their insatiate rapacity has
brought upon them. They will hold on to her with
the gripe of death; and she must and will struggle to
free herself, as from death.

" And now, how say you ? Are you prepared to
do your part in furtherance of this object ?"

" I am," replied Douglas promptly; " and I now
eagerly ask you to show me the means by which I can
advance it."

" You asked for men," said B——, " and you shall
have them. They are already provided, and want but
a leader."

" But what authority can I have to be recognised
as such ?"

" You have heard your uncle, aunt, or cousins,
speak of Jacob Schwartz."

" I believe I have; but what can such a fellow have
to do with such affairs as we now speak of. Is he not
an ignorant clown ?"

"He is all that," said B——. "But he writes as good a hand as Marshal Saxe, and has probably read as many books as Cincinnatus. But to speak seriously, he is no common clown. I picked him up, nearly forty years ago, a little, dirty, ragged boy, without money, without friends, without education, and without principles. All these wants I found means to supply, except that of education, which to him would be quite superfluous. But he now has money sufficient, and friends without number; and, what is better still, he has become an honest man, and discharges the duties of one none the worse for having had a pretty large experience in knavery. Such as he is, he is bound to me by gratitude, such as few men are capable of. More than a dozen years ago, he followed the bent of early habit, and retired to his native mountains, where he has married, and lives after the manner of the country, as if he were worth nothing in the world but his rifle. He has a good deal of money, which I manage for him; and as he has no taste for extravagance of any sort, and is generous as a king, he always has a dollar to spare a friend.

"When I tell you that the people of that district see so little money that they always count it by fourpence-half-pennies, you will readily believe that a little help goes a great way. They don't see that Schwartz has any property; but their opinion of his sagacity and enterprise takes away all wonder at the fact, that he is always able, as well as ready, to give aid to a friend at time of need. You will of course infer, that his influence among them is very great. Now that, and all his faculties of body, mind, and purse, are at my command. He is aware of the state of public affairs; adopts all my views, as far as he can understand them, and beyond that point trusts me implicitly. It is through his instrumentality that the minds of the mountaineers of that district are pre pared for action at this moment. No force is actually organized, but every thing is ready for the emergency. The dispositions of the people, and the strong fastnesses of the country, will make it a secure retreat to a partisan corps. The materials for such a corps may be found in part among the inhabitants. A nucleus is all that is wanting, and to that all the persecuted and distressed, from every quarter, will gather."

"You show me, then," said Douglas, "that you already have all you want—men and a leader. Your friend Schwartz must be the very man to command those fellows, and might not like to submit to the authority of another."

"He is not the man to command," said B——, "because he could not keep up intelligence with other parts of the country, though as a medium of intelligence there is none better. Indeed he cannot be spared from that branch of service. Besides, though he might command his neighbors, you will be joined by men who will not submit to be commanded by any but a gentleman. As to any reluctance on his part, go to him in my name, or in that of your uncle or aunt, and you command him, body and soul. You will find all his facilities devoted to your service, without envy, jealousy, or grudging; and you will do well to use his mind more than his body. In many particulars he is one of the most efficient men in the world; and as he perfectly understands himself, and knows what he is fit for, you may always leave him to choose his own function, and to execute it in his own way."

CHAPTER XXIX.

The heath this night must be my bed,
The bracken curtain for my head,
My lullaby the warder's tread,
    Far, far, from Love and thee, Mary!

"I THINK," said Douglas, "I now understand your general purpose, and the means to be placed at my disposal. Let me now know your plan of operations. What am I to do, and when?"

"The task I propose to myself," replied B——, "is one which requires that I keep myself out of harm's way, and free from all suspicion, until the time shall come; when I propose to act a part which shall make me a conspicuous mark for the malice or policy of our enemies. Hence I affect to live, and keep myself as much as possible on this side of the line. What you do there must be done in such a way as to indicate no connexion with me. I therefore propose that you accompany my friend here to South Carolina, where you may derive much benefit from seeing the first men in that State, with whom he will make you acquainted. From thence I would have you address letters to your friends (especially those in the army) so worded as to lead them to attribute your change of opinions (which should be made to seem progressive) to the influence of these new associations. A few weeks will be sufficient for this purpose, and you may return to Virginia early in the summer. Here," continued B——, pointing to a map which hung in the room, "is the point at which you will enter the State, and here will be the principal scene of your operations. You will there find Schwartz, to whom you shall be properly accredited, and from whom you will learn the resources to be placed at your command, and the capabilities of the country.

"Now observe. Our object is to organize a small force, under which the district may be protected in declaring for the Independence of Virginia, and prepared to afford a place of refuge to the Legislature, should they be driven from Richmond, before they have time to organize the operations of the Government. Of course, they must have an opportunity to assemble there, if but for a day. This it must be *our* care to secure, by a sudden movement from the midland counties on the southern boundary, and in this we *may* need your co-operation. On that point we shall take care to keep you advised.

"Now our first object being to free Richmond from the presence of the federal army, at the moment the Legislature is to meet, we must be careful to cause no alarm for the safety of that place. Any movement in that direction would produce a concentration of force there, and increase our difficulties. You should, therefore, be careful so to shape your operations as rather to call the attention of the enemy to other points; and if you can make them of sufficient importance to draw detachments from Richmond, a double purpose will be answered. You will have no cause to fear any force that can be brought against you. Your field of operations affords situations which may defy assault, and, the line of North Carolina being at your back, you may, at any moment, cross it and disband for a time.

"But I am not sure whether our end may not be answered best by giving to all your operations such a character as may exclude the idea of any political object. As none of those who are conspicuous as malcontents in the lower country will join you, this deception will not be difficult. In beating up the quarters of the troops near you, you may seem to act but in self defence; and should you extend your blow so far as Lynchburg, your mountaineers will hardly fail to levy such contributions on the camp-followers and Yankee pedlars there (who call themselves merchants), as to give the measure the appearance of a mere marauding expedition."

"I am not so very sure," replied Douglas, "that I should like to mix my little reputation as a soldier and a gentleman with an affair of that sort."

"I am not suggesting anything contrary to the laws of war," said B——. "The violation of them would be but in appearance. Care would be taken to indemnify any who might be wronged, whenever it shall be expedient for you to throw off the mask.

As to any temporary misconstruction, your name would connect you with your uncle, and, through him, with me and all our friends; and moreover, would whet the malice of your worthy friends, the Bakers, who would move heaven and earth to circumvent you. Better, therefore, to drop the last name. Archibald Douglas is name enough to satisfy the ambition of any reasonable man, at least until he can cap it with a yet more honorable addition, if that be possible."

While this conversation was going on, there was some appearance of embarrassment about Douglas, which did not escape the observation of his uncle. At length he said to him, in an under tone, that, before carrying the matter under discussion any farther, he would be glad to have a few words with him in private.

" I understand your wish," said the old gentleman, aloud; "it shall be indulged."

" I suspect you mistake me," said Douglas, coloring very high.

" Not at all," replied the other. " You only suppose so because you do not know that one of my friends here received his wife in marriage at my hands, and that the other stood father to mine. Hence I have no such reserves with them as you may suppose. *Now*, do I understand you?"

" I dare say you do," replied Douglas, blushing yet more deeply.

" Then I say, again, your wish shall be indulged. You shall not leave us until you are fully established in all the rights which it is mine to confer. But you must suppress your raptures until you hear the conditions. Our plan requires secrecy, and, above all, that there should be no appearance of concert between you and us, and no cause to suspect it. This thing, therefore, must be absolutely private; no witnesses but those here present, and your aunt, and Lucia; and in the next moment your foot must be in the stirrup. Are you content?"

"Content!" said Douglas. "Indeed I am not; but I see that you are acting upon a concerted plan, and that all expostulation must be vain. Let me at least see Delia now."

"I suspect she has gone to bed," said Mr. T——. "*Retired!* I believe is the word introduced by our Yankee school-mistresses, whose prurient imaginations are shocked at the name of a bed. Poor girl, she was glad to retire, in the plain English sense of the word, as soon as we got here, and, I dare say, has been in bed half an hour. She and your aunt were on active service all last night, while you were keeping a snoring watch over our friend Whiting. Come, my boy! You shall not infect her with the fever of your brain to-night. If you cannot sleep, it is no reason why she should not. And now let us turn again to other matters."

"The next question, then," said the southron, "is how we can aid you? By sword, or tongue, or pen, or purse?"

"By purse as much as you please," said B——.

" Our young friend here will need a small military chest, which we have no means of filling. As to the rest, keep out of the scrape. We wish to join you in peace, and then remain at peace, which will not be, if you strike a blow in our behalf now. As much *individual* aid as you please to our rendezvous just before the first Monday in December. A thousand independent volunteers, *pour le coup*, would be welcome. In the meantime, if you can send our young friend here a promising young officer from your military school, to be his second in command, it is all we would ask. Of course he will come as of his own head, for you must not seem to have anything to do with the matter."

Many other topics connected with our subject were discussed, but I deem it unadvisable to speak of more than is necessary to explain the subsequent situation of the parties. When they met again at breakfast, the swimming eye and changing cheek of Delia told that she had been made acquainted with all that had passed. The countenance of Douglas beamed with high excitement, at once pleasant and painful. A glance of triumphant encouragement to Delia, and her answering tearful smile, showed that they perfectly understood each other. Indeed, it was time they should, for it had been settled that B——, who was a resident and justice of the peace of the county, should perform the marriage ceremony, according to the unceremonious law of North Carolina, immediately after breakfast.

As soon as it was over, they adjourned to the parlor, where B——, drawing Delia to him, seated her
on his knee. " I don't half like this business," said
he. " I have no mind to take an active part in giving up my own little girl to this young fellow. I
am too old to think of loving and fighting all in a
breath, as he does, and I thought to wait till the wars
were over, and here he comes and cuts me out. But
I am determined to do nothing in prejudice of my
claim, until I find that I have no chance. Young
man," added he, in a tone gradually changing from
playful to serious, " do you love this dear girl with
that faithful, single-hearted love, which man owes to
a woman who gives him all her heart, and entrusts
to him all her happiness, and all her hopes ? "

As he said this he took the hand of Douglas, and
went on : " Do you thus love her, and will you in
good faith manifest this love, by being to her a true
and devoted husband, in every change and vicissitude
of life, so long as life shall last ? Answer me, Douglas," he continued, with a voice approaching to
sternness, and a fixed and searching look, while he
strongly grasped the young man's hand.

" Assuredly I will," said Douglas, somewhat hurt.

" And you, dear," said B——, resuming his kind
and playful tone, " do you love this young fellow in
like sort, and will you, on your part, be to him thus
faithful as his wife ? "

While B—— said this the blushing Delia tried to
disengage herself. But he detained her, and caught

the hand with which she endeavored to loosen his from her waist, and held it fast. At length she hid her face on his neck, whispering :

"You know I do. You know I will.

"Then God bless you, my children," said B——, bringing their hands together and grasping both firmly in one of his; "for you are married as fast as the law can tie you."

In a moment the whole party were on their feet, each expressing a different variety of surprise. Douglas was the first to understand his situation fully, as appeared by his springing forward and catching his bride to his bosom, imprinting on her pure cheek the kiss that holy nature prompts, and that all the caprices of fashion (thank God!) can never shame. From him she escaped into the arms of her mother, who, caressing her with murmured tenderness, looked half reproachfully at B——. Then smiling through the tear that filled her large blue eye, she shook her finger at him, and said, "Just like you! Just like you!"

"Fairly cheated you of your scene, Margaret. All the matronly airs, and maidenly airs, that you and Delia have been rehearsing this morning, gone for nothing. And there is dear little Lucia crying as if to break her heart, because sister Delia was married before she could fix her pretty little face for the occasion. Never mind, dear! When your turn comes there will be less hurry, and you shall have a ceremony as long as the whole liturgy. Well,

Douglas, you will not· quarrel with me, I am sure ; and I think Delia will forgive me for the trick I played her. You have but an hour to stay together, and where was the sense of giving that up to the flutter and agitation of a deferred ceremony ? I suspect if I were always to manage the matter in this way, I should have my hands as full of business as the dentist that used to conjure people's teeth out of their mouths without their knowing it, while he was pretending just to fix his instrument. But go, my children. Empty your full hearts into each other's bosoms, and thank me for the privilege."

CHAPTER XXX.

——Gathering tears and tremblings of distress;
And cheeks all pale, which, but an hour ago,
Blushed at the praise of their own loveliness:
And there were sudden partings, such as press
The life from out young hearts, and choking sighs,
Which ne'er might be repeated: Who could guess
If ever more should meet those mutual eyes?

BYRON.

AND so it was. I can add nothing to the language
of the poet. I can supply nothing to the imagination of the reader. Thus Douglas and Delia parted.
He accompanied his new acquaintance to the southern capital; he there met with men whose names
live and will live in the history of their country, and
whose memories will be honored while virtue is held
in reverence among men. From these, and especially
from the accomplished gentleman to whose friendship he had been introduced by his uncle and Mr.
B——, he received such lights as dispelled every
shadow of doubt from his mind. The wrongs of
Virginia, her rights and her remedies, became the
subject of all his thoughts, and he burned with
impatience for the time when he might draw his
sword on her behalf, and turn to her use, as he had

expressed it, the lessons learned in the school of her oppressors.

That time at length arrived. Returning by the upper road which skirts the foot of the mountains, he re-entered Virginia nearly at the spot to which his brother had gone in quest of him. There, as he had been taught to expect, he found Schwartz, whose reception of him fully justified the assurances of B——. To that gentleman he showed unbounded devotion, delighted to speak of favors received at his hands, and of "moving accidents by flood and field," which they had encountered together. Next to B——, in his estimation, stood Mrs. Trevor; then Delia, for whom when a child he had formed a passionate attachment; and last, Mr. Trevor himself, whom, after the rest, he respected and admired above all human beings. A hint from B—— that Douglas was the husband of Delia placed him at once in the same catalogue of worthies, and from the first moment he devoted himself not less to his personal service than to the advancement of the common cause. He had already organized a small corps, the command of which he unreservedly surrendered, making it his constant study to recommend the new commander to the confidence of the men.

No man could deserve it better, or was better qualified to win it. Frank, affable, generous, and kind, his deportment was marked by that self-respectful courtesy which has all the good effect of dignity, without ever passing by that name. With nothing repulsive, austere, or cold in his demeanor, he was a man whose orders no soldier would question, whose displeasure no gentleman would choose to incur, whose feelings no friend, however careless, would wound. Liberally supplied with money by his southern friends, and instructed by Schwartz in the judicious use of it, he took effectual measures to prevent distress in the families of his followers. A small sum amply satisfied their simple wants, and his men had the satisfaction of knowing that their families suffered nothing by their absence from their little farms.

Beside the small embodied corps I have mentioned, the whole population of that warlike district were placed under a sort of organization, so that, while they pursued their occupations of hunting or farming, they were prepared, at any moment, to join an expedition or to resist an attack.

Schwartz, who knew the country, inch by inch, made Douglas acquainted with all its strengths and all its passes, so that he soon became an expert woodsman, and an active mountaineer. His first care was to select a place for a stationary camp. For this purpose he chose a position strong by nature, which he made nearly impregnable. He next provided horses enough to mount a part of his corps. For these the rich herbage of the mountains afforded abundant subsistence during the summer months. Of ammunition there was no stint. The

lead mines were just at his back, beyond the Alleg-
hanny. Powder is made of good quality in all that
region, and the quantity necessary for the rifle is so
small, that the rifleman may be said to carry a hundred lives in his powder-horn. Of provisions he had
plenty, though wanting many things deemed necessary in a regular army. But the pure air of the
mountains, and the exercise of hunting and scouting,
preserved the health of the men, without tents, or
salt, or vinegar, or vegetables of any kind. Venison
and beef, dried in the sun, or over the fire by the
process called jerking, was prepared in the season
of abundance for winter use, and proved the best
sort of food for a marauding corps. Light, compact,
and nutritious, there is no diet on which a man can
travel so far or fight so hard.

Nothing now remained but to make his enemy
feel him. Stooping from his mountain fastness, he
soon broke up all the military posts in the adjacent
counties ; so that, in a few weeks, not a blue-coat
was to be seen on the south side of Staunton river,
Freed from the presence of their enemy, the people
were found ready to rise en masse. He dissuaded
them from doing more than to put themselves in
readiness for action, to furnish him needed supplies,
for which he paid fairly, and to give him notice of
the approach of the enemy. For this purpose he
established a sort of half military organization, and
had it in his power to increase his little force to five
times its number in a few days. His strength being

thus adapted to any occasion which could be expected to offer, after sweeping away the enemy from the south side of the river, he proceeded to break up the posts in the counties on the northern bank. In the end, though the enemy were nominally in possession of all the country between James river and Roanoke, they held no post higher than Lynchburg, nor any farther south than Farmville. Above this last place, their scouts and foraging parties showed themselves occasionally, but never ventured to leave the banks of James river for more than a single night.

At Lynchburg, not long before the time at which our story commences, two companies had been posted. As Douglas had never shown a force of more than a hundred men, no fear of an attack on that point was entertained. But suddenly collecting a number of auxiliaries, he struck at them, drove them from their post, enriched his men with every thing that the laws of war permitted him to seize, and retreated to his stronghold in the mountains. The supplies of arms, ammunition, clothing, and blankets, thus procured, put him in condition to increase his corps, if necessary. Thus, at the time of which we speak, having little more than a hundred men embodied, he could have marched five times that number to Richmond; and, for any service near at hand, could have commanded a yet larger force. Though unprovided with many of the conveniences of military life, they were not deficient in essentials. There was " not a bit of feather in his host," nor drum, nor trumpet, nor banner. But there were stout hearts, and strong hands, and fleet limbs, and good rifles, and knives and tomahawks ; and that system and harmony which spring from a sense of danger, a high purpose, and confidence in a leader. To the listening ear, a whisper speaks louder than a trumpet to the heedless. To the trusting heart, the chieftain's voice supersedes the spirit-stirring drum.

While Douglas thus maintained his position among the mountains, it became a sort of Cave of Adullam. His little corps was a nucleus to which the discontented and persecuted gathered continually. His embodied force was increased, while the organization of the neighboring population became more perfect, their confidence firmer, their zeal more ardent. So effectually had he broken the power of the Central Government in that quarter, that it had been deemed expedient to throw a much larger federal force into Lynchburg, to curb his progress in that direction, and to restrain the disaffected in the counties along the north bank of James river. Could he have co-operated with the friends of Virginia there, it was not clear that the flame might not spread on and on, in the direction of Washington, until the very seat of empire might be unsafe. Hence a regiment had been detached from the army at Richmond, and another from the North, originally destined for that place, was turned aside to Lynchburg. Aware of these move-

ments, Douglas had no doubt that the purpose of such
an assemblage of force was not merely preventive.
He saw that attempts would be made to recover the
ground which the enemy had lost on the south side of
James river ; and that, by remaining strictly on the
defensive, he might be forced to withdraw his embodied force to their mountain stronghold, and not
only lose the aid of his irregulars, but give them up
to the vengeance of the enemy.   Under these circumstances, attack was the most effectual form of defence,
and boldness was true prudence.

The time, too, was at hand for the decisive movement, in the lower counties, for the relief of Richmond.   The desired diversion had been effected, and
Douglas found himself capable of bringing into the
field a force, the presence of which would be no incon-
siderable aid to that about to assemble below.   To
strike at his enemy therefore, to overwhelm him if
possible, and, if not, to elude him and fall down to
the assistance of B——, seemed to be the surest plan for
preserving the safety and independence even of the
mountain region.   If successful, every desirable end
would be accomplished.   Even should he fail, his
duty to the faithful yeomanry and peasantry of that
devoted section, was rather to draw the enemy away
after him toward Richmond, than by falling directly
back, or even by remaining where he was, to invite
them to overrun the country which had afforded him
such zealous and efficient co-operation.

Influenced by these considerations, Douglas had

despatched Schwartz to lay them before B——, and
receive his instructions. He had long ago recognised
him as the person of whom his aunt had said that
"the destiny of Virginia depended on him." He had
received at his hands the sort of authority which he
wielded, now indeed by his own personal influence
and character, but originally as the trusted represen-
tative of B——. He had no mind to shake off that
character. He had seen that, by means not exactly
understood, that gentleman commanded resources,
both at home and abroad, which enabled him to
meditate plans, in which all the operations of
Douglas's corps, however brilliant, were but circumstances of less importance themselves than in their
relations.

Schwartz was the sole medium of communication
between the two. With nothing in his appearance to
attract attention—nothing in his manners or common
style of conversation betokening powers superior to
those of any other peasant—his intelligence and
fidelity supplied the place of letters. He understood
every thing, and forgot nothing that was said to him.
He therefore carried no papers, and passed unsuspected through the country, amusing with the most
harmless gossip, all he chanced to fall in with. He
was a man who knew how to have business any
where, and at any moment; and he passed along
more like a sparrow hopping from twig to twig,
pecking at a berry here and a leaf there, and never
seeming to have an ulterior object, than with the

strong-winged flight which indicates a distant and important destination.

In one of Arthur's visits to Lucia (his betrothal to whom was no longer a secret in her father's family), he was made acquainted with the history of Douglas's marriage. He was also entrusted with the important information that the gallant leader, with whose exploits the country rung, and whom his imagination had endued with almost superhuman powers, was his own best beloved brother. He was instantly on fire to join him, and Schwartz was instructed to convey to him the necessary intelligence; and, if possible, to fall in with him on the way. But he had been turned aside by objects of higher moment on his return and Arthur had got ahead of him. Having ascertained this fact in the county of Charlotte, where their roads came together, Schwartz travelled hard to overtake him ; left his tired horse at the entrance of the defile, and, following on foot, came up with him as we have seen.

CHAPTER XXXI.

It is, that she will cherish the renown
  Of noble deeds, achieved her name to grace ;
And prize the heart that beat for her alone,
  In Glory's triumph, or in Death's embrace.

ANONYMOUS.

LET us now return to the deep glen, at the bottom of which we left our friend Arthur, accompanied by his mountain guide. Schwartz was welcomed with cordial joy by his comrades, and, having asked for the Captain, was told he was in his tent. Arthur looked around in vain for a tent, but saw none. The beetling crags on both sides of the dell seemed to be the only shelter that the place afforded. But against the rock, a hundred yards below, and directly beneath the spot from which Schwartz had given notice of his presence, hung a piece of tent-cloth. One edge of this was tacked to a pole which lay horizontally against the rocky wall, the ends being supported by forks about ten feet long. This proved to be a sort of door to a wide-mouthed cavernous recess in the rock, deep enough to afford room for the few little conveniences which an officer can expect to keep about him in active service.

Approaching this, Schwartz lifted the corner, and our travellers stood in the presence of Douglas.

He was seated at a coarse table, poring over a rude manuscript map, and did not lift his head until he heard the word "brother" uttered by the well-known voice of Arthur. In a moment they were in each other's arms, and, in the next, the new-comer was overwhelmed with questions about his father, mother, and various friends. Some indeed were not named; for, though Schwartz was in the secret of the fact, he was incapable of being let into the deeper mystery of hearts like those of Douglas and Delia. To such the utterance of a beloved name in the presence of the uninitiated is an unpardonable profanation. But though that of Delia was not spoken, Arthur took care so to emphasize his account of the health of his uncle's family, as to convey to the mind of Douglas an assurance of all he wished to hear. But if Schwartz was not deep in the tender mysteries of refined and delicate love, no man better understood a hint, or better knew how to improve it. He accordingly interrupted the conversation, just to say that he brought important intelligence, which must be communicated that night; adding that he would leave them together for an hour. He now withdrew, and afforded the desired opportunity for unreserved conversation.

"My Delia," said Douglas; "I understand that she is well, and, I hope, happy."

"She is happy," said Arthur. "She hears of

you, from the impartial voice of public fame, in
terms that fill her heart with pride, and leave no
room there for alarm or melancholy. She feels as
becomes a soldier's wife, anxious for her husband's
fate, but confident in his fortunes. She has caught
this notion from Mr. B——, who is her oracle, and
who seems to have imparted to her, not only all his
sentiments, but all the energy and buoyancy of his
self-confident mind."

"Thank God!" said Douglas.   "Just so would
I have her to be. I knew it would be so. I saw
her noble mother, when danger threatened my
uncle; and I saw her too.   But this is the first positive information, on *that* point, that has reached me
since I have been here.   Mr. B—— and I can only
correspond by messages through Schwartz, and
though he is plain and accurate as a printed book in
repeating what he understands, yet ideas of this sort
are not in his line.   And my good and venerable
old father—are you here with his permission?"

"I am not; nor does he know where I am.   I
have no doubt that I should have his approbation if
he did.   I am sure *you* have."

"I!" exclaimed Douglas, with a start of violent
surprise.   "What does he know of me?"

"Nothing at all," said Arthur, smiling.   "But he
knows of a certain partisan leader, whom the world
calls Captain Douglas, and if I can read the old
man's eyes, when he hears that name, he would
rather call that man his son than any other on earth."

As Arthur spoke the eyes of Douglas filled, and, pressing his hand to his brow, he bowed his head a moment on the table. Then rising, he stood erect, and looking up with a rapt and abstracted air, his eye flashing through his tears, he folded his arms, and speaking in the measured tone of one who feels deeply, but in whose mind thought masters feeling, he parodied that noble speech which Shakspeare puts in the mouth of Prince Henry:

> "Then in the closing of some glorious day,
> When I shall wear a garment all of blood,
> And stain my favors with a bloody mask,
> I will be bold to tell him, 'I am your son.'"

"And my Delia!—my virgin bride! O! for that day,

> "When woman's pure kiss, sweet and long,
> Welcomes her warrior home."

"I tell you, Arthur, that, in thoughts like these, there is a rapture which makes this hole in the rock a palace, and this flinty couch a bed of down. Are you prepared, my dear fellow, to partake with me in such feelings? That, I know, depends in part on Lucia. What of her?"

"She is to me," said Arthur, "all that Delia is to you; though she is too young to have the same strength of mind, and I have no right to expect the same confidence in my prowess and fortunes."

"Never fear. It will not be wanting at the pinch.
A woman never fears for the safety of him she
loves but when she doubts his truth. Let her feel
that she is his second self, and self-confidence calms
her fears. Let her feel that she lives in his heart,
and, strong in love, she defies the dagger which as-
sails it. Calpurnia trembled for Cæsar. Why?
He was the husband of every woman in Rome.
Had he been true to her, she would have felt only
that prudent fear that he would not have derided.
He would, perhaps, have yielded to her discreet
remonstrance, and her love would have justified the
confidence which characterizes the love of woman,
by saving his life. But, what a rhapsody I am
uttering! You say my father does not know where
you are? How is that?"

"I was not at liberty to acquaint him with your
secret. Your absence has drawn on him some displeasure from those in power, and their minions are
all around him. It seems that you are supposed to
be in the South for no good purpose, and not without an understanding with him. My disappearance
will attract farther notice. For that he cares little;
but he is so scrupulous in his notions of honor and
truth, that, were he questioned about us, he could
hardly conceal any thing he might know. Your
letters, I see, still come from the South, though they
say nothing of your whereabout. Of course, he
thinks you are there; and I, without undeceiving
him, simply asked leave to go to look for you. That

his feelings are with us, I have no doubt. But he is so beset by spies, and so hampered by the position of our brothers in the army and navy, that he even tries to hide the secret of his thoughts from himself."

Thus the brothers conversed until Schwartz returned and claimed the Captain's ear; who began by asking what news he brought from B——.

" The Colonel (so he always designated B——) likes your plan mightily, sir," replied Schwartz, " if you can rub through with it. But he is afraid, from all he can learn, that them fellows at Lynchburg may be too many for you; so, he says, you must find out exactly how that is, and if you don't think it a pretty good chance, just slip down along the line, toward the middle of November, and join him."

" If I do so, where am I to find him precisely?" asked Douglas.

" Just where the Petersburg railroad crosses the line," said Schwartz. " You see the folks there are all friendly, because as long as things stay as they are, their railroad an't worth an old flint, and so they are patching up all the old cars, and fixing every thing for the Colonel, as soon as he can start a regiment or so, to make a dash at Petersburg, and so hold on there till the rest of his men join him. Now, if we were to be the first there, Captain, I have a notion that we'd be the very boys for them chaps at Petersburg."

" I should like that well," said Douglas. " But

I understand my old acquaintance, Col. Mason, at Lynchburg, has a great desire to see me, and I should hate to disappoint him."

"I don't think he commands there now," said Schwartz. "There is another regiment come from the North to join him, and they say the other is the oldest colonel."

"That is of course," said Douglas, "for Mason is the youngest in the army. But I am not sorry for the exchange, for they have hardly sent as good a one. There is not a man among them I would not rather meet than Mason. Have you been able to learn the particulars of their force there?"

"As well as I can understand," replied Schwartz, "the whole number is not far from a thousand, and may be a few more."

"A thousand! Can we raise men enough to strike at them before they think of it?"

"I have not a doubt of it, sir, if we could get at them on fair terms. The people along down between here and Staunton river don't like the thoughts of what them fellows may do to them, and they are keen to take them before they are ready. I talked to the head-men among them, as you told me, and they all see that the right way is to try to get the first blow. Because, you see, Captain, when we an't gaining we are losing. If we let the enemy hold Lynchburg, and they find two regiments will not do, they will bring four, and so on, till they get the upper hand, and then they will pay these poor fellows about here for old and new. But if we could make out to give them a real beating, and so drive them clean off, why all the country as far as the Rappahannock would rise that minute, and they'd have enough to do to hold their own at Fredericksburg."

"I suppose you said all this to Mr. B—— ?"

" To be sure I did, sir; and he thinks just as we do about it, only he is dubious about attacking a fortified camp, as they call it, just with rifles."

" He is right about that," replied Douglas. " Riflemen are the best troops in the world to defend a breastwork, but they are the worst to attack one. I had hopes, however, that we might have drawn out the enemy by some device, even when Mason commanded. He is too brave to be ashamed to be prudent. I wish I knew whom they have sent to supersede him. But, whoever he is, it is a hundred to one, that being set over the head of an abler man, he will be impatient to show his superiority by reversing his predecessor's plans, and shaming the prudence of Mason by some hasty display of valor. If I did but know who was in command !"

" I tried to find that out," replied Schwartz; " because I knew you were pretty well acquainted with the most of them. You remember, sir, you told me from the first almost exactly how this Col. Mason was going to do. But I could not find any body that could tell me the new Colonel's name. But, whoever he is, Mr. B—— thinks, and so do I (but that is nothing), and I have a notion you do too partly, sir, that if we mean to do any thing with them, we must try to catch them somewhere between here and Lynchburg."

"I am afraid that is all too true," said Douglas, "and if no such chance offers, we shall have to give them the slip as B—— proposes; and I should hate it."

"And so would I," said Schwartz; "and so, you see, sir, I have been trying to fix a sort of a plan to draw them out, and that is what I want to tell you about."

What this plan was, the next chapter shall disclose.

CHAPTER XXXII.

And yet I knew him a notorious liar;
Think him a great-way fool—solely a coward.
SHAKSPEARE.

"You must understand, Captain," continued
Schwartz, "that I had allotted to fall in with your
brother about Little Roanoke bridge, where our roads
come together. The people there are friendly, and
mighty clever people, and if they don't know all
about me, they don't want much of it; for they are
our own sort of folks, and true as steel. So I thought
I could depend on them to take notice for me when
such a man might pass, and let me know. When
I got there, by all I could learn, your brother had
not gone by; and, as I was pretty tired, and that is
one of the places where I commonly lie by to pick
up news, I thought I would stop a while.

"I had not been there long, before here comes
the Captain that commands the company at Farmville; and if ever I saw a conceited fool, you may
be sure he is one. What he was after, the Lord
knows. He said he was reconnoitring, but I have
a notion he was just looking for somebody to talk
to; and as the folks there ain't got much chat for

any body, he just claps to talking to me. And he
run on about one thing and another, and there was
nothing I wanted to know but what he told me, only
just I knew it all before. But I thought, may be, I
might get something out of him, so I let him talk,
and I sot and listened.

"After a while he gets to talking about you.
And, Lord! how he wished you would come in his
way; and how he would have served you, if you
had tried to beat up his quarters, like you did them
fellows at Lynchburg. But he was in hopes to
have a clip at you yet, only just you were always
hiding and skulking in the mountains, like a wolf,
and then coming down in the night to kill sheep.
And he reckoned *you knew* where the *dogs* was, and
took care to keep out of their way. And then he
laughed, and thought he was mighty smart. So,
thought I, 'stranger, if you have a mind to get into
hot water, may be you may have a chance.' So I
speaks up; and, says I, 'after all, that Captain
Douglas an't half the man he's cracked up for, no
how.' "

"Do you know him?" says he.

"I guess I do," says I; "he is cunning enough,
and he has got tricks enough, and signs and coun-
tersigns to keep out of harm's way; but," says I,
"if a man could just get hold of his signs, and
so get at him, he an't nothing for a right, real hard
fight."

"They tell me," says he, "there an't no such

thing as getting in twenty miles of him, or more, may be; and all the folks through the country there stands guard for him, and nobody else knows where he is."

"That's very true," says I; "but then you see, stranger, when too many folks has got a secret, then it an't a secret no more."

"It's a wonder," says he, "some of them don't tell."

"May be they cannot get any thing by telling," says I. "There's many a poor fellow there, to my knowing, that don't see a dollar once a year, and its mighty little the sight of a few yellow jackets would not make them tell, only just they never seed any, and don't know what they are. But they'll be right apt to find out."

"You talk like you know that part of the country," says he. "May be *you* know something about it."

"May be I might," says I. "But then," says I, "it don't become a poor fellow, like me, to know any thing that a grand officer, with his fine apperlets, all of solid gold, don't know. Lord!" says I, "if I had but half the money you give for your apperlets, I *reckon* I'd know something then."

And with that he looks right hard at me, and says he, "May be you'd like to list for a soldier."

"May be I would," says I, "if they pays me well. 'Cause, you see," says I, "sir, as to the country and the President, and all that, it's what I don't know nothing about; only I takes their part as takes my part. And that's the reason," says I, "I would not stay up yonder."

"Why," says he, "do you live there, when you are at home?"

"I cannot say," says I, "that I have got a home rightly anywhere. But I did *live* there, after a fashion; and they wanted me to do like the rest of them, and quit my business and keep guard, and stop every man that could not give the signs. And what was I to get by it? Just nothing at all. If I had any bread of my own to eat, why, I might eat it; and if I killed a deer, they'd take their share, and thought they did great things if they let me keep the skin; but as to pay, they don't think of such a thing. But that would not do for me," says I; "and, more than that, it won't do for more, besides me, whatever Captain Douglas may think of it, I can tell him."

"Well," says he, "if you'll list with me you shall have pay, and bounty, and clothes, and rations, and all. 'Cause," says he, "the President, he keeps the key of the treasury, and we are his soldiers, and we all live like fighting cocks, I can tell you."

"Well," says I, "I'd like to list well enough, only just I guess if once you had me for a soldier, you'd make me tell all I know, and ax me no odds; and," says I, "I have been a-thinking, if I could meet with any right clever gentleman, that would pay me for telling, I'd tell it all first, and then list afterwards."

"Well," says he, "do you know Douglas's signs, enough to carry a man to his camp as a friend?"

"I guess I do," says I, "and more than that, too."

"And what do you know?" says he.

"That's telling," says I.

"But," says he, "I *want* to know all about it," says he, "because Col. Mason, there, at Lynchburg, is determined to break Douglas up, if he can get at him; and he is looking every day for more men from the North to help him."

"Well," says I, "I can put him in a way to get at him, and not go up there into the mountains neither. 'Cause," says I, "that's an ugly place. It an't one regiment, nor two neither hardly, that could do much there. And then, again, if Douglas was to find too many coming against him, he'd be away t'other side of Salem before they'd get there."

"And how is a body to get at him?" says he.

"Ah!" says I, "that's a long story."

"Well," says he, "I see what you are after, and if you'll put me in a way to give Col. Mason a fair clip at him, it will make my fortune, and then I'll be bound to see you paid handsomely."

"That an't what I am after," says I.

"Why, don't you want money?" says he.

"To be sure I do," says I; "but that an't money."

"Well," says he, "tell me what you can do, and I will tell you what I'll do."

"That's something like," says I. "As to what I

can do, I can put you in a way to catch Captain Douglas out of the mountains, with as many men as you please to bring agin him."

"Well," says he, "if you'll do that, I'll pay you a hundred dollars."

"The dear Lord!" says I. "A hundred dollars! I never expected to have that much money in my life!"

"May be it's too much," says he. "May be fifty will do?"

"No, no," says I; "a hundred will do mighty well; so let me have the cash, and I'll tell you all."

"That won't do," says he. "How do I know that what you are going to tell me will do me any good?"

"Well," says I, "I reckon if one won't another will."

So, with that, he studied a while, and says he: "Well, I'll give you my note for a hundred dollars, to be paid directly after Col. Mason gets a lick at Douglas in the low country, by my help."

"Cannot you give me an order on Mr. Morton, here, in the same way?" says I.

"You are mighty tight," says he; "but may be I can."

So, with that he speaks to Mr. Morton, and he agreed to accept the order. You see, sir, Mr. Morton, as I told you, is a true-hearted Virginian; and he knows me, and I just sorter winked at him, to let him know all was safe. For as to that fellow paying him again after he paid me, Mr. Morton hadn't no thought of it, nor I neither. But he seed what I was after, and says he to the Captain : "To be sure, sir, it's nothing I would not do to serve the country." And with that they fixed the order all right, and gives it to me, and I slips it back again into Mr. Morton's hand. And then I takes the Captain out again, and tells him the way up here; and, says I, "Now, if you can get to see Captain Douglas, you must fix a good story to tell him."

"And what must that be?" says he.

"Why, you have only just to tell him that you have raised a parcel of men in Bedford county, or somewhere thereaway, sorter toward Lynchburg, and you want to know where to join him. Then he'll be sure to tell you when he is coming down out of the mountains, and he'll name a place for you to meet him at, and then if you don't fix him about right, it an't my fault."

"But how am I to get to him?" says he.

"That's it," says I, "and that's what you never could do without help. You see," says I, "sir, every man in that country lives by hunting, more or less; and every man has a rifle for himself, and one for every one of his boys, and may be more. And when a fellow is going anywhere, he never knows when he may see a deer; so you never can catch them without their rifles. But then you may travel all through the country, and you won't see a man that looks any ways like a soldier. And when they want to stop a man, they don't bawl at him and ask for the countersign. That sort of thing may do in an army, but it won't do with folks that have not got an army to back them. So you may fall in with ever so many of them, and they'll find you out; but if they choose to let you pass, you'll never find them out, nor know what they are after."

"But how are they to find me out," says he, "if they an't got no countersign?"

"They an't got no countersign, *rightly*," says I; "but it is pretty much the same thing, if a man asks you a civil question, and you don't know what answer to give him. Now, suppose you was travelling along there, and you meets one of them fellows, and he was to ask you, mighty innocent like, what parts you were from. What would you say?"

"I don't know," says he. "May be I'd tell him I was from down about Halifax court-house."

"And that minute," says I, "he'd know all about you."

"How's that?" says he.

"Why, that's the way they ax for the countersign," says I.

"What is the countersign?" says he.

"CURRITUCK," says I; "when they ax you that, you must say you come from Currituck."

"And is that all?" says he. "Why, that is a countersign, sure enough. But don't they never change it?"

"No," says I; "the men are too much scattered all

through the country, for that; but it answers mighty well, the way they fix it. They don't let you off with one question, just so, but they'll ask you a heap more; and they'll say a heap of simple things to you just to hear what you'll say; and just about the time you think you have fooled them, they'll find you out. There's a parcel of sharp fellows up thereaway, mind, I tell you; and you'll have to get your lesson mighty well before you go there. You see, some will ask you one question and some another. You don't know what it's going to be; so I must tell you all the straight of it, and you must practise before we part; and then," says I, " you can write it all down, and all the way you go you can be saying it over." So, with that, sir, I tells him the biggest part of our questions; but you may be sure I gave him wrong answers to every one of them. But then I told our people at the different stations along about him, and told them to pass him, and never let him know but what his answers were all right. So then I tells him that when he got to you, you would want to know, may be, how he came by the signs; and, says I, " when he axes you that, you must tell him you got them from Job Dixon," says I. " That's a fellow the Captain keeps busy recruiting away down the country, and when he hears that, he won't suspicion you the least in the world; 'cause you see," says I, " the man they call Job Dixon has got another name besides that, and that name an't nothing but a sort of a countersign for the Captain to know the men by that he sends in." You see, Captain, I fixed all this way, that I might let you know exactly, so that if the fellow should come when I was out of the way, you might know what to think of him, just as if I was here. And it won't do to let him see me, no how."

"*Job Dixon !*" said Douglas. " Well, let me make a memorandum of that name."

Saying this, he took a letter from his pocket, and endorsing the name of Job Dixon on the back of it, as that of the writer, threw it on the table.

"That will do," said Schwartz. " He will be here bright and early in the morning, and when he sees that, he will feel as safe as a rat in a mill."

"Here in the morning !" said Douglas. "How can you be sure of that ?"

" I seed him from the top of the mountain," replied Schwartz, " when Witt stopped him. I told Witt to keep him all night, and send him on in the morning, with a couple of fellows to show him the way, and guard him."

" If that is the case," said Douglas, " I can meet him at the piquet, and stop him there ; for I would rather he should not see this place. But what arrangement would you advise me to make with him ?"

" Why, the Colonel says," replied Schwartz, " that he wants you to join him at his rendezvous about the last of November, or may be a little earlier ; so whatever you do ought to be done time enough to fall back, if we get worsted, and slip along down the line, according to your old plan. So I am a thinking it would be well to fix the time for meeting this fellow about the tenth of the month, and then, if we can catch them in their own trap, we shall have time to follow up the blow and break up their whole establishment there at Lynchburg, and then march boldly down the straight road."

"Do you know of any crossing-place on Staunton river, in the direction of Lynchburg," asked Douglas, "that would answer for an ambuscade?"

"I have a notion," said Schwartz, "that Jones's Ford would suit as well as any other; because there's a deep hollow comes down on both sides of it, and thick woods on the hills."

"That will do then," said Douglas. "So now let us take our supper and go to rest; for I must be at the piquet in time to meet your man. Before you go to sleep, suppose you send one of our boys to tell them to stop him if he gets there before me."

The supper was produced, and fully justified what Witt had told Arthur of the fare he might expect. As to lodging, bear-skins were plenty, and so were blankets, which had been collected during the expedition against Lynchburg. But a rock is a hard bed, put on it what you will. Yet youth, and health, and high excitement, gave Arthur a most luxurious supper, and a night of such sleep as the best lodged prince in Europe might envy.

CHAPTER XXXIII.

The sunken glen, whose sunless shrubs must weep.

WHEN Arthur awoke, he found himself alone. The sun was high in the heavens, but a deep shadow hung over the dark glen, into which his rays never looked, except at noon-day. Arthur now walked out, and amused himself with gazing around on the singular spot which his brother had chosen as a place of refuge. It was, indeed, a place of strength, which seemed calculated to bid defiance to any thing but famine.

The glen, at this point, might be some two hundred feet deep. Above and below, the little stream filled the whole chasm, pouring furiously along between overhanging cliffs. The tops of these, except in the immediate vicinity, were crowned with lofty trees, which, nodding to each other across the gulph, in some places nearly intermingled their branches. The valley, just where Douglas had pitched his camp, was somewhat wider. Just above, the stream seemed to gush from the very bowels of the mountain, dashing, as it tumbled over a fall of twenty or thirty feet, against the dark evergreens which clustered both sides of the gulph. From

thence, flowing through a wider space, it still confined itself to a narrow and deep channel, scooped
into an almost cavernous bed, under the western
cliff. Thence, turning abruptly to the southeast, it
swept across the dell to the opposite hill, from which
it again recoiled in like manner. There was thus,
on each side, between the hill and the receding
stream, a spot of dry ground, or rather rock. It was
indeed nothing but a rocky shelf, a little above inun-
dation, jutting in a half moon from the base of the
cliff. About the middle of its passage from hill to
hill, the stream tumbled over a ledge, the highest
points of which, rising above the water, served as
stepping stones, and afforded a passage across, practicable indeed, but neither commodious, nor to the
eye of a stranger, even safe.

The sort of stair which afforded the only approach
to this savage den, hung directly over the stream, at
the point where, having crossed from the western
side of the glen, it again whirled back, leaving, as I
have said, a dry spot on its eastern margin. At the
upper corner of this shelf, where it touched the cliff,
the path reached the bottom ; and an hundred yards
below, at the lower extremity of the same platform,
hung the tent-cloth that indicated the quarters of the
chief.

The sort of cave, the mouth of which was concealed by this, was but a deepening of the recess
under the cliff, which every where afforded a partial
shelter from the weather, and a complete defence

against rocks tumbled from above.   Under this
were the rude beds and camp-fires of the men, and
in front of them a breast-work of logs, raised high
enough to afford protection from any shot fired from
the opposite hill.   Between the upper log and that
next below it, was a sort of loop-hole, made by cutting corresponding notches in each ; and as the edges
of the cliffs had been shorn of all their growth, a
man could not show himself on either, without
being exposed to the fatal fire of men directing their
aim with a rest, and in all the coolness of perfect
safety.

The most curious part of the whole establishment
was a sort of mill.   At the point where the stream,
breaking over the rocky ledge of which I have spoken,
swept away around the shoulder of the platform, was
placed a small log pen.   The end of a shaft, projecting from it, overhung the water.   Into this were
driven stakes, fitted at one end into large auger-holes,
and, at the other, spread out like a broad oar.   These
fan-like extremities dipped in the water, and, yield-
ing to its force, kept the shaft revolving night and
day.   Machinery equally rude connected its movements with those of a pair of light mill-stones, which
found no rest, and required no attention.   Though
grinding less than a bushel in the hour, it still ground
on and on, affording coarse bread for the whole
company and showing how true the old adage, that
" fair and softly go far in a day."   One man was
seen to replenish the hopper.   Others were passing

and repassing, each with his share of meal. The whole was covered with rude boards. Exposed to the fire of each cliff, it was, of course, capable of being made to command both, and some of its features showed that it was intended to be occupied as a tower of strength in case of attack.

In short, to the unpractised eye of Arthur, the whole presented the appearance of impregnable security and well arranged preparation. There was indeed no present danger, but the place had been chosen and fitted with a view to the last extremity. The course of the stream, tending to the south, led in a few miles into the State of North Carolina, and in that direction there was an outlet practicable, though difficult. Between the camp and the State line there was no point at which the glen could be entered; and Douglas, if driven to retreat in that direction, had none but natural obstacles to overcome.

Cold weather was now approaching, and there was no station where the troops of Douglas were so little exposed to the severity of the season as this. The soft air from the waterfall, though never warm, was never intensely cold, and no other wind but that from the south ever entered the glen. Hence as many men as were not engaged on active duty were assembled here. Still the number present was but small. Some were at the piquet, some on the scout. Besides, it was now the hunting season, and many were abroad in the woods, as the carcasses brought in during the course of the morning plainly showed.

Arthur now looked around for Schwartz; and hearing his voice behind one of the breast-works, passed around the end of it, and silently joining the circle, listened to his discourse, which seemed to be a sort of military lecture.

"You see, boys," said he, "as to *tictacs*, or whatever they call it, that sort of thing an't made for the like of us. When a parcel of fellows lists for soldiers, just because they an't got nothing else to do, and may be one half of them is cowards, and the other half not much better, they are obliged to have rules to go .by. Because, if once you can beat it into a fellow's head that after he has got into danger it is safer for him to stand still than to run away, why then the worse scared he is the surer he will be to stay there. But it an't so with us, because if any of us was any way scary, he would not be here no how. The only rule for us is the Indian rule.

"In the first place, it is our business always to know where the inimy is before he knows where we are, and then, if we don't want to fight him, keep out of his way. Now the right way to do that, is just to squander, like a flock of partridges.

"Then if you are going to fight, the only rule is to give the word, and let every man kill all he can, and take care of himself the best he can. Now that way the riglars fight; if one man in ten kills a man, they call it desperate bloody work. But I reckon if there was an inimy now coming up the valley to the foot of the Devil's Back-bone, and the word was, to kill all we could before he got there, any of us here would feel mighty cheap if he did not kill somebody.

"And mind, boys, whether we fight or run, whether we keep together, or squander, 'two and two, is the word. You must all mate yourselves two and two, to stand together and run together, to fight together and die together. One of you must call himself number one, and the other number two, and then, if there's a hundred together and the inimy comes number two never fires till number one has fired and loaded again. You see, men, a fellow takes good aim, when he knows there's another one by, to hit if he misses ; and fifty rifles in that way, will do more than a hundred when every one knows that's his last chance. Fifty rifles will stop a troop of horse, and a hundred cannot do no more. But if the guns are all empty, then here comes what's left of them slashing away with the broad-swords like devils. But let there be a few more guns to pepper away at them while the first are loading, and they will go to the right-about mighty quick.

" Now mind what I tell you, boys, and the first time it comes to the pinch, you'll say old Schwartz didn't fight Indians so long for nothing. And as to running, any man that's afraid to run when he sees cause, is half a coward, any how. Do you run just when you please. Egad ! I'd hate to depend on a man to fight that I could not trust to run. There is no harm in running, if you know where you are running to, and your friends know it too; and the right way is to fix a place, every morning, to meet at night, and let every man get there as he can, and do what mischief he can. But, mind, if it comes to that, always run two and two, and then one can help another; and if one comes up missing, the other can tell what's become of him.

"I'm telling our boys," continued Schwartz, who now observed Arthur, "some of the lessons I learned among the Shawnees. You see, Mr. Arthur (you must not think strange of my calling you so, sir, for all your family seem like my own flesh and blood to me—for all you don't know how that is); you see, sir, the Captain is a regular officer, built plumb from the ground up; but for all that, he knows that all this is true; and, before now, when he and I have been sitting over the fire, at night, he has told me about one Gineral Braddock, I think they called him, that got his men shot all to pieces, and himself too, just because he would not believe that there was any other way to fight but just his way. Now, you see, sir, the reason why he was taken at an *onplush* was, that he was fighting agin Indians. Well, suppose we fight Indian-fashion; will not that be pretty much the same thing? May be we an't exactly up to that, but we must do the best we can; for as to fighting the riglars just in their own way, why they'll beat us as long as the sun shines.

"Do you mind that night," continued Schwartz, laughing, "when the Lieutenant and his men came there to your uncle's to take him and the Captain? That was Indian play for you. Egad! if I had not *heard* that the Colonel was there, I should have knowed he was at the fixing of that business. You see, sir, that is what a man learns by living in places where a body is never safe; and the upshot of it is, that after a while he gets so that he never can be in any danger. It's like learning to sleep with one eye always open."

Schwartz now rose from the ground, where he had been sitting, and brushing the ashes from his leathers, joined Arthur, and they repaired to the tent where their simple meal awaited them. From him the youth learned that his brother had repaired to the piquet at an early hour; and to the piquet, gentle reader, *we* will now follow.

CHAPTER XXXIV.

―――――――――――― He has merit,
Sufficient for itself its own reward.
Why think of him!   An honorable fool,
He seeks no other guerdon.

ANONYMOUS.

DOUGLAS was at the piquet long enough before the arrival of his guest, to make such arrangements as should prevent the stranger from suspecting that this was not the camp he was desirous to see.   He had no mind that his enemy should know the real nature and precise position of his main stronghold.   Hence he had determined to give him the meeting at the piquet, and took pains to provide, as if for his own ordinary accommodation, such a breakfast as he would have been content to furnish at his own quarters for the most honored visiter.

The spy, who had learned little of his profession but that self-indulgent art which is technically called "playing old soldier," had been in no haste to leave his rest, and Witt, who understood Schwartz's game, did not hurry him.   The breakfast hour, therefore, had fully arrived before he made his appearance.   He came accompanied by Witt and another of his party;

and, in appearance and manners, fully answered the description of him given by Schwartz. He was a tall, red-haired man, vain, pert, and full of self-complacency. Indeed, so much did he display of a satisfaction, at once chuckling and childish, that Douglas, even though unwarned, must have suspected treachery. Besides, he never could have believed a being, manifestly so frivolous and foolish, capable of the high purpose of devoting himself to a life of toil, hardship, and danger. The vain and self-indulgent may receive momentary impulses, under the influence of which brilliant achievements may be suddenly accomplished; but from such the tasks of study, virtue, and enduring courage, must never be expected.

He seemed, at first, more intent upon his breakfast than anything else, and when it appeared, made faces at his coarse fare which ill accorded with his professed indifference to all personal inconvenience. But, bad as it was, he contrived to swallow enough to show that he was not prepared to play the ascetic any more in regard to the quantity than the quality of his food·

"You see," said Douglas, "the life we lead. If you are not prepared to submit cheerfully to privations, compared to which what you see here is luxury, you should not join us."

"Damn luxury," said the other. "What do I care about luxury? To be sure, I have been used to it all my life; coffee or tea, one, every morning for breakfast; and good light bread, and potatoes, and pies; and then, for dinner, pork or fresh meat, or codfish, at least every day in the week, and all sorts of *sass*, and then pies again, and cheese, and all that. But I am ready to give it all up to serve my country, and live as hard as any body."

"I am glad to hear it," said Douglas, drawing some papers from his pocket. Among these he affected to search in vain for a particular paper, and in doing so, carelessly threw on the table the letter endorsed with the name Job Dixon. He saw that it caught the other's eyes, and, expressing some dissatisfaction at his own carelessness, said : " You have a right to know, before you join us, all about our force, and I ought to show you my last return; but I have it not at hand, though I believe I know pretty well the number of my men. But stay," continued he, interrupting himself with a start, and looking at the gallant Captain with a keenness that made his very back ache, "how came you by my pass-words, sir?"

"I got them from a man they call Job Dixon," replied the trembling Captain.

" Job Dixon !" replied Douglas, immediately resuming his complacency ; " then all is right."

" O yes! all is right," said the other, recovering from his alarm, but more fluttered and confused than ever. " He told me that wa'nt his name, sure enough, and he said that name was only a sort of a countersign to you."

It cost Douglas some effort to suppress a smile at seeing the delicate and dangerous office of a spy undertaken by one so destitute of all the qualities necessary to it; but he commanded himself, and asked whether the other was now content to join him.

"To be sure I am," said he; "and not only I, but fifty more as good fellows as ever stepped shoe-leather. You see, that was what I doubted about. I thought may be as I had such a company, I had a right to set up for myself; but after I heard all about you from that man, Job Dixon, or whatever else his name is, I made up my mind to join you."

"Where are your men?" asked Douglas.

"They are all about home yet," said the Captain, "but I can bring them together any day, and any place you please to name. I suppose you don't mean to stay up here in the mountains all the time, and may be it might suit as well for me to fall in with you somewhere."

"That is true," said Douglas, "We are not so well off here for rations, as to want any body before we have use for them. As long as we stay here we are strong enough. A regiment of men could not climb the Devil's Back-bone before our faces. But I propose to move shortly, and should be glad of a reinforcement on the way. What county are your men in?"

"In Bedford county," replied the other, repeating his lesson exactly.

"That will do, then," said Douglas. "I propose to march against Mason, at Lynchburg, early in November, and on the fifth day of the month I will meet you at Jones's Ford, on Staunton river."

"I cannot say that I know exactly where that is," said the spy.

"It is little out of your way into any part of Bedford county," said Douglas; "and as I want to see some of our friends down in that quarter, I will ride there with you. I am told Mason is pretty strong, and I want to get all the force I can, and that is not so much but what I shall be glad of your help."

"How many men have you?" asked the Yankee Captain.

"I have but a handful *here*, just now; but I am sending out orders for more to join on the route, and I am in hopes to reach the river with four hundred at least. I shall stay there, at all events, till more come in; because it would be foolish to attack Mason's regiment with less than five or six hundred."

"That will do," said the other; "for Mason is not more than four hundred strong."

"Indeed!" replied Douglas, affecting surprise and pleasure. "Then I am pretty sure of him. I had heard as much before, but I don't trust every body. I was afraid there was a trap set for me; but now I am satisfied, and if I can leave Staunton river with six hundred men, I shall gather force enough before I get to Lynchburg to drive Mason and his regiment before me like chaff."

Having said this, Douglas set about the necessary arrangements for accompanying his new acquaintance to Jones's Ford. As the distance was too great for one day, he proposed to pass the night at the house of a trusty friend, from whence the Yankee officer would have it in his power to reach a tavern, two miles beyond the river, the next day. He now despatched a note to Arthur, saying that he wished to examine the ground at the river, in company with him and Schwartz. He therefore directed them to follow at a cautious distance, so as not to be seen by the spy; to pass them in the night, and take up their quarters at a house in advance, and the next day proceed to the dwelling of Mr. Gordon (a staunch friend), near the river, and wait for him there. Meantime a horse, that stood piqueted hard by, was saddled, and Douglas set out, accompanied by the treacherous Captain and the faithful Witt.

The journey was made without any occurrence worth noting. In the conversation of the stranger there was nothing to beguile Douglas from his own thoughts. The vain babble of the prating coxcomb was all wasted on the impenetrable Witt; and, after a few fruitless attempts to overcome the taciturnity of his companions, he followed their example, and the greater part of the journey was made in silence. Late on the second evening they reached the river. The spy was directed to the public-house on the other side, and Douglas and Witt returned to Mr. Gordon's, where they found Arthur and Schwartz.

As they were now in a land of civilization and comfort, Douglas was not sorry to obtain, once more, a good night's lodging, which his hospitable friend was delighted to afford. But this rare enjoyment did

not make him forgetful of the necessity of watching
the motions of his enemy. He accordingly despatched
a scout to the house to which the Yankee had been
directed, to make sure that he had gone on.

At a late hour the man returned, and roused
Douglas to inform him that the spy had indeed gone
as far as he had intended, and that he had there
fallen in with a party of a dozen dragoons, commanded by a subaltern, who were on a scout through
the country. With this officer he had been seen to be
engaged in private and earnest conversation, and
orders had been issued to the men to look well to
the condition of their arms, and to be in readiness
to move at day-light.

It at once occurred to Douglas that a new scheme
had entered the head of the vain and frivolous being
who had thrust himself into an affair requiring
qualities so different. It was probable that he wished
to avail himself of the presence of this little party to
endeavor to surprise his enemy, whom he had reason
to believe to be still near the Ford. The folly of risk-
ing the defeat of his favorite enterprise by joining in
the attempt, and thus throwing off his mask, was not
likely to occur to him. The question with Douglas
was, whether by abiding the attack he should afford
the bungling fool, whom he had been leading into
his own trap, a chance to escape from it by his own
blunder. In this apprehension, however, he did not
give that worthy due credit for his discretion. He
had indeed considered Douglas as his proper prey;

and though he had been unable to restrain his disposition to babble, he sorely repented his indiscretion, when he found the other officer disposed to anticipate him. He had accordingly earnestly dissuaded him from attempting any thing ; and, not prevailing in this, had determined to go on alone, and leave the other to execute his project as he might.

But though uncertain what might be the conduct of the spy, Douglas could not resist his inclination to throw himself in the way of the expected attack. It was necessary that he should examine the ground carefully, and he had not time to wait until the scouting party should have left the neighborhood. Besides, he was anxious to inform himself precisely of the force and position of the enemy, and the name of their new commander. For this purpose he was eager to make at least one prisoner. And, after all, perhaps not the least moving consideration, was his desire to taste once more the stormy joy of battle.

Upon the whole, he determined to turn the tables on his enemy, if possible ; and, instead of returning to bed, prepared immediately for action. All things were soon ready. The master of the house, his two sons, and three of the neighbors, who, hearing that he was there, had called to see him, added to his own party, made a force of ten men, with which he was not afraid to abide the attack of thirteen. At the head of these he took the road, and by daylight had occupied the ground where he wished to meet the enemy.

At the point of which we speak, the road, after passing for some miles over a broad and level ridge, at the distance of a quarter of a mile from the river, dives suddenly into a steep defile between two hills. The descent is rapid, and, in less than a hundred yards, the hills come down abruptly on either hand, leaving between them barely space enough for the road, which is quite narrow. They are steep, rugged, with projecting rocks, and altogether impracticable to cavalry; and are moreover covered with a heavy growth of timber and brushwood. At the distance of about two hundred yards from the plain above, the road turns sharp to the right. It then pursues a course nearly direct, for a like distance; and then, turning short to the left, the river, ford, and the opposite landing, are at once in full view.

A point a little below the first mentioned bend was selected by Douglas for his position. He posted Witt and three others on one side of the road, behind rocks and trees, while he, Arthur, and one more, disposed themselves, in like manner, on the other. Schwartz, with the rest, passed through the defile, with orders to hide themselves near the bank, and let the enemy pass without interruption. A pole had been thrown across the road, some twenty yards in front of Douglas and his party. The crossing of this, by the enemy, was to be the signal for firing: The officer was designated to be the mark of Witt. The right and left hand man of the leading file, had each his appropriate executioner appointed; then the two next, and then two more, were in like manner foredoomed, so that no shot should be thrown away. While these arrangements were making, Arthur bethought him of Schwartz's lecture on tactics, and was at once sensible of the vast superiority of untaught courage and sagacity, on occasions like this, over the sort of discipline on which the martinet is so apt to pride himself.

About sunrise, the enemy appeared, consisting, as the scout had said, of a dozen men, under the command of a single officer. To the great relief of Douglas, the redoubtable Yankee Captain was not with them. As the hill was steep, they advanced in a walk, while the officer, who was in the rear, occasionally turned his horse's head to the hill, seeming to examine for some recess in which his party might draw aside, and form a sort of ambuscade. But there was no such spot. The ground was every where too steep for cavalry; and, disappointed, he put spurs to his horse, and pushed forward to resume his place at the head of the party. They were now near the fatal point; every rifle was in rest, and duly levelled at its mark, and in the moment that the leading file were crossing the pole, six saddles were emptied, and six horses ran masterless. The aim of Witt at the officer, who was much more distant, and moving rapidly, was less fatal. But his ball took effect, as was plainly shown by the sword arm, which, at the moment, fell powerless. The men went to the right-about in a moment, and a shout, which the echoes of the steep gorge multiplied into a hundred voices, sent them down the hill at full speed.

The officer, though wounded, was not quite so ready to take to his heels, and called to his men to halt. With all but one, he succeeded; but that one, wild with terror, dashed on. In the mean time, Schwartz and his little party had planted themselves in the road, near the river, and their array was the first object that met the eye of the affrighted soldier as he turned the angle of the road. But panic is as apt to hurry a man into danger as away from it, and the sight of this new enemy only urged the poor wretch to a more desperate effort to escape, by breaking by them. In vain did the men throw up their arms, and call to him to stop. He rushed on, right upon Schwartz, who stood in the middle of the road, and who, as a *dernier ressort*, stopped his career with a bullet. The report of his rifle, and a glimpse of Douglas's men advancing along the side of the hill to get within shot, decided the officer that it was time to look to his safety. Turning the angle of the road, he saw the fate of his fallen soldier, and the cause of it. Immediately calling on his men to follow, he dashed on with an impetuosity which showed a determination to force a passage or perish.

The result was inevitable. Schwartz was in the act of loading his rifle. The other three levelled theirs. They had not been trained in Schwartz's school of tactics, and all three, attracted by the epaulette and plume and sash of the officer, fired at him. He fell dead, and the rest, perceiving their advantage, rushed on the mountaineers, who, of necessity, sprang aside, and let them pass. One of them was not so nimble, but that, as he clambered up the rocky face of the hill, a sweeping back-handed stroke inflicted a deep gash in the back part of his thigh. This was the only injury received by the party of Douglas in the affair, and dearly did it cost the man who gave it. Schwartz marked him, and coolly went on loading his rifle. By the time he had effected this, the soldier was half way across the river, and, the next moment, tumbled from his horse, and went floating down the stream. The other five gained the shore before another rifle could be loaded, and doubling a rocky point around which the road turned, disappeared.

CHAPTER XXXV.

THIS victory, though on a small scale, was complete in itself. It was a favorable omen, too, and might serve as a sort of rehearsal of the more important battle to be fought on the same ground. In one thing only Douglas had been disappointed, by the eagerness of Schwartz's men. He had made no prisoners, and the fallen enemy were all either dead, or not in condition to be harassed by such questions as he wished to ask. They were necessarily committed to the care of such of the party as lived in the neighborhood; and their horses and arms being secured, were placed in the same hands for safe keeping.

The feelings of Arthur, as he looked on this fearful scene of slaughter, were such as might be expected to possess the mind of a youth, who, as yet, had never seen the blood of man shed in strife. But these are nothing to the purpose of my tale. It is enough to say, that the contemplation of it wrought the usual change in his character. He now felt that to kill or be killed was the order of the day; and, though his next sleep was haunted by visions of the ghastly objects that lay before him, he awoke from it with a mind prepared for the stern duties of war.

Requesting the company and advice of his host, Douglas now proceeded to examine the ground. He found the river hills every where intersected, on both sides of the river, by ravines such as that I have described. The ford was shallow, but just above was deep water, which, on the north side, came down quite near to the gravel bar, which served as a dam. Here a steep and high rock bounded the river, and along the base of it, the water eddied in a deep pool, and then swept away in a strong but shallow current. At a short distance below was the mouth of a ravine, overgrown with lofty trees, and clustering with brushwood, at a distance of fifty yards from the landing place. The road, issuing from the river at the foot of the rock, holds a straight course for twenty yards, or thereabouts, and then turning short to the left, is no more in sight of the river. From thence a short but steep ascent through a deep cleft in the hills, brings the traveller to the top, where he turns again to the right, and resumes the direction towards Lynchburg. After a thorough examination of the whole, the party returned to breakfast at the house of Mr. Gordon.

Douglas rode slowly and thoughtfully. At length he said apart to Schwartz:

"Your plot is admirable; but I am afraid it will fail."

"What chance of that?" asked Schwartz. "They

will be ashamed to bring more than a thousand men against you, even if they had them. We can raise as many as they can, and we shall be on the ground, and have the same advantage we had just now."

"But suppose they come and take possession first," said Douglas.

"Oh! no danger of that. They'll be in no hurry to leave their snug quarters any sooner than they can help; and we can be here a day or two before the time."

"It may be so," said Douglas; "but I don't think Col. Mason takes me for an absolute fool; and if he does, he has reason to know that I have sharp-witted men about me. But any man's wits may fail him sometimes. For example, it has never occurred to either of us, that Mason will certainly not believe that we have been fooled by such a fellow as this Yankee of yours. Will he not, therefore, at once suspect the truth, and conclude that we are trying to catch him in his own trap?"

"Egad!" said Schwartz, "that is true. I had not thought of that. The fellow is too silly to be made bait of, sure enough. But then, you see, Captain, we can fix them any how. Mr. Gordon here can raise men enough, in three days, to keep them from crossing the river, until we are ready for them; and then you know, we can push across a part of our men, and toll them over. If once we get them into a right sharp fight, they'll follow us across the river fast enough."

"I have no doubt of their coming to look for us," said Douglas; "and no doubt of a fight; but we must be prepared to meet more men than we have bargained for. Depend upon it, they will bring every man they can raise. Why, would you believe it, the fellow talked to me about living at home on codfish, and potatoes, and cider, and pies, and *all sorts of sass?* Such a simpleton could not impose on a child. Col. Mason has talents worthy of a better cause, and he will see through the whole affair. I suppose he is superseded; but he is an honorable man, and will frankly give the benefit of his suspicions to his superior, who can hardly be such a fool as to disregard his suggestions. We must bestir ourselves, therefore, or give up the game and escape from our own plot.

"Gentlemen," continued Douglas, speaking aloud, and in a sustained and decisive tone, "this is our place of rendezvous; the time mid-day on the third of November. Every man must come prepared for action, and such as mean to accompany me to the lower country, must bring with them all their necessaries. Mr. Gordon, I must depend on you to hold this pass, and keep the enemy from crossing the river. I shall send a force to support you, if necessary. You, Schwartz, know what to do better than I can tell you. You, Witt, will return with me, and we will talk as we ride, of what is to be done. Mr. Gordon, *we* could travel without food, but our horses cannot. We must trouble you for something for all, and then we part until the day of rendezvous. Until that time, ' Vigilance and Activity' is the word; but then, ' FREEDOM, INDEPENDENCE, and GLORY.' "

As Douglas said this they arrived at Mr. Gordon's door. The ready meal was hastily swallowed, the horses fed, and they departed for the camp. On the way Schwartz, turning to the left, kept a southward course through the district, along the foot of the mountains, to rouse the inhabitants in that quarter, and to collect a party to support Mr. Gordon. The rest returned to the camp, from whence runners were despatched throughout all the adjacent country, and even beyond the mountain to the head-waters of the Holston. Leaving them thus employed, let us repair to the head-quarters of the enemy.

In the handsome parlor of a handsome house, in the suburbs of Lynchburg, we find two officers seated at a game of piquet. The hour is nine at night. The room is richly furnished. A bright fire burns on the hearth, and the blaze of sconce and astral lamps sheds its soft, luxurious, moonlight beams into every corner. Wine, cordials, fruits, and cigars, are placed on a table, and every thing betokens comfort and luxury, ease and indolence. The dress of these officers corresponds with the scene. Both glitter with gold and flutter in lace, and their richly mounted swords and highly finished pistols, which lie on the table, show that the owners abound in the means of display and self-indulgence.

Such was indeed the fact. The pay of the army, gradually increased by law during thirty years, had grown to a noble revenue. The *emoluments*, as they are called, under a system of fraud and connivance, had advanced (*without law*) yet more rapidly; so that to be a Colonel in the army of the United States was to be a rich man. Such was the rank of both these officers. It was true that the treasury had already begun to feel the drain of the vast sums accumulated under an iniquitous tariff, and now employed to fortify the tyranny that had enforced that pernicious system. The loss of the southern trade gave reason to fear that the supply now on hand, if once exhausted, would not be speedily renewed. But the rulers felt but the more sensibly that the energetic employment both of force and corruption was necessary to retain the little that remained, by holding Virginia in subjection. With this view, the same system of wasteful expenditure, commenced twenty years before, was kept up; and all who served the crown with becoming zeal were encouraged to hold open their mouths that they might be filled.

In another part of the room a company of subalterns fluttered around a bevy of fair damsels. To these young ladies the mistress of this mansion had of late become an object of much increased regard. No friend was so dear, no society so desirable, no house so pleasant to visit at as hers. Many an extra visit did she receive, since the abounding loyalty of her husband had invited the commandant of the post to make it his head-quarters. Many a wistful glance had been cast during the evening, from the assiduous subalterns, toward the handsome and unheeding wearer of two epaulettes, to whose authority all who approached him were bound to bow. But it was all in vain. Sufficient to himself, he valued not the admiring eyes which were bent upon him ; or if they occupied any thing of his attention, it was to be made the subject of invidious comparison with the ladies of the highest fashion in the northern cities, whose lavish attentions had rendered him totally heedless of the vulgar admiration of a parcel of half-bred Virginia girls.

These remarks, however, apply to only one of the officers in question. The other manifested no such insensibility, though his attentions to the fair were only marked by a staid courtesy, hardly more flattering than the perfect indifference of his companion. Still he paid such attention as it becomes a gentleman to pay to every thing that wears the exterior of a lady. But the day when he was himself an object of court to them was past. Indeed, the ladies had already begun to despair of thawing the coldness of his temperament, when being superseded by a younger and handsomer commander, he was laid on the shelf and condemned as quite *passé*.

But it is high time to make the reader acquainted with the two military gentlemen, to whose presence he has been introduced.

The reader, without doubt, already understands that, of the two officers before us, the elder in years, though the younger in commission, is Col. Mason, late commandant of the post. His companion is Col. Owen Trevor, whose impatience for distinction has been indulged by sending him to Lynchburg with his regiment. Here, taking rank of Mason, he has been in fact placed in command of a brigade, with an understanding that time and opportunity will be afforded him to show himself qualified for the rank, by discharging the functions of a brigadier. This post has been assigned him because in this direction is the only enemy actually in arms.

Although the force under the command of Douglas had been originally but a handful, Mason had seen that it possessed, in a marvellous degree, the faculty of occasional expansion. His intelligence had taught him to expect that it would ere long be greatly increased, if not crushed by a vigorous movement on his part. Hence he was desirous of acting on the offensive, especially as he had no doubt, from the past, that Lynchburg was the object of Douglas. But he had seen enough of the character and resources of his enemy to know that a small force would be unavailing, and had therefore earnestly desired to be reinforced. In answer to this request he had received, not the moderate aid that he had desired, but an order to surrender his command to Col. Trevor, whose well-appointed regiment was ordered to the post.

Col. Mason was a man of honor and talent. He was one of the many subjects of that strong delusion which had so extensively prevailed; and, under the influence of which, Virginia, for thirty years, had been sacrificing the *substance* of liberty and prosperity to the *forms* of a constitution devised to secure, but perverted to destroy them. He belonged, moreover, to that unfortunate class of partisans whom it is safe to neglect. Acting on *principles*, however erroneous, it was clearly seen that these alone were sufficient to bind him to the service to which he had devoted himself. It was at the same time little doubted that a change of opinions would be followed by a renunciation of all the advantages of his situation, whatever they might be. To waste on such a man the means of corrupting the corruptible, and securing the faithless, would indeed have been "ridiculous excess." He had won his way to his present rank by the strict performance of every duty of the subordinate offices, through which he had risen by regular gradation. In the shuffling and cutting of the military pack, he had seen junior officers placed above him by that sort of legerdemain which had so long before procured his master the name of the magician. He had not indeed acquiesced tamely in this, but means had been always found to soothe him, and he had been retained in the service by dexterous appeals to that magnanimity which they who knew not how to appreciate, yet knew well how to play upon.

But he had not yet forgotten how, ten years before, some pretext had been found for reversing the relative rank of himself and Col. Trevor, when both were very young and both subalterns. But on that occasion, as usual, some complimentary though temporary arrangement had been devised to reconcile him to that which gave the rank of Captain to one, whom he, still a Lieutenant, had once commanded. Having repressed his dissatisfaction at that time, he now felt bound to acquiesce in the circumstances which placed his former subordinate immediately in authority over him. If this occurrence made him repent his former tameness, now when it was too late to remonstrate, he did not say so, but addressed himself with grave precision to the fulfilment of all his commander's orders.

CHAPTER XXXVI.

Fortuna nimium quem fovet, stultum facit.

COLONEL TREVOR was the spoiled child of fortune and patronage. He was old enough to remember his father's rise in life. Hence, in estimating his consequence in society, he had formed a habit of comparing him with the class from which he sprung, and not with that more intellectual order of men, in which he had at last found his proper place, and where he had long remained stationary in well ascertained equality. This circumstance alone made an important difference between him and his younger brothers. The sort of retrospect with which he was most familiar teaches any thing but humility, however it may *impress* that lesson on the mind that has already learned it.

In the commencement of Col. Trevor's military career, the approbation of his father had been of more consequence to the usurper than now, when his throne stood strong on its own foundations. The character of that worthy gentleman, too, had been less understood. The President had not been aware how absolutely the convictions of his own mind and his high sense of duty supplied the place of those *douceurs*, the frequent repetition and continued expectation of which is necessary to bind the faith of the unprincipled. Before this discovery was made, Col. Trevor had been already advanced to a rank, and invested with an adventitious consequence, which made it important to cultivate him on his own account. His early training had taught him the grand maxim of the court: "Nothing ask, nothing have." He had discovered that any display of fixed principle, however favorable to the usurper's plans, was no passport to advancement; that rewards were only for the mercenary, and that they were always dispensed with a freedom duly proportioned to the eagerness with which they were sought. The caustic wit of John Randolph had unintentionally and almost with his last breath supplied the faction with a counter-sign not to be mistaken. If any man talked about his principles (as all men do and must at times), there was always at hand some dexterous pimp, whose business it was to ascertain their number. If they were found to be either more or less than seven, the discovery was fatal to his hopes of advancement.

The character of Douglas Trevor had been formed under circumstances directly the reverse of those which had operated on his elder brother. He only remembered his father in the same circles and the same place in society in which his latter days had been spent. No change of condition had led the youth to turn his back on the companions of his boyhood; no rapid promotion had filled him with a fond conceit of his own consequence, or an overweening eagerness for rank and emolument; and his unbought fidelity had shown that he was of the number of those on whom rewards would be wasted. Thus it happened (as it often does), that two young men, sons of the same parents, educated in the same school, and trained to the same profession, were just the reverse of each other, in particulars wherein nature had probably made little difference between them. So it was, that while the one was indifferent to duty, frivolous, self-indulgent, and mercenary, the other was assiduous, discreet, temperate, and disinterested.

It may be inferred from what I have said, that the rank of Col. Trevor was already above his merit. The consequence was, that having reached his present elevation by the force of causes not within himself, his own consciousness afforded no standard for his farther pretensions. He could see no reason why he should not be a field-marshal as well as a colonel. And so it was; for he had no just claims to either rank on the score of service or qualification. A stone thrown up, were it endued with consciousness and thought, could see no reason, as long as it was ascending, why it might not fly to the moon. If my experience in life has taught me anything, it is, that a man who sets no bounds to his aspirations, unless his daily intercourse with the world affords daily proofs of an intrinsic superiority over all he meets, is already raised above his merit.

The gentlemen, of whom I have been speaking, were busily engaged in their game, when the Orderly in waiting entered and announced an officer who wished to report himself to the commandant of the post.

"Let him call in the morning, and be damned to him," said Col. Trevor. "Is this an hour to disturb a gentleman?"

The Orderly saluted and withdrew, but presently returned to say that the officer had particular business with Colonel Mason, and wished to see him immediately. Mason accordingly left the room, and was gone but a few minutes, when he too came back.

"This officer, sir," said he, "asked to see me, supposing me still in command here. His intelligence is for you; and, from what I heard before I discovered his mistake, it may be important that you should receive it to-night."

"Well," said Trevor, in a tone at once lazy and peevish, "I suppose I must see him. But it is damned hard that I cannot have a moment's leisure. Let him come in."

He was summoned accordingly, and proved to be no other than our acquaintance, the Yankee spy, whom I now introduce to the reader, as he announced himself. He is Captain Amos Cottle, of the 20th regiment of infantry, in the army of the United States. His name, I presume (like that of the fourteen James Thomsons, in Don Juan), had been bestowed in honor of the illustrious bard immortalized by Lord Byron. He was invited to take a glass of wine, and, having seated himself, requested a private conference with the commanding officer. This was a signal for the dispersion of the ladies, and their assiduous attendants, who adjourned to another room. Mason was about to follow, but the Colonel carelessly requested him to remain.

Captain Cottle was then invited to open his budget, which he did by telling what the reader already knows. Not a sentence did he utter, in which some indication of folly, vanity, or indiscretion did not escape him. All this, however, passed unremarked of Col. Trevor, whose eyes sparkled at the welcome intelligence. Nothing could be more apropos to his wishes, or to the plan of the President. " Veni, vidi, vici." The exploit of Cæsar was the only parallel to that which he proposed to achieve. Occasionally he looked to Mason for sympathy and concurrence with his unexpressed thoughts. As often he withdrew his eye, chilled and perplexed by the cold, steady, thoughtful look of his companion. What could this mean? Could Mason be insensible to the advantage of the plot, or indifferent to its issue? Could envy so far prevail with a man heretofore distinguished by his disinterested zeal for the service, as to damp his ardor in an enterprise of so much promise? He was at first indignant at this idea, but a little reflection made him judge his brother-officer with more candor.

"Poor Mason," said he to himself. " I don't wonder that he is a little mortified at my good fortune. It is something hard that he should have held this post so long, without a chance to do anything, and that I should have come just in time to rob him of this. But then, damn it! it is his own fault. What did he want with a reinforcement against a parcel of ragged militia? It was right to supersede an officer who would ask more than one regiment to meet any number of such ragamuffins that could come against him. Besides, he ought to have broken up their den long ago. If Douglas escapes me this time, it shall not be long before I smoke him out of his hole, or there is no virtue in gunpowder."

Having thus reasoned himself into a state of exqui-site self-complacency, he heard the story of Captain Cottle to the end, and then asked the opinion of Mason.

"I cannot say," replied that gentleman, "that I am prepared to give an opinion."

"I hope," said Trevor, "that you don't mean to deny me the benefit of your thoughts."

"So far from it, that I make it a point of conscience not to speak without having first thought. When I have done so, I will tell you what I think. To speak now would be but to give you the crude suggestions of unreflecting and impertinent presumption."

"I cannot understand," said Trevor, "how you can require time to think in so plain a case."

"I might say, in reply," answered Mason, "that as the case is so clear to you, you can hardly need my advice. Indeed, I understand your request of it, but as a compliment to which I am not insensible, and which I shall not decline. When I am prepared to speak, therefore, I shall speak as plain as if the case were as full of difficulty to you as it is to me."

Having said this, Mason drew Cottle into conversation ; inquired the particulars of his visit to the mountain ; encouraged him to recite his conversations with Douglas; and, filling him full of vanity and conceit by his deferential deportment, made the light shine through him, so as to expose his folly to the most careless observer. At length he was dismissed for the night, and Mason, addressing Trevor, said : " I am now ready to give you my thoughts. I could not do so in Captain Cottle's presence; and, indeed, my mind was not clear until I had some more conversation with him. I am now satisfied."

" Let's hear, then, the result of your cogitations," asked Trevor, with something of a sneer.

Mason colored slightly, but said, in a calm tone : " I have had some experience of this Captain Douglas, and am morally sure he has not been deceived by this man, as he supposes."

" What ! " exclaimed Trevor. " Do you forget that Captain Cottle is an officer whose rank is a pledge for his honor, and who would forfeit his commission and his life by bringing false intelligence to his commander ? "

" I don't doubt his truth," said Mason, " but his sagacity I do doubt. The man is palpably a Yankee——"

" And the cunning of the Yankee is proverbial," interrupted Trevor.

" It is, indeed," replied Mason ; " but as he is not

only a Yankee, but obviously so, he could not have made Douglas believe that he was an influential inhabitant of Bedford, a native of the county, and a zealous stickler for the sovereignty of Virginia."

"You give your Captain Douglas credit for a great deal of sagacity."

"And not without reason," said Mason. "His plans, and his manner of conducting them, all show it. His intelligence appears to be always correct and ready, and his devices for the concealment of his own schemes are commonly impenetrable. It is clear, from many circumstances, that he has agents who pass through the country unsuspected ; and I should not be surprised if Cottle had fallen in with one of them. I have no doubt that Douglas will be found at Jones's Ford on the day appointed; but my life upon it, instead of coming there to be surprised, he proposes to come there to surprise you."

"*Surprise* ME!" said Trevor, scornfully.

"I have no apprehension that he will surprise you," said Mason, "because I am sure you will take all proper precaution. I merely mean to say that he will attempt it."

"And be punished for his presumption," said Trevor. "As to precaution, I must use it, to be sure, superfluous as it may be against a set of inexperienced militia."

"Of one sort of experience," said Mason, "and that not the least important, they have had more than we. They have tasted danger more than once; and their skill in the use of the rifle is such as men who live with the weapon in their hands, and they alone, can be expected to acquire."

" I hope to bring in some of them as prisoners," said Trevor, " and then we shall see how that is. I will pit a dozen of our sharp-shooters against a dozen of them, my horse to yours."

" I am not in the habit of betting," replied Mason, smiling quietly; " but, in this case, I dare say I may do it innocently, as the offence will hardly reach beyond intention; so I take your bet."

" How do you mean? " asked Trevor, sharply.

" I mean," said Mason, " that I am not very sure that you will take a dozen of them."

" Not sure! " exclaimed Trevor; " how can they escape me? "

" I don't profess to understand their craft," said Mason; " but they are hard to catch. In short, Colonel Trevor, my instructions require me to afford you all the information I have acquired here. It is therefore my duty, even without question from you, to assure you that you are in the midst of a disaffected country, and that you are going against an enemy not to be despised, and among a people universally hostile. Knowing these things, and invited by you to advise what is to be done in this affair, my advice is to march your whole disposable force to the appointed place, using every precaution to guard against surprise. It might be as well to anticipate Douglas, so

far at leastas to underst and the ground, and to occupy
it before the day."

" And so he takes warning, and escapes me."

" By no means. Cottle's scheme will have been
made available so far as to draw him down from the
mountains. You neither need nor desire any other
advantage. But I see that I cannot easily make
myself understood, because our minds are occupied
with different things. You are thinking about the
trap set for Douglas, and I am thinking about the
snare he has laid for you. Depend upon it, Colonel
Trevor, that the old story of catching a Tartar, may
be illustrated by catching Douglas among the river
hills. He may be caught; and yet, neither come
away, nor let you come. Observe," continued Mason, " when I inquired of this Captain Cottle about
the nature of the ground at the Ford, behold, he had
not taken notice of it! but, on cross-examination, by
finding what he did not see, I am satisfied that there
is no low ground, nor cleared land at the place ; that
the hills come sheer down to the river, and, by almost
necessary consequence, that the road leads through a
deep defile. The choice of such a place confirms my
suspicion of Douglas's plan, and affords the means to
counterwork it. If we occupy the strong points of
the ground, and he comes with only such a body of
men as Cottle expects, we take him without effusion
of blood. If he comes in force, our position will give
us all the advantage he seeks; and, trust me, in that
case we shall have need of them."

" *Need* of *advantages* against *irregulars!* " drawled Trevor, sneeringly, and emphasizing every word.

" Our discipline and experience are of little consequence," said Mason, " if we do not use them. One use of them is to know how to take advantages."

" Be it so," said Trevor ; " I shall seek none. A fair field and a clear sky are all I ask ; and I shall be careful to take no measures which may alarm this mountain wolf, and drive him back to his den before I can come up with him."

These words were hardly spoken when the Orderly announced that a sergeant of dragoons had just returned from a scouting party with important intelligence, and had come to make his report to the Colonel. What this was the reader will infer, when told that he was the non-commissioned officer on whom had devolved the command of the four men who had escaped with him from Jones's Ford. His information confirmed Mason's suspicions, and might have served as a damper to the flattering anticipations of a man less sanguine than Colonel Trevor. Its only effect on him was to sharpen his eagerness for the expected rencontre. Yet the Sergeant, when questioned, frankly admitted that his party had not been out-numbered. But it was clear that their design had been, by some means, disclosed to Douglas ; and his advantage had been the result of judicious dispositions, and the skill of his men in the use of that most terrible of all weapons.

But all this abated nothing of Colonel Trevor's

contempt for a foe unskilled in the manual exercise, ignorant of the grand manœuvres, and dressed in buckskin. Every attempt on the part of Col. Mason to bring him to listen to reason proved fruitless. Indeed the conversation occasionally took such a turn as to create a doubt in the mind of that gentleman, whether to press his advice any further might not make it difficult to reconcile with his own self-respect the deference which he knew to be due to his commander. He therefore determined to receive and execute in silence all orders which might be given, and leave the event to Providence.

CHAPTER XXXVII.

> More dreadful far their ire
> Than theirs, who, scorning danger's name,
> In eager mood to battle came;
> Their valor, like light straw on flame,
>   A fierce, but fading fire!

FREED at length from his troublesome adviser, Col. Trevor was left to the uninterrupted enjoyment of his anticipated triumph.   He seemed to tread on air, and, with a flashing eye, and spread nostrils, to look forward to the glories, and snuff up the carnage of the expected fight.   Such was his impatience for the adventure, that, in the eagerness of anticipation, he gave no thought to the necessary preparations. It was enough to issue the customary order for the troops to be in readiness for the march, with a supply of cartridges and rations suitable to the expedition.

The third day of November at length arrived, and the troops took up the line of march.   As they issued in glittering rank from the barracks above the town, the Colonel, proudly mounted on his stately charger, posted himself in the gateway of the house, where he had taken up his quarters, and received their passing salute.   The portico of the house was crowded with female figures;   the windows were clustered with fair faces; the noble oak-trees in the yard were hung with garlands, in token of the loyalty of the household, and of an anticipated triumph in his assured victory. But the Colonel saw nothing of this. His eye saw not the waving of handkerchiefs, his ear heard not the cheering farewells issuing in tones of music from rosy lips. He heard only the spirit-stirring drum and clanging bugle; he saw nothing but the stately steppings of his well-trained troops as they marched by; and then, his eye, following them, dwelt with delight upon their pictu- resque appearance as they wound along the slope of the hill, and crossed Blackwater-bridge. Beyond this, imagination presented objects of yet greater interest,—the battle-field, the tumult of the strife, the rout, the pursuit, the carnage, the vanquished leader led in chains to the foot of the throne, the gracious smile of approving majesty, and the rich rewards of successful valor. These things he saw; but saw not the gaunt figure of his host, who stood near, his strong features and manly person ill sort- ing with the abject part he condemned himself to act. He sought in vain to catch the eye of the excited commander, desirous, in his parting words, to convey some expression of loyalty and zeal. Colonel Trevor marked him not; and, as the rear of the column was about to pass, put spurs to his horse, and galloped to the front.

At this point of my story, I must crave the indul- gence of the reader, while I introduce my humble self to his notice. A native of South Carolina, and the heir of a goodly inheritance, which, during a long minority, had been at nurse in the hands of an honest and prudent guardian, I was just of age, the master of a handsome income, and of a large sum of money in hand. Having a taste for military life, my guardian had procured me a situation in the military academy, which had been established by the State, as a counterpoise to that institution at which the Federal Government had taught so many of our southern youths to whet their swords against the only sovereignty to which they owed allegiance. My proficiency had been seen, and gave entire satisfaction to my teachers. I had imbibed political opinions which made me a zealous advocate for the rights of the States, and a strenuous asserter of the unalienable independence of South Carolina. When, in compliance with the request of Mr. B——, inquiry had been made for a young man qualified and disposed to aid young Trevor in his enterprise, I had been selected for that purpose. I was invited to Columbia; made acquainted with the plans of the insurgents in Virginia, and provided with letters to my future commander. Journeying to Virginia by the route that he had pursued, on the evening of the first day of November I entered the valley described in the first chapter. I soon encountered a crowd of men who filled the road and the yard of a house contiguous to it. There were wagons, horses, and arms; and the men, moving quietly but busily, seemed all earnestly engaged in some important preparation.

I was presently stopped, courteously though peremptorily; and having expressed a wish to see Captain Douglas, was conducted to the house. There, pen in hand, and busily engaged in writing, sat a young man of small stature and slight figure. Though quite handsome, there was nothing remarkable in his features; but a bright gray eye, of calm, thoughtful, and searching expression, strongly contrasted with the dark brown curling hair that clustered over his brow.

Being accosted by my conductor, he raised his head; when I stepped forward, and handed him my letters. He glanced hastily to the signature of the first he opened, then read it leisurely, and looking at me with a beaming countenance, extended his hand. "You are welcome, sir," said he; "welcome to danger's hour. In the morning we march on an expedition which may decide the fate of the campaign. My engagements must excuse my seeming neglect of you this evening. But let me make you known to your future comrades."

Then turning to a fair-haired youth, already known to the reader as Arthur Trevor, he introduced him as his mother's son. I was then made acquainted with Schwartz and Witt, and several others. Among the number were a few young men from the lower counties, of good families and education, who, in this crisis, had left their homes to engage in this expedition. These, like their leader, had all learned to accommodate themselves to the fashions of that wild country, and its wilder climate, and especially to their own wild life. Each individual was dressed, from top to toe, in leather, no otherwise differing from the dress of the rudest mountaineer, than in neatness, and a certain easy grace, and air of fashion, which no dress can entirely conceal. In any dress, in any company, under any circumstances, Douglas Trevor would have been recognized as a gentleman.

I hardly remember how I fared, or how I passed the night. As a stranger, I presume somewhat better than most others ; but I took pains to show that I was content to eat what I could get, and to lodge as I might.

At daylight we were on the road. But little attention was paid to order. No enemy was near, and nobody was inclined to desert. There was therefore no necessity for harassing men and horses, by forcing them to keep in ranks. Each man rode where, and with whom he pleased, except that a few were directed to keep near the wagons, not so much to guard as to assist in case of need. It is impossible to conceive a military array, with less of the "pomp and circumstance of war." The horses were, for the most part, substantial, and in substantial order. Their equipments were of the rudest sort. Plough-bridles and pack-saddles were most common. The only arms were the rifle, knife, and tomahawk, with their appropriate accompaniments of powder-horn, charger, and pouch. Douglas, indeed, had a sword, and the few sabres taken from the dragoons had been distributed among the principal men. But they were all too wise to encumber their persons with these weapons, which might have been troublesome in their mode of warfare. A strong loop of thick leather, stitched to the skirt of the saddle, in front of the left knee, received the sword, the hilt of which stood up above the pummel. Two or three of the saddles were of the Spanish fashion, the horn of which served to support any trifle the rider might wish to hang on it. Douglas, in particular, carried, in this way, a leather case, containing his writing materials, and serving as a tablet for writing on horseback.

But rude as these equipments were, yet to one acquainted with the object of the expedition, there was an appearance of efficiency in the whole which gave the corps a truly formidable aspect. The perfect order of the arms, the strong rude dress of the men, their sinewy frames, their sunburnt faces; and, above all, the serious and resolved expression of countenance which generally prevailed, were tokens which none but a martinet would overlook.

As yet no duty had been assigned to me, so that I was perfectly disengaged. It was not until we had ridden several miles, that Douglas found leisure to converse with me. He then joined me, accompanied by Schwartz, to whom, in my presence, he explained my situation. Schwartz heard him with thoughtful attention, and then said : "It is all mighty well, sir, if Mr. Sidney will only just take it right. You see, sir," continued he, addressing me, "there an't no officers among us, and we only just call the Cap tain so for short. If he was a Captain or a Gineral it would not make much odds, because these fellows just go for what is right and hard fighting; and him they believe in, him they mind. But as to who is first and who is second, that's neither here nor there. I have not a doubt that you are the sort of a man we want; but all that we can do, is to give you a fair chance to let the men see it. The Captain can be asking your advice, now and then, and I and Witt will do the same, and when they see that, they will begin to find out what you are. And then, you see, sir, when once we get to fighting, a man is never in such a flurry himself, but what he can see who knows what he is about, and who does not. So, by the time we have had a skrimmage or two, the men will know all about you; and whenever the Captain is out of the way, they will all be looking to you to know what to do ; just in the way of giving your *opinion*, mind ; but, *after a while* it will get to be *orders*. And then, if any thing happens to the Cap- tain, and Witt and I don't see cause to change our mind, why, we only just have to follow you, and the men they follow us, and all will go straight. So you must just make yourself easy and keep quiet. We'll tell you when to speak, and after a while you'll find yourself second in command before you know it."

I had no difficulty in acknowledging the reasonableness of these ideas, though it seemed a new thing to find a man possessing the influence and authority of Schwartz, devising means to transfer them to another. But he knew, and the event showed that he was right, that there were some duties of a commander for which he was not fit; and that there were other things to which a chief could not devote himself, for which he was better qualified than any other.

On the third of November we reached the rendezvous, at the house of Mr. Gordon. On the way we had received frequent accessions of strength, and here we were joined by a yet larger reinforcement. Our whole number could not have been much, if at all, short of a thousand men.

Meantime scouts came in, from whom we learned that the same day had been fixed for the march of the troops from Lynchburg. It followed that we had abundance of time for our preparations. It so happened, that they had not learned the name of the new commander; but it was understood that a reinforcement had arrived, and that nearly the whole disposable force was on the march. This included a troop of dragoons and a company of artillery, with two pieces of cannon, in addition to a full regiment of infantry, and one battalion of another.

Having ascertained his force, and fixed on those on whom he could rely to understand and execute his plans, Douglas proceeded to make a temporary organization, suited to the occasion. The men were divided into corps, to each of which a post was provisionally assigned, to be occupied as soon as the approach of the enemy should be announced. Across the road, near the head of the defile, and just above the first angle next the top of the ascent, was constructed a barricade of logs, similar to those already described. This reached, on each side, to the foot of the hills, at steep, rocky, and impracticable points. It was long enough for twenty men to man its twenty loop-holes, and as it reached above their heads, they were quite concealed. An hundred men were allotted to this post, who were ranged five deep behind the barricade, and instructed to fire in turn, each man falling back to the rear to reload as soon as he had discharged his piece.

Others were distributed along the opposite faces of the hills overlooking the road, and directed to seek out hiding-places behind rocks, trees, and bushes. These men were under the immediate orders of individuals selected for the occasion, but attached to the command of Witt, who was stationed at the barrier.

About a hundred were placed in ambush in the mouth of the ravine, just below the road, on the north side of the river, under Schwartz. These were all picked men—our steadiest and coolest sharp-shooters—who were placed there for the purpose of attacking and carrying the guns of the enemy at the water's edge.

Douglas himself, at the head of the rest of his corps, prepared to occupy the road on the north side of the river, to bring on the action. These were divided into two equal bodies, and the whole ranged in platoons, at open order, across the road. Of the two battalions, as they may be called, the foremost was placed under my command. The other Douglas commanded in person. My orders were to post my headmost platoon just at the bend of the road, on the top of the hill where it turns to the right. They were instructed to fire *ad libitum*, each man choosing and making sure of his mark, and then to file away by the right, and, taking to their heels, to run down to the river, cross it, and dispose themselves on the other bank, so as most effectually to gall the enemy, should he attempt to cross. Each platoon, in succession, was to march up to the same ground, and, having fired, to execute the same manœuvre. The remaining column, under Douglas, were to stand their ground until the enemy should come in view on the top of the hill, and then to fall back fighting, and cross under cover of those who should have passed before. But the best account of what was ordered will be gathered from what was done.

CHAPTER XXXVIII.

The triumph and the vanity,
　The rapture of the strife;
The earthquake voice of victory,
　To thee the breath of life;
All quelled:—Dark spirit, what must be
The madness of thy memory?

WHILE these arrangements were in progress, scouts were hourly arriving. The country being altogether friendly, they were readily provided with fresh horses; and, before the enemy were half way from Lynchburg, we were fully apprised of their number, equipments, and order of march. First came a squadron of dragoons; then a light company; then Trevor's regiment, about five hundred strong; then a company of artillery; then one battalion of Mason's regiment, consisting of something more than two hundred men; the whole followed by a few light troops, by way of rear-guard. The whole might amount to a thousand men, well appointed and prepared at all points for efficient action.

On the morning of the fifth of November, the men were ordered to betake themselves to their allotted posts; and Douglas, having visited each, and seen that all was right, and rightly understood, addressed himself to his particular command. Where every man is an officer, each must be told individually beforehand what is expected from him. Panic apart, they will be apt to fulfil such instructions, and will fight with the terrible efficiency of individual animosity. Hence the formidable character of partisan warfare.

At length the enemy made their appearance. Clinging to the idea of surprising Douglas, Col. Trevor sent forward no advance, but determined to bring the whole strength of his corps to bear upon him at once. If he employed any scouts, they were either unfaithful, or were not permitted to approach near enough to learn any thing of the position or movements of Douglas. The consequence was, that Col. Trevor received the first intimation of his presence from a sharp firing in front, which sent his horse to the right-about and back to the rear. Pressing forward, he immediately ordered his sharp-shooters to disperse and take positions to gall us, while he pushed on his solid column of heavy infantry. The reception prepared for them was such as he had not dreamed of. His men fell like leaves in autumn ; and, as fast as one platoon of the mountaineers discharged their pieces, another was on the same ground to pour in again that terrible fire, of which the martinets of the regular service have so inadequate an idea. Instead of the deep-mouthed peal of muskets, discharged simultaneously, there is the sharp, short crack of rifle after rifle, fired by men no one of whom touches the trigger until he sees precisely where his ball is to go. The effect was suitable to the cause ; but yet the steady infantry pressed on,

" Each stepping where his comrade stood,"

to form an unbroken front, in order to charge with the bayonet.

Suddenly the firing ceased, and, behold, their enemy seemed to have fled from the expected charge. The fact was, that my last platoon, having fired, had withdrawn like their predecessors, and were running at full speed after their companions, down the hill and across the river. At the water's edge, I stopped and joined Schwartz in his ambush. It had been arranged that I should do this ; because, in case we should be so fortunate as to seize the cannon, my skill as an artillerist might be of great use. Meantime, my men having crossed over, dispersed themselves along the bank, the face of the hills, and across the road, to cover the retreat of those who remained.

The regulars had necessarily spent a few moments in repairing the wreck of their shattered column before they advanced. They then moved forward; but, before they turned the angle of the road, most of my men were across the river. At the same time, the column under the immediate command of Douglas was seen drawn up in the road, near the foot of the hill, with the rear resting on the water's edge. As the enemy advanced the front platoon fired, faced to the right, and filing along the flank of the column, entered the river and crossed just below the ford. They next filed to the left in the same way, and crossed above the ford. In this manner the whole column disappeared, one platoon after another, while their fire was answered by a roar of musketry, which, being discharged from the higher ground, did more harm to those on the farther bank of the river than to the nearer enemy. At length the last platoon was withdrawn, and the regulars rushed down toward the river for the purpose of annoying them in crossing. In this attempt they were again checked and driven back by the terrible fire of my men, who, having already crossed, were drawn up, as I have said, on the other bank.

Col. Trevor now saw the necessity of advancing his artillery, which was accordingly hurried down to the water's edge to clear a passage for the infantry. By the time the cannon were unlimbered, not a man of the mountaineers was to be seen. As soon as their companions had crossed, they dispersed with every appearance of confusion and alarm ; some scampering along the road, and some clambering up the hills on both sides of it.

The way was now open, and the infantry advanced to cross the river. At this moment Colonel Mason, riding up to Colonel Trevor, pointed out the advantageous position of the artillery as a cover to his rear, if he should be forced to retreat. " Give me leave to suggest," said he, " that it may be well to leave the cannon where they are. The cavalry, too, cannot act with effect among those hills, and the two together, should the fortune of the day be unpropitious, may be of more use here than on the other side."

"You say true," said Trevor. "It shall be as you advise, and you, Colonel, will remain in command of this reserve."

"I earnestly beg, sir," said Mason, "that you will not deny me a share in the work of the day. The Captains of artillery and dragoons are all-sufficient to the command of their respective corps."

"Pardon me, sir," said Trevor. "None can be so proper to execute your prudent and cautious device as you, its author. You will be pleased, therefore, to repair to the rear, rally the dragoons, and bring them down to the water's edge. Let them be ready to cross at a moment's warning, to assist in the pursuit as soon as I have driven the enemy into the plain."

Saying this, Colonel Trevor turned off, and giving the word to march, dashed into the river. Poor Mason, insulted and mortified, nevertheless patiently addressed himself to the duty assigned him. Thus was this able and brave man denied all participation in an affair which his arrogant and sanguine commander believed to be an abounding source of honor to all who might be engaged in it.

I have omitted to mention that, as soon as the plan of endeavoring to surprise the artillery had been adopted, Schwartz had requested me to draw the outline of a piece of mounted ordnance in the

sand, and to mark the proper positions of the artil-
lerists employed about it.   While I did this, some
ten or fifteen of our best marksmen stood by, looking
on attentively.   When my sketch was done, he
turned to one of them, and pointing to one of the
marks made to stand for an artillerist, said coolly :
" Now, this is your man ;" and to another, " this is
yours."   Thus he went on till he had doomed every
victim.

While we are supplying this omission in our narrative, the reader will please to suppose that Col.
Trevor's regiment have forded the river, and have
passed up the road and out of sight.   It will be
remembered that the hills on both sides of the defile
had been lined with concealed marksmen, and that
the greater part of the advance had, on recrossing
the river, thrown themselves into the same places of
concealment.   But the idea that they had done so
for any purpose but that of safety, entered not into
Col. Trevor's mind.   Indeed, if he had had any
doubt, it must have been removed when he found,
that as his column wound through the deep defile,
not a shot molested their march.   At the first angle
of the road he halted and let the column march past
him.   He could see, from this point, both the head
of it, as it advanced, and the rear as it came up.   As
the latter passed the spot where he stood, the leading platoon was in the act of turning the next angle
of the road.   At that moment he heard the startling
report of a volley of rifles.   He set spurs to his horse

to gallop to the front, when every rock and every
tree of the surrounding hills burst into flame, and
the deep ravine echoed to the report of a hundred
rifles. A shot struck his horse, and another piercing
his hat, grazed the top of his head deep enough to
lay bare the skull, and stun him, as he fell under his
slaughtered horse. He was thus placed *hors du
combat*, owing the preservation of his life to the insignia of his rank which had endangered it.

The sound of this firing was the signal for us.
Each of the selected marksmen fixed his aim on his
appropriate victim; and, at a word from Schwartz,
the artillerymen at the guns fell as if swept away
by the breath of a tempest. Rushing from our hid-
ing-place, the cannon were instantly in our possession. The company of artillery were not slow to
disappear behind the angle of the rock, and one or
two who peeped out, being instantly picked off, we
saw no more of them.

Presently we heard the heavy tramp of the squadron slowly descending the hill, accompanied with
the peculiar sound of dragoons, dressing the front in
preparation for a sudden and overwhelming charge.
While this was passing, our guns were all reloaded.
' Mind, boys," said Schwartz ; " all of number one."
The word was understood, and every alternate man
stood ready, with rifle cocked and trigger set, to
receive the enemy. The charge was sounded, and
the leading horsemen, wheeling around the rock,
were rushing on at full speed, when horses and

riders were seen to go down in one promiscuous heap. The greater number of the squadron were still out of sight; and, had the way been open, might have followed to share the fate of their companions, and finally to ride us down when our guns should have been all discharged. But the work had been done too effectually. The dead and wounded (both horse and rider) nearly filled the road; and for dragoons to pick their way among such appalling obstacles in the face of fifty loaded rifles at a distance of twenty paces, was out of the question. A few who made the attempt found this to their cost. The charge was not renewed, and some of our men advancing to the angle of the rock, and occupying inaccessible but commanding points on the hills, soon made them draw off to a safe distance.

While this was doing, I, with the few men selected for the service of the artillery, gave my attention to that. Glancing my eye along both pieces, I saw that both had been accurately pointed into the road on the other side. I had nothing, therefore, to do but to apply the port-fire, which was still burning in the clenched hand of a dead artillerist. By this time the column had fallen back, and the road below the first angle was fast filling with the retreating mass. I had never before witnessed the effusion of blood; and, heated as mine now was, it ran cold as I applied the match. As the smoke cleared off, I saw the enemy throwing away their arms, and stretching out their hands, some toward me, and some aloft to the unseen foe that galled them from the hills. The fire instantly slackened, and cravats and handkerchiefs being raised on the points of swords and bayonets, it ceased altogether. The mountaineers now poured down from the hills into the ravine, securing the arms of the enemy, mixing among them and hemming them in on every side. Douglas, whose place, since he had recrossed the river, had been among these concealed marksmen, was one of the first to approach the enemy. Advancing to those whose rank was most conspicuous, he made known his authority, and received their swords.

Meantime Col. Trevor had recovered his senses, and found himself fastened to the ground by the weight of his horse, which lay upon his leg. He was presently discovered, relieved, and helped to rise. At this moment he caught the eye of Douglas, who hastened to him, less from impatience to demand his sword, than to offer assistance to one who seemed to be an officer of high rank, and badly wounded. In the figure before him, all smeared with blood and dirt, he saw nothing by which he could recognize his brother. To the Colonel, the disguise of Douglas was hardly less complete. He had seen him receiving the surrender of others, and stood prepared to go through the same humiliating ceremony. He felt that his own disgrace was complete, and the form of surrender was thought of with indifference. He had already reached the lowest depth of abasement.

" But in that lowest depth a lower deep" seemed to open, when, as he extended his hand to deliver his sword to the victor, he discovered that the hand put forth to receive it was that of Douglas. He flung down his sword, stamping with rage, and immediately after called to his men to resume their arms. The voice struck the ear of Douglas, though dissonant with passion. The figure too, confirmed his suspicion of the truth; and he immediately rushed to screen his brother with his own body from the rifles pointed against him. Calling for aid to those around, he presently succeeded in securing the Colonel, and after one or two fruitless attempts to soothe him, ordered him away to the house of Mr. Gordon. To that gentleman he spoke aside, and explaining in confidence the strange scene that he had just witnessed, besought him to take command of the escort, and to pay all imaginable attention to the health, comfort, and feelings of the Colonel. He was accordingly led away, raging and foaming at the mouth like a spoiled child who has been deprived of his toy, or baulked in his amusement. The mortification of Douglas was extreme; but he had the satisfaction to find that Arthur was not present; and to no other person but Schwartz and myself did the name of Colonel Trevor afford a hint of the connexion.

CHAPTER XXXIX.

———————If thou didst but consent
To this most cruel act, do but despair;
And if thou want'st a cord, the smallest thread
That ever spider twisted from her womb
Will serve to strangle thee; a rush will be
A beam to hang thee on! Or, wouldst thou drown thyself,
Put but a little water in a spoon,
And it shall be, as all the ocean,
Enough to stifle such a villain!

I SHALL not detain the reader with a detail of the farther particulars of this skirmish. Indeed we hardly stayed to acquaint ourselves with its exact results. As at least half the men who had fought under Douglas on that day had no intention to follow him any farther, we left to them the care of the killed, wounded, and prisoners. The body of Col. Mason alone was selected for a more honorable burial than the rude hands of the mountaineers could bestow. It was dragged from beneath the incumbent mass of men and horses, placed on a suitable carriage, covered with the colors of his regiment, and taken to Lynchburg, to be there restored to his companions in arms. The band of his regiment were also marched to that place to assist in rendering the last honors to their late commander.

Having given the necessary orders, Douglas snatched a moment to ride to Mr. Gordon's, where he hoped to find his brother in a more reasonable mood. The Colonel had been confined in a private room; and, being treated with great courtesy and respect, had lost nothing of his arrogance. Such is always the effect of delicate attention to the undeserving. A man of merit would have been softened and melted by the deference with which Colonel Trevor was treated. To him it seemed but that sort of spontaneous homage to greatness which the heart pays unconsciously. The effect of it was, that being told by Mr. Gordon that his brother had come to visit him in his room, he sent him the following magnanimous note, pencilled on the back of a letter:

" I am your prisoner. Do with me as you please. Inflict on me any death, however cruel; but spare me the sight of one whose treasons have dishonored our common name, and who has deprived me of my only chance to restore its former splendor."

Douglas was inexpressibly shocked at this manifestation of a temper at once savage and coldly selfish. But he had no time to waste in parleying with the ungoverned passions of his brother, and wrote an answer in these words:

" You are *my* prisoner, and *mine* only, and shall be treated with all tenderness and respect. I am responsible to no one for your custody, and you shall soon be at liberty. Go home. Go to our venerable father, and comfort his declining years. If the instincts of your heart do not restrain you from fighting against your brothers (for Arthur is with me), let a sense of honor make you regard yourself as a prisoner on parole, not at liberty to fight again against Virginia. Meantime your sword shall be restored, and you shall be treated in all things as the brother of D. T."

While Douglas was engaged in this painful duty, Arthur was employed in preparing a formal report of the events of the day. This was signed by the Chief on his return, and with it the young man was despatched to B——, with instructions to ask his orders, and return with them, unless another messenger should be preferred. In the meantime all things had been made ready for the march to Lynchburg. I shall not give the history of this. It was triumphal, as far as complete success and the applauding gratulations of the people could make it so. We had no difficulty in adding to our numbers as many men as the fruits of our victory enabled us to supply with arms. Some joined us instantly, and others engaged to rendezvous at Lynchburg in a few days.

There was nothing to damp the pleasure of Douglas, but the conduct of his perverse brother, and the presence of the dead body of his old friend, Colonel Mason. On our arrival before the camp at Lynchburg, I received orders to present myself with a flag before the gate, at the head of a detachment which escorted the body, accompanied by the music of his band, and all the sad and imposing insignia of a military funeral.

An officer came out to meet us, and thus received the first authentic history of the fate of the expedition. I was instructed to deliver over the body of Colonel Mason with every circumstance of respect and courtesy. I was also charged to demand the surrender of the entrenched camp, and of the garrison as prisoners of war.

A negotiation ensued, which ended in a suspension of arms for five days, and an agreement to surrender if, in that time, no reinforcement arrived.

This arrangement was by no means unwelcome to Douglas. It gave him time to receive and organize the new recruits that were pouring in, and to await the return of Arthur. In the meantime, much of that sort of intercourse which is common on such occasions took place. There are few things in life more pleasant than it is. There must be less of malignity in human nature than is generally supposed, or men would not seize, with so much eagerness, on opportunities to lose the idea of public hostility in the kindly interchange of courtesy and good offices. Friendships are never formed more suddenly and cordially than under such circumstances. So we found it on this occasion. Major Wood, the officer in command, was a gentleman and soldier, honorable, frank, generous, and accomplished. I was brought much into contact with him, and found him enthusiastic in his acknowledgments of the merits of Douglas, and eager to become acquainted with him. But the time had not come when he was willing to be known by his true name; and besides that he was acquainted with the Major, there were many others in the camp who would have recognized him. He therefore confined himself to his quarters, on various pleas of business; and, to make his seclusion effectual, took lodgings in a house in the suburbs of the town. By his advice, I mixed much with the men; and, as I had acquitted myself to their entire satisfaction in the late affair, I found that I was in a fair way to be recognized as second in command. Schwartz and Witt made a point of consulting me publicly on all occasions; and this circumstance, together with my daily attention to the organization of the troops, obtained me full credit for all my military skill, and a great deal more.

The five days passed away quite pleasantly. The regulars, finding that they were not like to fall into the hands of savages, were becoming reconciled to the fate which now seemed inevitable; and we parted on the last night of the truce, with no unpleasant anticipations of the surrender which was to take place the next day at noon.

The morning came, and our men paraded in high spirits, and with considerable show of order and discipline. This was particularly the case with a small company which had been detailed for the service of the artillery, who took their stand at the guns with the air of men proud of their new acquirements. I had indeed taken great pains to train and exercise them, and, by universal consent, was recognized as the immediate commander of this corps, which was drawn up with the cannon planted directly against the gate of the camp.

All this time Douglas did not make his appearance. At length the hour approached for the garrison to march out, and lay down their arms, when Schwartz went to his quarters to receive his orders. He soon returned, and taking me aside, told me that Douglas was not at his quarters, and was nowhere to be seen.

We had already observed appearances in the camp not at all answerable to the expected surrender, and I was now startled at this intelligence. The character of Major Wood forbade indeed any suspicion of foul play. But the time was near at hand when the enemy should march out, and we heard nothing of their drums, calling the men to parade. We determined, therefore, to send a flag to the camp on some pretext. The officer who carried it was immediately warned off, and having said that he had a communication for Major Wood, was told that that officer was no longer in command, and that COL. TREVOR would receive no communication from rebels and traitors.

This was decisive. The quarters of Douglas were not very distant from the enemy, and such had been the appearance of perfect good faith in all their proceedings, that our camp had been guarded even more negligently than is common with militia. It seemed, indeed, almost incredible that Col. Trevor could have been guilty of an act of base treachery against the life or liberty of his generous brother ; but to Schwartz and myself, who knew the connexion, even this seemed hardly less extravagant than his former conduct. That he had escaped, joined the troops, and disclaimed the capitulation entered into by Major Wood, was certain. To have surprised and carried off Douglas could not be much worse.

We now consulted with Witt, to whom we communicated our suspicions, at the same time disclosing the true name of our young commander, and his relation to Col. Trevor. What was suspicion with us, was at once absolute certainty with him. I do not think I ever witnessed such a change as our communication made in the whole appearance and demeanor of the man. Heretofore, I had always seen him cool, cautious, deliberate, and thoughtful. There was, besides, a prevailing tone of benevolence in all he said, which, added to his sobriety and strong sense, gave him some claim to the title of philosopher. But now the expression of his countenance was terrible and awful. He had made no show of regard for Douglas; but his attachment was deep and abiding, and his alarm for his safety was in the same degree. He was impatient of a moment's delay, sternly protested against wasting time in discussion, and insisted on immediately storming the camp.

Schwartz was nothing behind him in zeal, though less disturbed by passion; and we presently determined to bring matters to extremities. As soon, therefore, as the hour appointed for surrender arrived, our captive drummer was ordered to beat a parley.

To this the only answer was a general fire of musketry from the whole line of the camp on that side, by which a few men were hurt. But the distance was too great for any serious mischief. Enough, however, was done to excite the men to fury; and without waiting for the word, they rushed to the assault. Their movement determined me. To rush up to the piqueted entrenchment, behind which the enemy were in comparative safety, was to expose themselves to destruction. It was indispensable to open a way for them. This I effected by a discharge of both pieces of artillery, which tore the gate away, and pointed their attack to this accessible point. The moment after, Colonel Trevor, with his untractable rashness, appeared in the gateway, shouting, and calling to his men to sally forth against us. He was instantly recognized by the incensed Witt, whose fatal aim brought him to the ground. His men fell back; and in a moment after a white flag was raised.

It was no easy matter to prevail on our men to pay any regard to this signal; but we succeeded in restraining them before it was too late. Of course we demanded the instant surrender of the place, which was unhesitatingly given up. Major Wood now came forward to apologize and explain. Col. Trevor, having made his escape, had returned to the camp soon after tattoo. His whole behavior was that of a man beside himself, and actuated by some inscrutable motive to some inscrutable purpose. Of these he said nothing to his officers, but peremptorily

disclaiming the capitulation, gave orders that all
things should be prepared for a renewal of hostilities
the next morning. Nothing more was known but
that he had summoned to his quarters a favorite
sergeant of his own regiment, who had been left
sick in camp when he marched against Douglas.
This sergeant and four soldiers, as it seemed from
the morning report, had disappeared in the night.

Major Wood assured us, that all that had been
since done had taken place under the immediate
orders and superintendence of Colonel Trevor, and
in spite of his own most earnest remonstrances. In
proof of his sincerity, he appealed to the fact of his
unconditional surrender the moment he was apprised
of the fall of the Colonel. With all this I was perfectly satisfied, and gladly returned him his sword,
with a proper acknowledgment of his gentlemanly
conduct.

"And now, Major," said Schwartz, "there is
another matter we want to talk to you about. Do
you know any thing of our Captain?"

"Of Captain Douglas?" said the Major. "Certainly not. But I hope I may now have the pleasure
of seeing him."

"Look here, Major," said Witt, whose eye still
glared with ferocity not at all abated by the fall of
Trevor; "that a'nt the thing; and we want a
straight answer. Captain Douglas is missing, and
we want to know what's become of him."

"Missing!" said the Major, with unfeigned amaze-

ment. " I assure you, upon my honor, I know nothing of him."

" Is there any body here that knows, or is like to
know ?" said Schwartz.

" None that I can imagine," was the reply.

" Is there not a Captain here," asked Schwartz;
" a red-headed fellow, that commands the company
at Farmville ?"

" Captain Cottle?   Yes."

" Well, I want to see him."

He was immediately summoned, and presently
made his reluctant appearance. His alarm increased
on seeing Schwartz and Witt.

" See here, Mister," said the former; " here is a
piece of villany that we want to know about; and
there is nobody, I reckon, so apt to tell us as
you."

" Indeed, sir," said Cottle, " I declare, sir, I don't
know a word about it."

" You don't, eh !" said Schwartz. " Well, any
how, you are mighty quick to *find out* that you don't
know ; that I must say for you."

" Did you ever see me before ?" said Witt, fixing
his terrible eye on the alarmed Captain.   " Did you
ever see me before?" repeated he.   " Do you remember where it was ?   Do you remember your business
there ; and did you ever hear of such a thing as a
man being hung for a spy ?"

The collapse of deadly terror came over Cottle at
these dreadful words. His face, already pale, became

livid; his eye no longer blenched under the fearful glance of Witt; but the lids opened as if by mutual repulsion, while his lip and under jaw fell power-less. He was roused from this state by Schwartz, who asked him what had become of Captain Doug-las.

He was now effectually scared out of all thought of concealment, and answered without prevarication that Captain Douglas had been surprised, during the night, by the order of Col. Trevor, and sent away immediately under the guard of a sergeant and four men, across the river. He could not say, certainly, where he was gone; but he suspected to Washington, as Col. Trevor appeared to have been writing busily all the time the party were engaged in the capture of Douglas. It was vain to attempt concealing that he had a hand in this, though the disclosure was made with great reluctance. It appeared, moreover, that he had been anxious to accompany the prisoner, supposing him to be ordered for Washington; but Col. Trevor had refused to send him. Indeed, he sent none but those who had not been engaged in the action at the ford, and was certainly right not to trust the vain babbler, whose idle garrulity could hardly have failed to rub off any gloss he might have thought fit to spread over the affair.

"How did they get across the river?" asked Schwartz. "We have a strong guard on the other side, and they had orders to keep a strict watch."

'Col. Trevor told the sergeant," replied Cottle,

"just to float quietly down the river and land away
below; and a handkerchief was tied over the Captain's mouth to keep him from making a noise, and
if he did, they were ordered to shoot him."

I have no words to express the horror with which
I heard this last circumstance. I trusted, and indeed
Major Wood seemed to be of that opinion, that Col.
Trevor had really been beside himself; but regarding
his conduct even as the effect of frenzy, it was hardly
less shocking. From Schwartz the communication
only called forth some pithy expressions of detestation, without seeming to interrupt the working of his
thoughts, which were at once busy to devise some
remedy for the evil.

Witt was differently affected. His whole frame
and countenance assumed an appearance of stony
rigidity, betokening fixed and fearful purpose. He
turned his glaring eye to the spot where Col. Trevor
had fallen, with an expression that showed his vengeance quite unsatisfied. A glance of fierce scorn
fell for a moment on Cottle; and then, with a searching look, he addressed himself to Major Wood.

" Major Wood," said he, with a voice whose deep,
stern tones, demanded the truth and the whole truth,
" did you know any thing of this business?"

" Upon my honor, I did not; and Captain Cottle,
who did know, will tell you so."

" I would hardly take *his* word *against himself*,"
said Witt, with cold contempt, and not even turning
his eye on Cottle. Then pausing a moment, he

added, with the same look of severe scrutiny,
" Major Wood, do you know who Captain Douglas
is ? Do you know that he is Col. Trevor's own
brother ?"

" Great God !" exclaimed the Major. " Douglas
Trevor ! That fine, intelligent, accomplished, noble
young man !"——

" Did you know him ?" asked the other.

" I did," said Wood, " and loved him well. Poor
fellow ! Poor fellow ! His doom is sealed."

" That's enough," said Witt. " I see now that you
had no hand in it. But is it not your duty, Major
Wood, to bring back Captain Douglas and set him
at liberty ?"

" Would to God that I could," said the Major ;
" but he is quite beyond my reach before this."

" See here, Major," said Schwartz ; " write an
order to that sergeant to bring him back, and give
me a pass to follow him without being stopped, and
I will have him back in no time. Them fellows lost
ground here crossing the river, and I can catch
them."

"That might do," said the Major, hesitatingly ;
" and I am bound in honor to do it, because his capture was a breach of my truce. But I shall never
be forgiven. No matter ; it shall be done if they
break me for it."

" *You* may thank the Major," said Witt, turning
his implacable eye on Cottle, " for that word ; for it
has given *you* a chance for your life. But for that,

you would have been hanging like a dog in half an hour.   Now, Major, I don't want you to come to any harm ; and so you shall have a fair excuse.   Bring Captain Douglas back to us, and we will let this fellow go.   But if the Captain is not here before the week is out, then, as sure as there is a God in Heaven, he shall be hanged for a spy, as he is."

There is a difference between the certainty of being hanged in half an hour, and a chance of escape, however unpromising.   To Captain Cottle, who had not ventured nearer to Jones's Ford than the rear of the dragoons, and who was now in greater peril than he had ever willingly encountered, the difference was of great importance.   Yet his hopes were faint, for he had heard the orders of Trevor, which enjoined despatch ; and he was equally earnest in hurrying the Major and Schwartz.   His impertinence was cut short by ordering him to close custody in jail ; and the credentials of Schwartz being soon prepared, he set out on his journey.

CHAPTER XL.

That lies like truth, and yet most truly lies.

LET us again intrude into the sanctuary of majesty.
The President is alone as before. He has the same
air of somewhat impatient expectation. A shade of
anxious thought is on his brow, and his cheek is
flushed with some little excitement. Yet these ele-
ments are all so mixed as to be scarcely perceptible;
and were he conscious that we are looking at him,
they would be completely concealed. On the table
lie a number of letters recently received. Two of
them are separated from the rest. He takes up one
and reads it a second time. Let us look over him.
It runs thus:

"The wisest may be deceived; the most vigilant
may be betrayed: for the MOST trusted are often the
most treacherous.   CAUTION."

" What means this?" said the President, musingly.
" Who is it that I am warned against? The word
'MOST' is underscored. Who does that point at?
Whom do I trust *most?* I trust nobody. But I
seem to trust; and whom *most?* Surely it cannot
be he. I should, indeed, be wrong to trust to his
fidelity. But he is too wise to be false to his own

interest.   But may he not have an interest that I am
not aware of ?   It must be considered."

He then took up the other letter, which I beg
leave to lay before the reader, as a specimen of the
art with which the truth may be so told as to make
others believe what is false.   I recommend it particularly to military gentlemen, reporting the results
of a battle.

HEAD QUARTERS, CAMP NEAR LYNCHBURG,
November 12, 1849.

SIR : I have the honor to lay before your Excellency an account of the operations of the troops
under my command, since the date of my last despatch.

In pursuance of the information I had received, of
which your Excellency has been already advised, I
marched on the third inst., at the head of my own
regiment, one battalion of the 15th, a company of
artillery, and one of dragoons, to meet Douglas on
his descent from the mountains.   At Jones's Ford,
on Staunton river, I encountered him, when about
half his force had crossed over.   I attacked him
immediately ; and, after a sharp conflict, drove him
across the river.   By the advice of Col. Mason, I
left the artillery and dragoons on the north bank, to
protect our rear, placing them under the command
of that distinguished officer.

Pressing hard upon the rear of the enemy, we
came up with him just as he had fallen back on the

reserve. Here he rallied, and the fight was renewed. I regret to say that, at the first fire, my horse fell under me, imprisoning my leg by his fall. At the same moment a ball struck my head, and I came to the ground insensible.

You will judge my astonishment, when, on recovering my senses, I found that all my men near me had thrown down their arms, and that I was in the hands of the enemy, who assisted me to rise. I immediately called to my men to resume their arms; but am sorry to inform you that I was not obeyed. As I had not surrendered, I was seized and hurried away to the house of a ring-leader of these rebels, where I was confined. From that time I had no means of receiving any information on which I could rely concerning the events of the day, as I had no intercourse with any but the rebels.

Two days ago I was so fortunate as to make my escape. Returning to this place, I find my camp, which had been left under the command of Major Wood, beleaguered by the rebels, and a treaty for surrender in full progress. I rejoice that I have returned in time to prevent a consummation so disgraceful.

It is now midnight, and a small party has been sent out to endeavor to surprise the leader of this banditti. In the meantime all things are put in readiness for a sortie in the morning. I shall not close my letter until I can give some further account of the success of these operations.

Two o'clock, A.M.—My scouts have come in,

and brought in the hostile chief, who proves to be the last man in the world whom I could have wished to find in arms against the generous master who so well deserved his grateful devotion. I speak of that unfortunate youth, whose fault (I must not use a harsher term), nearly twelve months ago, dishonored our common name and parentage. Your Excellency will appreciate the struggle in my bosom, between a sense of duty and the foolish but inextinguishable relentings of nature. I have determined to put an end to this painful strife, and to take security against my own weakness, by sending him on immediately to you, without awaiting the result of the meditated sortie in the morning. He therefore travels in custody of the bearer of this letter, under guard of a sergeant and four men.

Having returned to the camp this night, after tattoo, I am unprepared to give any account of our loss, or that of the enemy. I have nothing authentic but the lamented death of Col. Mason, who fell fighting bravely.

I beg leave to express an humble hope, that your Excellency will be pleased to attribute the partial failure of my enterprise to the unfortunate wound which put me *hors du combat*, at a moment, up to which we had successfully driven the enemy before us for nearly half a mile and across the river.

I remain, sir, with the most profound respect, your Excellency's most humble and faithful servant,

OWEN TREVOR, Col. 18th Inf.

"A worthy gentleman," said the President, folding up the letter. "A most worthy gentleman! Let any man doubt henceforth, if he can, that the only way to judge in advance of what a man will do, is to ascertain his interest. See how readily it settled this nice point of casuistry—this delicate question of conflicting duties. Trust! Yes, I will trust; but not as fools do. I will trust no man's honor, but every man's interest. The experience of my whole life has taught the lesson, and every day confirms it. Here comes a new example," added he, as the door-bell sounded, and was echoed by the single stroke in the room.

The door opened, and the honorable Mr. Baker appeared. His figure had lost nothing of its deferential bend; his step nothing of its creeping, cautious tread; his countenance nothing of its abject servility. But there was more of anxiety and less of hope, with a slight appearance of peevish dissatisfaction.

"You are very good, my dear sir," said the President. "You are always almost present to my wish. Government would be an easy task, were all officers like you."

"I humbly thank your Excellency," replied the Judge. "Were not your approbation precious to me, I might be tempted perhaps to look more than I ought to public opinion. Perhaps I do so, as it is; for though my duties are clearly necessary to the good of the State, I find it hard to bear the loud reproaches of a misjudging multitude, that reach me through a factious press."

" Let it not reach you, my dear sir. The storm does but rage without. Why need you hear it when it touches you not? Shut your ears and sleep soundly; or open them only to the more pleasant tones that issue from loyal lips. I take care not to know what is said of me by malcontent scribblers; but I hardly flatter myself that I should preserve my equanimity, if I read all that is written."

"It is sometimes impossible not to hear," said the Judge; "and there are words which convey reproach, which, though uttered in a single breath, reach the heart. I can never, I fear, make myself proof against such a phrase as '*judicial murder*.' "

" But you must find consolation in your own enlightened conscience, my dear sir. Some feeling must be expected when the edge of the law falls on victims whose offences demand punishment, and yet are such as those the world calls honorable and upright are most likely to commit."

" The misfortune is," replied the other, " that it is only for such offences, and on such victims, that my office seems to be made to act; and when the curse rises up against me, loud as well as deep, and uttered and echoed on every side, I pray your Excellency to pardon me, when I say, that I find its honors and emoluments a poor compensation."

" It will be some relief to you, then," replied the President, " that you are like to have a subject of a different sort to act upon. One whose crimes offend against the laws of God as well as man ; and who is not more obnoxious to State policy than to the detestation of all good men, and of none more than yourself."

" Of whom is your Excellency pleased to speak ?" asked Mr. Baker.

" Of no other than that young fellow, Trevor, whose ill luck snatched him away from our hands, when perhaps he was not quite ripe for punishment. But he has since made himself perfect in crime, by becoming the leader of a desperate banditti. In short, he is no other than the famous Captain Douglas, and is now in my power. I think you will find in his case a fair set-off against some of the mortifications of which you complain ; and think no more of denying your services to the public, at least until he has fulfilled his destiny."

The effect of this communication on the mind of the honorable gentleman, was such as the President had anticipated. To every being of the name of Trevor he bore a mortal antipathy. In the case of Douglas, this was rendered more intense by the sympathy of a father with a favorite son. An envious malignity was a striking feature in the characters both of father and son ; and this had been provoked to the utmost by that unfortunate young man. Both were sensible that the younger Baker had been in bad odor with the public, ever since the affair at the falls ; and hence, it was not only grateful to their malice, but to their pride, to fasten on Douglas a stigma so dishonorable as to have relation back, and to excuse his adversary with those who did not know all the circumstances, for not seeking such redress as *gentlemen* demand of *gentlemen* only.

The good humor of the Judge was now manifestly restored, and the President went on to give him some particulars of the late military occurrences. Douglas, he said, was on the road, and would reach Washington the next day. The letter, it seems, had been brought by a soldier who had orders to outgo the rest of the party, and ride express to Washington.

" It is well," said the President, " that I have this timely intimation of his approach. The custody of State prisoners cannot be safely entrusted to any but the military ; and that of this young man must be committed to no corps in which he had any acquaintance. It seems that he was a universal favorite among men and officers. I am about to take measures to guard against any such blunder."

In such conversation half an hour was passed, when the Minister made his appearance. He had been sent for, and to him the President communicated the history of the capture of Douglas. Had he turned an eye of close scrutiny on the favorite, at the moment when he uttered the name, and announced the fate of his victim, he might have seen a slight expression of countenance, which it would not have been easy to interpret. But this escaped him ; and he went on to direct that the true name of the prisoner should be kept secret ; that his arrival should be watched for ; and that he should be at once con-

ducted to a place provided for the separate confine-
ment of State prisoners. It was, moreover, ordered,
that a detail of officers and men for that prison should
be carefully made, so as to exclude any persons
whose loyalty was at all doubtful ; and especially all
who, from former associations, could be supposed to
feel any kindness for Douglas.

Finally, it was agreed that, should he arrive in the
course of that night, or the next day, he should be
brought, on the following night, before the triumvi-
rate, in the room where they then were.

" You were right," continued the President, addressing his Minister, " when you said that this
young man had talent. The discovery of his identity
explains the marvellous organization and efficiency
of that wild banditti that he commanded. His
capture must be fatal to their future success. They
must be powerless now that they have lost their
leader, and must soon disband. That is well. The
two regiments may now be marched from Lynchburg
to Richmond, and save us the necessity of sending a
reinforcement from this quarter. The troops there,
with this aid, will certainly be sufficient to check the
insurrectionary movements that we hear of in the
southern counties, and to cover the meeting of the
Legislature. Col. Trevor has certainly deserved well.
I am afraid his unfortunate wound may have occasioned the loss of more men than we could well
spare, who seem to have surrendered while he was
insensible. But the disbanding of Douglas's corps

will, of course, set them at liberty to return to their
duty.   But this takes nothing from Col. Trevor's
merit.   He must be brevetted.   As to Major Wood,
in the regular course he should succeed Mason ; but
I must hear more of this negotiation for a surrender
of his post, before he is promoted.   That affair must
be satisfactorily explained, or he will hardly escape
a court-martial."

The President now went on to give some farther
orders, and then dismissed his guests.

CHAPTER XLI.

Treason can never take a form so hideous,
But it will find a glass, that shall reflect
A comely semblance, on which self may look
With a complacent smile.

On his departure from Lynchburg, Schwartz had
been provided with a suit of clothes half military, to
prevent the notice which his rude mountain attire
would have attracted. The day was half spent before he was on the road, and the sergeant and his
party were already far in advance of him.

Colonel Trevor had been desirous, for obvious
reasons, that his letter and prisoner should reach
Washington as soon as possible, and had ordered
the party to proceed with all practicable despatch.
But, as they might be somewhat retarded by the
necessary care of their prisoner, he had directed that
the letter should be sent on, as we have seen, by a
single soldier, who had reached Washington on the
second night. But the sergeant was not far behind,
and had used such diligence that he crossed the
bridge the next morning at an early hour, just as
poor Schwartz came in sight.

He recognized the party by the peculiar dress of

Douglas, with which he was so familiar; but it was too late. He followed, however, disconcerted by his failure, but not desponding. At the farther end of the bridge he was struck with the countenance and manner of a fine-looking young man, of genteel but plain appearance, who stood gazing earnestly after the prisoner and his guard.

Observing Schwartz, he asked eagerly who the prisoner was, and was told it was Captain Douglas.

"Good God!" exclaimed he, in a tone of deep concern; "is it possible? But thank God! it is no worse."

"Did you think it was any body you knew?" asked the quick-witted Schwartz.

"Yes," replied the other. "I was almost sure it was a friend of my own."

"And what was your friend's name, stranger? if I may be so bold."

"You are bold enough," said the youth. "I am not in the habit of answering questions, unless I know who asks them, and why."

"I don't mean no harm, young man," replied Schwartz; "and if you tell me your friend's name and your own too, may be you won't be sorry for it."

The stranger looked hard at Schwartz, and in his serious, earnest, and sagacious countenance saw enough to make him curious to know what this meant. He therefore replied, that his friend was Lieutenant Trevor, late of the United States Dragoons.

"Then I have a notion," replied Schwartz, "that your name is Whiting."

"My name *is* Whiting," replied the other, in great surprise; "but how should you know it?"

"I have heard the Captain talk about you many a time."

"The Captain! What Captain?"

"*Him*," replied Schwartz, pointing toward the distant party.

"*Him!* And how was he to know any thing about me?"

"Just because he is the very man you thought he was."

"Douglas!" exclaimed Whiting. "Trevor! Douglas Trevor! Good God, what an ass I have been! O Trevor, my friend! how earnestly have I wished to know where to find you! Had I been with you, this might have been prevented."

"May be it is best as it is," said Schwartz. "The Captain did not want for friends where he was. May be one friend here will do him more good than a hundred any where else. That is what I am here for now."

"You are a friend to Trevor, then," replied Whiting; "perhaps one of his followers."

"You may say that," said Schwartz. "Any how, I'm his friend."

"Then come with me to my lodgings. You can tell me every thing, and we will see what is to be done. Trevor has friends enough here. Thank

God! I saw him. But for that we might not have
found out who he was till it was too late."

Whiting now showed Schwartz where to bestow
his horse, and afterwards conducted him to his lodgings. These were in an obscure suburb, humble,
plain, and poorly fitted up. Appearances showed
that the occupant spent most of his time with the
pen, although many of the relics of his former military equipments were to be seen about the room.
But the dust on his cap, which hung against the
wall, and the mould on the belt and scabbard of his
sword, showed that these had been long unused. In
truth, the escape of Douglas and his uncle had been
fatal to him as a soldier. He had been dismissed
the army; and now, as it seemed, earned a poor
livelihood by doing for small wages the manual
labor of those offices, the salaries of which are
received by men who do nothing at all.

During their long walk through the streets of that
city "so magnificent in distances," as Monsieur
Serrurier said of it, and while a hasty breakfast was
preparing for Schwartz, he gave Whiting the particulars of the late battle at Jones's Ford; of Douglas's
capture, and of his brother's death, and the surrender of the camp. As soon as he had seen his guest
provided for, the young man left him alone. Going
out, he proceeded to the first stand of coaches, and
stepping into one was driven to the Minister's.
Here he alighted, showed a ticket to the porter,
entered, threaded several passages, descended a dark

stair, and, going into a small room in the basement, touched the spring of a bell. No answering sound was heard; but in half an hour the Minister appeared.

"I am glad to see you," said he. "Have you heard that your friend Trevor is in the power of his enemies, and is expected here to-day?"

"I had not heard it," said Whiting; "but I have seen him. He is here."

"Indeed! That is well. We have the more time."

"Where will he be lodged, and under what custody?"

"In the state prison. I am instructed to select his guards from among those who are strangers to his person, and well-affected to the Government."

"That will be no easy task, as it seems that all the troops of that description have been marched into Virginia, and that, except raw recruits, there are none here that it was thought safe to trust on that service."

"That is true," said the Minister; "and therefore I must select those same raw recruits. Think you there are many here who could be relied on to peril every thing on behalf of your friend?"

"No doubt of it. I was long enough in the army after his disgrace to know that his whole regiment were indignant at it. A hundred can be found ready to wipe it out with the blood of the President, or their own."

"It is well. He will be taken to the palace this

night, under the cloud of darkness.   Have all things
in readiness, and watch for his return.   You will
know what to do.   Did you know those who had
him in custody ?"

   " I knew the sergeant, and he knew me."

   " All right.   You then must be charged with the
disappearance of Douglas ; you must therefore make
your escape with him.   I shall, of course, see you
no more.   We have no time for compliment ; but
you will have my best wishes ; and the time may
come when you may have it in your power to do me
justice.   My country is to me, Mr. Whiting, what
yours is to you.   When New England was permitted
to join in what you will call the plunder of the
South, I was not very scrupulous about the means of
securing her share.   But nearly all that was worth
having is irretrievably lost.   What remains can only
be retained by means which will but make it an
instrument of power in the hands of this man, and so
enable him to perpetuate his reign according to the
forms of the constitution.   Take that away, and leave
the matter altogether to the votes of the northern
States, and I shall not long have to play second to
him.   In order to preserve his power, he would be
compelled to break up the system of monopoly contrived for the exclusive benefit of his favorite Empire
State ; or perhaps to concur with me in severing a
Union, the benefits of which are now lost, by the
escape of our common prey, and of which *we* bear
all the inconveniences.   Of course, I do not pretend

that the place to which the favor of my countrymen may advance me in either event, has no charms for me. But you will see that I am actuated by no low and sordid ambition. I am desirous you should see it in this light. It is not my fortune to command the services of many whose esteem is eminently desirable. I am, therefore, the more ambitious of yours. Should I succeed, my acts will vindicate my motives. Should I fail (and if Virginia disenthrals herself I shall not fail), you will do me this justice. What news have you of the movements of B—— ?"

" He is about to take up arms, with the probability of assembling a force which, with the concurrence of the corps of Douglas, will secure his object."

" But is not the band of Douglas dispersed ?"

" By no means; but much increased. They have still their mountain leaders, and a young man from the South Carolina military school, who seems well qualified to act, for the time, as the *locum tenens* of the chief."

" Then farewell, sir," said the Minister. " You carry with you my good wishes for yourself and your cause, and I pray you to commend them to Mr. B——."

About the time that these gentlemen thus separated, the President was informed that a gentleman and lady craved the favor of a private audience. He directed that they should be shown into the room, the privacy of which we have so often violated, and soon after he entered it.

A lady, whose figure and dress denoted youth, was seated on the sofa. She was in deep mourning, and a black veil completely hid her face. By her side sat a gentleman far advanced in life, and of a most venerable aspect. His fair complexion had blanched by time into the cold dead whiteness of age. The color had, in like manner, faded from his pale blue eye; and the quivering of his livid lip, and the trembling of his eyelids, betokened deep and anxious distress. *His* dress also was of black, mournfully contrasting with the almost unearthly whiteness of his face.

At the entrance of the President both rose; and the trembling and agitated old gentleman might be seen to give way for a moment, as if about to throw himself on his knees before "the dreaded prince whose will was fate." But he recovered himself, and with an air of suppliant dignity, stood as erect as the weakness and infirmity of age permitted. The President approached him with a look of perplexity and doubt; and, gazing earnestly at him, said: "I beg to know, sir, who it is. Bless me! Mr. Trevor, is it possible that I see you here, at this moment?"

"I am here, sir," replied the old gentleman, "a broken-hearted, bereaved father, lamenting the loss of one son, and suppliant for the life of another; and this is my niece, who is come to join her prayers to mine, on behalf of her betrothed husband."

There was enough in these words to add to the maiden confusion of poor Delia, but not enough to prevent her from lifting a timid glance, in which there was as much of entreaty as her proud spirit could descend to. She met the eye of the President, as with an air of quick and eager surprise he turned towards her; and in his eye she read a meaning, which, in the moment, blasted her hopes, and confirmed her in all her detestation of the cold, selfish, and crafty politician, whom she now beheld for the first time. She saw, instantly, that she was the object of some subtle purpose; and felt, that by putting herself in his power, she had but prepared for her husband a deeper distress than all the severities of the law could inflict. But she quailed not at the thought. Her proud and bold spirit came in aid of her weakness; her pale cheek burnt with an indignant glow, and the tears were dissipated from her eyes in the bright and almost fierce glance that flashed from them. Even through her veil too much of this appeared to escape the notice of the President.

He instantly turned away; and, with an air and tone of the most candied courtesy, addressed Mr. Trevor: "You speak in riddles, my dear sir," said he; "I beg you to explain."

"My task is more painful than I had anticipated," said the poor old man. "Have I, then, to be the herald of my poor Owen's death, and of the yet more disastrous fate of my other noble boy?"

"Col. Trevor dead, sir!" exclaimed the President, "Impossible! I have just received a letter from him, written on the 12th."

" That day was the last of his life," said the afflicted father. " He fell next morning. I received the news yesterday by the railroad ; and by travelling all night by the same conveyance, I am here to entreat that the axe may not glean what the sword has left me. My poor boy Douglas, I am told, is in your power, and perhaps here.'

" I had *heard* of this; but I assure you your son is not here. I will not deny that I expect him; and regret that it is under circumstances which will not allow me the pleasure of extending to him the same courtesy I shall be happy to render to you. Compose yourself, my dear sir; let me beg you and your niece to retire to rooms which are always ready to receive you where I am master; and let me send for your baggage."

Delia, who thought there was something of hesitancy in her uncle's mind, instantly exclaimed : "No, my uncle! No, my father! The palace of a tyrant is a prison. There is no mercy here. No hope for my noble husband. Save yourself. Return home while you may, and leave me here to share his fate. Our friends *may* rescue us. They WILL avenge us. But in that cold eye there is no relenting."

"You are harsh, lady," said the President; "I will not add, unjust. I will prove that, by permitting your instant departure, without even inquiring where you lodge."

He now bowed them out, and immediately summoning a servant, said : "Take the number of that coach, and let the driver attend me this evening." Then, as the servant left the room, he went on: "Why, this is better and better. I think I have holds enough now on Baker to bind him to his task, however his heart may yearn after his beggarly estate in Virginia. It seems, forsooth, that after all that has passed, his son yet has a hankering after this girl; the only woman, as he says, that he ever truly loved. It may be but spite against his favored rival; or it may be, in truth, that every thing that bears the shape of man is susceptible of love, or what passes for it. Be it so. He may be gratified; but his father shall fulfil conditions."

In the evening of the same day the following letter was put into the hands of the President:

"Your captive has arrived. Beware how you remand him to his prison, when you dismiss him to-night. Order him to be confined within the palace; and when you give the order, mark well its effect on him you most trust. CAUTION."

"Why, here is *proof* as well as accusation," said the President. "Here *is* treason. How else is it known that Trevor was to be brought here to-night? I will improve this hint. A rescue is to be attempted! Is that it? Then the guard will be attacked on their return without the prisoner. Woe to the traitor if it prove so!"

* * * * * * *

I have been interrupted in my narrative. I have hesitated whether to give this fragment to the public, until I have leisure to complete my history. On farther reflection, I have determined to do so.   Let it go forth as the first *Bulletin* of that gallant contest, in which Virginia achieved her independence; lifted the soiled banner of her sovereignty from the dust, and once more vindicated her proud motto, which graces my title page,—SIC SEMPER TYRANNIS! AMEN. So MOTE IT BE.

THE END.